Book of Never

Collection Two

The Peaks of Autumn ~ Imperial Towers

Ashley Capes

The Peaks of Autumn
Book of Never: 4

Chapter 1.

Tsolde threw an apple over her shoulder.

The red orb spun through the air. Never stretched to catch it, the hard skin slapping into his palm. He ignored the slight twinge in his thigh as he lowered his arm. "You'd be more accurate if you faced your target, you know," he said before crunching into the fruit. A wind had picked up where they climbed the mountain trail, needles falling from the tall pine trees.

She tossed her curls. "The next one will give you a black eye."

Luis laughed from where he brought up the rear.

Never took another bite, slurping at the juice. "Well you can pay for your own. I didn't use the last of my silver to put up with such wanton insubordination."

Tsolde offered no response, adjusting the pack and striding on – though she probably rolled her eyes first. He grinned. The pack, along with his own and Luis' packs, were filled with supplies for the Folhan Range's perilous Iron Pass. Ropes, lamp oil, torches, even small hand shovels and a pick axe, along with food and water – though he'd also rely on mountain streams.

Leaving the Silver City had been easy enough – and now that he'd put a few days between himself and its walls of stone, he wondered whether Snow had taken a hand in the ease of escape? A fire had started south of the palace, drawing much attention from the guards, attention which was already focused around the damaged Temple of Jyan, and allowing Never to lead his small group through an underground passage.

Another expense that drained his purse. But then, had the innkeeper of the Silver Bell not told them where to find a man willing to sell a discreet way out of the city, they might not have escaped at all. Especially with his leg slowing them – yet today, it moved easily. Only minor quibbles; he was close to fully healed, most of the stitches had already fallen out. Elina had been right – he was healing too quickly.

Still, speed was important and if abnormal-healing helped, so be it. Prince Jenisan would surely send men in all directions. What Never wanted to know was whether the Prince would join the chase himself? With his father's death and a kingdom to protect from rebels and the ever-greedy Vadiya, it seemed unlikely.

And more, how would Elina and her grandfather fare?

"Never, I hear riders," Luis said.

"Off the road." Never ran for a stand of trees and lay in the undergrowth to peer through the branches. Tsolde and Luis were not far behind – barely a heartbeat passed after they settled before the riders appeared.

Steel clanked and the jingle from harnesses were audible beneath the pounding of hooves. The riders charged on, steel flashing, soon disappearing beyond a bend in the trail. Never swore softly. Steelhawks. What were they doing? On their way over the mountain to continue filtering down into Marlosa? Or, searching for someone?

"They're after me," Tsolde said, her mouth set. "Bastards; they don't give up, do they?"

Never nodded. "They're quite disciplined." He stood, brushing leaves from his tunic and pants before striking a parallel course to the road, keeping within the treeline. Luis and Tsolde followed. "What makes you think they were for you?" he asked her as they resumed walking.

"Floriak met with them. I told you; they want the port. It saves them a long overland journey." She kicked at a stone. "I told him I didn't want them staying in my inn and he hit me, Never."

He stopped. "What? You didn't say that before."

"The bruise is gone." She shrugged. "He tried to lock me up but Augim..." she trailed off. Tsolde had offered little about her escape but Augim hadn't survived, Never knew that much.

But it hadn't been without a cost to Floriak either; somehow she'd stolen his purse and then his horse on the way out.

"And you think he wants you that badly?"

She met his gaze. "When he looked at me it was clear what he wanted."

He put a hand on her shoulder. If that was the case... then what trouble was it truly, for the man to tell Steelhawks – men who were already heading to Marlosa – to keep an eye out for Tsolde? "I'm proud of what you did."

"I had no choice."

"Well, you do now," he said. He glanced at Luis. Both had a choice now. "And you, Luis." Was it right? Could he really take them both into whatever danger lay ahead? Snow would use them as leverage; Never knew that. And of course there was Jenisan too, who would punish them for travelling with Never.

And his curse... he had more control of his blood now but accidents were accidents for a reason; they disdained the illusion of control.

The treasure-hunter shook his head. "I'm staying, Never. You've tried this before, on Ferne's ship and at the Silver Bell – you're stuck with me."

Never had to smile, even as a twinge of fear tugged at his heart. Could he truly protect Luis? And Tsolde both? Or was it vanity that let him believe it?

"What about you, My Lady?"

Tsolde folded her arms. "You're not leaving me in some mountain village in the middle of nowhere. I can handle myself."

"Then it's settled; we'd better keep going," he said. "The way my luck has been changing of late, Jenisan will be the next one up the trail."

Chapter 2.

The dark, purple mass of mountain peaks roared up to the sky; the rising autumn wind trapped there, moans hidden within. It whipped at Never's cloak and cast hair into his eyes. He'd cut it when they stopped for the evening; if the mountain decided to let them survive.

A deep chasm plummeted down one side of the winding road. Though it was wide enough for wagonloads of iron and silver to run down to City-Sedrin, he fancied the wind was trying to pull him toward the drop.

Naught but a fancy; yet it seemed the kind of trick the Gods would play.

He shook his head. Even if Snow believed the Gods were gone... who else would revel in such misfortune? Perhaps it was Never's own bitterness that sought something to blame. A familiar routine.

"We need to find shelter," Luis shouted. He pointed to their back trail. Black clouds massed – an autumn storm. Grand. Never nodded, and pushed into the air current, squinting at the dust. Tsolde walked beside him, using his bigger frame as a partial shield. Even so, she soon had to fight for every step.

He steered her nearer the rockface and continued climbing. There was a cave somewhere ahead, yet what if the Steelhawks had already taken it? If luck held; the Vadiya would have already ridden beyond now that the storm had hit.

And if they turned back to seek shelter...

"Well, that's up to you, isn't it?" he murmured to the Gods. Pacela should be watching out for him. But then, the Steelhawks would have prayed for exactly the same thing from Osya. Maybe the dice would know? He could roll them, high for the cave, low to pass, but the storm would devour them if they risked pressing on.

When the cave mouth finally did come into view he signalled for Luis to watch Tsolde while he scouted. She frowned at him, saying something, but the wind snatched her words. Luis nodded and Never slunk around the bend. He kept himself close to rock but if anyone lurked within the darkness of the cave mouth, they'd see him approach.

The cave rested beneath an overhang where the mountain road widened. There was little to stop the gale when it blew across the face of the range, striking down from the east as now, but inside the cave lay a half-screen of wood and brush. A new feature. Whoever had built it knew their business.

Never slowed as he neared the opening. He drew a knife and let the blade hover over the back of his hand. His blood wouldn't help if there were Steelhawks within. Or ten men of any country for that matter. At the best, he could draw them out and head away from Luis and Tsolde. Find a way back later.

He crept within; raising the dagger as his eyes adjusted.

Blackness resolved to grey, a stony floor underfoot. Further in lay a wide space with shelves cut into the stone. A ring of brick encircled years of ash and soot but there was no store of fuel for a fire.

Nor were there any people.

He sighed. Finally, some luck. He returned to the mouth of the cave and waved Luis and Tsolde into shelter.

*

Out of the storm, screen raised, it was possible to at least hear one another, even when the rain started. It slashed across the face of the opening, but could not reach them. They'd lined their packs before one wall. With no fuel for the fire, the best they could do was use bedrolls and cloaks as blankets and sit close together.

Tsolde put her water flask down. "You haven't told me what you're looking for in the mountains above Marlosa."

"Something to help with my curse," Never said.

"I know that. But what is this thing exactly? How will it help?"

Never shrugged. "The Altar of Stars is the something I need to locate by the night of the new moon. It will help; that's all I know." Snow had no reason to lie; but doubtless there would have been reasons he held back.

Luis looked up from where he was cleaning his nails with a belt knife. "That's all? The library had nothing else?"

Time for another half-truth – how many had that been? And when would they all add up to a lie? Yet, to protect them it was still the best way. "I was interrupted; but I did learn something else from the Amouni books – I can read some runes, after a fashion."

"Like on the river?" Luis asked.

"More like being given images in my mind when I see them."

"So what did you see?" Tsolde asked. Her curiosity had not warn off since first learning of his curse as a child.

"Nothing good."

"You don't have to hold back, Never. I thought we'd agreed."

Luis was grinning.

Never sighed. "It's not pleasant – but I'm not telling you only because there's no reason to believe we'll ever encounter what I saw." And yet, only a fool didn't expect the worst. Such an attitude had saved him a great deal of disappointment over the years – not to mention keeping one step ahead of death. Always a nice side-effect to such pessimism.

Or realism.

"You're trying to spare us," she said. She pointed. "I saw your expression; you're not sure."

"You don't give up, do you?" He shook his head. "I saw a... creature in a cave. Like a skeleton with grey skin stretched over its bones. It faced off against one of my ancestors, who held two globes of blood, but there was no attack. I could tell that it wanted the man's organs – but I don't know what for, truly."

Her face had paled. "In a cave?"

"Yes." He gave her a smile. "But there's no way to know which cave – or how old the vision was. You've lived in Hanik all your life – have you ever heard of such creatures in the Folhan Ranges?"

A frown. "No."

"And neither have I."

Luis nodded to himself. "Who's to say such creatures didn't die off centuries ago?"

"Exactly," Never said.

Tsolde still bore a furrow in her brow. "But people have always been afraid of the Iron Pass. They say it's haunted."

Never shrugged. "It didn't seem to be the last time I passed through."

She didn't answer but Luis had another question. "What can you tell us of the Pass? There's a way through the collapse?"

"There is. The avalanches blocked most of it but Mal showed me and my brother the way, when we were young. Some passages within the mine are intact."

"When did you last take it?" Tsolde asked.

"All was well two years past," he said.

"And if it isn't, this time?"

"We try the long way – the Silver Pass, and hope we are swift enough. And that we don't all freeze to death in an early winter storm."

"And once we emerge on the Marlosa side of the range? Where is the Altar?"

"I only know that it lies beyond the border. I have a feeling I'll be able to sense it."

"That's all?" Tsolde asked. Her expression was not one of confidence.

He grinned. "You can head back down the mountain and try your luck with Jenisan and Floriak if you like."

She glowered at him. "No, thank you."

"Then we'll worry about the Iron Pass once we reach it.

For now, we should rest until the storm grows bored; there are still several days to the pass – including some pretty long climbs. I want us well-rested."

Chapter 3.

The wind finally died off near dawn. Never woke to the silence – something which had become rather unnatural. No movement or light beyond, only the soft glow of the blue-stone.

"Couldn't find my flask," Luis said softly.

He nodded. Tsolde still slept nearby, her face at peace. Good. If she was lucky, they'd stay ahead of Jenisan and Floriak and she could remain that way. Until reaching Marlosa. Then who knew what was in store.

"I might as well take what's left of your watch," Never said.

Luis grinned. "Feeling well-rested?"

"Actually yes." He shrugged. "Which hasn't been the case lately, not with my leg." He stood, stretching it out. No pain. Not even a niggle.

"You've healed awfully fast." There was a trace of awe to his voice.

"Agreed." He moved toward the entrance. "I'm going to stretch it some more while I think."

A lavender streak crossed the sky at the horizon and misty cloud buried the peaks to cast a diffuse light across the stone. The road was quiet, trees only stirring to let drops of dew fall. He paced before the cave mouth.

Tiny cuts had always healed quickly but this was something new. An injury like the one he'd sustained in the forests should have taken weeks to heal, not days. And yet, here he was, strolling about the mountains now without even a twinge.

He'd not solved anything when it was time to wake the others, but the problem continued to nip at his heels as they climbed the trail.

By mid-morning the wind had risen again, though it was gentle, no longer a force dragging his feet toward the sheer drop. Tsolde had braided her hair to keep it from her eyes, the breeze still strong enough to be a bother. It did little, however, to cloak a persistent sound of stone clinking against stone, somewhere above.

Craning his neck, he spotted an eagle's nest. Perhaps the bird was cracking one of the stubborn rock-feet, trying to break the large insect's shell.

"Bird of prey?" Luis asked.

"Probably."

When the path ahead came to a fork, one side shrouded in light and the other in shadow, Never paused to glance to the sun. It was probably high enough for noon. "Let's stop to eat," he said.

Tsolde slumped to the ground and Luis slung his own pack down, kneeling before it.

The earth shook.

Never spun, bracing his legs. Yet the rumbling did not

last and a column of dust soon rose from the path in the slopes high above. An avalanche? Or a smaller rockslide?

Neither bode well if debris covered the road.

"We're going to have to dig our way through that, aren't we?" Tsolde asked.

"I hope not; I'd hate for you to break a nail," Never said with a grin.

She rolled her eyes and even Luis' expression had turned darker, but he said; "It might not have blocked our path. There has to be more than one trail leading to the Pass, right?"

"There might be. I remember only the King's Road but don't despair yet." He removed a parcel of hard-bread and unwrapped it, taking a bite. "Let's see what we find up there first."

The sun was setting – simply disappearing beneath the horizon with barely a single blush – when Never reached the slide. He drew in a deep breath and hissed a curse. Rubble covered the road in a great, grey heap, completely blocking their way.

Above, a mighty gouge appeared in the wall, clean, pale rock revealed – as if a giant had cleaved part of the very mountain and below, left shattered stone piled across the road. Never approached, placing a foot on the heap. Rubble shifted and a stone trickled down the heap to plummet into the abyss beside the road.

No way to climb around and no way was he going to try climb over and risk having the whole thing collapse and slide into the chasm.

"What now?" Tsolde asked.

"We turn back and try one of the smaller trails – I marked two as we climbed," he said.

Luis nodded, shifting his pack on his shoulders and turning from the rubble. Tsolde joined him but Never paused at a faint sound. "I hear something," he said. The others paused.

A cry for help?

He moved to the rubble and leant close.

"Please," a voice spoke from within – the word soft but unmistakably Vadiya.

"I hear you," he answered in kind.

"You have to... save me."

Never tested a few pieces of stone, shifting one he felt was safe. The slide held. He moved another and paused, a chill falling over him. Steel glinted on the dying light within the slide, a large piece had created some manner of shelf, protecting a man. The Steelhawk was crammed within the slide, his waist buried in darkness and stone, his arm pinned beneath another slab.

A huge dent rested in his helm and the man's head was turned away from the light – Never doubted the fellow could move. He was probably paralysed and certainly dying. Blood pooled beneath his torso, staining the armour.

"I'm here. What happened?"

"Get me out."

"I will," Never said.

"We never had a chance... there was a crack and then... I don't even know what happened next... Screams." The fellow twitched, a slight scraping of armour on stone.

"You turned back?"

"Yes... we missed them, somehow... commander... ordered..." The man groaned. "Did you get the bastard?"

"Who?"

"The one who caused... the slide." The Steelhawk's voice was growing softer. "I saw him... he was up there... he made it happen."

"Up where?" Never asked, urging the man to hold on.

But the Steelhawk did not answer. Never straightened with a sigh. "Poor bastard."

"What was it?" Luis asked.

"A Steelhawk," Never said. "Probably all of them, they'd turned back. They realised they'd missed us," he said.

Tsolde's eyes were a little wide. "A man survived that?"

"Caught on the edge of the slide perhaps," Never said with a shrug. "He did say something else. He claimed he saw a man cause the avalanche."

"How?"

"He didn't get a chance to tell me." Never looked up to the surrounding peaks and outcroppings. Empty, all of them. "Maybe he was confused, maybe not, but it can't hurt to keep our eyes open."

Chapter 4.

Never led them down the King's Road to a blasted tree stump, crumbled to the ground like a broken man, one jagged arm cradling a new shoot of hardy green. The sun had just set when they started up, climbing the narrow trail in the near-dark until he called a halt in a small stand of pine trees.

Dead needles carpeted the stony earth, soft underfoot. "Tsolde, can you find us kindling?"

She nodded and moved around the trees.

Luis stepped closer and lowered his voice, keeping an eye on Tsolde. "So how much stock do we put in the Steelhawk's words?"

"I don't know," he said. "But I'm not going to risk ignoring him."

"I can take the last watch, if you'd like?"

"I'd like a bed with deep pillows, Luis."

"Maybe once we get home," he said. A trace of bitterness entered his voice. "If there's any of it left."

Never glanced at his friend. "I think there will be. I've

met the Empress; Crisina will fight tooth and nail."

He blinked. "You've met Empress Crisina?"

"Some years back now. She personally had me thrown from the palace," he said with a grin.

"Why?"

"Mostly because I was snooping around; looking for clues to my past, that sort of thing. I must say, she seemed more at home in her garden than I imagine on a battlefield but she's determined."

Luis sighed. "Is that enough, Never? You know as well as any what the Vadiya are like."

"I do."

"I wonder if Peat is still fighting them."

"He'd smell trouble and avoid it, wouldn't he?"

"Probably." Luis smiled, a faint whiteness of his teeth showing in the dying light.

But it quickly faded. He strode to a small boulder and climbed up, shading his eyes. "Never."

Never joined him and followed the man's gaze. Far below, where the King's Road curved around the mountain, lurked the red glow of campfires. Several campfires. "Travellers or something worse, I wonder," he said.

"Like Jenisan?"

"Exactly." If it was... well, a curse upon the prince. Or king. And if the ingrate had forced Elina to be part of the chase then two curses upon his head.

"I'd judge them to be two days behind at least."

"For now." Never said. "And our path will likely be slower than theirs, so we'll have trouble staying ahead."

"What are you looking at?" Tsolde appeared beside him.

He pointed. "Someone follows. My gold is on Jenisan."

"Then we should keep moving," she said.

"Not in the dark, we could slip and fall, break something. Or worse."

"What about your blue-stone?"

"We need rest. We sleep while they sleep and post a watch as before."

A cold camp and a colder watch; Never paced the perimeter of the trees. He watched the campfires below, but did not let them blind him to other concerns. The night was quiet, the wind had fallen away to reveal only the small sounds of night creatures. An owl overhead – or at least, talons on branches – and creeping things but nothing sinister.

When he woke Luis and sought his rest, sleep was slow to come. He turned often and it wasn't simply the deep chill to the air.

Something was amiss.

Not like the sea-creatures, not the new unease he'd experienced around Snow – something different yet vaguely familiar. On a whim, he lifted the crystal marble free and held it up to the moon, where a beam slipped through the canopy.

The figure stood with arms spread to each side but the tilt of the head gave no indication of the expression.

"And what are you trying to tell me?" he whispered.

The figure did not move.

He returned the ball to an inner pocket and lay back and closed his eyes. Too bad he couldn't force himself to fall asleep.

And yet sleep he must have, for his head was heavy and eyes bleary when Luis woke him to darkness. "Never, they're moving."

"Who?" Never groaned. By the smeary-stars overhead, only a few hours had passed. He rubbed at his eyes.

"Jenisan. Or whoever it is down there – the lights are climbing the road."

Never fumbled for a flask, took a drink and started stuffing his bedroll into his pack. "Then so are we. Wake Tsolde, can you?"

Luis did as instructed and Never moved back to the edge of the road. The red glow moved slowly up one of the ridges. Soon they'd be lost as the King's Road curved with the mountain but something had to be driving them on to take the road at night. They were well-provisioned. By the line of lights, he estimated a score of men.

Disagreeable odds.

"Will they find our trail?" Tsolde asked when she moved to stand beside him.

"Possibly." He glanced back up at the night sky. "They'll pass this point during daylight hours and may see some evidence. Whenever they hit the avalanche, I expect they'll turn back for a thorough search in any event."

"We'll be long gone by then," Luis said.

"Let's hope so," Never replied. "Who knows what waits ahead; I've not had much occasion to leave the King's Road often on this side of the ranges."

Tsolde put her hands on her hips as she turned to face the shadowy trail beside the stand of trees. "Whatever it is we'll deal with it."

"Hold on to that stubbornness," Never said. "I fear we'll need it soon enough."

Leading with his blue-stone, which he periodically rubbed between his hands, Never took them up the winding trail. In places, the looming ghosts of calf-high fern lined the path. Rough-cut steps climbed in a long zig-zag. At each landing he paused a moment to catch his breath as the air gradually thinned.

When dawn lightened the sky, they stopped where a mountain stream flowed from the very rock-face. Deep and quite wide, it was also short, the current slow. It soon disappeared beneath stone again. But he bent to drink and refill his flask. The water chilled his teeth and banished the slight haze he'd been walking under. How quickly sleepiness had crept up on him.

"We should rest here," Luis said. "While there's no wind or rain."

Never paused. A moment to ease the ache in his limbs would be welcome... and yet, best not to tempt fate. "Let's push a little further."

He appraised Never a moment. "You look more tired than I feel."

"Now, now, Luis. Mother-Hen doesn't suit you."

Luis laughed. "Well, I'm keeping an eye on you just the same."

He climbed higher. The path was old, disused it seemed, yet it did have the look of something that had once been important. He'd never travelled it before, but there was a chance it would run parallel with the King's Road long enough to see them safely beyond the slide.

And it seemed likely all the way until noon, when the path ended.

A huge door of stone and steel blocked the wall. The trail had narrowed into a passage, walls surging up around them, but in the shadows with the sickly green and white lichen lay only the great door. Pebbles and shards of stone lay before it. A broken haft of some tool rested beneath it too. Never frowned at the door as he ran fingers over the rough marks on the surface. "Shall I knock?" Nothing about it gave the impression that it had been opened recently and the axe or whatever tool someone tried in the past had certainly failed.

Tsolde exhaled. "Try something."

He placed a hand against the cold surface. Unyielding. He knelt by one of the large hinges – buried in lichen. There were no symbols carved across the face of the door, no handle either.

He gave it a thump.

A deep boom rang out but the door did not open.

"Something better," Tsolde said.

"Sound advice, Lady Tsolde," he replied.

Luis was prodding different parts of the wall and the door itself with the butt of his spear, but there were no hidden switches or levers. Despite the absence of the five-pointed leaf, Never pricked his finger with a dagger point and pressed against the door.

Nothing.

He drew the symbol – and nothing again.

"Why did you do that?" Tsolde asked.

"Just in case. It worked often enough on the Isle."

She glanced over their back-trail. "If this is useless, shouldn't we hurry and take that other path you mentioned?"

"If we can reach it."

He led them back down, unease growing within his gut. The closer they came to the King's Road, the greater chance they had of running into pursuit. It all depended on whether Jenisan had reached the avalanche and turned back. Who knew when or even whether they'd stopped to rest?

The sun began to set as they neared the rush of the stream, where he paused to drink the cold water – the chill once again waking him a little.

"I'm going to scout ahead again," Luis said, dumping his pack.

Never waved a hand as he sat against a stone and unhooked his own pack. Tsolde continued to pace, one hand on the dagger her father had left her.

"You'll wear it out," he said.

"What?"

"The mountain," he replied. "Why don't you stop the pacing and take a moment."

At first she seemed to be about to retort, but she only shook her head. "I cannot go back, Never. I won't. We have to stay ahead of them somehow."

"We'll find a way."

"And if we don't?"

"Then pretend we captured you. You've never met Jenisan, have you?"

She shook her head.

"Then the new King won't know any different. Simply tell him we took you from some village and he'll have you returned."

"Good plan, Never but there's a flaw. You'd be captured. Or worse."

He grinned up at her. "True, and I'd hate that – we'll have to avoid it."

Footsteps approached – someone moving swiftly. Never stood and Tsolde narrowed her eyes in the growing darkness but it was only Luis. His eyes were wide and his chest heaved.

Trouble – hardly surprising, really.

"We have royal company I take it?" Never asked.

Luis shook his head, sucking in a breath of air. "Worse. It's Elina, Never. She's the one leading the hunting party."

Chapter 5.

"She looks furious," Luis added.

Never began to pace, echoing Tsolde. Was Elina furious at being forced into the position of chasing him down, or just furious with him? Hard to say with her; she seemed to have strong feelings for the King and no doubt Jenisan had been quick to exercise leverage over her. "How close?"

"They're moving slowly, in case of ambush, but we need to do something."

"Damn."

Tsolde caught his arm. "Think of something, Never."

"Did you think I was writing a ballad?"

"Of course not!"

"Listen. We cannot pass them and there is nowhere to hide. The door is sealed – that leaves negotiation. She will spare the two of you if I surrender," he said.

Luis shook his head. "No. That's not a solution."

"It is, my friend – just not one you were hoping for," he said. "I won't have either of you hurt on my account."

The treasure-hunter muttered a curse. Tsolde resumed

pacing, twisting the ends of her braid.

The clicking of stone on stone broke the silence.

A rock-turtle was climbing from the stream, its heavy feet clacking across the path. The name was deceptive – it was no true turtle, but its slow gait and stony skin gave it enough similarities. The creature stood no taller than a turtle but its head was broader, flatter – the hard ridges of its mouth were used to crush tough beetle shells and crack the scales of fish.

In the water, it was far more agile – on land it was slow, four feet gripping the stone. But its rock-like skin allowed it to blend in. He'd once sat upon one by accident, something it didn't appreciate if the rasping growl had been any indication.

Tsolde waved to the creature. "Look – a Tremasch. We're saved."

He frowned. "How?"

"They often live in pods, under rocky streams like this."

"I can't hold my breath very long, you know."

She shook her head. "No. Listen – they only choose safe places, always two exits. It stops them being caught by mountain-trappers."

Never brushed aside the question of why anyone would hunt such creatures. "How can you be sure?"

"Just trust me," she said. "If we swim down, there will be a way out."

"But how far?" Luis asked. "What if the other exit is halfway across the mountain?"

"I'll check," she said.

Never frowned. How dangerous was it? The echo of voices from below drifted up. No time. "Quickly, then."

Tsolde dropped her pack to the stone and stepped into

the stream, diving below with a muffled cry at the cold, no doubt. Never strode forward, bending by the edge. Tsolde's figure swam down into the murk, a pale smudge.

"We're running out of time," Luis said. "If she doesn't find anything..."

"I can still surrender."

Luis only glanced over his shoulder to where the voices had died down. Never followed the man's gaze but no-one appeared – yet. Back to the water and Tsolde was breaking the surface.

"There is a way – I see light," she said. Her lips had already turned faintly blue.

A shout rose from their back trail.

"Go," Never cried, dragging Luis toward the water. The spearman fell with a splash. "I'll hold them off then follow," he added when Luis surfaced, eyes wide.

"Never, wait," Tsolde said.

"Don't waste it," he hissed. She clenched her teeth but took a deep breath and ducked below the water.

"Swear it," Luis said, his mouth a firm line.

"I swear."

Luis followed Tsolde and Never stood to fold his arms. Men climbed the trail, slowing and spreading out as they noticed his figure standing in the near-darkness. The lead soldier, a stout fellow with a heavy beard, signalled to those behind him. The Hanik men bore bows and short swords but did not draw.

Though the leader's words were in Hanik, he'd obviously sent for Elina.

"Long night, eh?" Never asked them.

No-one spoke. Some of the men shifted their feet as

they waited. One knelt to ready a lantern, its warm glow soon spreading over the rocks. What were their orders? Still no-one had made a threatening move but how long would that last? Perhaps they were afraid of his curse. More likely, Jenisan wanted him alive – a public execution seemed the man's style.

A shorter figure approached, resolving into Elina, her hair tied into a plait and her bow gripped in a gloved hand. Dark rings of weariness circled her eyes. Her expression was one of surprise. "Never? Where's Luis and the girl?"

"I sent them back down the mountain," he said. "It was safer."

She shook her head. "We didn't pass anyone."

"Must have been while you were napping."

"You know why I've come."

He took a chance. "I know you were forced into this."

Elina pressed her lips together. She nodded to one of the men behind her. The fellow brought forth a net with weighted points. "Never, I want this to be peaceful. Don't make me hurt you," she said.

He spun a knife into his hand, slipping it from an inner sheath, and held it poised over his palm. "I make you the same offer."

"Each of these men have families, Never. People who care for them. Many have children – I know you won't hurt them."

Never smiled a sad smile. "Only if you force me."

Silence fell between them. One of her men swallowed and Elina cast her bow down where it clattered across the stony trail. "Damn you, he won't accept failure, Never. Even from me. Surrender."

"And walk merrily to my death?" There was no-one to

protect now, Luis and Tsolde would have had time to escape. Giving up might have kept Elina from following them, but giving up also meant giving up on answers. No. He'd searched too long.

And there was still Snow to confront.

Time to make his own exit.

"I can try and convince him, Never. He will listen –"

"His Royal Highness does not care for my kind, Elina. He would kill me no matter the accident that led us here."

She glanced away – was it shame? She knew she couldn't convince her King, knew her words had been empty; he saw it in her posture. But when Elina turned back, her eyes had hardened. "You're not leaving me any choice."

"True." Never grinned as he sheathed his blade. "Careful if you follow."

Confusion registered in her eyes. He spun and dived into the stream. Cold enveloped him, numbing his hands and face, and darkness ruled. He swam down, kicking hard with hands outstretched as he searched for the opening. Distant cries faded above as his fingers closed over the rim of a narrow opening. Never dragged himself into the tunnel, scrambling for hand-holds. He pulled himself along, kicking until his lungs began to strain.

But there was light.

It glowed above, streaming down in pale green.

Never reached for it, fighting the pain in his chest and exhaling a stream of bubbles as he neared the light source – and exploded forth with a gasp.

He blinked water from his eyes.

A luminous cavern surrounded him, a high roof covered in glowing stone shapes. Something in the stone possessed its own glow, he'd seen it before; an eerie light. The pool he treaded water within was lined with more of it and he swam over to a gap, pulling himself free where he lay across the stone, shivering a moment.

"Never?"

He looked up. Luis and Tsolde, both miserable-looking and drenched, rushed around from one of the green columns. "Who else?" he said with a grin, unable to stop his teeth chattering.

Chapter 6.

"Where are we then?" he asked. He brushed a finger across the nearest stone and it came away with a faint glowing powder. Nearby, a groove in the ground revealed recent scuff marks – the dwelling of the rock-turtle?

"An underground cave of some sort," Luis said. "Bigger than I was expecting, that's for certain."

Tsolde jerked a thumb over her shoulder. "The Tremasch has a path, it leads outside – I can feel the air further along."

"Elina?" Luis asked.

"She's up there with a dozen men, maybe more. I doubt anyone will follow at first, but we should hurry. If they all swim down they'll probably stage then set out together – they're afraid of me," he said. And why shouldn't they be? Yet he kept most of the bitterness from his voice.

Tsolde led them quickly between the green columns to the sound of their boots squelching. It echoed in the cavern until the faint stirring of air met his face and Tsolde brought them to a halt. She knelt by a small opening – again, something they'd have to crawl – or wriggle – through in order to reach the other side.

"I'll go first," she said, sticking her head into the tunnel.

"Careful," he said.

"I know, I know."

Once Tsolde was through, Luis followed, pausing at one point. "Trouble?" Never asked.

Luis shifted and dragged himself forward. "It gets tight in the middle – just take a deep breath."

Never sighed but when he reached the narrow part of the passage he was able to reach for handholds ahead, suck in the night air and haul himself through with little difficulty, and only a moment's discomfort as what seemed to be the weight of the entire mountain pressed upon him.

And then Luis was helping him to his feet on the banks of another stream, this one empty of water, and only a jumble of rocks beneath. New starlight softened the hard edges. The scent of pine drifted across from the opposite bank.

He shivered. How inviting, the pines – whatever shelter they offered would be most welcome. And with no supplies, no climbing equipment, food or fire-making tools – they were in for a rough night.

"Can we close the opening?" Luis asked.

Never pointed to the dry riverbed. "If we pile up enough heavy rocks, we'd slow them at the very least. How's your back feeling?"

"It's shivering in anticipation."

Never chuckled as he climbed into the riverbed.

Tsolde straightened. "Won't that block the Tremasch?"

"He'll find another home," Never said as together, he and Luis lifted the first stone. The largest they could handle, they carried it to the edge of the bed then started to build a pile. Tsolde joined them, collecting smaller pieces and stacking them beside the tunnel.

Once they had enough stone, Never and Luis used the pile to help themselves lift the biggest ones out, grunting and muttering curses as they worked. Once the tunnel was half-covered, they returned for the stepping stones and added them to the top – sealing the opening as Tsolde added the smaller pieces, wedging them between gaps.

Never leant against the wall, breathing hard a moment. "Not bad." It would hold up any who tried to follow for some time. Without any way to bring leverage of bodyweight, let alone grip the stones well, Jenisan's men would be hard-pressed to clear the blockage.

With luck, they'd give up and seek a different path.

Or head back.

Which might mean trouble for Elina... yet Jenisan would be disappointed, yes. Not crazed, surely? She was a smart girl; she'd be able to take care of herself.

He made to push himself from the wall but his limbs were slow to respond. How long since he'd slept? No matter – he had to keep moving. If they tried to set up a camp, they'd all freeze and die from exposure while they slept. "We have to keep walking," Never said.

"How long?" Tsolde asked. Her hair still clung to her head, braid glistening.

"Until we dry off or come across a nice, warm forest fire," he said.

"Into the trees then?" Luis asked. "I think I see a trail."

Never waved a hand. "Lead on."

The wood on the opposite side of the dry riverbed

climbed with the mountain, pine needles littering the ground. Enormous branches spread over the trail, blocking the stars. The path twisted back around on itself, sending them downhill for a little while. When it began to climb again, Luis stopped, flipping his spear into his grip.

A white owl screeched, flying soundlessly overhead.

Luis chuckled then continued.

They moved higher into the wood.

Near midnight a waning moon peered through the needles and Never found himself blinking at the dark trail before him. His clothes had dried somewhat but the air still chilled him as he walked. Tsolde was muttering to herself and Luis strode on without complaint, soon slipping into a crouch and waving them forward.

Never knelt beside Tsolde. "Luis?"

He pointed with his spear, moonlight glinting on the blade. "I think there's a village ahead. See, beyond the fallen tree."

A tiny glow rested between dark shapes. They might have been buildings, they might have been more trees and the light was hard to pinpoint. Was it simply moonlight reflecting off something? A slight breeze rustled the needles, bringing with it the faint scent of woodsmoke.

"Woodsmoke," he said.

"Is it safe?" Luis asked.

"Some of the mountain-folk are quite standoffish," Tsolde said, frowning toward where the glow had been.

"We might have to risk it – we need shelter," Never said as he pulled himself upright courtesy of a low-hanging branch. "My legs are beginning to feel like water."

Never drew a knife and led the way along the trail, closing

in on the first large shadow – which was a hut. His boots crunched and he stopped. No movement or sound from the building.

He lifted his foot and squinted in the dark.

Something pale, thin... bones.

"Tread carefully," he said, keeping his voice low.

Further along, more bones, strewn about the path between buildings. All small and thin, most birds or small animals, it seemed. Fragile rib cages were broken and skulls peeked from piles of needles. In a patch of moonlight ahead, a collection had been arranged into something of a small shrine.

A clearing appeared.

Ringed by more shadowy shapes of houses, it was easier to discern uneven thatch in the rooves, sagging eaves and boarded-up windows.

Deserted? Or something worse? The clearing appeared to be a bone-yard, littered with slender bones, the larger pieces made into small piles. Some were crowned by skulls – he saw fox, deer and even something that might have been a cracked bear-skull.

"What is this place?" Tsolde asked.

"Abandoned, I hope," Never said. He approached the nearest home, its door ajar and called softly within.

Nothing.

He nudged the door open with the butt of a knife. Rusted hinges screamed and he winced. But nothing stirred within. The moonlight revealed an empty floor and another collection of bones; this time rodents, which was obvious, since one pile had been arranged into an accurate reconstruction of a rat.

"Luis, start checking the other houses. We're looking for something secure and easily defended," he said. Tsolde looked up at him. "You're staying with me," he said.

She put her hands on her hips. "Don't do that."

"Try to protect you?"

"I can protect myself – I shouldn't have to remind you of all people."

"Humour me while we're here and once we've found a good spot you can take first watch."

She caught his arm. "Never."

He met her fierce gaze and couldn't help smiling. Her mother had the same look whenever she'd tried to convince Tsolde to follow her wishes. "I'm not being careful because I doubt your ability to take care of yourself."

"Then let me help."

"I will. And don't forget who got us out of trouble back there. How do you know so much about rock-turtles?" he said as he led her to the next home and glanced inside. Another bone collection – this time they formed a pattern where they rested upon a table.

"A regular. He's a hunter and he stays at the Stag once a season and he's a good storyteller."

"Well, I'm glad he is."

"Me too," she said. The tension had left her voice. A good thing too – he didn't need her pushing so hard.

"How about this one?" Luis called from the opposite side of the clearing.

He'd found a two storey inn built beneath a huge pine, its limbs spreading over the roof, generations of needles covering the thatch. At least it had a better-looking roof than the other homes.

"There's a stove; looks like it'll burn. We can use dried needles for kindling and there's plenty of fuel around," he said. "The upper floor gives a good vantage point of most of the village too."

"Let's try it out," Never said. "Can't be worse than any of the others."

Luis gave a grimace. "Well, there are some strange bones in this place."

"Stranger than out there?" Tsolde asked.

"You decide," Luis said, pushing the door open with one arm.

Chapter 7.

The first room was empty of all but dust on creaking floorboards. Two doors led out – one into a cloakroom where a single, oiled cloak hung on a peg. Musty, but still whole.

The common room, in contrast, was full.

Men, women and children sat at square tables in the silence of death, their bones pale in the moonlight. Some held empty cups, others had been posed as if talking. One mother had an arm resting around the shoulder of a smaller skeleton; and at the bar, the innkeeper's skull had fallen askew.

Never shivered. Who would do such a thing and why?

"They're held together with a resin and sticks and string," Luis said. "Someone has slept upstairs in one of the rooms but I cannot say when. Some time ago, it seems."

"Then we must be on our guard," he said. "What of the stove?"

Luis took them behind the bar and into the kitchen. Empty shelves and cold steel only, with a giant table between.

No knives or ladles, not even a frying pan remained. But the stove did appear functional, with flint and tinder in a box nearby, so Never sent Luis and Tsolde outside to collect fuel while he barricaded the back door.

Upstairs he found enough bedding in the empty rooms to make the kitchen floor comfortable and then checked on the room with the unmade bed. An empty water flask and a blunted dagger lay beside the cot.

He crouched, lifting the blade. No unique markings. Who had slept here? Why had they left? And more importantly, why visit such a place to begin with? Perhaps it was a final survivor of some calamity that had befallen the village. If so, was the person who'd slept here the same who'd made bone-shrines all over the village? The scene in the common room?

Never returned to the kitchen to find a flickering light. Luis had started the fire and Tsolde was laying her still-damp tunic across the table near the stove. Her undergarments clung and revealed a little too much of her figure.

For years now he'd been watching out for her, whenever he'd passed through Lenan he made time to visit, and it was a little unnerving to see her changing. He'd grown accustomed to thinking of her as a child, despite evidence to the contrary. After all, she'd been running the Young Stag for years now. He should have known better.

"Stop staring," she told him without looking up from where she was arranging her boots before the stove.

"You'll catch a cold."

"Not with that fire," she said as she moved to her section of floor and pulled the blankets over her with a frown, no doubt at the musty scent of the unused fabric. "And I'm taking the last watch, so my clothes will be dry by then."

"And I'll take first watch," Luis said. He loaded a few larger pieces into the stove and gave a little nod of satisfaction.

"Wake me when it's my turn then," Never said, then removed and arranged his own cloak, tunic and boots before crawling into his makeshift bed where he lay back, the crackling of the fire washing over him, its growing warmth a blessing.

Even the strange bones were not enough to keep him from sleep.

***

"All clear," Luis said when he woke Never.

"Good. I'm not in the mood for a surprise."

Luis grinned, keeping his voice soft. "I left that cloak up there too. It's no stove but it's better than nothing."

"Thanks."

Never climbed the stairs and found the cloak draped over a chair which Luis had obviously taken from the common room. It had been set before the dusty window-pane and Never shivered as he wrapped the garment around his shoulders.

Only the stars graced the clearing below, the bones hard to discern, the other buildings mostly lost in shadow. If anyone was out there, they were holed up somewhere themselves.

The watch passed slowly and he stood to check downstairs twice, returning to his chair each time. The seat was hard and unforgiving – that and the cold kept him awake at least. Never lifted his legs and stretched them on the window-sill, releasing a long sigh.

"That's my cloak."

The voice had spoken in Hanik, soft and raspy. The following words seemed to be about an arrow.

Never froze.

Had Jenisan's men caught up to them? Never might not have understood all of what the voice said, but he answered as best he could. "My Haniker is poor."

"How about Marlosi?" the voice asked, the words clear but slow, as if unused for a long time.

"Better."

"Are you planning to stay in Garmedl long then?"

Never frowned. The fellow didn't seem to be one of Elina's men. What did he want? "Just until morning. We are merely travelling through."

"Ah. Like all the rest." A creak of wood. "Few come to Garmedl any more, you see. I'm waiting for the others to return home."

The other villagers? Never resisted the urge to turn. There was still the threat of the arrow and who knew what else. The fellow had entered the room without making a single sound.

"Are they due to return soon?"

"Any day now." Another creak, as if the man shifted his weight. "So, stranger. What brings Marlosi folk like you two and a young Hanik girl together in these parts?"

"We're heading for the Iron Pass," Never said. "But an avalanche forced us to take a bit of a detour. Would you know of a swift path we might take by chance?"

"Might do. Head north out of the village and take the trail marked with an old snake. You'd better watch out however, there's a strange fellow up that way. Seen him a few times and he doesn't like anyone going near his caves."

"We'll steer clear of him then, thank you."

"As well you should." He cleared his throat. "Stranger, I want to ask. Have you seen..."

Never waited.

"No, never mind. I'll check myself, seems best. Don't want to trouble you folk."

"Can I help?"

"Just little Ali's pet; she's missing."

Ali? What pet? "I don't mind helping search, but wouldn't it be easier in the daylight?" he asked.

Nothing. Was the fellow mulling it over? Raising his bow, drawing the arrow back?

"Hello?"

Never turned his head, slowly.

An empty doorframe behind him. He stood, letting the cloak fall from his shoulders. Not a single trace of the man. Never crept into the hallway and followed it to the next room. Within, an open window and just beyond it, one of the arms of the great pine. The needles were still, their scent sharp in the night.

Where had the man gone?

Never returned to his post and leant up against the window. Had that been a flicker of movement in the house with the rodent bones? Too hard to tell. He strained his ears in the dark but there were no sounds either, just a faint snore from Luis below. Never sat back. Odd.

When it was time to wake Tsolde he warned her about the man. "I don't think he'll return or that he even means us harm somehow, but be prepared."

She nodded. "I will."

He handed her the cloak then added a few more pieces

of wood to the fire before lying back and closing his eyes. If the stranger was waiting for the village to return, it seemed he'd be waiting for a long time.

And maybe that explained the skeletons.

Chapter 8.

Standing in the common room, Never groaned as he rubbed his temples. A fitful remainder to his night's sleep left him battling an aching head but water would probably help. The stove had done its job drying everything out; shame that included his mouth.

"No more visits from strange men then?" he asked Tsolde. She was tying sheets together into a makeshift knapsack, to which Luis was adding flint and tinder. A similarly constructed sheet seemed to contain blankets.

"None," she said. "Sure you didn't imagine him?"

He shook his head. "Not a chance. I'd remember if a man appeared and told me he'd made these shrines."

Luis paused. "The man told you that?"

"Not in so many words, though I have a theory about the village of Garmedl," Never said. "But I need water first. Luis, check the back trail, I'll see what I can find in the way of water. Tsolde, finish up here and join me."

"Right."

The rising sun cast a green tint across the clearing before

the inn, revealing the grime and dirt clinging to many of the bones. As he'd assumed in the night, all were animals. The little shrines had not been disturbed overnight and there was no sign of fresh animal droppings anywhere. Did even animals avoid the village?

None of the houses contained water barrels or anything else of use but a well-worn path led between two buildings and ended at a dry riverbed. The same waterway they'd found near the rock-turtle's lair, no doubt.

And maybe that explained why Garmedl was deserted.

Footsteps approached. Tsolde moved along the trail, arms full of their knapsacks. "What did you find?"

"The river is empty here. Something must have blocked it higher up. That's why the people left the village."

She nodded. "But it doesn't explain the skeletons."

"Perhaps it does."

"How?"

"Our mysterious friend is waiting for people who will never return. I think he tried to make up for it in a somewhat troubling manner."

Her expression fell. "If that's true... it's sad."

"Yes."

He continued his search, heading north of the village where he found a crossroad – a slab of chiselled rock shaped as a snake had been placed in the centre of the trail heading northeast.

It left two other directions, both marked by a wooden sign.

Tsolde pointed to the fading words. "King's Road to the east and west lies another village – Drylh. Perhaps that's where the people of Garmedl went."

"And the snake?" Never asked.

"No idea," she said. "It looks like a warning, doesn't it?"

"Indeed. Let's find Luis before we make any decisions, but our mystery man did suggest the Snake-path was a detour we might take."

"Do you trust him?"

"Well, I don't imagine he would want to mislead us."

"That's something."

Luis was waiting back in the village clearing. "No sign of pursuit," he said.

"Let's hope they've given up on the tunnel then."

"But I did find a cemetery," Luis said. "Which you'll want to see. A rivulet runs beside it too."

"More surprises?" Never asked.

"For a cemetery, it's pretty empty." Luis led them down another path, this one running behind the inn.

As they walked, Never caught glimpses of headstones of old wood, rotting where they stood. When he entered the graveyard he sighed. Empty holes beneath most of the markers. A shovel still stood in the earth beside one grave, silvery cobwebs strung within the handle. The sound of trickling water filled the hush.

"Now we have an explanation for the skeletons," Tsolde said softly.

"We do."

Luis glanced at him. "Your lonesome friend?"

"The fellow who spoke to me last night, yes. He is lonely, it seems. There's an empty riverbed that likely drove the villagers to abandon this place. The man suggested a way around the avalanche, if we want to try it." He added the warning the survivor of Garmedl offered, about the man seen around the mountain caves.

"Ah." Luis paused. "Then do you think we can take his word about the path?"

"He didn't strike me as one for guile," Never said. He moved around some of the markers and knelt beside the tiny stream, no more than a trickle within another dry bed. "And the Iron Pass is, essentially, northward. The snake trail heads in the same direction. I think we can trust his word for now."

Luis nodded as he joined Never and handed over a flask. "From the kitchen," he said.

Never filled it. "Good."

Then it was back to the trail, climbing through the wooded snake-path until the vista opened up around mid-morning. The trail swung around an outcropping, offering a view down to the King's Road.

Far below, steel reflected off the still-rising sun as figures marched the twisting road. Vadiya. Even from a distance, the sheer bulk of their armour was clear. The line of soldiers would soon be lost to sight, heading beneath an arch that served as a gate to the higher peaks and eventually the silver mines.

"There's someone Jenisan should be more concerned by," he said.

"Have they taken the mines then?"

"Hard to say. If Jenisan hasn't caught all the traitors, the Vadiya might have it already."

Tsolde was glaring down at them. "So are they leaving or arriving?"

"Hard to say. They might have been sent down but the avalanche stopped them. If so, they'll be back with tools, that's for sure."

"If Elina's party has the same thought, that will put them in each other's path," Luis said.

He was right. And there was little chance her small force would survive such an encounter. And she didn't deserve that. But there was no way to help her. Never rubbed his neck. No way to warn them either. His fear was not only for the knowledge he might lose if Elina were killed. Despite all the promises he'd made to himself about letting others grow close, he didn't want to be responsible, however indirectly, for yet another death – he simply didn't want her to die.

Not in any circumstances.

"Don't underestimate her, Never," Luis said. "I doubt she'd let herself be surprised."

He nodded slowly. "True enough. We keep climbing then."

Each step had the dull thud of betrayal... but he strode on anyway. Luis was right; she'd take care of herself. And if he tried to find a way down, she'd only try and clap him in chains for His Royal Majesty the Fool.

Although, the man was only a fool if he was wrong about the Amouni.

And Never didn't know enough to truly agree or disagree with the man yet. Jenisan was only trying to protect his people and seek vengeance for the death of his father. Mistaken, but understandable.

"Still, you're not having my head," he muttered.

Noon came and passed when the trail sharpened into a set of steps leading up to a huge carving of dark stone. A snake's head at rest. It looked as if it were protruding from the very mountain. Fangs peeked from its mouth and the eyes were sealed shut, moss crawling across the surface and grey pine needles caught in the ridges of brow and the slits of the nose.

Never paused to stare, circling the base of the steps. "Magnificent," he said.

"Must be fifteen feet easily," Luis said.

"See here," Never pointed. The body curled along the mountain, darker ridges of stone almost like stripes. It followed the bends of the King's Road far below. From that vantage point, doubtless few would be able to discern what lay high above them, obscured by trees or mist.

"I think there are gaps in the stone," Luis said.

Tsolde snapped her fingers. "I know what this is. It's the Serpent's Tail; the old mountain kings made it as an escape from their keep. You can reach the ruins but I don't know if anyone has found the way down the tail."

Never frowned up at the closed mouth. "And it looks like we're going to have some trouble with the head."

"Didn't the man from Garmedl say this was a path?"

"Maybe he hasn't used it in the last hundred years," Never said. "And that's why he didn't realise it was closed."

"Very funny."

"There's the man he warned us about too," Luis said.

Never hefted his makeshift pack. "Let's eat first. These berries and nuts we found are just the thing I need to solve this problem."

"Whatever closes your mouth," Tsolde said sweetly.

Chapter 9.

"Well, I'm out of ideas," Never said, slapping one of the snake's fangs.

He did his best to unclench his jaw. Nothing had worked – no hidden levers or buttons, no false stones, no trick with weights or pressure that he or Luis could discern, nothing to do with blood either.

The slithering stone bastard had beaten them.

"Do we turn back?" Tsolde asked. Her expression was no less frustrated as she kicked at a rock. It tumbled down the steps.

Never glanced to the sky. The sun was dipping between distant peaks, golden light crossing the gorges to splash against the snake, creeping along the body toward the head. Hours! All afternoon struggling with it. A waste of time in the end. "I don't know. We'll lose time – days even, if we do. And that might not matter in the short term, but one bad storm and who knows, we might be in serious trouble."

"Have we tried everything?" Luis asked.

Never sighed. "Boost me up again, I'll take one more

look on top."

Luis did as instructed. Never gripped the lid of the closed eye and pulled himself the rest of the way up. Atop the snake's head waited little but scattered needles and the damp remains of what was once a puddle. The body extended along as if emerging from the very cliffs but that was no help. It ended at a sharp angle of walls, swallowed within, and possessing no climbing material, they had little chance of scaling the sheer rock face.

The cracks further along the body, those that gave the appearance of stripes, were too narrow to squeeze between and again, there were no heavy tools on hand to break in, if that were even possible. It left the head or mouth of the serpent itself.

He knocked against the head, kicking at odd-coloured patches of stone as he searched. Nothing new. No hidden switches.

"Any luck?"

"Nothing," he said. He stamped a boot against the head. "Pacela's Curse." He stamped again, hitting harder this time.

A boom echoed and stone cracked against stone, dust rising.

Never fell into a crouch, arms outstretched… but nothing else happened. He looked up to the stone walls before him. Nothing.

"You two hurt?" he called.

Luis laughed. "No, but you should see this."

Never peered over the edge. The jaw had fallen open – sinking into the ground to reveal steps leading up the throat. A clever mechanical device? No matter – it was open! He climbed down and dusted his hands. "I should have stomped on his head earlier."

Tsolde snorted. "Look at the snake's eyes."

Golden light now covered the serpent's head and the eyes were open, some manner of onyx set as pupils. "The sunset opened the way?"

"I'd say so," she said.

Never shook his head but he was smiling. "In we go then."

"Can we be sure it's safe?" Luis asked.

"No. But I'm confident neither Jenisan nor the Vadiya will bother us here. And the hermit of Garmedl thought this path could take us to the Iron Pass."

"And the strange man he mentioned? The one who doesn't like visitors?"

"We'll be watching for him too."

Never stepped into the mouth and into the body. A broad tunnel stretched before them, thin pillars of golden light cutting across from the sunset. As he walked, his feet stirred dust which climbed into the air to glitter. Beautiful.

Behind him, Luis gave a cough. "Damn dust."

The snake's body continued to turn with the mountain, naught but dust on the floor. Orange splashed across the opposite wall and a chill breeze snuck in through the same openings. He knelt once to examine the floor.

"What is it?"

A brass button, tarnished from rain, lay in a small crevice. "Nothing of note," he said and moved on. "But people have been in here after the old mountain kings."

Night began to fall, and shadow with it. The tunnel grew dark, but not so dark that he did not see a gaping hole in the floor. Wind stirred up from the mighty drop below, the dark green of pine climbing the crevice. The gap was wide enough to leap across but as the evening darkened, any similar holes might come as a nasty surprise indeed.

"Once we've passed this it might be time to consider stopping for the night," Never said.

Luis nodded. "Agreed."

"Too bad we can't start a fire – it's going to be cold in here," Tsolde said.

Never backed up. "Better than outside at least."

He ran forward then leapt across the gap, landing easily. Tsolde followed, then Luis. They moved away from the hole and the cold wind, picking a spot some distance from openings in the wall too, and spread their bedrolls.

More berries and nuts for their cold meal, all of which had been foraged while struggling to open the snake door, along with some of their dwindling water. Never took first watch. It was cold and uneventful, he sought his thin bed, stone eating through the blanket, and wrapped his cloak around his torso.

By dawn he was ready to leave, aching and cold, breath steaming in the air despite having slept close to the others, he and Luis protecting Tsolde. "Onward," he said, after they'd each sipped from the flask.

"We'll need more of this soon." Tsolde passed the flask to Luis.

"If it looks like this path is going to take us nowhere we'll turn back and resupply," he said. "We have enough for two days if we're frugal. I'm hoping this passage climbs to the surface well before then."

"Can't hurt to look a little further," Luis said.

Never led them further along the serpent's tail until reaching another hole in the path, this one wide enough that it could not be leapt. Instead, he had to cling to the sides of the snake's body and inch his way across uneven footing. Sometime in the past, someone had bolted handholds into the wall, making the task easier. A cruel wind threw his cloak about but he crossed without looking down. Luis followed, leaving Tsolde on the other side.

Her face was pale but she took the first step after a deep breath, gripping the rusted rungs with white knuckles.

"Just a little farther," Never said when she reached the halfway point.

"Let me concentrate," she snapped. "Why did they make such a dangerous trail anyway?"

He waited by the edge of the stone. Tsolde reached for the last hand hold, stretching her foot toward firm ground.

Stone cracked.

She screamed, limbs flailing. Never lunged. He snapped his hand over her wrist, jerking her to safety. She gripped him, whole body trembling. His own heart thundered. With her cheek pressed against his chest, it probably deafened her.

"You're safe," he told her.

She took a shuddering breath. "Thank you, Never."

"Need a moment?"

"No, let's keep going. Get me away from the edge."

Never led her further along, passing through bars of light where they cut through the wall. Ahead lay only darkness where the mountain swallowed the tail. Too bad the bluestone was lost. Elina probably had it. Had she avoided the Vadiya? He could only hope.

He paused at the limits of the light. Barely visible was a series of steps – leading up. Hope? Or a fool's hope? "If there's no change by nightfall, we turn back. We'll still have enough water to reach that mountain pool back beneath the entrance," he said. "Objections? Ideas? Anything?"

"You could roll those lucky dice of yours," Luis said.

Never patted an inner pocket of his vest – drawing out die and the marble figurine. "Hold this a moment, will you?" He asked Tsolde. She accepted the crystal, glad of the distraction it seemed by the way she examined the figure within.

"Think this will help?" he asked Luis.

The spearman shrugged. "Why not? I seem to remember them getting you out of a few shifts at the oar back on the Carene."

Never grinned. "Very well." He turned back and held the Amouni die up to the faint light and pointed to one side. "See this symbol – like three fingers on a hand? It's lucky. The coil is too, if you're playing Houses."

"What about that one? Looks like a lightning bolt hitting a V," Luis said.

"In some games if you roll that you lose your hand."

"Ah."

Never crouched across from Luis and tossed the die. It rattled over the stone and bounced from Luis' boot.

Luis bent and paused, hand hovering over the die a moment.

"Well?"

"Maybe you should roll again," he said, lifting it to show the side with the lightning bolt.

Never scratched at his beard. Whenever he and Snow had rolled the bolt in the past, the outcome had been trouble. Like the first time they'd attempted to scale the walls of the palace in Isacina. Or when the scum took Zia into the tar pits, he and Snow had used it to decide who would try follow and who would return to ask Mal for help. Never had been the loser that time and Snow the eventual hero, but at a cost...

Hard to imagine a poorer omen.

"Never, something's happening." A hint of concern filled Tsolde's voice. "Is the little man supposed to move?"

"At times."

She placed the marble into his palm. In the dim light the fellow cowered, hands over his head. Something in the air changed – a tightness, a sense of indrawn breath. And heat. Heat? He turned to the stair. Nothing but darkness.

"Something is happening," he said. "Be ready."

"For what?" Tsolde asked.

"Anything. Everything."

Luis set his tied blanket aside and flipped his spear into both hands, holding it across his chest. Tsolde lifted her dagger. Never drew his own blades. He nearly swore when his blood pulsed in his veins, as if eager to meet whatever danger was coming.

The sense of warmth grew – the change in air came from their back-trail. Never swallowed. Something wrong approached. There was no sound, no light but it was clear enough; his very blood was responding.

Silvery light flashed. A heavy thud followed, vibrations running along the tunnel. Never took a step forward. "Be ready to run. Up the stair."

Light faded, revealing a black figure glimmering with an iridescence that seemed to lurk beneath oily skin. Heat surged from it, buffeting Never's face, even from a distance. The thing was stout, round and bore no visible eyes. Its legs and arms seemed to burst from random points in the body, striking the stone and heaving the thing forward. It quickly gathered speed, the heat pouring forth as it approached.

Never hurled a dagger at the bulk.

The steel slipped into the body with barely a pause, as if swallowed whole. The creature did not so much as flinch. "Go," he cried.

Chapter 10.

Never spun as Luis dragged Tsolde up the first few steps. The faint silver light offered enough help that they did not stumble. Never leapt after them, glancing over his shoulder. Could the thing fit in the stairway?

"Damn." Easily.

How to slow it? The heat seared his back as he charged up the stairs – only to ease suddenly. He spun. The dark, seething creature of silver and shadow had come to a halt and was turning, legs slapping the walls as it shifted its bulk.

Something... someone stood behind it!

Never held his breath.

The newcomer stood tall and dark, yet the whites of his eyes were clear and his expression was one of determination in the silvery glow. How was he withstanding the heat? The ball of death surged forward and the man threw himself against the wall – but not to evade. His legs and arms, his chest even, sank into the rock as he side-stepped then swung them at the creature, as if pulling a curtain down.

Stone followed.

It flashed down from the very roof, smashing the thing into motionlessness. Steam hissed and silver pooled around a huge column of stone which now blocked half the Serpent's Trail. The stranger emerged from the stone wall, chest heaving where he stood a moment, before shuddering and collapsing to the ground.

Never ran back. "Can you hear me?"

The man offered no response.

Never knelt. Beneath a dark grey tunic, the man's skin was hot to the touch, like a wall of stone blasted by sun all afternoon. Never gave the fellow a shake. Nothing. He took the man by the shoulders and braced himself, straining and failing to move their saviour. Like dragging a stone!

The hissing silver was spreading and the man lay in its path.

"Luis!" he called.

The echo of footsteps followed and Luis appeared, eyes wide as he took in the scene. "Never?"

"Help me roll him over."

Luis knelt beside him. "What happened?"

"He's heavier than he looks, so we go together, right? Roll him toward the stairs, I doubt we could carry this guy."

Luis nodded, then took a firm grip on the man. He grunted when Never gave a nod, pushing as Luis pulled, leaning his body weight back. The stone-man rose and teetered, then thumped down as Luis jumped back.

"Nearly lost my toes."

"Again. We have to save him – he stopped that thing," Never said.

They rolled the man once more, then a third time, eventually breaking into a sweat when they hit the steps.

"What now?" Luis gasped.

The pool of silvery liquid was slowing, spreading where the man had lain, but did not seem as though it would move much further. "Find Tsolde. We'll figure out the next step as soon as this guy wakes."

"Will he?"

"He's breathing, that's something."

When Tsolde returned she shook her head as she glanced at the strange man. "Do you think this is the one the hermit told us about?"

"Could be," Never said. "Let's hope he's not in a bad mood when he wakes."

"We'll soon find out," Luis said.

The man of stone's eyes fluttered and he flinched, but upon seeing the apparent absence of the silver-creature, sighed, closing them again. "You are fools to come here but I am glad you survived," he said. His voice was surprisingly normal – Never had expected a deep, gravelly growl.

"Thank you for saving us," Never said.

The man sat up with a smile that was half wince. "I imagine you have many questions – let me answer but one for now. I am Darom."

Never made the introductions. He wanted to ask 'what are you?' but resisted, instead going for the next most pressing question. "Darom, what was that creature?"

He stood. "Let us find a safer place, follow me and I will tell you what I know." He started up the stairs, moving slowly at first, and Never followed at an even slower pace, hands reaching for the walls in the darkness. By the slight fumbling, Luis and Tsolde were having the same trouble.

Darom paused. "Ah. I apologise." Never waited. Soft

creaks followed and pinpoints of light appeared high above, popping into existence and leading up. They cast enough light that he could see the steps again.

Their strange saviour removed his hands from the wall, took a breath and resumed his climb. Never kept pace after checking on Tsolde and Luis, both of whom followed not quite close enough to trample his heels, but near enough.

"The creature that attacked you is a... mistake, perhaps. It came about long ago, when the mountain kings dug too deep with their mines. I do not know much more, other than that they rarely climb so high."

"I did not think we were so close to the mines," Never said.

"You are right. They are still a few days travel north east, which is what concerns me about the Black Ember's appearance here."

The stairs ended at a landing with a single door. "The Mountain Kings' Palace, the ruins of Kathuer, such as remain, lie beyond this door, only a little way further now. However, I would request something of you each, if you would consider it I would be pleased."

"Please," Never said.

"Would you permit me to accompany you there and beyond a little ways? I am travelling near to where you doubtless travel and would be happy to offer my protection in exchange for the company." His expression suggested sincerity.

Never glanced at Luis and Tsolde. If another Black Ember appeared, Darom would no doubt earn his keep, even as he had done so already. "No objections from me, Never," Luis said.

"Nor I," Tsolde added.

"Welcome aboard," Never said with a grin.

***

A warm wind cut across the ruins of Kathuer, stirring dark clouds and dried leaves alike as Darom gestured to the nearest building. "There is a well in the courtyard beyond."

Never blinked when his eyes adjusted to the new light. Their guide's skin was no longer a dark earth, but more the paler wash of exposed stone – its shade not unlike the surrounding walls.

But Never did not mention it, instead, heading for the well. The rope and bucket were well-maintained. He lowered the rope as Luis and Tsolde waited. "I wonder if Darom is the one who takes care of this place?"

"Who else might?" Luis said.

There was no evidence of recent visitors in the ruin. The walls were chipped and scarred from weapons and fire when, at one point in the history of Elina's ancestors, Hanik settlers had come and began, then ended a war with the mountain kings. A stripe of purple stone ran along the base of the wall and even that of the well.

"Do you know what the purple is for?" Never asked Tsolde.

"No. I've never travelled here, only heard of it." She turned back to the clearing and the other, smaller structures, none of which amounted to a full room. "To be honest, there isn't much left. Less than I thought."

Never hauled the bucket up and drank, then passed it around. Darom approached as they filled their single flask. "There is a road out of the palace grounds that will lead down to what is now known as the King's Road but it is busy of late. I doubt you will want to cross paths with the Vadiya."

"Not truly."

"There is another way, should you wish it." He paused. "There is danger enough there too and I cannot guide you through it."

"What danger?" Never asked. "Another Black Ember?"

"Not the Yimash, no," he said. "It was once called the Narrow Way. It is a gorge that will take you to the Giant's Bridge."

"I know the bridge," Never said. "It will bring us very close to the mines. At the bridge, most travellers will turn toward the Silver Pass but there we can continue higher to the Iron Pass," he said.

Darom drew in a breath. "The Iron Pass? You plan to take it?"

"Yes. I know the pass well."

"Find another way, Never."

"I cannot. We're racing time – I must reach Marlosi before the new moon."

Darom frowned. "Is the risk worth it?"

"Yes," Never said. "No doubt in my mind."

"Then my advice would be to steer clear of Night Lake," he said.

"We will."

"What of the gorge, Darom?" Luis asked. "You mentioned danger."

"So I did. The Narrow Way is a thin path of stone that will take you to the bridge but it is a deathly drop and the winds are strong. If you weigh yourself down with rock, you will pass safely."

Tsolde didn't appear too pleased at his words.

"And you, Darom?" Never asked.

"I will take you to the gorge but then I must leave. I am... needed elsewhere and it is a natural point for our paths to diverge." The stone-like man started from the ruins and Never kept pace, the others following.

"Forgive my curiosity," Never began. "But you can imagine that we might be curious about how you came to be so... strong."

Darom chuckled. "Tactfully put, Never. I am descended of the Mountain People and it seems the old blood no longer hides. I have always been... strong, as you put it."

Old blood. A familiar problem. Or gift, perhaps, in Darom's case. "And it allows you to pass into the mountain?"

"Yes. But at a cost. I believe my ancestors were more adept than I. I will rest long tonight."

"And have you always protected unwary travellers?"

"No. In truth, I see few and reveal myself to fewer."

"But you saved us?"

Darom nodded.

"Through luck?"

He glanced at Never. "Your blood. I could feel your blood. It was old, even to me."

"I've been told I have Amouni heritage."

"I suspected as much," he said. There was no surprise in his bearing – did Darom know something?

The man gestured up ahead, to where the path split into two stairs. One led up and the other stepped down the mountain, doubtless toward the King's Road. "There is your path. Gather what stone you may before crossing."

"Thank you, Darom," he said, Luis and Tsolde echoing his words. "Before we go, I'd like to ask one more question,"

Never said after a moment.

"Yes?"

"You weren't surprised to hear the name Amouni."

"Not truly, no."

"Why is that? I am searching for whatever truths about them I might find. Have you met more of my kind during your time?"

"None. But my guess was true – few seem old to me, you understand."

"Ah." Another quiver of false hope. To be expected perhaps.

"And the Yimash?" Luis asked.

"Yes," Tsolde added. "Is there anything we can do if another appears?"

He smiled sadly. "No, young lady. You are best to flee or at the least, place stone between you and the creature. They are few in number now, but should you travel the Iron Pass as you plan, you may come across one. Sometimes, I have seen them roam that far." He glanced to the stairs leading downward. "And now I must leave; for I must do my part for my master." He started down the steps.

"Your master?" Never called after.

Darom gestured to the stone around him. "I am but a cog in this great mountain."

"Ah." Never started up the steps, skipping a few to catch Luis and Tsolde. And then he stopped.

Cog.

That word. Darom had used the word 'cog' to describe himself – was it a coincidence? Or something more – the man of smoke in the inn had called himself 'Cog'. Gods, had Snow interfered here too?

Never spun.

The path to the King's Road lay empty.

Chapter 11.

Never was still shaking his head by the top of the stair, where Tsolde had stopped to drink from the flask while Luis scouted the shadowy gorge. Had Darom's use of the word 'cog' been innocent or was it something else? The man seemed honest, could he really be another of Snow's pawns?

When he ran his theory by Tsolde she shrugged. "It doesn't seem likely, does it? I mean, why would your brother even want to control a man like Darom?"

"That's what concerns me; I have no idea."

"Snow might have gone crazy, from what you've told me about the Bleak Man, but it doesn't seem like he'd do something for no reason. And there's no reason to use Darom, is there?"

"I would have thought not." He sighed. "I'm probably just seeing his hand in everything now, warranted or not."

"Could be."

"Come and see this," Luis called.

Never and Tsolde joined him by the edge of the gorge. A narrow walkway of grey and purple stone extended across the dark chasm. Sheer sides led down to certain death, the floor of the gorge lost in darkness. The walkway was wide enough for one traveller at a time only – save for a central area which spread into a circle, visible at the very limits of his vision.

Wind rushed up the sides, whistling between stone and tugging at Never's hair when he caught the edge of his cloak.

"What is the circular place in the middle for, I wonder?" Never asked.

"Human sacrifice," Tsolde said, her lips pressed together as she stared. "No-one does so anymore, but my ancestors put a stop to it when we conquered these mountains."

"Then we'd have a lot of company down there if we fall in," Never said.

"That's not funny."

Luis chuckled. "Well, here are the rocks Darom mentioned. Doesn't seem like anyone has used them for some time."

Twin piles of stones, from fist-sized pieces to slabs the length of his arm, sat piled near the path, pale and worn from wind and rain. "Load up your pockets and the bottom of your pant legs," Never said. "I don't know how much we'll need, but make sure you can actually walk. Keep the weight toward the bottom, I don't want either of you tipping over because you're top heavy."

"We're not stupid, Never," Tsolde said.

"My mistake," he said with a grin.

Once he finished loading himself up he lifted a leg, testing the weight. Tough, but he could move his limbs at least. The others were ready. Good. Time to find out just how strong the wind was.

"Tsolde, you're lightest so you're in the middle," he said.

"Fine with me," she replied.

Never clomped onto the path. His first few steps were easy enough, despite the gaping emptiness to either side. The wind ruffled his clothing but it didn't buffet him until much farther along, where it forced him into a crouch. He glanced over his shoulder. Tsolde had crouched too, and Luis was on one knee, his eyes wide.

The wind continued to whistle, rising to a shriek before easing.

Never rose to press on.

The stones did help; they gave a little confidence but by the time he reached the circular space in the centre of the narrow way, he wasn't convinced they were making all that much of a difference. Although the added sense of security was welcome.

An altar sat squat in the centre of the space, dark with centuries of bloodstains.

He moved on.

The rest of the narrow path was easy enough to traverse – until a point two dozen feet from safety, when a gust of wind slammed into him, hard enough to tip his torso. He straightened himself and fell to the stone with a shout. "Down."

Wind continued to howl. It dragged at him, as if trying to pluck him from the walkway and cast him into the gaping maw. Never gripped the earth; arms aching. A shrill screech joined the howling and he shuddered. It was as though the screams of the dead echoed up from the pit of inky shadow.

His hands grew chill.

Would it ever ease? Still he clung to the path, fingers

growing numb, not even daring to turn his head back to check on Tsolde and Luis. Any change could give the wind something additional to tear at. Instead, he closed his eyes to the stinging dust and waited.

When the gale finally fell away he climbed to his knees, twisting his neck.

Tsolde, her face drained of colour, was crawling forward – eyes unseeing. Luis signalled from behind her and Never nodded, crawling the rest of the way himself. On the other side, he rolled away from the edge of the chasm and lay back a moment, breathing deeply.

"Keep going," Tsolde said.

He lifted his head. Tsolde was striding for a winding trail that led up to the top of the ridge – something which ought to have done a better job at sheltering them. He groaned, dragging himself up to join Luis, who walked after her.

"Wasn't that fun?" Never said.

"I'm not convinced you know what the word 'fun' means, Never."

He laughed. "You're probably right."

Thin, yellowing weeds lined the trail and at the top of the ridge waited another steep descent, the path tumbling down to something steel that caught the afternoon light. Beyond, the Folhan Mountains stretched on, purple beneath the black clouds spreading across the sky.

Farther below, a haze of smoke and even the hints of darker stone from a man-made structure. A few steps down the trail and he'd see what was, hopefully, the Giant's Bridge.

"Bad weather out there," Luis said. "Though it might not reach us."

"It's welcome to come," Never said.

"Why?" Tsolde asked. She'd regained some composure and a little colour to go with it.

"It will shield us, keep idle Vadiya within their tents."

She straightened. "Vadiya?"

"Look again," Never said. Luis was already nodding and Tsolde's eyes soon narrowed. "Let's see what we're dealing with."

Never climbed cautiously down, sliding a little. "Careful," he warned the others. Thankfully, the few stones trickled down to a natural curve in the slope. The steel he'd seen from above was revealed to be huge bolts driven into the stone – a pair of chains, each link descending down toward exactly what he'd predicted.

Below, too distant to hear voices, the Vadiya camp spread across the stony ground before the closest side of the Giant's Bridge. A dozen rows of tents, possibly more, were broken by evenly-spaced campfires with huge cauldrons. Other fires pumped warmth and smoke into the air. A soundless whoosh of smoke and flame flared when an armoured man dumped pine branches atop one of them.

But above it lay the Giant's Bridge – it still gave him pause.

Stone pillars guarded entry to the bridge; the smaller pieces of stone larger than the wagons that should have been passing over it. Each pillar had been carved with rigid symbols unlike any he'd seen before – not those he was now coming to think of as Amouni, but more harsh. The bridge spanned a chasm, broad and solid, entryway to the nearby silver mines.

How had it been built? And by whom... he'd shaken his head in awe upon first seeing it, years ago now. The arches beneath were magnificent in their own right – such knowledge seemed lost now.

"Where is the garrison? We should have troops swarming over these snakes," Tsolde said.

"More traitors?" Luis suggested.

She nodded, her expression dark. "They want the silver, don't they?"

Never exhaled. "Most likely. They have a lot of soldiers to pay."

"Cocky, aren't they?" Luis pointed. "Not much in the way of defence on the permitter of the camp. Still, it looks like we need to sneak past about two... maybe three hundred men."

"I don't like our chances," Tsolde said. "Giant's Bridge is the only path to the mines, save turning back and detouring for weeks to approach from nearer the side of the Marlosi border."

Never sat, untying his knapsack. No food, just his blanket. "Time I cannot afford, if I am to meet the deadline."

"Any ideas?" Luis asked.

"Subterfuge. And boldness," he said. "I have an idea but we need three things first. One is food – we hunt before we try this. Two, we need to be sure these chains are safe. And three, we need a volunteer from the Vadiya."

Chapter 12.

"He's broken his neck," Luis said, face surprised in the growing dark.

"Saves us doing it," Never replied. "Hurry, help me."

Together they dragged the sentry off the trail and into a stand of pine where Never started on the buckles of the man's breastplate. Luis stopped to massage his ankle, having twisted it on the way down – the iron chain had not reached the King's Road, forcing them to drop the remaining feet.

"How do you know so much about Vadiya war camps?" Tsolde asked without turning from the road.

"I was held prisoner in Vadiya for over a year," Never said.

"Truly?"

He started on the greaves. "One of my fonder memories."

"How?"

"I got into trouble trying to steal a horse. The owner of the horse was creative enough to want a foreign slave." He looked to Luis. "I'll have to carry your spear and Tsolde's knife."

"Shouldn't one of us at least conceal a weapon?" Tsolde

asked.

"If you're found with a knife we're finished."

"I don't like it."

Luis frowned too, but handed his spear over. "He's right, Tsolde."

"Fine." She gave her blade to Never.

"Good." Never switched boots, stashing his own behind a trunk with a shrug. He'd never see them again but that didn't really matter, did it? "Vadiya have two sets of sentries, pairs close to camp and outliers like this one." He lifted a horn. "Outliers will be spread along the back-trail and before the camp; they sound an alarm for advance warning, giving the camp more time to prepare. It's only a few men more than many other armies, in truth. The same men also serve as advance scouts."

"And this one?" Tsolde asked.

"We were lucky to surprise him – I imagine he wasn't expecting trouble from the direction of the Bridge, too focused on the King's Road." Never had completed most of the transformation. When he started to strap on all the weapons, he swore. "This is ridiculous." He dumped the bow and hatchet. Sword, daggers and spear was enough.

"And you really think you can fool them?" Tsolde asked.

"My Vadiyem is perfect," he said.

"Keep your hood raised then," she said. "You're not pale enough for this."

"It's getting darker," he said. "If we hit the camp before they light too many torches, we'll be fine. Probably. Now tie the rope like I showed you, remember to keep enough hidden in your palm to tug the slipknot free if –"

"We get it, Never," Tsolde said.

"Good." He pulled on the gauntlets with a snap. "How do I look?"

She gave him a nod. "Not bad."

"Ready then?" he asked.

Luis hesitated. "You're sure about this, Never? We're risking a lot – if we're caught..."

"I know," he said. "They won't take prisoners if they're trying to cover up what they're doing here." He flexed his hands in and out of fists. "Everything will be fine if you follow my lead. I've bluffed my way out of worse." And if the Gods were kind for a change, he'd be able to do so once more.

"Yeah?"

"I once convinced the King of the Lappodi Islands that I was his long lost nephew."

Tsolde frowned. "Is that true?"

"I'll tell you once we reach the Iron Pass," he said. "Now, I'm leading you so take it slow. Don't speak to anyone, even if you're asked a direct question. The first trick will be the camp sentries."

Never directed them up the road as darkness continued to fall. Luis still limped a little, but appeared to be holding up well enough. "Ready now," Never whispered. Adrenaline surged through his body and he grinned before scolding himself. Idiot – he was on a tightrope and others depended on him.

Ahead, two men rose from where they'd been sitting on the roadside.

"That you, Hedyk?" one asked. His hand rested on his sword hilt and the second man had an arrow set to his string.

"Synav," Never answered in Vadiyem, choosing a common

name. "We traded shifts."

The man grunted but turned his gaze to the 'prisoners'. "What you got there?"

"Found them trying to sneak up the road," Never said. He nudged Luis, who did not react. "This one said something about looking for work in the mines."

"And the girl?" the second sentry said.

"Same story," Never said. "Look, I'm cold and hungry, friends. Best if I take them to see the captain, yes?"

The bowman snickered. "Think he'll make time for you?"

"Doubtful."

The first man motioned for Never to enter the camp and the second called after. "Bring us back something hot, will you?"

Never waved a hand in acknowledgement. He lowered his voice. "See, easy enough."

Neither of his 'prisoners' answered, which was for the best.

Warm glows spread across the camp as braziers were lit. One near a line of stores and another at the crossroad he passed through, turning his face away from the light. Most of the men, regular soldiers rather than Steelhawks, gave them glances only before returning to card games or idle chatter – about the weather or their commanding officer or home – suggesting that a couple of new prisoners was nothing noteworthy.

The bridge towered over them, a black hulking thing in darkening sky, close now yet if they were caught it might as well be on the other side of the world. And beneath the bridge, difficult to discern in the poor light, a large pavilion for whoever had been given command. He squinted...

slowing his step.

A red talon flew over the pavilion.

Never resumed a smooth gait. The Red Talon of the Isajan family. Sacha. Was she actually here? He could have screamed a curse. Of all the hideous luck. If she saw him… everything would be ruined. Sacha; her name hadn't crossed his mind for years.

He clenched his jaw and set a new pace, brisk but not too much so, as if hurrying to meet orders, as they passed an infirmary. Several men lay on stretchers within open tents, sleeping or dead he could not tell. A healer held one man's arm across a bench as he sewed the wound, the soldier's expression stoic.

"Halt."

Never stopped, barking an order at Luis and Tsolde, who froze, before turning to the voice, keeping out of the light.

A Steelhawk with a Captain's striped insignia resting over the heart of his breastplate. The man stood expectantly, helm under his arm. His red cloak was covered in dust, as if he'd just returned to camp.

"Captain?" Never asked, keeping his tone respectful.

"Rank and Family."

"Synav, Captain. Second Ranger," he said, again, choosing a common standing for an advance sentry, not too lowly, but not a First Ranger, either, who'd have been equivalent to a Lieutenant.

"And these prisoners?"

Never repeated his story. Then played his gamble. "I have orders to take them to Lady Isajan."

He frowned. "I have just come from her tent and I was not aware of any such orders."

Never affected a look of apology, hoping to convey embarrassment that a Captain had not been kept in the loop. "I see, Captain."

The Steelhawk swore, as if realising he was losing face before a sentry. "Get on with you then," he said and strode away.

Never relayed an order to his prisoners and noted the slight change in both Luis and Tsolde's shoulders – but he couldn't relax yet, not even a little. Any misstep could land him in Sacha's lap. And not in a pleasant way.

She'd probably throttle him as soon as invite him back into her bed.

Hard to blame her.

The pavilion appeared ahead. Two Steelhawks were posted before the large tent, which also possessed an awning over the entry flap to provide shelter for the Lady – who was hardly dainty, but had obviously not given up her luxuries.

It was also well-lit, unlike the bridge itself, which was mostly dark. But all he had to do was walk his prisoners right by, as if he had every right to do so. As he directed Luis and Tsolde, he angled himself to use Luis's taller frame as a screen, a shadow cast upon him.

At the bridge, another pair of guards. One raised a hand. "No-one crosses the bridge at night. You should know that."

"Lady Sacha's orders," Never snapped. "You want to be the one to contradict her?"

The man frowned. "I haven't been told –"

Never folded his arms. The fellow bore a bull as his insignia. Lofaner family – well-regarded but not powerful. The man had probably fought hard to earn such a posting. "Some things are above your rank. You think every decision she makes is going to be passed down to a Bull?"

The man flushed.

Never pressed on, doing his best Harstas impersonation. "The last man that interfered with her was cut to pieces and fed to his commanding officer. I assume you don't want that to be you, yes?" The claim was a lie of course – he'd heard the same rumour about Sacha years ago but when he asked her, she'd only laughed, saying, "It's just another way to control them."

The second guard's eyes had widened. "Just let him go, Muthis, don't be a fool."

"Go and check with the Captain, he'll know," the first said.

"Fine."

Never glanced after the fellow, who didn't have far to go. Time to move. He gave Luis a prod and they started forward. The sentry moved to block them. Never sighed. "Don't do it, Muthis. I've seen what she can do."

Still the man hesitated.

"Look, I'm not going to let you stop me. It's my head on the line too, you know," Never said.

The fellow stood aside with a glare.

"Wise choice, old sport."

Into the darkness they went. Never strode after his prisoners, keeping control of his limbs. The urge to run was strong – just as was turning back. But that wasn't going to happen. Why spoil the bluff? So far, everything had worked out wonderfully, aside from the little surprise with Sacha.

The giant's bridge was broad and it stretched into the dark. A smaller guard post with a single torch fluttering in the wind waited ahead, a pool of yellow light.

"This is working," Luis said softly. "Keep it up, Never."

"I will."

Only a single guard stood within the light. He straightened from his slouch when Never appeared. "Hold it, what's happening here. Off for a stroll, then?"

"Just taking the prisoners to the mine," Never said. "Stuck with a thankless task. Would rather be in my bedroll."

The man grinned. "Tell me about it, friend."

"Well, I'd better get these jenaek up there," he said. "You know what Lady Isajan is like."

A figure wrapped in a crimson cloak stepped into the pool of light, flanked by hulking Steelhawks.

"And what is that exactly, soldier?"

Sacha.

Chapter 13.

She had barely aged – only slight crinkles of smile lines at her eyes, her feathery eyebrows – now raised – still a faint blonde. Short hair had been cut close to her head, somehow drawing more attention to the vivid blue of her eyes.

The archetypical Vadiya woman.

A sword hung from her belt, knives too, yet she was under-armed for a Steelhawk. Though from the new insignia on her breastplate, the old Vadiya rune for 'one', she was now a First Hawk – the camp was hers, just as he'd suspected from the pavilion.

Never fell to one knee, pulling Luis and Tsolde down with him. "I apologise for running my mouth, My Lady," he said, lowering his voice. Would it be enough to disguise his voice from her? "I humbly request that you punish me but allow my family to be protected from my shame."

A moment's silence.

"Speak again, soldier," Sacha said. Her voice held a note of curiosity mixed in with the disapproval.

He cleared his throat. "What would you have me to say,

My Lady?"

"My name."

"Lady?"

"Speak my full name and title."

She knew. Never swallowed a curse. He was trapped – no way to fight free, nowhere to flee to and no chance of using his blood, encased in steel as he was. And anything he tried would get Luis and Tsolde killed. "Lady Sacha, First Hawk of Family Isajan, daughter of Lady Natasiv and Lord Dakan."

Another pause. "Stand. Show me your face."

Never rose, then drew back his hood.

Gasps from the men but her eyes only widened just enough to reveal that she'd recognised him; beyond that she did not react. She turned to her bodyguards. "Take him to my tent and the others to the cells," she said.

"Shall I call for the Interrogator? They may be spies," one of the Steelhawks said.

"No, Fernov. I think I'd like to get to the bottom of this myself. Search and bind them all."

The fellow grinned as he set to work. Never didn't resist and exhaled in relief when Luis and Tsolde kept their cool, though both wore expressions of deep concern. As well they ought to – and yet, Sacha's reaction had been if not promising... enough to give him a touch of hope.

Of course, the Gods were wont to stamp his hopes into dust for decades now.

Fernov started Never toward the camp. He glanced over his shoulder, Sacha was following, eyes upon him but the other Steelhawk was taking Luis and Tsolde up into the darkness, toward the mine.

Cells? Were the miners and other Hanik imprisoned at the silver mine?

Never opened his mouth to demand they stay together but Sacha met his eyes and shook her head.

He said nothing, looking ahead without seeing until he was shoved into the warm pavilion, knees striking a heavy rug. More of her luxuries. A brazier burnt in the corner, partially blocked by a table spread with maps in the centre of the room. Opposite lay a wide cot, heaped with heavy blankets and soft pillows.

The scent of cedarwood lay about the tent – she was obviously burning it in the brazier.

"Leave us," Sacha told her guards once they'd removed his stolen armour and weapons, including his knives.

In the quiet that followed she studied him for a long moment, leaning on the table.

"Hello, Sacha. You look like you have something on your mind," he said from where he knelt.

Her mouth twitched, as if to smile, but she leant down so that she was face to face with him, where she reached out to grab his chin and squeeze. His heart skipped a beat – her skin; there was a faint trace of lilac. Images flashed in his mind, her bare legs in candlelight, entwined with blankets. "Yes, Never. There is something on my mind. I'm trying to decide whether to strip you naked and take you outside for my men to tear to pieces or strip you naked and take you to my bed."

"I see."

"Do you?" she let him go, straightening again, eyes flashing.

"Yes," he said, keeping his voice earnest. "No-one likes to

be deserted."

She narrowed her eyes. "You had better be sincere."

He would have raised his hands, only they were tied behind his back. "I am. You know I play the fool but I'm not doing so now. I had to escape, Sacha. I know that must have hurt you."

Now she chuckled. "Don't you have a high opinion of yourself."

He grinned. "See how well you know me?"

Sacha began to pace the tent and he relaxed into his bonds a little. If she was chuckling, maybe he'd survive this yet. Tsolde and Luis were still in trouble. At the very least, they were alive, and Sacha had made it clear there was to be no interrogation... for now. Who knew if they were unhurt? Or how long that would remain true.

But he wasn't willing to risk the fragile peace in the tent with a question. Yet.

Besides, Sacha would be asking enough questions for the both of them soon enough.

"Very well, Never. Time to keep up that refreshing new tendency of yours toward honesty, yes?"

"Yes."

"Good. First, why are you here? I find it hard to believe your obsessive search for your true name would lead you to my camp."

"It's leading me back to Marlosi, actually," he said. "We just hoped to pass through, you see, I'm on a bit of a deadline."

"A deadline?"

"The new moon."

"Why?"

"I've learnt that something will be revealed to me there,

only during the new moon. I must reach the Marlosi side of the Folhan Mountains on that night."

"And you believe this because you found some manner of sign, directing you as such?" She shook her head. "It sounds thin, Never."

"I'm driven, not foolish," he said. "I found murals in the Amber Isle, do you know it?"

"I've heard of the place; I'm surprised it exists."

"Well, deep within, I found clues to my heritage. The murals led me to Hanik and now they're leading me back home."

Her interest returned. She'd always been supportive of his search – deep down, even when it came between them, he believed she wanted him to learn the truth. "You have a copy of these murals?"

"No, but I remember enough – and I suspect there will be more at my destination." Hopefully activated by the moon, as Snow seemed to hint, and just as the symbol on the Amber Isle.

"And your friends?"

"Two who have agreed to help me. Luis is a treasure-hunter and Tsolde a runaway," he said. All reasonably truthful.

"I see. And the Hanik girl, Never? She might be a spy; you understand I must be sure. When did she join your little party?"

"In Lenan," he said. "Weeks past." Inside he frowned. It was a link back to Tsolde's home that Sacha probably didn't need to know. And yet, he had to convince his former lover that the young woman was no threat. "She was driven from home by her family," he said. "Escaping an unwanted marriage." Again, truthful without revealing too much.

"I will speak with them, you know that. And I will check their stories."

"No stories, Sacha, just the truth. Luis and Tsolde are who I say they are." He rolled his shoulders. "Feel like untying me?"

"Not truly."

"Very well. How about you tell me what you're doing here?"

"Leading my forces."

"Indeed. But why?"

She laughed. "Are we talking objectives now, Never? It should be obvious; the silver and the bridge. We control both and we cut off Hanik and Marlosi from aiding each other and open a path for any... further incursions."

"We?"

"Since when did you care about things like war and invasions?"

"Truly spoken. But what I was really asking is 'why' Sacha? What do you care about the size of Vadiya's borders?"

"Oh, Never." She moved closer, then placed a foot on his chest. Impossible not to see how shapely her leg was. She gave him a push and he fell back. She loomed over him. "Somehow there's still something naive about you, beneath all that cockiness."

"It's not charming?"

"Never, you might have been my father's prisoner for months but so was I, only all my life," she said, her brow furrowing and her blue eyes flashing. "Maybe I didn't run when you did but I soon found the courage to leave. And see now, I've already become everything he said I could never become."

"Yes, you have." He met her gaze. "But you had help."

"Of course. I'll spare you too many details but Prince Tendov transformed me from a spirited, angry young woman into a First Hawk. A leader of men."

"You were already a brilliant soldier when we met."

"True. And now I am more." She pulled her cloak around her shoulders and strode to the exit. "Stay put, Never. My guards have orders to kill you if you run, and I wouldn't want that."

"Where are you going?"

"To check on your friends – and when I return, we'll talk some more and you can convince me that you're useful. How does that sound?"

He closed his eyes, in fear or anticipation? "Like old times."

Sacha chuckled and the rustle of the tent flap followed.

Chapter 14.

Never twisted his legs out from under his body and stretched as he rolled onto his side. With his arms still bound behind his back, he didn't relish the idea of being the only Marlosi man in Vadiya armour running through a camp of three hundred men.

Their voices washed over the pavilion, loud in the night, yet it was only those nearest he could make out; Sacha's guards, both of whom appeared concerned about Prince Tendov's impending visit.

"Word is he'll be here tomorrow," one said.

A grunt. "I heard. And knowing him, he'll appear tonight, just to keep everyone on edge."

"She'll keep him busy though."

"Yeah, well – not long enough, Stasn. He'll be stalking about the place looking for faults to point out before we know it. And guess who he'll scrutinise first?"

"You're right about that," Stasn said with a sigh.

A moment of silence passed between them.

"Think he'll have us move on Jenisan soon?" Stasn said.

"Only if that fool Floriak has done as he claimed. The Prince won't want to lose the advantage of the twin strike, right?"

"Right."

Another pause, then, "How long you think she'll be?" Stasn again.

"Why?"

"I need to visit the latrines."

A snort from the first guard. "You've got time, she took her kit and her bodyguards with her. She's going to be thorough."

Never shifted. Powerless. Sacha wouldn't need to torture them; Luis would know they had nothing to gain by hiding anything. He had to. He had to. Come on, Luis, don't be a fool. "And Tsolde, you better keep your temper under control," he murmured.

"Think they're spies?" Stasn asked.

"Who knows."

"And the one inside? What did you make of him?"

"Now that's curious – maybe she just wants some sport but they seemed to know each other. Had a lot to talk about."

"Right. And you know what Prince Tendov will think of that," Stasn laughed and his fellow joined in. Footsteps receded.

Never rolled onto his other side with a soft groan. Wonderful. On top of everything else, a jealous boyfriend to contend with. Sacha had better return before Tendov dropped in. Especially if the man was likely to surprise the troops. More, Tendov seemed entirely lacking tolerance, not the kind of fellow who would respond well to finding a man bound in his lover's tent.

While he waited, Never rotated his position, sometimes on his side, or his knees, or pacing the tent as the night wore on, he spent a good deal of time glancing over the maps on the table where he noted several planned invasion routes in Hanik. Shading indicated conquered territory in Marlosa, most of the central but little in the north, where the Empress would hopefully still hold out. The imperial city was shaded too, but the southern reaches had little to reveal of Vadiya movement.

Quisa.

Home? Perhaps, but only slightly more so than Marlosa itself. The Quisoan would not have fought long, being a smaller collection of villages and nomadic tribes, rather than a single force. And they possessed no resource the Vadiya would want – except for, perhaps their horses. Quisoan horses were prized.

A woman's voice.

He turned as the tent flap opened. Sacha strode inside, then leant back to speak to her guards, voice lowered. She smiled at Never as she unclasped her cloak and threw it in a corner, her sword belt following. No trace of blood on her body or hands. Either she cleaned up or she didn't actually hurt them.

Some of the tension in his body eased. Some.

Sacha approached and placed her hand on his cheek. "I'm surprised – it seems you really were just caught in the wrong place."

"My friends?"

"Relax, Never. I barely threw a punch – they were very forthcoming, and concerned for you. Which I found touching."

"Then they're alive?"

"Of course, which is how they'll stay as long as I will it. Understood?"

He nodded. It was too soon to smile, to allow relief in, but at least they were alive. "And now?"

She pushed him toward the bed. "No more talking."

Never stumbled, but kept his feet. She grinned and pushed him harder. He crashed into the pillows. Sacha was moments behind, straddling him and pressing her lips against his. He kissed her back, blood surging and his body responding to hers.

She broke the kiss, pausing to draw a thin knife free from where it had been concealed in the small of her back. "Don't think this means I'm untying you – try something foolish and I will kill you, Never. Your blood isn't faster than my knife."

"You're in charge."

Her eyes were hard. "I am."

She kept the knife in hand but leant in close, her free hand gripping his tunic. She cut through the fabric, exposing his chest and running her lips across his skin, up to his neck where the heat of her breath caused him to shiver.

He felt her lips change shape, as though she smiled.

***

Never lay in the cool dark of the tent, Sacha's breathing washing over him where she lay across his chest.

The brazier had died down and shadows pressed in around the red glow, as if suppressing the very embers. Beyond the canvas walls the camp lay quiet, awaiting dawn with only soft sounds, a gentle wind stirring a tent flap or a distant bird waking somewhere high above.

He shifted his arm slightly and Sacha stirred. She had untied him after a time, thankfully, though his wrists were still a little raw. Would it have been easier to tell himself she'd given him no choice? She had been in control, any attempt at resistance would have been pointless, considering where he was.

Yet he always had a choice – he could have fought and she would have killed him.

But that was no choice at all, surely?

No, the real problem was simple enough. He'd enjoyed it. Every moment was a moment of bliss. The memories of the firmness of her body, her scent, the lightness of her touch, her forcefulness, all were naught but shades compared to actually sharing her bed once more.

And even though the last time had been years in the past now – the night before he'd taken his chance to escape her father's keep in fact – it seemed he'd forgotten nothing by the way his senses were overwhelmed during the night, the way every emotion flooded back.

Vivid, yet tinted with the desperation of youth.

Things were different now.

And what sort of night had Luis and Tsolde spent? He had to find them; there was a way out of the camp if he took the time to find it.

"I can hear you thinking. Stop it," she said.

He laughed softly. "And what am I thinking about?"

"Running away – what you always think about," Sacha said. She rolled away from him, reaching for water. Her back was smooth in the faint light and he reached out to stroke it.

"Are you going to try and stop me again?"

She lay back, pulling the blanket up to cover her breasts. "I can't let you simply walk out of my camp, Never. You know that."

"Then let me sneak out. Pretend you killed me, I'll figure something out."

She appraised him a moment. "No. Nothing like that. Things have changed."

Even Sacha was echoing his thoughts. "I know you don't plan on keeping me in your tent forever."

She glanced away. "No, I do not."

"And I assume you don't want me to meet him, either."

Now she smiled. "I doubt you two would enjoy each other's company – you're too alike."

He raised an eyebrow. "I'm like Prince Tendov?"

"You're both driven by something... and neither of you give up," she said, then stood and began to dress. "Otherwise you might be opposites."

"Well let's hurry. He'll be here soon, won't he?"

She glanced at him, hands busy with the laces on her shirt.

"Your guards were obviously feeling chatty while you were gone; I heard enough to know they're afraid of him."

"As they should be."

Never stood, reaching for his own clothing. "Why don't you have me transferred to the mines as a prisoner – it's close to where I'm going. You can save face and I can escape – leave me one of my knives."

"You still wish to cross the border?"

"Yes. There is something there, Sacha, something that will give me another clue as to my true name."

"You still believe that? What if you don't ever find

anything, Never – what then?"

"I die searching."

She shook her head. "I'll arrange the transfer. Dress quickly. Take my knife, hide it well because you'll need it. I'll be sending you to the cells bound. It won't be a picnic."

"Life has never been a picnic," he said, "though last night was pleasant enough."

"So it was." She'd finished with her boots and strode out of the tent.

Never leapt into the rest of his clothing, that which remained in one piece, and slipped the thin knife within the seam of his pants. Then he drank from her water and searched for food – how long since he'd eaten now? His hunger roared back. There was a hessian bag of apples beside her travelling chest, he took one out and bit into it.

"What are you doing, jenaek?"

One of her bodyguards, Fernov, stood in the entryway, a regular Vadiya soldier joining him.

Never swallowed his mouthful. "Eating an apple."

The Steelhawk frowned as he strode over and held up a length of rope. "Hands."

After another bite, Never tossed the apple to the soldier, possibly Stasn – who caught it with a blink – then held out his hands to be bound. The Steelhawk was hardly gentle, but he didn't take the opportunity to lay into Never out of sight of his mistress either.

He caught Never by the shoulder. "You might not be a spy but you are a fool. Now march."

Never left the pavilion, the steely light of dawn covering the rows of tents. Smoke from new fires added to the grey of the world. Sacha was nowhere to be seen and a jerk on the arm from his guard didn't give him time to look.

He was herded to the Giant's Bridge and then escorted across it at such a pace that he was climbing the trail beyond before he'd had a chance to adjust to the rising sun. At the top of the ridge his guards paused while one shook a stone out of his boot, tossing it into one of the wagon-ridges in the road.

Below spread the entrance to the silver mine, bustling with activity despite the early hour. Campfires burned clean, spread around tents and wooden buildings. Dozens of Steelhawks walked the length of the mine, hands on their weapons. Hanik men in plain clothing, their faces almost black with dirt, pushed empty carts along steel rails into a gaping maw in the rock face. Lanterns disappeared within the dark slope.

Other men pushed carts laden with grey rock onto nearby platforms where the contents were lifted by a series of ropes and pulleys and cursing men. The cart was then pushed along a constructed rail that ranged over the heads of the workers, to be tipped into something of a quarry, where men with hammers and shackles shattered the stone.

Somewhere out of sight, the crushed rock was obviously fed into a sluice or perhaps directly into a furnace. The furnace wasn't visible from his position, but its smoke stained the sky. Even from some distance the scent was noxious; the sooner the wind changed the better.

"Get going," one of his guards said.

At the bottom of the gentle slope Never was met by a heavyset man with a large hammer swinging from his belt, a set of keys on the opposite hip. He grunted as he accepted Never, hauling him around one of the buildings and through a heavy door into a long corridor. Miner's barracks, converted into a prison – fresh bolts and brackets affixed to each door.

Two pair of guards stood at either end of the prison.

"Soup, bread and water twice a day," the jailor said when he stopped at one of the makeshift cells. He frowned when Never didn't respond, then held up two fingers and repeated the information in broken Marlosi.

"I speak Vadiyem," Never said.

"Then answer me next time – else I'll break a leg with my hammer, got it?"

"Yes."

The man grunted again, then unhooked his keys, opening the door and shoving Never into a tiny room with a cot, a bucket and nothing else.

The door slammed shut and then the lock clicked. The heavy clank of the bolt sliding home followed.

Trapped.

Chapter 15.

Two days had already passed and while he still had his knife; he'd accomplished little else. He'd only seen Luis twice and Tsolde once. Luis had been pressed into service in the mine; Never caught a glimpse of him while being allowed to walk about in chains one noon.

The treasure-hunter had emerged from the mine's dark mouth, pushing a cart with another man. Never caught Luis' eye – and hope sparkled – before Luis lowered his head as his cart passed a Steelhawk.

Never would be heading for the mines himself soon, once he'd finished digging the new latrine behind the barracks. And less pleasant work he could not think of off-hand. Tsolde had been pressed into service as some manner of bookkeeper, it seemed from a conversation he overheard between guards. She'd held her composure when they saw each other, revealing nothing, but as she followed Bendlav the jailor back to his office, taking down the figures he barked, her shoulders had straightened.

At least she appeared unharmed.

"Such confidence," he said to himself, laying atop the blankets of his cot, arms and back aching from the day's digging. "Nice to know they believe in me." But escape was proving tediously difficult. Opportunities were scant, and with two friends in two separate places, a clean escape was looking doubtful.

Sacha hadn't lied.

She hadn't made it easy on him. The knife was a gift but what he really needed was a thousand Marlosi Calvary. Or a precision avalanche.

Instead, he left his empty bowl by the door and sought some rest.

Tomorrow, he'd have a chance to plan – to get a good look at the mine, see what holes would be possible to slip through.

When dawn came it was to the rattling of steel in adjacent cells. Luis was in one of them but Never hadn't been able to figure out which one yet. The other prisoners were miners and a single Vadiya, a soldier who'd obviously upset his superiors in some way. The fellow had been digging latrines and was due to return to duty.

Which was useful – it left no-one to tell tales.

His own cell soon opened, the guard handing Never a bowl of steaming soup with a sigh – presumably a sigh of boredom. "It must be tedious, all that freedom," Never said to him in Vadiyem, the first time he'd spoken to the fellow.

The guard blinked, then scowled as he scooped up last night's empty bowl and slammed the door.

Never chuckled and blew on the soup until it cooled.

By the time he'd been hauled off to the mines, assembled with the other prisoners before a balding Steelhawk, all

Hanik men save for Luis, who stood a head taller than the rest, the meal seemed a distant memory.

The fellow growled his orders; no talking, no-one leaves the mine until sundown, two breaks for water and one for lunch. Anywhere deeper than the statue of the Mountain God was off-limits. "The tunnels aren't safe – we've already lost men there to cave-ins. Keep to the lamps." He frowned at Never. "New man?"

"Yes, sir."

"Work hard and we'll let you free once we've emptied the mine – same deal for everyone. And keep to the areas with lamps. I have men down there with whips and chains. Don't make them use either."

Never nodded.

The Steelhawk waved his hand and men paired off, some to head into the darkness and others for the empty carts nearby. Luis drifted over and gestured for Never to follow him. He did so, heading toward the dark.

"Did she hurt you?" Never whispered, speaking Marlosi.

"No worse than a bar-room brawl," he said, gesturing to a fading bruise on his cheek. "She likes her answers swiftly, doesn't she?"

"And Tsolde?"

"She didn't hurt her – but I do not know where she is."

"I do. The jailor is using her to do his bookwork."

The track that sloped down into the mine was gentle enough and steps for foot traffic ran alongside. A glow from a pair of lanterns soon appeared ahead, a single guard stationed there. Luis stopped speaking and the whispers from the other men died away when the guard appeared, then resumed once the fellow was out of earshot, the trail

levelling off. Here the torchlight led to active tunnels –
the others, Luis told him, were mined out, dangerous or
collapsed long ago.

"The foreman was making a poor joke, of course. Where
we are now there's enough silver for another half a lifetime.
If we don't escape, we're dying here," he said.

Never slapped his friend on the shoulder. "Leave that to
me. What else can you tell me?"

"I was estimating the time it takes for a cart to reach the
surface," Luis said. "For when I figured out where Tsolde
was." He shook his head. "It would be tough, but I think
no-one would miss us for most of the morning."

"That long?"

"The tunnel we're mining is deep and the carts are heavy.
It takes a long time for two men to push it back out."

"Good, that's something."

"Where we actually dig, that's harder. We have weapons
– shovels and pick axes, but the Steelhawks down here carry
crossbows in addition to the whips. I don't like our chances
with a show of force."

"Stealth it is, then."

"The disused tunnels?"

"Not something I want to explore at length, but if we can
use them to divert any search parties..."

At the next set of lights there stood a pair of soldiers and
once again, the whispers died away to silence, leaving only
the echoing tread of their feet

"There's still everyone above. And Tsolde," he said once
they'd passed out of earshot.

Never nodded. "Let's see what else we have to face."

They eventually reached the mining site, where enough

lanterns hung from the walls and buttresses to set the silver ore gleaming. Not unlike the Amber Isle, after a fashion. More Steelhawks armed with crossbows waited beside sets of axes and shovels. "You know what to do," one of them shouted.

Luis joined the queue and Never followed, accepting an axe. Together they found a section of wall away from the nearest prisoner and began. Never swung at the wall, ignoring the shock it sent through his arms. A hunk of rock threaded with silver fell to his feet. He swung again and within moments he was sweating, despite the cold underground.

When the Steelhawks called for the first halt he drank his ration of water greedily.

Then it was back to digging into the bowels of the earth.

Noon came and passed in a blur of hacking – at one point he switched to shovelling the stone into one of the carts, and then it was one more drink before heading toward the surface. His arms were near-to crumbling and new muscles – muscles that had surely not been in his body prior – had begun to ache. It was much worse than digging the latrine, and a perfect way to drain the men's strength.

After a day in the mine, most prisoners would barely have the strength to eat, let alone plan an escape.

But he was not most prisoners.

Between guards in their pools of light, Never spoke over the grinding of the cart's wheels. "This will never work. It needs to be at night, which is your cell?"

"Second from the western entry of the barracks."

"Tonight I am going to release you. We'll take Tsolde once I have imprisoned the jailor – I think, in the dark, I can impersonate my guard, and fool the jailor."

"That easy, huh?"

He grinned. "Let's hope so."

"Then what?"

"We head for the high ground. The road to the Iron Pass and the old mine lies above us – there's no other path."

"This is a bigger gamble than the others. They'll know we haven't tried to cross the bridge."

"I'm betting they will but we'll be too far ahead by then. The moon is still visible at night, we'll be able to see well enough to travel."

"Do we have enough time to reach Marlosi?"

"Let's hope so. Just be ready after midnight."

After pushing their cart up the final incline and into the setting sun – more sweating and cursing and now squinting too – Never and Luis were directed back to the barracks, locked up once more. With nothing else to do but rest, Never slumped into his cot, limbs like sticks of lead, and closed his eyes.

Soon enough, he'd make his move, after which he might not sleep for days.

Best to take advantage of the free room while he could.

Chapter 16.

Near midnight Never called for the guard. He'd been practicing with his blood for an hour and was finally ready. If he remained careful, no-one would have to die – or alert the others. Yet he would kill if given no choice.

After his first call there was no answer so he called again, and then raised the pitch of his voice. Other prisoners roared curses at him but he kept on until his guard wrenched the door open, face red with rage.

"What is it? And give the shouting a rest, damn you."

Never opened his mouth to answer, only to have blood spurt forth – which, with a lot of concentration, was exactly what he wanted. It splashed down the front of his tunic and filled his mouth as he hit the floor, feigning panic. "Help me," he gurgled. "Take me to... healer."

The guard gaped, then knelt by his side.

Never whipped Sacha's knife free – holding it to the man's throat. "Don't move now," he said, blood sliding between his teeth.

The man froze, a look of horror crossing his face.

"You're going to go to sleep now. If you struggle, I will cut you and drain your blood, do you understand?"

"You're a vampire?"

Never grinned. The fellow turned pale, then shuddered to the floor. Fainted cold. Never chuckled – that part was easier than he'd hoped. He spat excess blood then raised his voice to mimic the guard, shouting for the jailor, claiming to need help moving a sick prisoner.

Bendlav's keys jingled to signal his approach. Never propped up the guard and as the heavyset jailor peered inside, Never shoved the guard forward.

The jailor caught his countryman with wide eyes, stumbling.

Never slipped into the corridor and spun around Bendlav, shoving both men into the room. He leapt atop the jailor's back, where he slipped his arm around the fellow's throat and squeezed.

The jailor grunted, thrusting himself up – lurching back and slamming Never into the cot. He swore, pain shooting through his head where it thumped against the stone but he did not let go. Bendlav drove his elbow back into Never's abdomen, each strike causing him to curse again but the blows soon weakened. The man grew limp.

Never held the pressure a little longer, to be sure Bendlav was unconscious, then stood and kicked the jailor. "Bastard." It might have been too much, the fellow might die, but he didn't have time nor the inclination to check.

Move.

He snatched the key chain and jogged down to Luis' cell, wrenching the keys in the lock and sliding the bolt free. When he swung the door open; Luis was already standing.

"Ready?"

Luis flinched. "Are you hurt?"

"Just part of the ploy," Never said, wiping his mouth. "Quickly."

He strode across the way to the jailor's room. While bigger than the cells, it was still small, crammed with furniture; a desk, cot and a series of pegs hung with clothing.

And one important absence.

Tsolde.

"Where is she?" he hissed.

"Try the next cell," Luis said.

Never leant close to the door. "Tsolde? Are you in there?"

A shaky voice answered – a young woman's voice. "Never?"

"We're getting out of here."

He jammed the key into the lock and turned it as Luis pulled the bolt all the way free, hefting it like a weapon. How the man still had the strength to carry the bar was a wonder but it was a clever idea.

Tsolde tumbled out of the cell, shock covering her face. "Are you all right?" he asked. "Did he hurt you? Did he touch you?"

She wrapped her arms around him. "No," she said, speaking into his chest. "Bendlav doesn't like women, Never. He was actually quite kind."

Never exhaled, relief washing over him. "No time to talk, but I'm glad. Come on."

He led them out of the barracks and detoured the pool of light from a torch burning before the other buildings, keeping close to the darker mine. Using the moonlight, he was able to avoid crunching on the gravel and find firm ground, climbing the ladder that led to the quarry – which

Luis had told him would soon join the King's Road and the Iron Mines, still half a day away.

By dawn, no-one would know where they had gone, let alone when. The search would be spread thin, restricted to the immediate area for hiding. Others would waste time in the mine itself, maybe even sending word back to the main camp.

If they could simply pass through the quarry.

Luis caught his arm. "Never, I took a turn here. There are no guards at night but sentries watch the trail leading out."

"Very well."

He slowed his pace, checking on Luis and Tsolde once more, and over her shoulder to the still-quiet camp before starting along the path. No sign of trouble. Good, let it stay that way. The trail hugged the edge of the quarry with its silent structures before climbing up toward the King's Road – a broad path in the moonlight. A pair of huge pines grew beside the road.

The sentries would be near.

A horn blasted in the camp below. Cries followed, new light blooming. Never swore, charging toward the tree trunks. If he could rush the sentries there might be a chance. He skidded around the tree – only to crash into the armoured man rushing toward the sound of alarm.

Never was flung back. His head struck the stone, crippling pain spreading like fire. Sprawled on the unforgiving earth, Never fumbled for his knife as the sentry blew his own horn, answering the call. Then he threw it aside and raised his own weapon.

Luis stepped over Never's shoulder, lifting his steel pole and catching a sword blow. "Tsolde, run," he cried.

Never found his knees, waving Tsolde around the struggle. She hesitated after only a few steps. He echoed Luis' words with a shout as he circled the sentry. The soldier was swinging blow after blow at Luis, who met each strike with his makeshift weapon.

If Never could take out the man's legs... he crouched, ready to dive, when something struck the man's breastplate and bounced into the night. A stone! The strike caused the man to hesitate long enough for Luis to land a blow that drove the fellow to the ground. Never snatched the sentry's sword and set the point to the man's throat. "Stay."

Beneath them, lights were converging on the quarry.

"Quickly," Never shouted.

Luis chased after Tsolde, who still held a stone where she stood up the trail, and Never cracked the soldier across the head before following. He frowned as he ran. In the past, he probably would have killed the sentry to be sure. And probably done the same with the jailors.

What had changed?

Ahead, Luis stopped. He held his iron bar in both hands, facing off with a second figure. Never thundered up the path... and stumbled to a halt.

The advance sentry had obviously headed toward camp, hearing the horn blasts. And now he held Tsolde, a knife to her throat. Blood trickled down her skin, black in the moonlight. "Drop your weapons or she dies, yes?"

Luis didn't move. How good was his Vadiyem? Though the meaning was clear enough. Never checked on their back-trail – torches were climbing the path, at least a dozen men. Never raised his knife to his wrist.

Tsolde screamed. The sentry growled. "Need me to spell

it out? Drop them."

"Never? What do we do?" Luis asked.

"Leave me," Tsolde gasped.

"No," Never said. His knife clattered to the stone. "We're caught."

Luis swore but flung his bar into the quarry.

"That's better," the sentry said. "Now turn and walk slowly to meet my comrades, keeping your hands in sight."

Never started down the trail. The first Steelhawk caught his arm, twisted it and drove him to his knees. Never grunted but didn't fight. There was a chance to talk his way out of it if he could convince them he was acting on Sacha's orders.

And yet, would that compromise her position?

"Who are they?" someone asked.

"Prisoners escaped from the barracks," another voice said. "Kill them and leave the bodies at the entrance to the mine, I say. Make an example."

A third voice joined in. "Jailor's probably dead – they're the ones who killed him."

An angry swell in the muttering.

Never started to speak but his captor cuffed his head. He bit into his tongue, blood filling his mouth again. He spat, the taste of iron strong. Familiar.

And useless.

"Kill them now," yet another voice demanded. "I remember what Lady Isajan said. They aren't spies, they're just travellers. Kill them and be done with it. I'm cold."

"Let's not be so hasty."

Never tilted his head.

This new voice was familiar, softer than the shouting men, yet it remained audible. The muttering of the soldiers transformed into a respectful tone and the Steelhawk holding Never drew in a breath. "Prince Tendov."

Never tensed.

"Leave these to me. Go now, all of you."

"But, Your Highness. We must protect you," one of the hawks said.

"Your concern is... misguided, but I appreciate the sincerity. Go." A hint of steel had entered his voice. Never was released. Footsteps shuffled away, light receding with it, until only Never, Luis and Tsolde remained. Never stood and turned.

The prince waited before them, a cloak and hood concealing his face.

He raised pale hands and pulled the hood back with a smile.

"Hello, brother."

Snow.

Chapter 17.

"Snow."

His brother raised an eyebrow, blue eyes catching the moonlight, seeming to glow as if sending the light back into the sky. "You shouldn't be surprised, brother. You're getting obsessed with your search."

"Snow." Never had no other words.

Snow was Prince Tendov. Snow was Sacha's lover. Never swallowed. Was the sense of betrayal greater at that thought – or the knowledge that Snow was part of the invasion that had thrown Marlosi into turmoil and was now seeking to do the same to Hanik. A random, greedy little king was one thing – but his own brother?

Was there no end to the lengths the man would go? Would he topple all kingdoms in his search for Amouni artefacts? Or was it simple conquest? Or not simple at all, perhaps. There was all the ranting about breaking down humanity in order to rebuild it...

"You're not a prince," was all Never could say. Stupid.

Snow laughed. "Getting right to the important things,

I see. Of course I am not, but King Rachinam was kind enough to adopt me as his own after my parents were most tragically killed during my youth."

"He adopted you? He has so many sons already."

"Yes, years ago now, Never. And why not? My Vadiya is flawless and of course there's my appearance," he said. "No-one turns an eye in Vadiya. It's... refreshing."

"I see there's no end to your duplicity."

"Say rather that I encouraged him."

Never glanced to his side – there were things he wasn't sure Luis or Tsolde should hear – but both had fallen to the ground. When? Never dashed to Tsolde first, then Luis, but both were in a deep sleep, chests rising and falling evenly.

He looked up to his brother. "What is this?"

"Privacy."

Never stood, striding up to Snow – close enough to catch the scent of meat on his breath. "What are you doing?"

"That we have already discussed."

"Humour me."

Snow threw his hands up. "Use your head, brother. What is the quickest path to my goal? Unity, Empire, Obedience."

Never clenched his teeth. At least Snow couldn't simply annihilate humanity with Amouni powers. A small mercy perhaps. "I will stop you."

"I'd rather you join me. You're in the dark, Never. There's still so much for you to learn. Go to the Altar of Stars as I instructed. Discover the truth about the Amouni. Then we will speak again."

"What? You're letting us leave?"

"If you hurry, yes. I told you in the Temple – you are my brother. I would not do this alone, you deserve to know what

I have learnt but I am not foolish enough to think you will believe my word. You must hear our ancestors – go, Never. I will handle the Vadiya; they obey me." He paused, a faint smile playing across his lips. "And I will send your apologies to Sacha, if you wish?"

A stab of jealousy hit him – harder than he expected – and he clenched a fist. Snow only raised an eyebrow, as if curious about the possibility of violence between them.

A groan from Luis stopped him. Never knelt beside the man, helping him sit.

"Never? What happened?"

"It was my brother. He's letting us go," Never said. He turned back to the trail, only to find it empty. Not a single trace remained – but a single white feather drifted down to the stone as an owl flew to the pine tree, claws gripping the bark.

"Snow?"

And there it sat, watching him help Tsolde to her feet and watching still as the three of them reached the King's Road and started up, leaving the silver mine behind.

Chapter 18.

The journey to the old iron mines floated by in a haze of daylight and stars, thinning moons, cold meals, shivering and scattered conversation. Never tried to explain what he knew of Snow to Luis and Tsolde without terrifying them but it was a difficult task.

"What are you saying?" Tsolde asked the first night, after they'd left the camp far enough behind to be reasonably sure there was no pursuit. "If he's trying to create a single Empire and you might be able to stop him, why let us go?"

"I'm saying he's mad... But still in complete control of his thinking," Never said. "He needs me for something and I don't know what, exactly. But there are things he has done – and things I suspect he has done – which go far beyond our shared curse. He knows so much more than I. If he continues on his current path, he could pull the whole world into war. Or worse."

Luis frowned. "What's worse than the entire world fighting?"

Never glanced away. "The entire world dead – save for

those few he approves of. If any."

Luis gasped. "That's possible?"

"I don't know. But I'm afraid it could be."

Tsolde was still gaping. "He is mad."

Never looked from one disbelieving face to the other. "You must both promise me not to anger him, if you encounter him, no matter what, even if you think I am in danger. Let me deal with him; it's not worth the risk."

Luis spread his hands. "Never, I won't let him simply kill you. You're my friend."

"And mine," Tsolde added, her expression firm.

Never swallowed down a surge of crippling fear and a swelling of warmth. How long since he'd had friends who were willing to risk their lives for him? He'd almost forgotten how it felt.

And yet, how long too, since he'd been foolish enough to allow such a wonderful thing to happen?

He couldn't be responsible for their deaths should Snow lose control.

The best way to protect them was to send them away now... yet how could he? Would they even listen? Or simply trail him? Be taken by the Vadiya to be used as bargaining pieces or to be captured by Jenisan for the same purpose. For now, weren't they safer with him?

He smiled, unable to keep a little sadness from his voice. "Thank you both, but I wish to protect you just as much and that's why you must swear it. Both of you. Swear you will let me deal with Snow."

Luis and Tsolde exchanged a glance, both expressions conflicted. Luis' shoulder slumped first. "I swear it."

A weight on his chest eased. "Thank you, my friend.

Tsolde?"

She sighed. "I swear it too."

He clapped his hands together as another knot of tension unravelled. "Grand! It's settled. Now let's get some rest."

***

When they finally stood before the shadowy entrance to the old mine – with a mere matter of days left until the new moon, Never called a halt beneath the rising sun, which was still battling through towering pines. He had to clear his head; he couldn't stop Snow. Pointless. There was no way to second guess his brother, no way to get ahead. Snow and his secrets were always going to have the jump on him.

He had to catch up, or at least come close.

Reach the Altar of Stars, learn what he could and then decide a new course of action.

Which meant focusing on the trial ahead. The Iron Pass was dangerous enough even when he gave it his full attention.

He pointed to the overgrown staging area. No carts, but in places, grey, rotten wood from tracks remained. No iron either; that had been taken for use in other mines. "The old entrance. If we'd kept travelling, we'd come to the Iron Pass, still suffering the effects of the earthquake or avalanche, all those years ago, the same one caused some cave-ins here. Hopefully there have been no new ones. Our path will dip into the mines before we see the other side of the Folhan Mountains."

"We're not prepared, are we?" Luis said.

"Not truly. I hope to find rope within and any tools we might need. They'll be old but folks made steel true in the past. We'll manage."

"What about food and water?" Tsolde asked. "Or proper clothing – I can't remember the last time I was warm. I've got scratches all over my arms and legs from blasted leaves and branches."

"All good questions," Never said. He rubbed his temples, closing his eyes as he did. "We hunt before we enter the mines. Sharpen a spear from saplings on stone, Luis. I'll start a fire again, even if it takes another hour of rubbing wood. We'll have a warm meal before we leave at least. There are plenty of streams too. Before we enter, Tsolde, your job is to find some way of carrying the water. There will be debris within the mine, I seem to remember something."

"Fine," Tsolde said, sounding pleased.

"And what can we expect in the way of danger?" Luis asked.

"Possible cave-ins, unstable floor. The usual food, water and light concerns – though it's a three day journey, I'm more worried about light. If I hadn't lost my blue-stone back at the stream..." He shrugged. "Most people say evil lurks deep within – the reason the Hanik abandoned the mines in the first place."

Luis grunted. "That's rather vague, Never."

"I didn't encounter it the last time I took this path, nor the first."

"It's supposed to be something old," Tsolde said. "Father used to tell me tales about the mine when I was a child and asked him to scare me. He said no-one agreed on exactly what was down there, only that miners simply began to disappear without a trace – often a man would report a disappearance of someone he had been working beside. All agree that we went too deep and woke something."

"Maybe it was Black Embers, like the one Darom saved us from," Luis said.

Never put a hand on each of their shoulders. "Well, my bypass isn't so deep that we'll be waking anything up."

"Good," Tsolde said.

Luis added his agreement. "So why have you travelled it twice? You didn't tell us before."

"One time I was hiding from Vadiya Steelhawks who were most keen to find me. I'd stolen something from them." Although, he hadn't done such a good job of stealing Sacha's heart after all. He kept a rueful smile to himself; what a fool to think she'd love no-one else in the years between. He himself had found others, why shouldn't she? Only he hadn't counted on it being Snow. "The other time was chasing yet another dead-end clue. Legends spoke of a silver necklace and clasp, buried deep within the mountain. It was said to pre-date Hanik times." And now he did laugh. "The amount of times I've tracked down something simply because it was old and might be related to my curse, I could have opened a museum."

Luis straightened. "A clasp of silver? Not Aleeta's Silver Rosebud?"

"That's the one."

"And you found it but didn't take it? Never, the Rosebud would be worth a fortune," Luis said. "No-one's seen it in hundreds of years. It's said to be so beautiful that people who look upon it burst into tears."

Never held up his hand. "Exaggerations I'm sure. And despite Mal's help, we didn't find it, only another dead-end."

"Besides, it's supposed to be cursed," Tsolde said. "I don't want to unearth it if it's truly down there."

Luis started to pace the road. "That's right. Princess Aleeta was held to ransom for it, wasn't she? And when everything went wrong with the exchange, the King cursed the Rosebud and sealed the criminals within the mines and no-one has found even a trace of the princess, thieves, or the Rosebud."

Never grinned. "Let's worry about food, water, and light first. We need to build some torches and spend a bit of time hunting. I'm hungry enough to eat my own hands."

Tsolde snorted, but set off into the trees where she bent to the ground, sifting through the pine needles for material suitable for their torches.

"Want to do a bit more hunting?" Never asked Luis.

"I'll do my best – just don't expect steak."

"Understood. I'll see what I can find in the mouth of the mine."

"Anything will help, won't it?" Luis said, then set off with a grin, no doubt thinking about finding the Silver Rosebud.

Never approached the mine and ducked beneath the sinking arch into the shadows. His feet stirred thick dust, a musty scent rising with it. What was once an open space where carts could unload then follow the loop of their steel tracks was now scattered with animal droppings, clumps of leaves and grey pine needles.

A short distance within stood a lone cart, pick hanging over the edge, blade rusted.

Never walked farther along, bending by a dark shape on the ground. An abandoned pack. One buckle was missing from the strap and when he lifted the flap and brushed away old spider webs, he found a tin flask and rotting, frayed rope nestled beside flint and tinder.

Rats had chewed their way into the bottom, obviously to eat whatever food had remained within before it was abandoned.

Would the fire-making tools work? One way to find out.

He returned to the bright daylight with a slight frown on his face. Odd that no travellers or scavengers had taken the pack before – a testament to the fear surrounding the mines? Or an oversight perhaps. But then, for any treasure-hunter, it wasn't much of a find, nor would they be quite so unprepared to need it.

By midday he'd found an old shovel – its handle was hardly perfect but it held together at least, along with a thin chisel. Both coated in rust, but he could clean them a little at least. In addition, he uncovered a lantern but without oil it was useless and he left it where it hung from one of the dust-coated support beams.

Tsolde had bundled together kindling, dried pine needles and resin into tight bunches, tying them with strips of fabric torn from the hem of the prisoner's grey tunic the Vadiya had given her. Never handed her rope from the old pack. "Un-weave this," he said. "I doubt it's strong enough to use for climbing."

"That's more like it," she said.

Luis had stored his findings on a reasonably flat collection of stones; mostly sour rock berries and nuts once again. Even with the added roots in the pile, their prospects were looking grim. Never climbed between the trees toward where he'd last seen Luis searching, slowing when he caught sight of the man crouched before a ridge.

When the stirring of grass alerted him, Luis turned and

waved Never closer.

He pointed down below. "Look."

Someone had set a snare on a thin trail – a grey hare lay trapped within, unmoving. How long had it been there? Had trappers come to the mountains looking for fur? Or travellers in need of food?

"Whoever set the snare could return at any moment," Luis said.

"And yet, the hare looks to have been there for some time, probably caught earlier this morning."

Luis nodded. "And if so, why hasn't anyone come to collect it?"

"How long have you been watching?"

"Long enough – I think they've moved on, or forgotten."

Never rose. "Let's eat."

He slipped down the trail and collected the hare, giving its neck a twist when it struggled, then returned to the mine with Luis. Using some of Tsolde's kindling, he started a fire with the flint and tinder, explaining to her what they'd found while Luis used Sacha's knife to skin the rabbit.

"So they might return at any moment?" she asked. "Won't they be upset that we've stolen their rabbit?"

"I'm predicting as much."

"And if they're nearby – or if your brother changes his mind? Won't the smoke lead them right to us?"

"We'd know by now if 'Prince Tendov' had changed his mind. Just enjoy the meat, Tsolde – it's the last hot meal we'll be having for some time."

Chapter 19.

Once they'd eaten the rabbit – the scant but hot flesh most welcome – and supplemented it with some of the nuts Luis had found, it was time to enter the abandoned mine. Nearly a hundred years had passed since the Hanik fled.

And just what was left behind?

Never paused before re-entering, glancing at his companions. Tsolde had the chisel looped through a belt of rope and a makeshift pouch contained their store of the woody nuts and the berries. She held a burning torch, the sweet pine scent filling the area. Luis carried the pick and the rest of their food slung over his back within the newly repaired pack. A flask of precious water also lay within, flint and tinder too – along with the rest of the torches. Only a dozen, but it would be sufficient to find other supplies; he'd seen enough on the last visit to know there should be something.

With luck.

"Ready?" Never asked.

Luis nodded. His face was apprehensive but there was an

excitement below it – the lure of the hunt. Tsolde had been biting her lip but she stopped. "I don't like this place... but I've seen you do some unbelievable things, Never. Get us through, all right?"

"I will."

He led them within, raising his torch and starting down into the depths of the mountain. For most of the afternoon there was little to see. The tracks wormed deeper and deeper, passing support columns of cold wood and jagged runs of cut stone in the walls, occasional scraps of steel or cloth along with dozens of empty lanterns.

Chill air hung around them, damp in the silence that filled the mine, broken only by their footfalls. They rarely stopped save to light new torches or once, around nightfall as best he could judge, to eat a portion of their rations. Not once did he turn from the main, broad tunnel, bypassing all side passages – some only a few feet deep and others tangled into the mountain.

"No need," Never had said when Luis asked. "It's not until we actually leave the new mine that we have to start taking note of passages. Stick to the main tunnel – it's in the best shape in any event."

"The new mine?" Luis asked.

"As I understand it, there's an older mine that had been emptied of resources before this one was dug," Tsolde explained. "Others say it was the old mine that first contained whatever it was that eventually led everyone to abandon these mines."

When it was time to sleep a watch was set. Whoever took on the role had two tasks: listen for anything out of the ordinary and protect the fire. His own watch passed without incident – just as it had the last two times he'd been to the mines. In fact, the only time he'd been concerned, even for a moment, had been near the Night Lake. Just as Darom warned.

But it had only been a feeling all those years ago – nothing certain.

Not a pleasant feeling, however.

When he woke to a dark morning and the flickering torchlight, Luis and Tsolde offered similar experiences – nothing to report. And so he took a mouthful of water, skipping breakfast, and led them deeper into the silver mine.

***

Little changed until, near late afternoon, they began to climb – the steel rails leading toward the surface.

"Where are we?" Tsolde asked.

"Ascending to what the miners used to call 'the air hole' from memory," Never said.

"Memory?"

"I once read a crumbling journal down here and that's what the miner called it."

Luis switched the torch to his other hand, casting new shadows across the walls. "What was it for?"

Never shrugged. "Respite, I believe. It serves no real purpose from a mining standpoint. The quarries are not close by. I think the miners simply wanted to see the sky again and so they followed a vein up to the surface."

"And we'll take it?"

"Yes. It opens into a glade that may have food. There's a stream there."

"And then?"

"Back down here."

Tsolde turned back to him from where she'd been watching the shadows beyond the torchlight. "Why? I thought you said we're travelling to the old mine?"

"A passage connects them."

Tsolde frowned. "I thought the mines weren't connected. Why would they do that? They were afraid of whatever was in the old mine."

He spread his hands. "Something made the tunnel." Never glanced from grim expression to grim expression. "You'll feel better when we can see the sky again, feel the air at the top."

When they climbed free from the mine, a bitterly cold breeze met them – enough to slice across the skin of his nose. But somehow, for all its sharpness, it was better than the damp below. His lungs pulled in the air as if in thanks.

The glade was as he remembered; wide, grassy earth ringed by towering pines.

They spread into it, walking beneath the starry sky, Tsolde rubbing her arms and Luis heading for the trickle of the stream between dark trunks. Never crossed the grass and entered the treeline, foraging for more berries. Each bulb was chill in his palm but he collected as many as he could find in the dark before choosing a suitable clearing to set up camp.

Luis and Tsolde soon joined him and they made a fire within the trees, sitting close. The heat crept through his bones and he closed his eyes. Only the crackle of flames. Soothing, despite his near-empty stomach.

After the meal, Tsolde poked Never's boot with a stick. "This seems like a good a time as any," she said. "Have you decided what you're going to do about your brother?"

He sighed, resisting the urge to stand and pace. Instead, he took out the dice and toyed with them. The question had been troubling him for too long already – and he was no closer to answering it for himself. "His bitterness has consumed him," Never finally said, shame deep within. For once, in the past, he'd been proud of Snow. His strength, his determination. And now...

"But he let us go," Luis said. "What is he playing at?"

"He has a purpose, of course. Beyond that which we can guess. He's working toward something... I don't know. He told me, while you were affected by his magic, that he wanted an empire."

"And it will spread from Vadiya," Tsolde said.

"He appears to have Marlosi added to that – next comes Hanik, it seems."

"Are you sure it's Snow behind all this?" Luis asked. "Just as Cog is Snow's servant, there could be someone directing him."

Never smiled. "Trying to see the best in my brother? I don't think he has the temperament to be anything but the man in charge."

"Perhaps... but we should be careful. I don't think we should assume too much. Maybe we're simply believing what Snow wants us to believe?"

Never nodded. "Possible, and that would suit him too. But I fear Elina was right to be wary of my blood. The same Amouni blood runs in his veins; he already knows so much. Snow might want the world for himself and he might be able to take it, if our ancestors are any indication of past success." Yet still he held back his true fear – that Snow might just be able to take the world and recast humanity in his own image.

"But they, too, fell," Tsolde said.

"Yes, and it's my job to find out how to do the same for Snow," Never said, flicking the die into the air and catching it. Soon he would have to confront the possibility that stopping his brother might mean killing him. Never glanced back into the restless flames. "We have to reach the Altar of Stars in time."

"And if this trip is part of a greater ploy?" Tsolde asked. "If he wants you there for another reason?"

"No. Snow needs me to learn the truth for myself because he wants me to join him of my own accord."

Luis gave a low whistle. Tsolde shook her head, curls bouncing.

Never couldn't grin. "I think he needs my blood, my potential. He can't achieve his full goal without it, I suspect. And hope."

"If it was only about your blood he would have stolen it by now," Luis said.

"Yes," Never answered softly. "But I may have to take his first."

"Can you?" Tsolde asked.

"I do not know." He jammed the dice back into an inner pocket. "Tomorrow is soon enough – I need to sleep. Wake me for my watch," he said.

While Tsolde and Luis discussed how to split the rest of the watch Never brushed stones clear and collected pine needles for his bed, then more fallen wood for the fire. Arms full, he started back toward the orange glow.

Come to us, Amouni.

He froze.

A slithering voice had spoken within his mind.

He turned slowly, scanning the looming shadows of the pines. Nothing. No-one near; he felt nothing, sensed nothing, not even the wind in the needles. "Who are you?" he asked, keeping his voice low.

Silence.

Chapter 20.

Never did not mention the voice.

Instead, he lay in the dark where embers lit the underside of the pine trees as he fought to decide whether he'd truly heard the voice. It had sounded awfully real – uncanny. There was something else about it too, something... not the sound of the voice, no, it was the sound of the words.

The voice had not uttered Marlosi. Nor Vadiya.

He sat up.

The words had been spoken in the Amouni tongue.

"Never?" Tsolde's voice was tight with worry.

"It's nothing," he said. "An odd dream is all. Try to get some sleep."

Amouni words. And he understood them – how? There was no answer to that question. And the call itself. Not a true welcome. If there were other Amouni or others who knew the lost tongue, they were not inviting him closer for pleasant conversation over the dinner table.

And it wasn't Snow either, of that much he was certain.

After taking the middle watch, he lay down again and

sleep eventually came. Yet it hadn't been restful, since when Tsolde woke him to the pale dawn light he was sure only a moment had passed. He groaned but thanked her when she rose from her crouching position.

"Poor sleep?" she asked.

"Very."

In comparison, Tsolde's eyes were bright. She didn't stumble on her way to the river the way Luis did. There was at least one benefit to taking last watch. If you didn't fall asleep – you were wide awake when it was time to leave.

At the stream he splashed cold water over his face, then drank, wiping the water from his growing beard. No chance to shave – it wasn't long yet, but it still itched his cheeks and chin.

"You look a little like a mercenary," Luis said. His own beard was lighter, matching his hair. Added to his moustache, the man's face had also been transformed.

"I feel about as dirty as one too," he said.

Tsolde nodded. "You could both use a bath."

Luis laughed. "There's no way I'm getting into that bed of ice-water, Tsolde."

She sighed.

Before leaving, Never collected the extra torches Tsolde had made and the few roots Luis had been able to collect. At least they had gained a little. Then it was time to light the torch, the resin burning-sweet, and head back into the mine.

The trip down the long shaft was swift. They soon strode along level ground again, heading farther – but not deeper – into the mountain. Never held the torch aloft, the heat bouncing off his face. It spread light through the tunnel and revealed a changing mine. Scarred walls and aborted tunnels still appeared but each passage grew narrower and there were fewer.

Abandoned tools appeared more often – three carts they passed, all full of stone thrust through with glittering iron and even a vein of silver. Luis trailed a hand over some and chipped a piece free with his axe, then tucked it into his pocket. "For when we get out of here," he said with a shrug. "I know someone who can melt it down."

Never nodded, leading them down a passage barely wide enough to swing an axe and paused at a blank wall. He slapped a hand against it. "Here is the passage. It ends in the other mine, in a… room that overlooks an underground lake."

"The Night Lake that Darom warned us about?" Tsolde asked.

"I suspect it is – I didn't stop to name it last time I was there."

"That's not what I mean," she said.

"We don't have to go very close to it at all – there's a walkway that hugs the wall. From it, we will have to climb across an underground river. The bridge was in fair condition so we'll be crossing into Marlosa in good time at this rate. It's a steady climb after, up a beautiful staircase."

Luis gestured to the wall. "Why didn't anyone from this mine find the older one?" he asked.

"I wondered that myself, and I suspect not just anyone can pass through," Never said as he gestured to a point where the floor met the wall. A tiny square of stone protruded. "Luis, step on that, will you?"

Luis did as instructed. Nothing happened. He put a little more weight on it then looked to Never. "It won't move."

He waved Luis aside. "But when I do so…" He pressed

down with his boot and a muted click followed. The silver outline of a door appeared as if burnt into the surface. Never squinted as he pushed it open and stepped through, turning back. "See? But we shouldn't tarry admiring the fruits of my heritage, it doesn't stay open long."

Tsolde and Luis hopped through and paused as the stone ground shut, silver light dying away. The torch revealed a wide room, empty of furniture but the floor was tiled. A pattern of darker pieces led toward another door – this one visible. The rush of moving water echoed from beneath them.

"Come to the balcony," Never said and pushed open the door to lead them into an enormous cavern. The faint movement of air, the dampness from the water and the echo of his steps as he moved across the steel balcony to lean on the rail, it all surprised him once again. The torchlight did not illuminate much – his blue-stone offered more during his last visit – but it was enough that Tsolde gasped.

The surface of the Night Lake was a bare winking of slow-moving water, far below, far enough that a fall would break bones at the least.

"Who could have built this?" Luis breathed.

"My ancestors?" Never pointed along the wall nearest to balcony. "It rings this side of the lake and then there's another door leading to the bridge. Once we cross the underground river it's just the stairway. We'll be back on the mountain top before you know it."

"And the lake?" Tsolde asked as they walked.

"I'm hoping just a lake, in spite of Darom's warning. Nothing happened last time I was here, remember that."

Tsolde glanced over the rail's edge often enough but when Never followed her gaze he saw nothing. The surface, as best he could tell, remained still. When they finally reached the door to the bridge, Never stepped upon its switch. The shimmering silver followed.

A pleasant evening for a swim, is it not?

Never jerked his foot back.

The same slithering voice – the same language. The word the voice had used for 'evening' bore a familiar echo – like estayeta, part of the phrase he saw on the river? But not quite... estay only. Eta meant something else, didn't it? He couldn't be sure. And the invitation in its voice... somehow it was hideous.

Like death itself.

"What's wrong?" Luis asked.

Never drew in a deep breath. If he was going to protect them they needed to know what he knew – which was nothing, truly. But one thing had been confirmed; he had not imagined the voice.

"I just heard a voice. In my head."

He frowned. "What do you mean?"

"It invited me for a swim – and it spoke Amouni," he said. "I understood it."

Luis blinked. "Does that mean... ?"

"I don't know," Never said. He placed his foot on the switch again, the glow rising. "We have to hurry – I don't trust it."

Tsolde caught his arm. "What if the owner of the voice is on the other side of the door."

"It's lower," he said. "I can feel it down there... staring up at us."

Indeed.

Never shoved the door open with a shout. "Quickly."

Beyond, he crossed the staging area and ran to the bridge – a graceful span with a low steel rail – but stumbled to a halt. A dark mass sat in the centre, a hiss just audible over the rush of the river. Scorch marks covered the bridge where it rested – silvery light boiled beneath the greasy skin.

Heat drove Never back a step and he spread his arms to shield Luis and Tsolde.

"What can we do?" Tsolde shouted.

"Back," Never cried as he spun. Luis was already stomping on the floor before the sealed doorway. "Let me." Never pressed the switch. Leaping through after Luis and Tsolde, he slammed the door shut just as a wave of heat hit.

But the steel held.

He fell back with a gasp.

Back already?

Never ignored the voice, casting about for anything to block the entry. Nothing. He tugged on one of the railings. Maybe he could –

"Never." Luis' voice was strained.

He spun back to the door. The steel was turning red; a pulsing light started to fill the room. The centre of the door quickly grew white.

Isn't the Yimash persistent? Best you hurry now.

"Run," Never shouted, waving them through. They charged across the long balcony, breathing hard, until a booming crack rocked the steel. A flash of white-hot pain tore into Never's leg and he crashed to the ground with a shout.

He rolled, gripping his bloodied calf. Fragments of hissing steel, still glowing, lay scattered across the balcony and shards were embedded in the stone wall. The Black

Ember bore down upon them.

Quickly, up you get.

The slithering voice sounded amused. Never ground his teeth, scrambling after Luis. The spearman had already turned back, feet pounding across the steel walkway toward Never. Luis slung an arm beneath Never's own, hauling him after Tsolde, who held the door to the empty room open. Her voice urged them forward.

Heat bore down on his back. "Into the mine," Never gasped at her.

Horror covered her face as she waved them on with the torch. Never swore as heat intensified around him – they were too slow, the Black Ember would have them at any moment.

Ahead, a figure loomed from the very wall.

Tall, dark skin blending with the stone around him – a man... Darom!

"Down!" the mountain man roared, his voice echoing.

Luis dove, carrying Never. They hit the balcony and rolled apart. Never reached his elbows then froze, mouth agape.

Darom wrested the Yimash. He'd gripped the bulk of its body, ignoring the blows its stout legs rained upon him, and was dragging it toward the rail. The man of stone grunted as he struggled with the creature. Why wasn't Darom screaming in agony? The heat, even from where Never lay, was enough to steal his breath.

The creature's hiss rose to ear-splitting levels as it broke free. Darom leapt after it, beating one of the eyes until it winked out. A silver burst of blood followed and now Darom roared in pain, but he did not release the Black

Ember. It continued to struggle, blackening the steel as Darom pushed it closer to the edge of the rail. Stooping, he placed a shoulder beneath its bulk then thrust upward with his legs.

Silver light flared and limbs thrashed as the Yimash flew over the rail.

A whistling scream rose as it fell, hurtling toward the Night Lake.

Never crawled forward in time to see it hit the surface.

Steam exploded.

White and grey clouds of steam rose from the lake's surface, a furious bubbling followed as part of the lake was set to boiling. The cloud climbed until it obscured the very rail, covering the shape of Darom, who leant against the steel, chest heaving.

Never dragged himself to his feet and lurched forward but the steam seared his skin. There was no choice but to wait. He turned to Luis. "As soon as it's safe, we check on Darom."

Luis nodded. "Do you think the creature is dead?"

"Gods, I hope so," Never said.

The steam soon eased enough that they could reach Darom. The stone-man had slumped onto his side, stretched out across the scorched steel. His body twitched and his chest rose and fell. There was not a single burn mark upon his bare chest but the charred tatters of his clothing still clung to him.

"Darom?" Never crouched by the man's head. He drew in another breath. Darom's hair had been singed to soot and eyes had simply melted away. "Can you hear me? Can we help?"

"I'll find water," Luis said, slinging his pack free.

"No need," Darom rasped. "I have served my purpose."

"Darom. Why?" Never asked. "We owe you our lives, let us try and help you."

"I helped... because it was the right thing to do," he said, pausing to shudder. "And because... those were my orders."

Never reached out to take the man's shoulder but stopped. It would only cause Darom more pain. "Someone ordered you to watch over us?"

Darom turned his sightless face a little. "Your brother."

Snow. Snow again – always Snow, using those around him for his own purpose, never caring at the cost! "Darom, I –"

"No, I am glad," the man said.

Then his chest rose no more.

Chapter 21.

Never and Luis carried Darom to the empty room, each step a struggle. Even without an injury it would have been difficult. Not only was Darom heavy beyond a normal man but his flesh remained hot to the touch. It was as if his skin had resisted – like stone – the heat from the Yimash but his insides had not been able to withstand the onslaught.

They lowered him then Never arranged Darom's arms across his chest and stood. A brave man – a good man, the last of mountain blood? How had Snow controlled him?

"Never, where is Tsolde?" Luis asked.

He spun. An empty room, torch burning where it lay on the floor – fool! He limped over to stomp on the switch. The mine door swung open as Luis raised the torch. The stone bore no traces of her, no fallen supplies, no scrapes from boots, nothing.

"She didn't cry out. What's happening?" Luis asked. "She couldn't have opened the door either."

"The balcony," Never said. Outside, steam still rose in an invisible hiss far below, but a much gentler sound now.

No rewards for such a guess.

The slithering voice was tight with suppressed laughter.

"Where is she?" he roared, voice echoing across the Night Lake. Not again – he couldn't be responsible for the death of more innocents. And not Tsolde. He'd promised her he'd get them through the mines. And worse – he'd been so sure. Too sure; the reward for overconfidence was always failure. Idiot, idiot, idiot!

"Never?"

"It's the voice," he snapped. "It's taunting me."

Now, now, we can be fair too. Why don't you cross the bridge and start on the stair. You'll find the door that others miss. Then you can see your precious girl again. A long pause. Aren't her curls beautiful? Not to mention all that skin and blood. And her organs, of course – we mustn't forget those.

"Don't you touch her," he screamed into the dark.

Do hurry.

Luis grabbed him by the shoulders. "Never, tell me what's happening? Where is she?"

Never slammed his fists onto the rail. He knew who – or what – owned the voice. Brushing against their minds, even in such a faint manner, was unpleasant enough. But he knew their name now, or at least, the Amouni name for them. Leschnilef. "They have her, Luis. The Leschnilef. The Grey-Faced things I saw in the Amouni book."

"Who?"

"Leschnilef. It means Stone-Wraiths. And it's a trap – they told me how to find them. They want us to chase her so they can take us too."

"But we're going anyway, aren't we?"

"We are." Never sped along the walkway, the pain in his

leg pulsing with every step. His blood was already trying to staunch itself, like for a minor wound, but it wasn't enough. By the door to the bridge his boot was slick with blood. He stopped, tearing at his now frayed cloak until he had enough to bind his calf.

Then he was leading Luis over the span, the rush of water a distant sound despite its closeness. The great stairway, which he ought to have marvelled over once more, he barely saw. Patterns carved across the tread of each step, forming grand scenes of gardens in green and wondrous flowers, flashed by beneath him as he took the stairs two at a time.

When he stumbled, Luis caught him. At the first landing he slumped against the wall, breathing hard. The next flight of stairs was carved to show a desert scene, warm and barren-seeming in the torchlight but he recalled, from his last visit, that tiny animals were camouflaged within.

No time to seek them out now.

"Never, where are we going?" Luis asked when he caught his breath. "You have to slow down."

"They said I'd find a door that others would miss."

"On the stair?"

"Right."

"And this landing?"

Never shook his head. "I don't know. I just needed to rest."

Luis started examining the walls and steps. Never checked on his bandage before joining his friend. Nothing stood out as remarkable and after a time he swore. "It's not here."

The next landing was the beginning of a seascape, blues and purples woven into the murals, all manner of fish great and small covering the steps that led up. Luis removed and lit a new torch before resuming the search. "It's the last torch," he said.

Never nodded as he examined the wall, pushing and prodding odd shapes and patterns in the stone. All to no avail.

"Never, look at this," Luis said. He knelt before the point where the first step met the landing. Each landing had, so far, been free of coloured stone, of patterns or images. Yet here was a curved splash of blue and silver, not unlike a fish. "It's raised against my fingertips," he said.

"Press it."

Luis paused. "It won't be like in the Amber Isle, will it? Some sort of trap?"

"No. They want us to find them."

Luis took a breath and pressed down. He waited. "Nothing."

"Let the Amouni try," Never said as they switched places. "Every other door seems to need my touch." He pushed and a deep click echoed beneath their feet. Never stood. The wall before them glowed with a silver line in the shape of a door.

A staircase leading down.

"In we go," Never said, and took the first step. He gestured for the torch. "Keep that axe ready." It was the best he could offer. He knew nothing about the stone-wraiths, save for their name and their desire for organs. And that his blood appeared to be a weapon against them – yet their grey, emaciated forms didn't seem to possess much in the way of blood to respond to.

And he couldn't manage anything like Snow's demonstration in the temple.

The torchlight revealed a long descent into more shadow.

Down he went, boots clapping against the stone, echoed by Luis'. The stairs did not deviate from their straight and steady descent. A half-hidden rushing had to be the river, but it was hard to be certain.

"We must have reached the level of the lake by now," Luis said.

Never nodded. "I think –"

A pale figure passed the very edge of the torchlight. He stopped – holding his breath. No footfalls, only Luis' breathing. "Did you see that?"

"I didn't see anything."

"As if someone turned a corner ahead of us," Never said.

"Let's find out," Luis said, though his expression was set.

But there was no corner. Only solid wall and more steps. Never glanced at Luis. "I saw something."

"I believe you, but where did it go?"

"A good question. Keep going." Never continued downward but slowed, his heart doing the same. Locating the path into the wraith's lair didn't mean he had to rush. Tsolde would be alive – it was still a trap after all. He had to spring it without getting snared.

And protect Luis.

And save Tsolde.

And then get everyone out of the wraith's lair and into Marlosa to the Altar of Stars before the new moon.

Thanks for nothing, Snow.

Finally the stairs ended in another balcony, only this one overlooked not a lake but a collection of buildings... a whole city. He exhaled. An underground city... an Amouni city? Yes. A shiver ran through his very limbs, just being near. Something about the place stirred deep, fragmentary memories.

A word or a voice, a flash of colour, mere echoes as time continued to chew away at the lives once residing within. Naught he could truly understand, but he knew it was an Amouni place – just as he knew the Leschnilef were not welcome in the city.

Light from soft-glowing points spread throughout the streets and atop buildings, the city sprawling across an enormous cavern. The roof was lost to darkness, as were the outer edges of the underground city, but he saw enough to know it'd take half a day to cross it end to end.

Most buildings were shaped as circles, the stone possessing rounded edges. Windows were hard to discern. Other buildings stood taller. Most of these were typical-looking towers but others, those with bases shaped more like triangles, might have been temples. They each possessed strange, open platforms spreading from their centres, like outstretched arms.

One temple-like building reared above the others, its arms wider than seemed safe, great, dark spheres resting at the ends. Tsolde would be held within.

"What is this place?" Luis asked.

"A lost Amouni city," Never said. "And the stone-wraiths are unwelcome guests here. I can feel it. It's as if the very streets are singing it to me."

"How do we find Tsolde?" Luis asked.

Never gestured to the ladder that offered access to the ground. "We climb down and head for the largest temple in the centre."

"And what about the wraiths? There could be dozens down there. Hundreds, how would we know?"

Even thousands.

The voice was louder in his mind now.

Never ignored it. "They don't like my blood – we stay close together, right?"

"No argument."

Never dropped the torch and stepped on it. "We re-light it on the way out," he said. He didn't add the following thought, the one Luis too probably left unspoken.

If they made it out.

Chapter 22.

The first few buildings were sealed. No doors, no windows. Never touched the walls, but not a single silver line appeared to slice the stone into an entry, not even when he tried his blood or the five-pointed leaf symbol. The cobbled streets were paved to a neatness beyond what he'd seen anywhere else, the seams between the stones were regular and so narrow as to prevent any weeds pushing through – assuming plant life could survive so far beneath the earth.

He glanced at one of the glowing spheres mounted on iron stands.

It was some manner of crystal or even quartz – and the pale blue glow simply seemed to reside within. Most flickered and flared when he neared. He and Luis began to detour them, keeping to the darkness between such spheres.

The first empty sphere they came across still stood tall but only shadows loomed within. Nearby, another bore a faint glow only, just a sheen to the crystal. How had they burnt out? Or a better question – how did the others still burn?

Not a single building admitted him. No matter the shape or size, from tiny pods that appeared big enough to hold one person only, to the smaller temples they passed on the way toward the centre of the city. Arches supporting the great arms that towered over them as they passed beneath were thick with shadow – yet more than once, he almost pointed something out to Luis. Some sense of movement. Each time, he did not, unsure of whether he'd truly seen anything.

The stone wraiths had not spoken for hours either. When he entered a courtyard with a huge, empty fountain and its shattered centrepiece, he found his first clue as to why. "Luis, look."

A corpse lay slumped over the edge of the fountain.

Head and shoulders taller than Luis, it was thin, grey skin stretched to breaking over elongated bones and long, scraggly white hair flowered from the mottled skull.

They had not spoken because they were few.

Because they were dying.

And they were planning their attack, a final, desperate attack for their own survival.

Unable to control an expression of disgust, Never rolled the body over. A grey face, deep slits for eyes and a toothless mouth. A huge rent tore through the side, revealing a brittle ribcage.

"How long has it been dead do you think?" Luis asked. His eyes searched the shadows beyond the courtyard, and he held his pick axe ready, knuckles whitening.

"There's no way to tell with a thing like this." He nudged the Leschnilef with his foot. The head lolled to one side with a dry creak. "But it's clear why they want our organs."

"And Tsolde?"

"The centre."

Beyond the courtyard the streets continued to drive directly toward the main temple, which soared above the other buildings. Huge globes of glowing light now blazed from the arms, and doubtless below too.

Decay swept over the buildings the nearer they came to the temple – the very stones were crumbling within. When he touched one, his fingers sunk, as if into firm sand. He pushed harder, until his hand met unyielding stone. An inner shell of protection? "Something failed here," Never said.

Farther along, they entered a patch of darkness where the buildings were now smeared with dark stains. Blood? Never reached out to touch a smear. Pain flashed and he flinched back.

"Never?"

Despite the pain, there had been a fleeting image. "I saw something, Luis."

"I'll watch the streets," he said.

Never reached out again, placing his whole palm over the ancient bloodstain. A stabbing along his arm followed and he blinked, but held steady. "Show me," he urged it.

Images followed.

Two children in light robes ran across an intersection. The crossroad was lit by the same globes as now, but these were a mixture of shades. Orange and purple, soft blues and bright greens too – they painted the very walls in a manner that added life to the underground, yet did not distort the faces of the children.

Both smiled as they ran, chatting about how they would spend their gold.

And the words were Amouni, clear to him but not so that he could repeat any if asked.

Pain increased but he did not release the wall.

The boys were still running. The blond had a handful of coins and the dark-haired lad carried a soft pouch.

And then a light bloomed overhead and the boys skidded to a halt.

Another stabbing jolt ran up his arm and this time the children disappeared. Never ground his teeth and pushed back. The image returned, along with a sharper pain. Light blazed, growing into a sharp blue, and the boys screamed until the light overtook them. Never screwed his own eyes shut but the glow was too strong and the throbbing ricocheted within his very skull.

When it faded, the boys lay motionless on the stones, not a single mark upon their bodies.

And then the vision was gone.

Never dropped his arm to clutch throbbing temples and nodded when Luis, voice faint, asked if he was well. "I think it will pass," he said.

"What did you see?"

"An enormous blue light killed a pair of Amouni boys, it bloomed over the city. I imagine it killed everyone."

Luis glanced around. "With no skeletons... the stone wraiths must have taken the bodies."

"With everyone dead, there was no-one to stop them," Never added.

"So what was the light?"

Never rubbed at his temples, leaning against a patch of wall without blood. "I don't know but I doubt it could happen again. It seemed final."

"Then we have to keep looking," Luis said.

"That we do."

Never pushed off into the streets once more, passing building after building rife with decay and blood. At one intersection he pointed to a light globe – shattered. The only one they'd seen broken so far.

At the next intersection the street widened where it joined the thoroughfare leading to the huge temple. It revealed the first open doorway. Never signalled to Luis and they split apart, each taking a side of the dark egress. Never had already sliced into his hand and Luis held the pick axe ready.

Never leapt inside.

Empty.

The square of light revealed a bare room only. Beyond waited a second doorway of steel, this one sealed. But when he touched it, silver light glowed and it opened, revealing a circular room lit by a pale glow from smaller spheres mounted on the walls. Two beds with thin blankets occupied each wall. A crystal cabinet stood between the beds, a pair of swords, one slightly longer than the other, were housed within.

Both blades shone with the same glow as the spheres – only brighter.

"Is this a barracks?" Luis asked, blinking as he shielded his eyes a moment.

"Or a home?" Yet there was little evidence of such. Never approached the case. "Strange that the stone wraiths have not been here. Could they not open the door?"

"Maybe only Amouni can," Luis said.

"And what of the crystal cabinets?" Never murmured as

he reached out, placing his palm against the cool surface. The crystal slid open and he reached in to clasp a hilt. Cold. He drew the blade forth. Light, yet the balance was impressive and the strength of the blade... it poured forth, surging into his hand. The forging took it beyond what had been created by other peoples.

He tossed the second weapon to Luis, who caught it, marvelling at the craftsmanship.

"How are you with a sword?" Never asked. "There don't seem to be any spears."

"I'll manage," he said as he tucked the axe into his belt.

Back onto the street, they found several other open buildings. Some with doors that opened and others that would not, no matter what Never tried. One more had a similar sword cabinet but the others were more domestic, ornaments, usually of animals, in the place of weapons.

A book had been left open on a bed but unlike those in the library at Hanik, he was not given any images when he lifted it. Never paused on the way out. "If the great light killed the people of this city, what happened to the bodies that would have been inside these homes at the time – those the stone wraiths presumably could not reach?" he asked.

"Someone had to have claimed them, for ill or good," Luis said.

"I agree."

Never strode back into the street, heading for the huge temple. The answers would lie within – and more importantly, so would Tsolde. And any wraith that stood between him and her would feel the sting of his sword.

Chapter 23.

Never examined the temple's base. The stone here was not like the decaying homes – it was strong where he tapped the sword's hilt against it. But no door opened either. He circled the building, Luis close behind, until he found himself directly beneath one of the arms.

The near-seamless pattern of stone had changed. He pushed against it and the familiar silver line of light appeared as the door swung inward.

The temple was a shell, a perfect ruin.

Faint blue light from the huge spheres poured in from above – the temple possessed no roof. Blackened rubble lay strewn about the floor, piled in beneath the walls, casting ugly shadows. Still clinging to the walls were twisted steel frames, burnt down to stubs, mostly. The scent of charred wood remained – and yet, how could that be so? The ruins were ancient.

"Something was burnt here, recently," Luis said. "Is that even possible?"

He shook his head. "I haven't seen a single scrap of wood, have you?"

"No."

"Let me check something," Never said, drawing the marble free. The small figure within was shaking its head. Never frowned, exchanging a glance with Luis, whose expression was not one of confidence.

"That's clear, isn't it?" Luis asked.

"It is, but we don't have a choice."

"True."

A whispering crossed the empty space between them, but no source appeared. In the centre of the huge room, stretching the limits of clear vision, rested a single stone table – someone lay upon it.

"Luis." Never raised his sword and advanced, flanked by his friend.

He kicked at a piece of blackened stone as he walked, eyes roving. Still no sign of the stone wraiths. What was their game? It was a trap; it had to be, but he couldn't simply skulk around the buried city forever. Instead, he had to act, had to force them to make their move.

Was it Tsolde? She was still too far away for him to be sure; the interior of the temple appeared larger than he'd have guessed from the outside.

As Never drew closer to the still-distant table, a slight whispering joined the sound of he and Luis' footfalls. His sword glowed brighter. Never slowed when a figure was reflected in the blade. Ghostly and pale.

When he glanced away, nothing stood before him.

In the blade, the figure rose through the air. "Look at your sword, Luis." He tilted the sword, tracking the spectre's ascension.

Luis caught his arm. "I don't think I need to."

Transparent figures were rising, leaping from equally diaphanous chairs and tables, from beds, from circles, from stone benches, rising like a thin forest of saplings. At first they rose slowly, robes still, faces serene as they passed.

Then the ghosts began to pick up speed. They were being torn from the temple and drawn up into the darkness high above, eventually becoming faint white streaks. Never blinked.

The past could wait; Tsolde still needed him.

He resumed his approach. When he passed through the

slower ghosts, he felt nothing but there was sadness reflected in the eyes that turned to regard him. He couldn't fight a shiver and even the oft impossibly-cheerful Luis remained silent.

A dozen paces from the table and the ghosts disappeared.

Fine, let it be so.

He had to be sure. The figure on the table... he slowed. It was small, too small. A tattered collection of rags covered a pile of stones.

"And so the trap is sprung," he said.

Luis swept the stones from the table with his free arm, spinning on the temple. "Where is she? Face us!"

Never strode forward, adding his own voice. "We are here. Come and meet your fate, you dried up worms!"

Only silence.

Never spun on his heel. In every shadow, behind every heap of rubble might they wait... but none came forth. He leapt atop the table and scanned the walls high above, the entrances to the arms, but still nothing.

Movement caught his eye.

Behind Luis, who was examining the floor for tracks, something stirred.

Finally.

A torso was rising from the stones, as if sitting up from a grave. Two more to the left of the first, and three more opposite them. Grey-Faces, all. They were sitting up, rising to their spindly feet.

Never clenched his sword – the Leschnilef had been lying in wait, lying within the very stone itself. The shuffling whispers of dry skin soon filled the temple from all directions. Luis had looked up with a frown, and seeing the stone-wraiths rising, leapt to Never's side.

"What now?" Luis asked, eyes wide.

"If they come close, kill them," Never said.

"That's our plan?"

"For now."

Most of the figures were emaciated beyond that of the vision he'd received in the Hanik Library. Skin hung from their bones in thin strips. Their narrow eyes were deep-set, a weak glow within. Few possessed a full set of intact limbs; others were missing whole arms or legs, their limping supported by crutches made from yellowed bones.

The Leschnilef gasped and hissed with each step, as though their lungs were straining. One of the things ran a maggoty-white tongue over cracked lips.

In the forefront stood a stronger stone wraith – taller, his grey skin taut but whole. Still not the creature of Never's vision, but moving fluidly enough. Talons tipped its fingers. Worn leather belt and dark pants, torn to the knees, made up the only clothing – its chest was little more than a wall of visible ribs.

"Give her to us," Never said.

The leader raised an arm to point. *You are most welcome, young fools.* Its mouth had not moved.

"Where is she?"

Your sacrifice will be remembered – we have waited long for this, long indeed.

Never held the sword up to the light and the glow flared. "You will be the first to die by this."

So be it. The leader gestured around him. *My brethren will feast upon me and then you and your friend, Amouni. We live long, on even a little of your bodies.*

"Will you?" Never raised an eyebrow. The thing was afraid, beneath the indifference. There was a hint of desperation. What could he do? His blood? But he could make no orbs, could not do what Snow had done.

And killing them would not reveal Tsolde.

If she lived.

We must survive.

Never spat. "And why is that? You are filthy scavengers, no more."

How quick to judge – typical Amouni. He drew himself up. *We had lived in the earth for generations before your kind came. We tended to the dark, to the great bones of the earth. Above, mankind thrived, even with our hunger. We knew when to limit the crop, how to steer them, to raise a bounty so none here would go without and yet maintain fair harvest.*

"What is he saying?" Luis asked.

Never glared at the leader of the Leschnilef. "Fair harvest – they were lives."

Do you not eat?

"That's enough. Show us Tsolde or die. Choose quickly."

There is another choice. The slithering smugness of its voice returned now. It twisted its torso and flung both hands into the air. The creatures opened their mouths in unison and a deep groan rose, a hundred voices – more, he couldn't tell.

The sound swelled, fogging his mind.

"Attack," he shouted as he leapt from the table. Luis' boots slammed after him.

The leader fell back.

A wraith moved to intercept Never but he swung hard

and the thing's head spun free, bouncing across the stones. The faint blue glow stayed in the air moments after Never's swing, as if tearing at it.

Never kicked the next thing to the ground and stomped on the chest, caving it in with a crunch. A third stone wraith lunged at him – more of a stumble, truly – and he pivoted, driving an elbow into its back, shattering the spine.

The press of creatures grew, even as he cut them down.

The chant continued and Luis was shouting as he swung, the sound of steel slicing through bone filling the temple. Never hacked and slashed his way to the leader, who stood in an open space, flexing his talons.

Never broke free and charged, swinging the sword in an overhead arc.

The wraith fell into the stone. Faster than Never's eyes could trace, the thing was gone, swallowed by the very temple floor, though nothing had collapsed.

An indrawn breath behind him.

Never managed half a turn before something hard cracked into the back of his head.

Chapter 24.

Never woke to the same shadows broken by the faint blue glow of the orbs.

He lay on stone, arms bound behind his back. Throbbing pounded in his head from the blow he'd been dealt. At least his leg no longer hurt – in fact, he'd long since lost his limp. Little use his new, swift healing would be now. He twisted, searching. Stone wraiths milled around the table, near enough that he could hear the hiss of their flaking skin rubbing against one another. Another sound grew in the darkness too, the gnawing of teeth on bone.

Gods, no...

Nearby, a group of the wraiths crouched over a body of their own kin, scrabbling for bones and chewing on the pieces they won. The same sounds drifted from various parts of the temple, as if the living had dragged corpses away for privacy.

He thrashed against his bonds.

Shadowy figures continued to move beyond the light, sneaking behind other shapes. The weaker ones, scavenging for scraps? A few were certainly smaller.

Luis.

Never glanced up at the table. As the creatures shifted, he caught a glimpse of a cloak. Luis. Never rolled to his knees. A nearby wraith spun its back on him, hunching protectively over a severed arm. Another pair of the creatures paused, long bones gripped in shaking hands.

His sword lay on the ground between them; they'd been shifting it with the bones.

Couldn't they touch the blade?

He swore. It hardly mattered, he was caught, bound firm. And it wasn't rope – some manner of cold substance kept him without the use of his hands. "Leave him be," he shouted.

The wraiths grew still.

They parted and the leader strode forward, covering half the distance between them.

Awake already? We've barely had time to begin.

Never reached his feet. "Begin what? If Luis isn't alive –"

You will have your turn. Amouni blood is difficult to manage, it takes care. Preparation. Unlike your friend.

No way to cut himself and use it against them.

"And Tsolde? What have you done with her?"

The thing's face did not change but the smile was clear in the words. We have no idea; she escaped one of our... former brethren, shall we say. We will retrieve her later. First, your friend and then, once the instruments have been collected, you.

He clenched his fists, all he could manage. A pitiful, futile act. Damn them! They'd used his assumptions about Tsolde as bait; they'd never held her in the temple. He was a fool. And now he'd dragged Luis into the heart of their lair. "You are but a husk. A mockery of life," Never growled.

Perhaps. But your efforts to bring us food remain most welcome.

The gathered crowd, those that weren't feasting, rubbed their limbs together in a sickening display of anticipation. Never charged the leader, dropping his shoulder.

Foolish.

It sidestepped his charge, a long arm flashing out. Talons raked Never's back and he stumbled again.

But had the creature made a mistake?

Blood welled in the wounds. The wraiths hissed now, flinching back. Never urged his blood forth... only to let it fall, splattering around him. There was no blood to draw from his captors.

The leader threw back his head and laughter rang in Never's mind.

Movement.

A flash of blue. The leader's head hit the stone with a wet slap, a glimpse of black blood sneaking out from under the neck. Narrow, slitted eyes fell dark.

Tsolde stood in the light, glowing blade in her hand. Her face was smudged with dirt and she bore half a dozen cuts and a large bruise on her head. When she turned on the nearest stone wraith, it flinched back.

The entire group had frozen – even those eating, all simply staring at Tsolde and the corpse at her feet. None spoke. Could any speak at all? Had only the leader been able to communicate? Never watched them until finally, one of the Leschnilef stepped back. Another, as if deriving courage from the first step of its kin, began to slide away from the light.

And then there was a mass evacuation, wraiths fleeing or sinking into stone – many taking detached limbs or flaps of skin or greyed organs with them. In moments, the temple was empty.

Tsolde grinned down at him. "That's three times I've had to save you, Never."

"Any time you decide that I need saving, feel most welcome," Never said.

She cut him free of his bindings, some manner of hardened mud, then they ran to Luis. He too, had been bound to the table at wrists and ankles by the dark mud, with its hard surface. "Is he alive?" Tsolde asked as she cut through the mud.

Never felt around Luis' neck for a pulse and uttered a prayer of thanks when he found it. "They may have drugged him. Or it could have been their song – it nearly had me blacked out before the leader hit me."

"What now?" she asked. "Can you carry him?"

He nodded. "I'll manage. You just keep the wraiths away."

He lifted Luis across his shoulders with a grunt, his recently healed leg wavering a moment before he straightened and started across the now-cluttered floor where he paused to accept the second blade from Tsolde. There were many more pieces of bone and half-corpses than he recalled killing.

How many had died in the fight over the first few bodies?

The stone wraiths did not follow them out and down the streets, or if they did, the things remained out of sight. All the better. Doubtless they would soon be fighting over their master's remains.

During the walk through the streets, between houses and through squares ringed by the odd, single-homes, he paused to rest often but none of the Leschnilef dared attack. During such rests, Tsolde prowled the immediate area, glowing sword in hand. The second he'd belted around his waist and together the two weapons provided more than enough light in sections of the city where the crystal spheres had darkened.

Luis woke with a deep groan before they reached the ladder. "My head..." He squinted against the glow from the swords. "Never? Tsolde! You're alive, I thought..."

"Thanks to Tsolde we're all alive." Never explained what had happened, finishing with a smile. "And so now I owe Tsolde once more and I can't imagine she'll let me off lightly."

"No way," she said with a grin of her own.

"Count me in on the debt," Luis said. He glanced to the ladder. "Think you can help me up that? That song from the wraiths, it's echoing in my head. It was like fighting my way out of a clinging fog."

"Agreed," Never said. "I'll go first and pull you up. Tsolde, rear guard."

He climbed to the balcony and then leaned down to grip Luis' arm when the man climbed, with careful movements, into reach. Hauling him up, he patted Luis on the back, then caught Tsolde when she neared.

Then it was a long climb up to the World Stair with its images and empty landings... Never frowned as he walked. The World Stair? Since when had he known its translated name? There was more, the true Amouni for the stair being Vi Mon.

Mon, world and Vi, walk.

By the landing other words had crept back in. Mother, father, brother. Greetings and curses, sometimes whole phrases. As if the leader of the stone wraiths had unlocked memories of the Amouni tongue.

And for a time, centuries at least, the thing had probably been the only living creature to utter the words.

Now, who knew? Snow might know a little of the language, perhaps even more, but he wasn't going to share his secrets unless it played to his advantage. And so far, almost everything had. Whoever Snow came into contact with he changed – for the worse, of late. Cog was one, Darom another. Would he destroy Sacha too? Never himself?

Finally, they exited the passage and resumed the trek up the World Stair, passing the ocean steps and across another landing; then it was the waving grasses and wheat of the Marlosa plains and the imperial city itself, smaller than he was accustomed to.

The next landing took them through other cities, cities unknown – one might have been Kiymako, with its lattice-work of interconnected walkways between buildings, but it was subtly different, narrower somehow, more fanciful.

Another city was a glistening wonder of rose and another perched on the edge of a great desert. Where did such a desert lie? The Empty Sea in Vadiya did not own such a city.

"These places," Tsolde said. "Are they even real?"

"A dream of the Amouni?" he suggested. "Perhaps, but I feel they must have – at one time at least, been true places."

The final landing revealed another door – sealed shut. Yet, again, as with all the others, at pressure from his foot the switch caused a silver line to split the stone. Unlike the others, a blinding light waited beyond.

Never shielded his eyes, grunting at the pain.

In time, his eyes adjusted and he moved into the open air, still blinking at the afternoon light. A glade similar to that found in the centre of their long path, spread before him. Grass and red toadstools peered between a heavy carpet of pine needles. No pool here, but from memory, he knew a stream ran down the mountain beyond the wood.

Never stumbled deeper into the clearing then lowered himself to the earth with a long sigh, lying in the grass and staring up at the clouds, a white and grey patchwork with only glimpses of blue between. "I'm sick to death of caves and tunnels," he announced.

Luis chuckled from where he sat nearby. "You've said that before, you know."

"At least The Amber Isle had jewels."

Tsolde walked by, stretching her arms and rolling her shoulders as she breathed deep. "It's cold up here too but I can feel the air at least."

"We'll start a fire soon," Never said. He sat up. "So tell us, Tsolde. What happened down there?"

"I don't really know. One moment I was frozen in shock, watching you run toward poor Darom and then something cold took my arm and I was inside stone. It was heavy, weighing against my arms and legs, my chest and face, everywhere, yet something pulled me through as if the rock were water." She shivered and it no longer seemed about the cold. "When we broke free it was in the underground city and a thin, husk of a creature was dragging me along the street. I screamed but it wrapped a dry hand over my mouth and its voice spoke within my mind, threatening me."

"How did you escape?" Luis asked.

"I fought free when it paused to rest – I think I was too heavy for it to drag along."

Never nodded. Had that been the first creature he and Luis had seen? "They're a dying race; it probably didn't have the strength."

"Well, I panicked. It screamed after me. There was so much despair and rage in the sound that I just fled at first, but it seemed they waited at the end of every street I chose. It wasn't until I stumbled into one of the temples that I was safe. Doors snapped down, closing behind me and I was sealed within."

Never leant forward. "The temple did that by itself, you didn't touch anything?"

"No. All I did was run within and collapse."

"Perhaps it protected her," Luis said. "The place certainly felt alive, in a strange way, to me."

"As good an explanation as any," Never agreed with a nod.

"When I finally caught my breath I explored in the dark, but found nothing, only stone benches. The creatures spoke in my mind the whole time, taunting me." Her jaw was clenched. "I don't know for how long, but eventually they stopped and something... urged me out. It was as if I knew you were in danger; the doors opened when I approached." She shook her head. "I nearly didn't go out there again but by the time I saw the light from the big temple I knew that I had to go. I snuck inside and they were... feeding on each other."

Luis blinked. "I don't remember that."

Never slapped him on the shoulder. "Be glad that you don't."

"I found the sword and you know the rest."

"We do." Never smiled and Luis grinned.

"Well, now it's your turn," she said. "What next, Never?"

"We take the trail through the pine there. It follows the peaks of the Folhan into Marlosa. Half a day to the Marlosi side."

"And the border?"

"Who knows now that the Vadiya are here. We'll sneak around," he said.

"And what about the Altar of Stars – how are we going to find that?" she asked.

"I'll know when it's close," he said, toying with the strange sword. In the daylight, its glow remained absent.

"Will we reach it by tomorrow night?" Luis asked. "I think I've kept track of the days and nights but I'm not certain."

"We will." He closed his eyes. "We need sleep first. And food somehow. I don't suppose anyone's been hiding a piece of roasted chicken, have they?"

"Yes, but I ate it already," Luis said with a straight face. "Sorry."

"What about you, Tsolde?"

"Nothing."

He sighed as he removed the Amouni sword, tossing it to Luis. "Well, how about you start the watch and wake me in a while. As soon as it gets dark, we'll see if we can't borrow something nice from whoever's camped at the border."

"If someone is camped at the border," Luis said.

"Don't forget, I'm usually quite lucky." Never lay back with a smile. Free of the mines, free of the Leschnilef, finally close to his goal. Relief mingled with joy. "Someone will be there."

Tsolde snorted. "With your luck it will be the entire

Vadiya army."

He rolled onto his side. "Then there'll be a bigger menu to choose from, won't there?"

Chapter 25.

Never shivered as he crouched behind a line of stones in the starlight, Luis and Tsolde close beside him. They'd had to fashion make-shift scabbards from the last of his cloak to conceal the glow from the swords; it seemed the blades simply responded to darkness.

Below, a large camp spread across the King's Road. Smoke lifted the scent of bubbling stews and roasting meat. He could have wept; a decent hot meal, it would have been a gift from the Gods.

But the Vadiya troops seemed rather less likely to spread their bounty than Hanik or Marlosi folk. While not the size of the force deeper within Hanik, two score was still too many. And that was only the tents he could count. More would be stationed behind the glowing windows of the watch-tower. Once jointly manned by both Hanik and Marlosi forces, it was unlikely either group remained within the stone tower now.

"I could steal another uniform and –"

"No," Luis and Tsolde said together, cutting him off.

"Fine," Never said, affecting a hurt tone. "There's a ravine leading around the King's Road, it's steep going but up this high, we'd probably have enough starlight to show us the way."

"It won't be guarded?" Luis asked.

"Won't know until we get there."

"Then we'd best get started," Luis said. "It won't be night forever."

Never led them down the slope and through the stony maze that lined the side of the King's Road that concealed their passage. They'd rejoined the road at a point behind the advance sentry and his horn. That left two others, who paced the immediate perimeter of the camp.

Never signalled for a halt when the sentries drew near.

"...and you know they're going to cause trouble, it's what they do."

The other man spat. "They aren't any different from the other cults back home. Forget about them."

"No, these Red Seeds are more organised. I'm telling you –"

"Give it a rest, will you?" the second sentry said. "I feel terrible right now and our shift has barely started."

Laughter. "It's your fault – you ate too much. Anyway, like I was saying..." the man passed from earshot. Never waited a little longer then crawled across an open space near the torchlight. With the edge of the outcropping so close, there was no choice but to move slowly.

But they passed through and reached the path that hugged the wall. Narrow but short, it ran beneath the outcropping supporting the tower. A steep drop was the reward for a misstep; a dozen or more broken bones being the best outcome.

"Stay close to the wall," Never said as he inched out.

Save for a shadow that passed over the moon as he started, unobstructed if thin moonlight offered a clear view. It wasn't until half-way across when a gaping hole appeared in the path. Jagged edges and chips near the base of the wall suggested deliberate sabotage. Had they lobbed huge stones at the path? Built and removed a platform to hack at it with hammers? Whatever the case, the Vadiya had done their job well enough.

"If either of you were thinking the security on the border could be better, I know why they weren't guarding this path."

"Why?" Tsolde whispered. Her face was unnaturally pale in the starlight; she didn't do well with heights.

"Someone has smashed part of the path," he said.

"Can we jump?" Luis said, his voice doubtful.

Never shook his head. "I don't think so. It's not that large but there's no way to get a run up. Unless..."

"What?"

"A stout plank – that's all we need. Turn back, I have an idea."

Once they were concealed within the stones once again, Never outlined his idea. "All I need to do is take a crate from the camp. We can pull it apart here then lay the pieces across the gap."

Luis nodded slowly. "It'd have to be a large crate for the plank to be long enough, right? I'll help you carry it."

"And I'll keep watch," Tsolde said.

"If there's trouble, back to the World Stair," Never said, then started toward the edge of the camp. At a dark point between two torches, he paused near a tent. Footsteps approached – the sentries had already finished their circuit? He reached for a weapon, but the steps faded.

Someone else then.

Peering up and down the line of tents, he caught a glimpse of barrels and crates stacked together. He gestured to the others and crept down the line, stepped over tent pegs and detoured torches that burned on stakes driven into the hard earth.

He passed the barrels, which would have been filled with arrows or crossbow bolts, and moved to the next stacks. Most were square, too short. From the markings, they housed breastplates. Further along, there waited three sets of rectangular boxes.

Longswords.

Perfect. Creeping along the stone, he lifted one end of the first box, pausing for Luis to grip the opposite end. Together, they took a few steps toward the deeper shadows beyond the camp.

A voice groaned from a nearby tent.

Never froze.

Muttering continued, following by a scrambling as if for a tent flap. A soldier burst from the tent and stumbled into the row, then fell to his knees, retching. Never kept still, watching. Luis was frozen too, but Tsolde had a hand on her own blade and was circling the tent.

If she had to use it, would the glow of the sword be concealed by the tent?

The fellow continued to empty his stomach, eventually falling down.

He did not move.

Never met Luis' eyes. Poison? Never lowered his end

of the crate and waved Tsolde back. She joined them and lowered her voice. "What happened?"

Horns rang out in the night.

Torches blazed and figures leapt from the darkness, converging on the camp from beyond the tower. Fire bloomed and cries soon followed, joined by the clash of steel on steel. An attack, but whom?

Best not to find out until the fighting had died down.

Never waved Luis and Tsolde into the stones but they'd barely taken half a dozen steps when a voice cried for them to halt. "I'll shoot you all," it promised. "Do not move." The man spoke from the opposite end of the camp, as if he'd approached from the Hanik side of the King's Road.

Never did as he was instructed, Tsolde and Luis following.

Light bloomed.

"They're not Vadiya, sir," the same voice called. "Just like I thought."

More footsteps and a rasping voice. "Very well, hold them, Mondesa. We'll clean up and see what you've caught."

Never blinked when he realised that Mondesa and the raspy fellow were speaking Marlosi.

"Drop those weapons and kneel," Mondesa continued. He sounded young, but his voice was still hard.

Never complied, the blade clanking with a vaguely metallic sound, but one unlike regular steel. "We're not working with the Vadiya," Never said. "We'd be happy to talk to your Captain," he said.

"He's just as anxious to speak with you," Mondesa said. "So save your breath for then; no more talking."

Again, Never complied. It wasn't time to try anything bold. And besides, the Marlosi were not likely to detain them, not when they had a common enemy. Waiting quickly grew painful, the cold of the mountain seeping into his knees, but he did not complain. Luis and Tsolde were equally stoic as the sounds of the Vadiya being slaughtered soon faded away.

The sentry who'd complained of feeling unwell and the man who'd lost his last meal, the relative ease with which the Marlosi force appeared to have subdued the camp, all now made sense.

All that wonderful-smelling stew had obviously been laced with poison.

A classic tactic but one most armies would have guarded against. Had the Vadiya camp been over-confident? Or did the Marlosi possess some undetectable poison?

Never shifted his bodyweight. No matter – in the end, the result was the same. The Vadiya were dead and he would be able to leave soon enough to find the Altar of Stars before the new moon tomorrow night.

All they had to do was convince Mondesa's superior that they were no threat.

Easy.

Chapter 26.

"I don't believe them; they're hiding something, I'll bet my sword on it," said the rasping voice of Captain Sirgeto. His dark hair had been hacked off near his shoulders, a grey streak running through it. Unshaven, the man appeared a mercenary but the battered imperial breastplate suggested otherwise – as did the red stallion engraved in the hilt of his longsword.

Never looked to Luis and Tsolde, bound beside him in the quiet watchtower. Neither refuted the Captain's claim. The man hadn't appeared to listen to much of what they'd had to say thus far – dawn was already breaking outside.

The last day Never had to find the altar.

The Marlosi soldier continued to pace the interior of the watchtower's ground floor, passing before the flames and casting shadows as he did. At least the room was warm; though Sirgeto no longer seemed inclined to stay long. Eventually the Captain stopped, turning to the young, clean-shaven Mondesa and the other soldier. Unlike the Captain and Mondesa, the third man did not wear imperial clothing of white or red. Instead his mismatched armour and worn scabbard suggested an actual mercenary. "Your thoughts?" Sirgeto asked.

The mercenary shrugged from where he sat atop a row of barrels. "Hard to say. Travellers is unlikely, and then there's the strange swords," he said, gesturing to the corner of the room, where the Amouni blades rested, their glow diffused somewhat by fireplace.

"Mondesa?"

The young man spread his hands. "I don't think they're spies. And I believe them when they say they hate the Vadiya as much as we do."

Sirgeto grunted. "That might be true but it's not enough to satisfy me and we don't have time to waste finding out the truth."

Never straightened. "Set us free; we will not interfere with your cause."

The Captain dragged a chair from a table and sat near the fireplace, stretching out his legs. "You want that to happen you'll have to come up with a better story than what you've offered me so far."

Never sighed, letting his shoulders slump a little. "Very well, Captain. Luis and I are swords for hire. Tsolde hired us to sneak her into Marlosi."

The man still frowned but he did lean forward a little. "You look ragged enough to be plying the same trade as my friend, Vantinio here. Why did she hire you?"

Vantinio chuckled.

"To escape a marriage. Her husband-to-be is a piece of slime."

"And your noble hearts just couldn't resist helping her, I

take it?"

Never shrugged. "She did offer to pay us."

Sirgeto faced Tsolde. "That true?"

"Yes. Baron Floriak will never lay another finger on me – I'd rather you kill me than send me back," she said, a seething but controlled fury clear in her voice. Never knew she wasn't exactly acting; she truly loathed the man.

Sirgeto raised an eye-brow. "Floriak?"

"Yes."

The Captain stood and headed for the door. "Bring them."

Never was nudged toward the exit, Luis and Tsolde too. "No sudden moves, now," Vantinio said.

Weak light spread across the wreckage of the camp, trampled tents and bodies everywhere. They passed a blood-stained bedroll, its edges torn. Char filled the air and Marlosi soldiers picked through the mess, salvaging supplies. Never only got a glance before he was pushed along again, but the imperial force numbered half those they'd defeated.

Beyond the watchtower the King's Road started to slope down into Marlosa, though nothing was truly different, same grey stone and pine trees, their needles near black in the dawn light.

Yet there was one notable feature.

Three bodies swung from a recently constructed gallows. Two men were Hanik and one wore Marlosa colours. The Captain signalled for Tsolde to move closer to the purple faces.

Tsolde glared at him. "What do you want?"

"It's not full light, you need to be closer to see," he said, and studied her as she stepped forward.

Never added his own frown to the collection of unhappy

faces gathered. What was Sirgeto's game? Tsolde examined the faces a moment... and then her shoulders began to shake and she lurched forward, expression one of rage.

"Tsolde?" Luis asked.

Sirgeto caught her by the shoulders, and held her back, meeting her gaze. His voice was gentle. "We can leave him there, if you wish?"

Tsolde swallowed. "No. Cut him down and cast him into a ravine."

Sirgeto released her and nodded to the others. Mondesa reached up to cut through the ropes and Vantinio caught the bodies of the first two, laying them across the stone. The third body, the man Tsolde had reacted to, slumped to the gallows and rolled to an ungraceful halt.

Baron Floriak.

Never had not met the man, but it was the obvious explanation. Which meant the other two were commanders of the border. All had no doubt been killed by the Vadiya; Floriak discovering that reward for treachery was simply more treachery.

Tsolde turned away and Luis moved closer, letting her lean against him a moment.

"You believe us," Never said.

Sirgeto scratched his cheek. "One more question. Those swords, where did they come from?"

Never hesitated. If he told them and they went down there looking for more... they'd not be able to open any of the doors but the stone wraiths remained. "Beneath the earth," he said. "We were forced to take the Iron Pass thanks to the large force of Vadiya that we told you about," he said.

Vantinio gave a low whistle but Sirgeto didn't react.

"Enchanted blades in the Iron Pass sounds crazy enough to be true. And I'll be letting you go but keeping the swords."

Never drew in a breath but did not object. The blades were ancient and no doubt powerful beyond what they'd revealed so far. They were part of his heritage... but they were not the Altar of Stars. He knew where many more swords could be found, if he truly cared.

"Something to say, Never?" the Captain asked.

"Only that you should be careful with them. We don't know if they are dangerous or not."

"Don't worry about us," Sirgeto said. He waved a hand as he started off, calling over his shoulder. "Mondesa. Set them free and help them along – take from the Vadiya supplies but be quick about it. We have another trap to set."

The young soldier took Never's hands and sliced through the ropes, doing the same for Luis and Tsolde. He smiled when he gestured they should follow. "I'm glad we don't have to kill you."

"That makes four of us," Never said.

Mondesa wove through the wreckage and stopped near the crates, where he rummaged around a moment, before coming up with a serviceable-looking Vadiya blade. Shorter than the Marlosi swords, it was still a killing tool. "What do you think?"

"I'd prefer knives, if possible," Never said.

The man dropped the blade. "No problem – why don't you look around and I'll work on some supplies."

Never thanked him and started collecting what he could from the crates, then it was time to pilfer from the dead. Unpleasant enough with all the blood and the lingering stench of old vomit, but at the end of his scavenging, he'd replaced his missing knives. Not his preferred cast, but he'd adjust to extra weight quickly. He also found a new belt, some coin, a black cloak and a pack which he filled with water, tasteless but nourishing travel rations and cooking tools.

When Mondesa returned to add more food and tightly-rolled tents to their plundering, Luis and Tsolde joined him. Luis now carried a spear once again, and the weapon suited him like a long lost partner. He also bore a new blue tunic over a Vadiya breastplate. Tsolde wore a short sword in addition to a new belt knife. He couldn't recall whether she'd taken any training for sword play – hacking the stone-wraiths was altogether different to fighting a trained swordsman.

Something he would worry about later.

"If you're heading deep into Marlosa, watch yourselves on the plains; they're crawling with Vadiya. You might be better hiding out in Quisa."

"How goes the resistance?" Luis asked.

Mondesa sighed. "A small victory such as today is all we seem to manage. The problem is, we aren't coordinated. Sirgeto says if we could find the Empress, she'd pull everyone together."

"Then Crisina lives yet?" Never asked.

"So we think," he said. "She was last heard from near Monasema Mountains."

A voice called across the camp. "Move it along, Sergeant." Captain Sirgeto was striding through the corpses, heading back toward the watchtower.

"Pacela watch over you then," Mondesa said as he hurried after his commanding officer.

Never flipped a blade into his hand then tossed it up, snatching it from the air. "Time to finally find the mysterious Altar of Stars."

"Any ideas yet?" Luis asked.

"Nothing, but if it's anything like the buried city, I'll feel it, Luis. Of that I'm sure."

Chapter 27.

Nightfall landed across the King's Road – called the Folhan Highway on the Marlosa side – the worn trail sloping ever-downward but revealing no Altar of Stars, no altars of any sort. Yet he did have the urge to drag his feet onwards. Something lay near, some space that had once held meaning for the Amouni.

Full dark and the new moon unrisen yet, time remained on his side for the moment.

"Hope we're getting closer, Never," Tsolde said.

"As do I." He turned toward a stand of trees beside the road. He increased his pace as best he could in the uneven light. "Maybe sooner than I thought."

Hidden at the end of a narrow trail and tucked between two spurs, lay a grove. It was set back far enough from the road to make an ideal campsite – something others had done, many times over the years, if the generations of ash on the ground were any indicator.

Yet it would not be perfect. A clearing within the towering pine trees did not offer full shelter. It lay open to the elements on one side, the pines offering a screen in a half-circle only.

"This is the place," he said. "I cannot say why, but we are here."

The trunks were broad, open to the sky – branches did not begin until nearly half-way up the tree. He approached the first, placing a hand against the rough surface. There, a ridge, as if bark had closed over an old wound. Someone had sawn away the lower branches a long time ago.

Shrubs crowded the area beneath the trunks, though some of the taller sections of undergrowth had been cleared. Again, some time ago, but far, far more recently than the shorn limbs.

The tree second from the end seemed to have fallen prey to some manner of wood-land disease but the sixth stood tall and smooth. He slapped a hand against the wood, a smile shifting his cheeks. A good feeling. "We're here. This is the altar."

"It doesn't look like a traditional altar," Luis said.

"No. But this is the place. We just have to wait now," he replied.

"And then what?" Tsolde asked.

"Excellent question."

Never helped set up camp while he waited for the new moon, shielding their small fire with the tents as best they could. Then it was simply time to sit, fire warming the night as the meat sizzled on the pot lid.

Luis appeared happy enough, leaning back to eat with a contented smile, but Tsolde had taken little and her expression was flat. When she eventually stood to walk into the trees, mentioning something about standing watch,

Never exchanged a look of worry with Luis before following. Her short figure stared across the empty road.

"Never, I'm fine," she said without turning.

"So I see."

"No joking around, all right? I just want to be alone."

He checked for sap then leant against a tree. "I really should keep an eye on you, to be safe – and you don't need to say it, I know you're thinking you can take care of yourself. And you do, you're good at it too."

She drew in a breath then nodded, her curls near-to-black in the night. A small stone clinked across the ground beyond the tree-line, illuminated by growing starlight. Tsolde threw another, then her shoulders slumped. "It's nice to hear that, Never."

"Want to talk about Floriak?"

"No. Thank you."

Never turned to footsteps. Luis appeared, waving his arm. "Never, something's happening."

He dashed back to the clearing, nearly trampling Luis' heels before skidding to a halt. Starlight was still splashed across the tree trunks but now something stirred in response, like the five-pointed leaf responding to the moon on the Amber Isle.

He stepped closer.

Images swam in fiery blue lines, as if small ghosts were trapped within. The scene was wide enough to cover each trunk, and while watching it, the thin gaps between the trees offered black lines of emptiness – and part of the scene was missing, due to the fifth tree.

But the images were clear enough.

War, slaughter.

Blood.

A swarm of armoured men hailed arrows, spears and sword blows upon a circle of robed Amouni. Where the Amouni stood, it was behind a thunderous force of blood – the torrents shattered bones and cast men aside, seared them where they screamed.

Yet the Amouni were heavily outnumbered.

And the armies were not without their own magics. Some hurled lightning down from the sky or threw fireballs of their own. Lightning shattered against an unseen barrier above the Amouni, others struck with explosions of dirt and limbs flickering on the tree trunks.

Next, the scene leapt forward in time, and the leaders of the armies were sifting through the robed corpses. When they lifted their bounty from the ash and blood, it was to show a companion a jewelled amulet, sometimes a dagger or other weapon, but always the sense of power was clear. Men and women from Hanik, so it seemed, and Vadiya, Marlosa and Kiymako too, from all lands, were pilfering such objects.

It was not long before the first fight broke out.

Scuffling over a shining pendant, two men struggled for the treasure, shouting until they could shout no more and only knives would do.

And then others joined the fight and more bodies piled across the plain.

Another jump in time and the armies were disappearing in opposite directions, their spoils with them, wounds bandaged, faces grim.

The images died away to darkness, leaving behind only the rasp of a long, slow exhale as he turned from the pale, clean trunks.

Chapter 28.

"So what does it mean?"

Never cleared his throat. Had he spoken aloud? He hadn't meant to. Luis and Tsolde were sleeping undisturbed in their tents, yet he could not join them, even were he not on watch. Instead, he paced the clearing, arms folded, cloak offering some – but not enough – protection from the cold. Even his toes wanted to curl up, hide away from the mountain chill.

Had the Amouni left such a message behind? And if so – was it a warning not to follow in their footsteps? Not to take on folly such as that which it appeared they had done in the past, if the images in the Amber Isle were an indication, the very same folly such as Snow seemed to be embarking upon? It was clear, by their fate. Such a living memory would not have been allowed to survive without good reason. Whoever had nurtured and hidden it for so long... descendants of the Amouni?

Or the rest of humanity?

Never approached the smooth surface of the pine

trees, resting a hand against them. Had it been their great knowledge or a great arrogance that led the Amouni to assume the mantle of rulers?

"Neither, brother," a soft voice answered. "Their sense of duty."

Never spun.

Snow stood in the camp, his own cloak pulled around him. He did not wear his Vadiya disguise, but instead a robe not unlike that which appeared in the vision. The sleeves were long, slightly flared and a five-pointed pattern adorned the hem. A large leaf symbol was repeated on the chest, gleaming in the starlight. His expression was expectant but there were also... traces of sympathy?

Before Never could answer, Snow turned to walk into the pines.

Never followed and once they were out of earshot of the camp he caught Snow's shoulder. "That is what you wanted me to see? You think that will convince me to join you in your madness?"

"Did you not see the fools? How eager humanity was to destroy knowledge, to slaughter our forebears for mere trinkets? To shatter prosperity such as has never been seen since?"

"At the cost of freedom."

"So you assume."

"And you know better?"

"Of course. You think this is the only Life-Memory to have survived? I have found others, Never, yet this ought to be enough."

He folded his arms. "And I'm simply to take your word then?"

"Come with me and I will show you the others. You will judge for yourself and you will come to the same conclusion I have. Humanity is not fit to govern itself."

Never spat. "But you and your Vadiya dupes are?"

Snow offered a thin smile. "I'm the closest thing the world has to a god and each time I recover a piece of our heritage, I grow closer still."

"This isn't who you are, Snow."

Anger flashed in his eyes but it faded quickly. "Who I am is unfinished."

"I don't need philosophy."

"But you need to open your eyes, brother. I have given you chances enough. No, a better question is to ask yourself, who are you?"

"I know who I am."

"You know what humanity wants you to see. You have let yourself become what they see. Freak, outcast, dangerous – riddled with guilt and fear, and all of it for naught." He made a fist. "But you are more than that, Never. You are beyond such feeble constructions. You are Amouni. That means more. You are of a noble line; you are all the potential that has been lost."

Never could not deny the momentary comfort that washed over him – Snow's oldest belief confirmed; they were gifted. To hear such words again... it was like hearing a trusted friend speak. What comfort, their blood was no curse, they were not the butt of cruel jokes from the Gods.

But that was not the truth. "We are not so grand, Snow."

"Do not believe their lies," he cried as he charged forward, gripping Never by the shoulders. "Let me show you what I have learnt about us."

"About Father?"

Snow's arms fell away but his expression remained firm. "I know I offered that... but you do not want to learn it – I was wrong to promise as much. Come with me to Vadiya now, I will show you another Life-Memory that explains –"

Never shoved his brother back. "No. Do not toy with me."

"There is no jest; I will share all."

"Then tell me now, here," Never snapped. "Not weeks away in some distant city."

Snow laughed. "Not weeks. Let me carry you," he said as he threw back his cloak. A pair of white wings unfurled. Their span was wide enough to smother Never in feathers, and they gleamed in the starlight, as if possessing their own luminescence.

Never gaped. "How?"

"Let me show you."

Did the wings explain how Snow had appeared soundlessly? The feather he'd mistook as being the owl's back near the Vadiya camp? The winged shaped that covered the moon before the Marlosi attack? And further into the past – on the Carene River. Had it been Snow, the large creature with the wingspan? Watching over him?

Or simply watching him.

"On the river – that was you."

"You may not believe it, but I worry about you, brother."

Never shook his head. "You worry about my blood, not me. You want to know where I am because you cannot afford to lose me."

His wings twitched. "Do you think so little of me then?"

"I don't know what to think anymore – all those you've killed, the Bleak Man – and Darom, did you send him down there to die?"

"He saved you and your friends," Snow hissed. "I worked too hard on him for you to let his sacrifice be for nothing."

"You what?" Never frowned. "What does that mean – what did you do to him?"

"Nothing he didn't agree to," Snow said. He held out a pale hand. "Come with me, Never. You must accept your legacy. I have given you time, let you discover the truth on your own but now you must shoulder the burden with me."

"No."

His brother kept an arm outstretched. "Don't be a fool."

"Leave me, Snow. I don't want what you want."

Snow cursed. "I'm not leaving you to ignorance, to the half-life we led before. You are Amouni. Your power – our power – was given so that we might restore the world to its former glory. I will not let you ruin that, brother."

Never folded his arms, jaw set.

"I do not want to force you," he said, and there was no anger in his voice – instead, there was sadness. Never stopped a retort of his own. Snow's eyes were pleading, his voice trembled. "Brother, I know what they will do to you. What they did to us before, I cannot let that happen again." He lowered his voice, almost as if speaking to himself. "I must not."

Sudden tears built – even as Never drew a pair of knives and spread his feet. "Then we must shed blood, it seems."

Snow covered his face with his hands a moment, wings twitching. When he raised his face, his eyes burned ice. "So rash, so very rash. There is no need to shed precious blood." He glanced back toward the clearing. "But blood might be shed yet – it would only be human blood, after all. And I do think they are holding you back, brother. Perhaps it is time to remove any lingering impediments to your Ascension."

"No." Never cast a knife – aiming for a wing.

Snow twisted and the blade sailed into the night. Then he snarled, launching himself across the space between them. His wings bore him down upon Never, blocking his vision – the bright blue of Snow's eyes continuing to bore into him.

Never slashed with his remaining weapon.

Snow caught his wrist. Never reached for a third knife but Snow snapped a punch across the jaw. Pain shot along his skull and Never growled, striving to get his existing blade back into play. He kicked out, connecting with Snow's knee.

His brother stumbled, but did not let go, dragging Never to the stone.

They rolled, struggling for control of the blade until his brother hissed and raised his free hand – blood pooling within, to create a furious sphere.

Something hurtled into his brother, tearing him from Never's chest.

Never sprang to his feet.

Luis fought Snow, but his brother quickly overpowered the treasure hunter – lifting him above his head and casting Luis aside. Luis crashed into a tree, the snapping of bone ringing through the clearing.

"Imbecile," Snow roared, striding forward, wings flared as he raised a bloody hand.

Luis struggled to rise, his face drained of colour as he clutched at his side. It was clear that whatever resistance he could manage would be as nothing before Snow.

Never thrust himself between them, hand raised. Snow drove the blood down and it splattered as their hands met and locked.

The drops seared Never's skin but he did not budge.

Snow flinched, his eyes wide. "Let go."

"Leave us," Never demanded through clenched teeth. More pain shuddered down his wrist and arm, heat growing in his fingers and palm. It seared and he screamed a curse as his muscles locked into spasms.

Snow jerked his arm back but could not break away – and the blood continued to burn. Never fought to free himself now, as his whole body shook and the pain intensified, burning his skin, flesh and very muscles until only a claw of pink bone appeared beneath the raging blood.

And then it was over.

Snow had fallen back, expression mortified. Tears stood in his eyes and he shivered, wings shrinking close to his body. "Never, forgive me," he cried, his voice broken.

"Go," Never roared – and roared again, the pain of his throat tearing most welcome. He screamed the word until it echoed from the very trees, until Snow stumbled back, fleeing into the shadows, starlight catching on a pair of feathers as they floated down to the stones.

Never gripped the stub of his hand and collapsed to the ground, Luis' voice distant as the night rushed in around him.

Imperial Towers
Book of Never: 5

Chapter 1.

Pale morning light broke across the camp, streaming down from between mountain peaks, gleaming on the mist. There was a hush beneath the trees, as the fire slowly re-awoke, eager flames curling around the piece of wood Never had placed within the ash. No birds chattered yet and neither Luis nor Tsolde stirred within their tents.

It should have been beautiful but Never couldn't enjoy the peace.

He flexed his fingers, one at a time. Each responded perfectly – no pain. His entire hand was whole, as if the terrible blood-fire had not seared it down to bone. But when he'd removed the bandages earlier, there it was.

Healed.

Only now, his hand was pale with black marks here and there, exactly like the bark of a birch tree. And while his skin remained smooth, it had grown hard as wood. It was a gradual change that blended perfectly into his natural, tanned complexion by the time his wrist met his forearm.

A gift from the Bleak Man's tree?

Surely it was the reason he'd been healing so fast of late – the tree's powers of regrowth had somehow melded with his own Amouni magic. Fortuitous indeed. It should have been pleasing and yet he felt no rush of satisfaction at a mystery solved, and only the barest hint of relief at the restoration of his hand.

A grim truth could no longer be denied or even half-acknowledged.

His brother was lost.

Never had no choice; he had to destroy Snow.

And perhaps it shouldn't have been so difficult to accept. After all, he'd known for a long time that Snow was unhinged. Yet it was still a shock to learn just how broken Snow had become. More so than the impossible fact that his brother had wings. Even the question of how was dampened by the chill of his newfound realisation.

He glanced up to the sky. *Gods, but you are cruel, aren't you?* He stood and walked to the broad pine where the Life-Memory had appeared in fiery blue. He rested his hand – his newly restored hand – against the bark with a sigh.

Something stirred within him. The slow spread of wood and leaf over decades and even, it seemed for these trees, centuries. A benevolent sense of their age washed over him, bringing something more, an awareness of the earth itself. The roots of the trees ran deep and there they wrapped the relics of the past, old stone, old rivers now long since filled in, old roads broken and buried.

But within those places echoes of the Amouni lingered.

Somewhere beneath they had once gathered upon a podium to... travel. Far beyond and far more swiftly than what could be achieved by horse or boat. Powerful magic indeed. Yet the how was not clear from the mere traces that remained.

"Never?"

Tsolde stood nearby, wrapped in her blanket.

He gave her a smile, holding up his hand. "I wonder if I could grow back a head if I needed to?"

Her eyes widened and she strode forward, reaching out to take his hand. "It's completely healed..." She met his eyes. "It looks like bark but it feels like skin and flesh. And it's hard too."

"Quite the parting gift, isn't it?"

She shifted her feet. "What are you going to do?"

"About my brother?" He leant against the tree and closed his eyes a moment. How to answer? "Kill him. But I won't lie; I don't know if I can."

"Because of his power?"

"Because he is still my brother."

She gave a weak smile. "You'll work it all out when the time comes."

"I'm glad you're confident in me," Never said. "Since I don't think I am. How is Luis?"

"He hasn't woken yet."

"Well, let's get something hot ready for when he does." Never started for the camp. Luis was lucky, if a broken rib could be called lucky. But it was better than internal bleeding, which, so far, it seemed he'd avoided. What he needed was some batena or stone-bulbs to dull the pain, but while the bulbs were possible, the batena wasn't likely.

"Boil some water, can you?" Never asked. "And see if Mondesa packed any medicine for us. I'm going to look for some herbs for Luis, just in case." If his luck held he'd be able to find some stone-bulbs to crush down to powder. The paste was a fair painkiller but there was an unfortunate secondary effect; hallucinations. Still, better than nothing.

He strode into the trees and crouched in the undergrowth covering a depression, brushing aside needles from the cold earth until he found the tear-shaped bulbs, half-buried by years of decay. Two only, each no larger than his fingernail, but he harvested them and kept searching until he had enough.

Back in the camp, the pot simmered as Tsolde prepared their meal. "Did you find anything?"

Never nodded as he sat across from the blaze, rummaging around his pack for a second pot and his flask. Placing the stone-bulbs into the pot he added a little water and drew a blade, using the pommel to crush the bulbs into a paste.

It would be applied to Luis' torso then bandaged – allowing its properties to seep through the skin and dull the pain. Not as potent, perhaps, as ingesting the paste but the hallucinations that tended to result from such a method were far more vivid, even terrifying. As it was, Luis would still experience some strange visions.

"Are we still safe here?" Tsolde asked, glancing to the trees that climbed the ridge.

"We ought to be. I see no reason why any passing Vadiya would take such a detour."

"What about Snow?"

"No. He'd not set them on our path; he needs me."

"Not to kill but to capture."

Never paused. Hadn't Snow tried as much, back on the river with the thugs? Ever-since, Snow had tried reason but that wouldn't always be the case. "Perhaps. I'll scout the road once we have Luis comfortable."

In the tent, he knelt beside Luis, whose chest rose and fell beneath the blankets. The man rested with a furrowed brow, as if in pain even while he slept. And he probably was. "Luis?" Never placed a hand on the man's shoulder.

Luis opened his eyes and groaned. "So I didn't magically heal overnight," he said.

Never grinned. "No Amouni blood."

"Maybe that's not such a bad thing," he said, wincing when he shifted. "What happened?"

"After Snow hit you we fought some more and he flew away. Tsolde and I got you here and you've been unconscious since. Oh, and my hand healed itself."

Luis blinked rapidly. "Ah…"

"A lot to take in, right?"

"That's an understatement."

Never lifted the pot. "This is a paste to help with the pain, I'll apply it to your skin then we'll bandage you up again."

"Do it."

Never offered his friend a sympathetic smile. "Ready to sit up?"

Luis sucked in a breath and pushed himself slowly into a sitting position, gripping Never's outstretched arm and grinding his teeth. Never unwound the bandage, working quickly to reveal black bruising running along the man's lower rib. He applied the paste, re-bandaged Luis and helped him back down. "It won't work fast but it'll make a difference," he said. "But you might hallucinate because of the stone-bulb."

"As long as it doesn't cause more pain."

"If you stay still it shouldn't. Just don't chase anything you see."

Luis frowned. "This is the best medicine you could find?"

"Well, we might be able to come up with something that will help with the actual healing. The paste is only for the pain."

"So long as it works."

Never paused at the tent flap. "About last night – don't do that again, you fool."

Luis smiled despite obvious pain. "You're welcome."

Chapter 2.

"I'm going to try add some meat to that," Never told Tsolde, once he stood before the fire again. She glanced up from the hardbread and nuts they'd taken from the Vadiya camp.

"How's Luis?"

"Holding up. Keep an eye on him though, he might see some strange things."

"Exactly how much did you use?"

"Enough to let him actually rest," he said.

She snorted. "Well, I found some grenvera to give him when he wakes."

"Good – how much?"

"A few draughts, no more."

Grenvera would work wonders, but it was less potent in small doses, it needed time and repeated use to be fully effective. Still, better than nothing. "Well, it could be worse," Never said.

He returned to the trees to set snares. Hopefully they'd catch something in time for lunch. Then, while Tsolde and

Luis rested, he performed some of the more tedious of life's tasks, mending torn clothing, preparing travel rations, sharpening blades – anything to keep his hands and mind busy while he waited.

Anything to stop him thinking about Snow.

Near noon, the fire concealed and rabbit stew set to simmering, Never rose. "We need to find out what's happening around us. If I'm not back by nightfall, set a watch and lay low until Luis heals enough to flee into Marlosa; try and find Mondesa and Captain Sirgeto."

"You want us to head into a warzone?"

He shrugged. "Everywhere is becoming a warzone."

Never slipped along the trail, pushing aside low-lying branches as he did, until he came to clearer walking. Keeping low, he threaded his way down to an outcropping of rock and lay in the ferns to peer down onto the Folhan Highway. A shiny beetle began a trek up his arm and he nudged it back into the dead fronds that covered the stone.

With his eyes closed, he waited. Listened.

There was no hint of sound coming from either end of the highway – which meant he had two choices. Wait for the possibility of an advance scout from Vadiya forces or venture back toward Giant's Bridge to see if he could learn something that way. Sacha would know whatever 'Prince Tendov' was planning next but that might not give him Snow's next move at all.

Assuming he could actually speak to her without being clapped in irons.

Risky.

Time passed.

He removed the beetle several more times, he checked

on the figure in the marble and sipped at his water. Perhaps he was better off heading for the watchtower and sneaking in to see if forces from the bridge had come across the slaughter.

Never pushed himself up – and froze.

The thunder of hooves. Growing louder. Coming from the direction of the watchtower. Never stood with a sigh. No time for deception or anything clever. If the rider was a Vadiya messenger, then he was going to be stopped by force alone.

Never spun, searching the undergrowth until he found a heavy log. Rolling it free of fern-shoots and moss, he carried it back and crouched at the outcropping. "Closer now," he urged the rider.

The horse soon appeared, charging around a corner. The rider was a Vadiya messenger, travelling light compared to a Steelhawk, but hardly unarmed, carrying bow and blade. The man's attention seemed to be focused on the road ahead – and little above him.

Never hefted the log in his hands, tensing his legs.

The rider neared.

Now!

Never shot up, heaving the log down. It crashed into the messenger's breastplate, knocking him clean off his mount. The man clattered to the stony road and his horse reared and turned back, though it did not bolt. Never leapt down to the road and charged forward, knife drawn. The messenger was still. He was either dead or unconscious – both served Never's ends. No sign of a scroll case or written missive either.

The mount.

Never called to the horse in Vadiyem, keeping his voice low and soothing. The animal snorted but let him approach. Once close enough, he caught the bridle and continued to speak softly. Faint steam rose from the mount's flanks as Never searched the saddlebags, lifting a hard scroll case free. Sealed with the Hawk of Family Isajan.

He tucked the scroll into his belt, liberated food from the bags and silver from the messenger before leading the horse up into the trees, where he paused to break the seal. The scroll within was covered in the hard, rigid Vadiya script, which made it easy to read at the least. Sacha was reporting to home and requesting more men, little of use there. Never read on. She also expected to meet Tendov's forces further south than City-Sedrin. He frowned. Why not besiege the city? A force like Jenisan's left undefeated would be a serious thorn. At the very end, Sacha mentioned a group of three travellers that the Prince was extremely interested in finding for questioning.

Descriptions of he, Luis and Tsolde followed.

"Gods be damned," he muttered. Snow was indeed planning to capture him – whatever he wanted could obviously wait no longer.

If Never decided to force the issue, it left two directions from which to choose – yet Snow could just as easily head for either, or both, and make much better time than Never.

After all, his brother was the one with wings.

Never returned to camp before darkness, hailing softly as he did. Tsolde stood, knife in hand, from where she'd been sitting before the clean-burning blaze. "Where did you find the horse?" she asked, a smile crossing her features.

"At the very convenient travelling horse-trader I happened

to come across."

"Very funny."

"Vadiya scout. We're quite lucky; since Luis can ride, we can leave sooner than I thought."

"And where are we going?"

He tossed her the scroll. "According to that, I think we have only one option."

She frowned at him. "I can't read Vadiyem, you fool."

"Right. Lady Isajan is expecting Prince Tendov south of the Silver City and she also wants more men, so we can expect a lot more activity on this highway soon enough if they draw them from Marlosa."

"Why? What is in the south?"

"I have no idea," Never said. "But it's worse. The 'prince' is also looking for us, handing out descriptions in those messages, and you can be certain it isn't the only messenger he'll send. I think the safest option is to head into Marlosa. We can put some distance between us and Isajan and get Luis to a proper healer at the same time."

"Could we stay here too? We seem well hidden."

"It's a bigger risk, since there's a small army behind us and limited medicine if Luis worsens."

She nodded slowly. "And Snow doesn't need us, he needs you. We're expendable to him."

"But not to me," Never said. "So we'd better break camp and see if we can keep ahead of him."

"It's getting dark, Never."

"True, and we'll have to go slow for Luis anyway. But it's better than staying still and the dark should make it harder for Snow to see us if he decides to search himself."

"You mean, from the sky?" her voice was a little awed.

"Hard to get used to isn't it?"

She nodded. "I'll wake Luis then. I hope he'll be able to ride."

"As do I."

Chapter 3.

Never led them down the mountain and into the foothills, tension growing with the changing scenery. It was not the easing of the chill wind or the disappearance of ferns in the undergrowth, the dwindling pines, the swathes of yellow grain spreading beyond the foothills or the scarcely visible line of the Ebina River – all the things that signalled a homecoming.

Any fondness that could have warmed his heart was held at bay by the lingering scent of smoke on the afternoon air.

"We're still too high to smell smoke from a ransacked village on the plains, aren't we?" Tsolde asked, her brow furrowed.

Never nodded. "Perhaps a mountain hamlet. There are several nearby."

Luis said nothing. Sweat lined his brow as he held the reins, but his expression darkened. He'd been riding without complaint, but with the last of the herbs gone, it was clear he was now suffering.

The highway bent around a stand of trees and the scent

of smoke grew, still no more than a bitter taste on Never's tongue rather than a spectre within the trunks. But the source was soon revealed. A pile of blackened bodies rested beside the road, surrounded by hewn earth. Near as tall as a man, it had to contain at least two score, possibly more men. Ash and char littered the highway. A gauntlet peeked from mud in a ditch beneath the pile.

No faces were discernible, merely black shadows within the heap of half-formed limbs and armour. A blackened breastplate hung from a stake that had been driven into the stony earth before the pile.

Vadiya script was scratched across the surface.

"What does it say?" Luis asked.

"It says 'We hunt you now'," Never replied. "Or close enough – there's a mistake in the word order but the meaning is clear."

"Captain Sirgeto and his men?" Tsolde asked.

"It's certainly possible."

Never led them beyond and down into the foothills. Though their supplies were holding up well enough, Luis needed more medicine. And the deeper they headed into Marlosa the greater chance there was of running into Vadiya forces. Even following Sirgeto's trail of death as they were, didn't guarantee they'd avoid enemy soldiers. It probably increased the chances of running afoul of the Vadiya, if any had caught wind of Sirgeto's frenzied resistance.

And frenzied it seemed.

At the sites of three more skirmishes it appeared that Vadiya scouting parties – and a once larger force – had been wiped out by the Captain and his small band. Good on him. Never had to acknowledge a twinge of pleasure, but there was a fair chance such strikes would draw more attention to the area.

And he couldn't afford that.

Barley and other grains stood in the fields, tall and golden but much of it brown and decaying too. In places, husks littered the roadside and the kernels were beginning to wither as the pending winter harvest would likely go unheeded.

"Let's take a moment," Never said as he paused on one of the low, wooden fences that lined the road. A breeze rustled the stalks behind him and somewhere in the distance a bird cried out. "This road is still important to the Vadiya – we're going to run into them sooner or later, whether it's forces heading into Hanik or the other way around, whether they're looking for us specifically or not." And there was even a chance one of those forces would be led by Sacha, something else he needed to avoid.

"And that's going to be true on any road, isn't it?" Tsolde said.

"Less so, but you're right. It's just one reason why I think we need to rest again." He looked to Luis, whose hair was sweat-dampened once more. His eyes bore a glazed look, something that hadn't been evident earlier that morning.

"I'm fine, Never," Luis said. "I can go on."

"Very well, to the nearest farmhouse then," Never replied. He glanced along the highway, which was half-torn by hooves and boots. A crossroad sign stood dark against the afternoon light. Nowhere could he see woodsmoke on the sky, but nor would he if people were laying low. "Let's see what's down there."

The crossroad offered more grain stretching forth, yet the

western fields had been razed to the ground, no more than blackened stubs remaining, dotted throughout the gentle contours of ash-choked earth. In the distance, a barn stood but nothing else.

Tsolde looked to it but Never shook his head. "The first place anyone will look if they're sweeping the area."

Further east waited simply more fields. The crops were a little shorter, but the path heading north, running almost parallel with the Folhan Ranges, was more promising. The wheat stood taller and the land seemed to dip. "This way." Never started down the path, Tsolde leading Luis. The man swayed a little in his saddle but was staying upright.

For now.

Never turned down the first narrow trail, which eventually led to a large farm set off from the fields and surrounded by a square of dying grass. The building was quiet, still. White walls bore no scorch marks or otherwise, the doors were closed yet there was an emptiness to it. No smoke rose from the chimney, no sense of movement between windows.

"Let's see if anyone's home," Never said.

At the door he drew a knife and leant against the wood, straining his hearing. No sounds from within. He pushed on the door but it remained shut. "Around back," he said. Never glanced into each window he passed but curtains blocked his view.

The rear door was closed. Never forced it open, calling a greeting.

Silence.

"We'd like to shelter here, if we may?"

He moved from room to room, finding only emptiness. A table set, a new wick in a tallow candle, chairs in place, an unmade bed in one room and two more atop a loft. Only the pantry revealed evidence of hasty retreat; bare shelves with naught but crumbs left on a piece of cloth. A thin trail of ants led from the crumbs to a chink in the wall.

Had the people here fled before the Vadiya? Or, been taken?

Outside, he nodded to Tsolde. "Seems empty. Think you could look after the horse and get some water boiling?"

"I can," she said.

Never helped Luis from the horse, taking his friend's weight with a grunt of surprise.

"I'm not that heavy, am I?" Luis gasped.

"You've probably lost weight," Never said, glad Luis couldn't see his expression, since the man's eyes were squeezed shut in pain. Tsolde took the reins and led the mare into the stable, mouth pressed into a firm line.

"That's not a good sign, is it?" Luis said.

"Not really." Never supported his friend as they walked inside and to the bed, where he lowered the taller man down. "We'll find something."

Tsolde soon appeared with a cup of water, her eyes full of worry. Luis drained the cup and lay back, his breathing easing a little.

Never took Tsolde back to the kitchen, lowering his voice. "He won't be able to travel much further, that fever is growing. His injuries are worse than we thought."

"Do we have anything left?"

"No."

She glanced around. "These people don't appear to have any herbs; I haven't checked everywhere yet but I don't like the look of things."

Some Red Clove would have done it, but better to wish for the moon. "I might have to try to find a village."

"And leave us here?"

"Unless you want to go?" he asked.

Tsolde glanced toward the room where Luis lay, the sound of his laboured breathing still audible. "I don't know Marlosa like you do."

"Then we have to think of something if you're found." Never scratched at his beard. Did the farmhouse have a razor somewhere? Hardly important. "Is there a cellar here?"

"Will Luis even be able to climb down if there is?"

"You'll help him," he said. "I could teach you some Vadiyem too. Enough to claim you have information worth keeping you alive for. It might buy some time if you're found by forces that haven't been given Snow's orders."

"But maybe not for Luis," she said. "They'd have no use for him as he is."

Never sighed. She was right. "Do as you see fit, Tsolde. I don't think we have many options. I'll be swift."

"Where are you going?"

He moved to the nearest window and parted the curtain, pointing along the road. "Perhaps half a day north and west lies a village... named something like 'bowl', I can't remember. There are larger settlements farther away but I don't know if they will be standing."

"And if your village has no medicine?"

"Disan lies beyond it, another day."

"Three days at least – would Luis survive that long?"

"He must." Never started toward the stable, striding into the shadows to check the mare over. He tossed Tsolde a spare knife. "And so do you."

Chapter 4.

Never reined the mare in, mud splattering from her hooves.

Misty rain clouded his view of the road and the village ahead – what was it called? Still he couldn't recall its name, but perhaps it didn't matter anymore, he realised as he squinted.

There was little left of it.

Afternoon light was failing, smothered by the rain and dark clouds overhead but he saw the black stumps and skeletal walls in place of homes.

"Gods be damned."

Never paused. Water continued to trickle down the back of his neck, but he'd long since been soaked through. What was a little more water now? He nearly tugged the reins back toward the farmstead but there was no point returning empty-handed. He had to press on and find something for Luis.

And squash down the possibility that when he returned, Tsolde and Luis would be gone.

Or worse.

He tapped his horse's flanks and passed through the blackened husk of the village – Oroluca, that's what it had been called. Oroluca, which meant Golden Bowl. Named after the sun as it would descend into the wide depression the village sat within and light the grass and surrounding fields; he'd passed through once, years ago. It had been beautiful.

The road drew him deeper into the plains as the afternoon wore down to darkness. There was no sign of the Vadiya, neither slinking about beyond the miserable-looking fields, nor charging along the trail. There was only more rain, more mud.

Overnight he huddled beside the mare in an abandoned hut, various leaks in the roof letting enough rain in to keep him chilled – and worse, to keep the smell of wet horse present. By noon the next day, after a chill wind had dried him off for the most part, he slowed the horse once more as Disan appeared ahead – or smoke from its chimneys at least, visible beyond a rise in the road and swirling up to join the iron-grey sky.

Never slipped into a stand of juniper beneath the rise, tied his horse to a low-hanging branch and climbed to peer down on Disan.

A few dozen white houses with red-tiled rooves, all slick from last night's rain, surrounded a well. Folks in typical Marlosi robes had queued up, the red, yellow and green stripes muted from a distance. The inn, a sprawling building with a small watch tower, stood at one end of the well's square. From his vantage point he also indentified the red glow of a smithy, it coloured a figure walking back and forth before the forge. Beside it stood a building with the sign for healer above its door.

Aside from the well, the town was quiet. Even the fields surrounding Disan showed no movement between the rows of grain. Was that a good sign? Hard to tell. At least here he noted some signs that the Vadiya were organising or allowing harvest. Never pulled out the crystal marble and held it within his palm.

The wooden figure within held up two hands, forefingers crossed – a common gesture for danger.

Never replaced the crystal with a sigh.

Trouble it would be then.

And soon enough it came – as a Vadiya Steelhawk strode up to the well, demanded someone fill his pail with water and returned to one of the houses once the job was done.

"Ah, there it is."

Never leant against a trunk a moment, then pushed himself off and left the treeline, approaching the town at a walk. The one Vadiya he did see hadn't seemed in the midst of a killing frenzy, but had demanded water of the residents. More like the actions of an occupying force.

Perhaps that meant the Vadiya were letting the town operate as normal?

He didn't have time to formulate a convoluted plan – a certain amount of boldness would have to do. Which meant walking directly into Disan, buying whatever he could from the healer then walking out again without being questioned by the Vadiya. Anything else probably meant Luis wouldn't survive.

Even so, a robe wouldn't hurt when it came to blending in.

A soft rain began to fall when he reached the first home. Never left the road and moved between two buildings, their high windows holding drawn curtains. The murmur of voices came from within, words indiscernible. Nearer the smithy, he paused when a figure hurried along a garden path but the woman did not look around, her dark hair beaded with water.

He walked a little quicker now, stopping along the side of the smithy at the sound of raised voices.

"Don't talk about that," a man said, his voice gruff.

"Maybe they'll come here. You never know," replied another man, sounding younger, sounding as though he was fighting to keep hope from his voice. "Those travellers that came through yesterday said Captain Sirgeto is actually winning. Said that they've started chasing down the Vadiya now and they're driving them out of the villages."

A snort. "Score of ex-Imperial troops won't win anything, Pio."

Pio lowered his voice. "They say he's up to a hundred men already."

"Farmers and fools flocking to join him," the gruff man snapped. "And all they'll do is bring the full force of the Vadiya down upon themselves. Or us, so I don't want to hear another word."

Never turned back, moving around the rear of the building to approach the healer's home from the other side. He didn't want either of the men to notice him, if possible. Their conversation had been educational at least. Sirgeto was drawing men – and attention – upon himself. Even more reason to avoid the fighting, yet Never had to wish the man luck. More useful however, was learning that the Vadiya did seem to let travellers into and out of Disan. Maybe there was a chance – assuming the healer had something powerful enough to help Luis.

And that Never could bring it back in time.

Before stepping into the street he checked for signs of Steelhawks, then knocked on the healer's door.

"Yes?"

"I am a traveller seeking medicine," Never said.

"You're welcome, but be quick," came the reply.

Never pushed the door open and stepped into a dimly lit room, the spicy scent of grenvera strong. An iron-haired woman sat behind a counter, hands busy as she tied several pouches for a waiting customer.

Something about the man was familiar – Never tensed.

What was it? The hair? The clothing? The stranger glanced back over his shoulder, revealing a plain face and a small smile.

"I won't be long, traveller."

Cog.

Never reached for a blade but the man turned and shook his head, tilting it toward the woman. "Be calm," he said. "We wouldn't want anything untoward to happen, would we?"

"Indeed," Never said with a frown. What was Cog up to? Snow had sent him to Marlosa, surely, but why? There was no way Snow could have known where Never would be... so it had to be something else.

The healer paused at her work, glaring at them. "I don't need you fools causing a fuss. Those damn Steelhawks will tear this place apart if you keep on."

Cog turned and sketched a bow. "No trouble, we will

take our discussion elsewhere once our business is complete."

She grunted and finished up, handing over the pouches and accepting the money Cog offered.

The man gestured to the door. "Let's return to check on your horse."

"You can wait," Never said. "I must buy medicine first."

Cog shook his head – and there was a touch of sadness in his eyes. "Healer Alippa was gracious enough to sell me the last of her chila powder." He lowered his voice. "By far the most potent remedy for serious fevers and as I understand it, among other things, internal bleeding."

Never glared at the man, pushing past to address Alippa. "Do you have anything else that would battle a life-threatening fever? I have tried grenvera and stone bulbs but my friend can no longer walk; his rib was broken and he is not healing."

"Chila powder is the best chance for your friend. If you cannot convince this man to part with the last of what I had, you could try Hilisa."

"I see." Hilisa was days to the northwest, there was no way he could reach it and return in time. "Have you any batena, by chance?"

She raised an eyebrow. "That won't be enough for your friend, you know."

"For me." He would need it.

Alippa prepared a pouch and he paid before turning to point at Cog. "I know he put you up to this and I expect you to tell me how. And why."

Cog offered a slight bow. "Of course. Follow me."

The man of smoke exited the healer's shop and slipped immediately between the buildings, circling around toward the inn. Never followed closely, eyeing the man's pack. Once they got into the trees, out of sight of the village, Never would have a decision to make. He might simply take the medicine, if he was quick enough, but that meant either killing or leaving Cog behind; Luis could not wait.

Yet if he did so, what answers would he miss?

For Snow was no doubt attempting to direct events once again. Well, no more.

The hum of voices bled through the wooden walls of the inn as Cog increased his pace, leaving it behind. Never matched the speed as the man turned a corner, leaping over a garden bed as to move between two homes.

An armoured figure stepped out from one of the buildings. Steelhawk.

The man stiffened in shock but before he could speak, Cog raised a hand. Grey smoke rushed up from the ground, smothering the man. Cog leapt forward, catching the fellow with a grunt before lowering the soldier to the ground, preventing the clanking of armour. "Onward then," he said.

Never pushed aside unease – Snow had done something to the man who called himself Cog, surely, what else explained such strange magic?

By the time they stood within the stand of juniper and Never checked on his mare, he was clenching his teeth once more. His unease had been replaced by simmering fury. He needed the chila powder. How dare Snow interfere once more!

Never turned to face Cog, who leant against a trunk. "Speak."

"You should know well that your brother can find you whenever he wishes; he senses you," Cog said. "By the way he has spoken of this sense, I assumed you could sense him."

No surprise. "Where is he now, then?"

"Perhaps at the Imperial City by now – I cannot be sure."

"Fine. Then answer me this. Why? Why come here ahead of me and take that which I need?" Never demanded. "If Snow thinks he can sway me by killing my friends, he is a damn fool."

"Think of it more as a bargaining chip," Cog replied. "Your brother suspects that you would not wish to hear from him directly at this time, so soon after your last meeting." The man glanced at Never's hand.

Never folded his arms. "Bargaining chip?"

Cog nodded, waiting.

"And if I simply take the medicine instead?"

"One or both of us may die, I do not know." The man shrugged. "But if so, the secrets your brother has given for me to share will die here."

Never shook his head. When it came down to it, he didn't know whether he could harm Cog at all... "Then you would die for him, like the others?"

"Of course."

Never shook his head. He couldn't risk it, could he? Any delay might cost Luis his life and yet if Cog did have something worth learning he had to take the chance. At the least, Never would hear what the man had to say. "What are you offering then, Cog?"

"Simply come with me to the river. There I will take you to a place where you will learn more of your heritage. After which, I will give you not only the chila powder but also the means with which to return to Luis in time to save him."

"And all this is what Snow desires?"

"Yes."

"And he thinks I trust him?"

Cog shrugged once more then turned to walk between the trees. "That I do not know. Come, Never, if you will. The river waits – it is not far."

Never stared after the strange man. Was it all simply another of Snow's ploys? A way to distract Never and to separate him from his friends? At best, Snow considered Luis and Tsolde a hindrance, that much was clear.

And yet, Snow wanted cooperation, not bloodshed.

No, not a single drop of precious Amouni blood could be lost, as far as his brother was concerned. And Snow also had to be aware that Never would not cooperate if it meant losing Luis and Tsolde. Whatever Cog – and Snow – offered now would doubtless serve them in some way, but Never needed the powder. Also, he couldn't deny that the temptation of being given another piece of his heritage was strong.

"Fine, brother. Let's see what you offer."

Chapter 5.

Noon had not waned by the time they reached the Ebina, an old, deep river of restless grey beneath the clouds. The banks were empty of fishermen. Upstream were what might have been darkened remnants of a campsite, and across the water a narrow trail ran alongside the rows of drooping grain.

"Don't be afraid, even though what follows will be strange," Cog said as he secured the pouches of chila powder within an oil skin, which he replaced in his travel pack. Then he removed a pendant from around his neck and spoke softly, facing the water.

Never led his horse closer. The words were familiar... the Amouni tongue? Though he could not discern individual words, the meaning was clear. It was a call for assistance – a deeply respectful call.

"And now we wait," Cog said, replacing the pendant before Never could get a clear look at it. Made of bone?

"I don't have a lot of leisure time, you know, Smokey."

"Be sure to protect anything that you do not wish to become temporarily soaked," Cog said.

Never raised an eyebrow. "You're a patient fellow, aren't you?"

Cog chuckled. "Does it bother you that I am not easily ruffled?"

"It certainly does." Never secured his batena and then glanced around – there were few places to tether a horse. Best to simply let her go free. "But we won't dwell on that now. Would you care to tell me what's happening?" He had his own suspicions but did not volunteer anything – better to keep Cog, and therefore Snow, in the dark about what Never knew.

Or thought he knew.

"We are about to travel a great distance."

"Very well," Never said.

Cog turned back to the water. "Here."

Something stirred beneath the dark surface, a golden colour grew... and a fish-head broke free, followed by a human neck and shoulders. A man-like figure, draped in deep yellow robes, soon stood on the surface.

Bare arms remained at his side, but the fish-head regarded Cog expectantly.

Just as Never had expected.

Yet how could Cog call such a figure forth? Surely he had no Amouni blood? No, the pendant. Or something Snow had taught the man – the Amouni words? Again Cog spoke, and still Never could not catch the meaning.

It shall be so, Guest. The fish-man said. To Never, he nodded. Welcome back, Master.

Never affected a look of shock, which Cog appeared to accept. "Simply take his hand when offered. We will enter the river and the guide will take care of the rest."

"Which is?" Never asked.

"Visiting a place of great potential," he said as he stepped into the river. The water reached his knees only. "Come quickly. Not all guides are fully present in the world after such a long time dormant."

Never followed, grimacing at the chill river and reaching for the guide's outstretched hand.

Do not release my hand. The guide's toneless voice rang in his head.

Never obeyed, and gave a gasp when the guide drew him beneath the current.

Cold, blackness enveloped him.

Did even his bones shiver? Yet there was air aplenty in the darkness and the streaking colours he'd experienced on the River Rinsa in Hanik returned. Yellow and purple, orange slicing through as the inky world consumed them. Cog was nowhere to be seen, yet the guide remained close, a strong presence that only began to dwindle when the colours slowed and faded. The surface of the lake appeared above and soon the pale glow from a red and white tiled room was revealed. Surely it was the same room as he'd come across on the Rinsa? And if so, how far had they travelled, and at what speed? Were the rivers even directly connected? He couldn't recall.

As before, when Never climbed from the pool – Cog beside him – he found his clothes drying quickly. The guide stood within the black pool of water, not a single drop of dew beading on its alabaster skin.

Cog thanked the guide – shajul – this time Never caught and recognised it, and the yellow robes faded to black as the fish-man disappeared.

"Where is this place?" Never asked.

"It is known as the Vestibule, located in Hanik," he replied, approaching the podium. "We must complete a ceremony swiftly, for you to learn what Snow has permitted me to offer."

"Lead on," Never said, waving a hand.

At the podium, Cog removed a vial of blood from his pack and with careful, even reverent movements, allowed a single drop to strike the surface.

Silvery light appeared in the wall, allowing a door to open. Cog led him into a circular chamber and the sight of the strange, steel furniture confirmed Never's suspicion. As with his last visit, Never eyed what he thought of as 'transfer tables'. What was their true purpose? Still dust-covered, they surrounded the wide, centre-dais and each table sloped toward the tiled floor, where a central drain lay concealed beneath the tiles.

The tables narrowed even further at the top, before spreading in a circle as if for a head to rest.

A chill ran across his shoulders.

Cog gestured around him. "You now stand within one of the only Amouni spaces to survive the Eradication. Its functions remain intact – see the Preparation Tables, how they have not rusted?"

Never raised an eyebrow. So Snow had been to the Preparation Chamber. "What does this place prepare then? What have you brought me here to tell me? How will I be able to return to my friends? Via that... strange fish-man?" He had nearly said guide but it was still best to hide the extent of his familiarity, limited though it was.

"This chamber prepares the Amouni."

Never couldn't fight a glimmer of curiosity. "For what?"

"Flight," Cog said with a smile. "Here, if you are willing to trust me, is where your wings, long-dormant, will finally be awoken."

Chapter 6.

Never blinked. Wings? That wasn't possible... even for the Amouni, surely?

Fool, of course it was.

Snow had wings and they came from somewhere. Why not an ancient Amouni preparation chamber? Yet that didn't explain how. Or why? Apparently Cog was going to claim he knew 'how' at least. And more, claim that Snow wanted Never to find his wings.

Never rolled his shoulders, an itch growing in the middle of his back. Gods, did his body believe it? There wasn't a single moment in all his life that might have hinted at the fact that he – or Snow for that matter – had wings hidden somewhere within his body.

"You don't believe me?" Cog asked.

"It's rather difficult to do so."

"Understandable."

"I assume wings are natural within the Amouni?"

"No, not all – but you and the Master have special bloodlines, even among the special."

Never raised an eyebrow. "Trying to boost my sense of self worth, Cog?"

"Perhaps – your brother mentioned that you still believe the lies humanity tell about you."

"Let's stay focused on the subject at hand, shall we?" Never approached one of the tables, running a hand over the cold, smooth steel. "What exactly is Snow offering?"

"As before. You Ascend, as fated, and I will give you the medicine and the means to return to Marlosa in time to save your friend. If you disagree, you leave, with or without the powder, but you will not reach Luis in time."

Never shook his head. He'd been manipulated once again – he had no choice now. He could not let Luis die; he had to gamble that Cog was telling at least a partial truth.

"Fine. What does my brother want? What does he gain from giving me wings?"

"That he has not shared with me."

Never chuckled. "How like him." Yet Cog had not denied it. Granting Never wings was merely another step in Snow's greater plan. Whatever that was.

"Then you accept?" Cog asked.

"It seems I must." Never glanced around the room. "What next? Take me through the process."

"Follow me then." Cog headed for the deep alcove, near-hidden in darkness. At the silver-handled door, Cog once again used a drop of Snow's blood to enter, his movements precious, even tense. As if he did not wish to waste even a single drop. Within, he leant over one of the steel stools and lifted free the strange instrument Never had seen on his previous visit.

Cog handed it over.

Long as Never's forearm, it bore a blunted hook at the end. "This?"

Cog lifted one of the ceremonial knives, its blade set with Amouni runes. "And this. It will be painful, but you will not be harmed, truly."

"How truly reassuring. Go on."

"I make two vertical incisions down your back. On the table. The Claw you hold pulls your wings free and light from an opening above the dais dries them. There, Snow posits, Amouni took their first flights, back when the dais was fully functional and could still rise."

"That's all? I feel nothing within my back that leads me to believe I bear wings."

"They are dormant, as I said," Cog replied.

"Meaning?"

"That the Awakening Ritual must occur before the procedure itself. You will not recall much of it but when it is over you will have Ascended." He gestured back to the circular room. "If you are ready, shall we begin, davishca?"

Never paused. "Davishca? Meaning Great One? None of that, Cog." He tossed the Claw across the small room to the man.

Cog caught it with a nod. "Very well."

"Let's begin," Never said. He strode back to one of the narrow tables and straddled it, facing the dais, where he removed his cloak, coat and a knife he'd strapped to his side before looking to Cog. A slight shiver crossed his skin in the cool chamber. "All right, Cog. Awaken me and do it swiftly. I have a friend to save."

"Of course." Cog produced the vial of Snow's blood. "First, drink this."

"My brother's blood?"

"Yes. The blood of an Ascended Amouni is required to Awaken dormant wings."

"So be it." Never took the blood and raised the vial to his lips, pausing. Was that all it would do? Could Snow's blood have some other effect, something... controlling? Or dangerous.

Perhaps it would teach him something of his brother's plans.

"It is safe," Cog said.

"Good to know," Never replied. "Especially coming from such an impartial fellow."

"It will have a disorienting effect, admittedly. And I have mixed in enough painkiller to keep the procedure tolerable."

"And you've done this before? For Snow?"

"My Master did not wish for me to reveal such details."

"Yes, isn't that good of him." Never glanced at the vial again. He had to do it for Luis. And he had to know if Snow was lying. Never muttered a curse then threw his head back. Warm, coppery liquid slid down his throat and he fought back a gag, but forced it down somehow. The blood surged through his body, seeming to find a way to join his own so swiftly, that Never broke into a sweat and his vision blurred.

"Lie back," Cog said, his voice muffled.

Never did as instructed, letting the back of his head lean against the cold steel. The room swam and Cog's unremarkable face loomed above him, a slight frown marring his brow.

"Something wrong?" Never asked, each word a struggle.

"We just need to give it a little time," he said, then moved out of sight once more. Never turned his head – again, a slow movement – and found Cog nearby, running the ceremonial blade across a whetstone, honing the edge. Good, a sharp blade would sting less, leave cleaner scars.

But another image competed with that of Cog, fleeting though it was – Ziana, standing on the edge of an autumn-coloured wood, wind-tossing her hair and her expression one of fury. Breathing grew more difficult. Then came a new vision, one of Snow standing over him, arms and cloak spread to shield Never from rain, while he coughed himself into a tight ball... and in the preparation chamber Never's pulse doubled, blood finally merging with Snow's until they flowed as one. It seemed also that Never had won some piece of knowledge too... about their blood, yet it faded before he could grasp it.

Never's pulse slowed and his breathing eased, yet his vision remained blurry and he could not form words.

A weight began to build around his shoulders, blood flowing and building, something... growing and rearranging. Pressure built, along with discomfort. Was his very body going to tear itself open? He grunted at the rapidly rising pain and Cog reappeared. "Nearly time. I'm going to tilt the table up now, so use the stirrups and grip the edges of the table. Do you understand?"

Never made a sound that he hoped suggested the affirmative.

The man ducked out of sight once more and an oddly disembodied sensation of movement followed as the room tilted and then Never felt the probing touch of Cog's fingers around his shoulder blades. Cog was muttering to himself, but again, the words were indistinct. Pain continued to build, as if something was pushing against his skin from the inside, trying to escape. Never fumbled for the table edge, grasping it, the cold steel digging into his fingers.

Something hot sliced into his skin, running down his back vertically – the new pain a step removed from his awareness. Blood flowed and a second cut followed. As with the first, the pain was present but not unbearable – in fact, it eased the pressure. Steel clattered to the tiles and a moment later something else pushed against his back, tugging at his very insides, tearing the incisions.

Never growled. "Hurry it up," he tried to say.

The room was spinning now and Cog shouted something but the words were lost. Never tried to turn his head, to ask for help but his strength was gone. Had Cog made a mistake? Amouni symbols, he recognised the lightning bolt and the five-pointed leaf, flashed before his eyes and he cried out as a sudden darkness smothered him.

Chapter 7.

Never sat on the dais and stared at the black feathers.

Light streamed down from the cylindrical opening above, soaking into his wings, long-since dry now. Each feather bore a depth of colour he had not expected; a blue-black yes, but when he tilted his wing just so, purple rested within too.

Even the fact that he could tilt his wings – that he had wings – had barely sunk into his still-groggy mind. Wings where he should have had only shoulders. Impossible. It should have been wondrous... yet something about the pleasure Snow would take from the change did its work to sour the whole thing. If Never wasn't fully human before, now he was something else entirely.

A cloud passed over the sun, darkening his wings.

The day was wearing on.

Never stood, his wings momentarily pulling him off balance. He folded them closer to his body. The additional warmth was welcome but he couldn't prevent a frown. Getting used to having wings was going to take longer than he'd imagined. Where did Snow hide the things when he paraded around as Prince Tendov? Snow was rarely without a cloak, and yet when Never stretched his wings they extended well beyond his arm span.

"You must have many questions," Cog said. His eyes shone from where he stood within the alcove. The fool was proud; no doubt overjoyed to have been a part of an Amouni Ascension – which meant proud to have helped his 'master'.

"Yes, but I doubt you can answer them all," he said. "How do I return to Marlosa? You mentioned a way before, do you mean the fish-man?"

"Yes. But once you reach Marlosa, you will have to fly."

Never burst into incredulous laughter. "Cog, I can barely walk with these, let alone fly."

Cog unhooked the pouches of chila and threw them across the room. "It is the quickest way."

Never caught the powder. "And who will teach me to fly?"

"Don't worry; it is in your blood, Amouni."

Never rolled his shoulders and beat his wings, stirring dust. The motion was just like moving any other limb, the muscle and bone within responded well enough. And it seemed they would grow weary just as his arms might.

"At least they feel natural," he said, unable to keep a trace of awe from his voice.

"But they will not seem so to casual observers," Cog said, bringing Never's clothing and weapons over. He pointed to the tunic and vest, where two slices had been cut. "This will enable you to spread your wings quickly, if needed. Keep your cloak intact, however," he said. "Your brother wanted me to tell you, your wings can be 'retracted' for lack of a better word, not unlike a cat's claws. Yet he did not explain how this could be achieved."

Never paused. Retracted? If he... slowly, and with a grimace, he drew his wings in and back, and they folded within his shoulders, like slipping into place – as if they had always been there. Enough of the feathers remained protruding that he had to flatten them against his skin, but with Cog's help he was able to thread his clothing through. The cloak covered everything and he shook his head. How strange, of a sudden, not to sense dark feathers at the edge of his vision.

Light crept from the other alcove and he hesitated. Was there time to look once more at the strange... thing or things that rested at the bottom of the large domed chamber? What would it tell him? Nothing doubtless. And there was no guarantee he'd be able to access it, wings or not. In fact, there was every chance he'd plummet to his death. New wings did not mean instant ability to fly.

And more importantly, Luis needed him; he'd tarried long enough.

"Tell Snow I forgive him for the hand," he told Cog. "But if Luis dies I am holding him responsible."

"I will tell him."

Never started back toward the entryway.

"Do you need –"

"No, thank you, Cog. I can call the guides myself," he said. He did not look over his shoulder to see the man's expression, but surprise would have been most welcome. Hopefully that surprise would be passed along to Snow.

At the water he paused to ensure the batena and chila powder were protected then called the guide. The fish-head man in his robes flickered into existence, standing waist-deep in the black water. Master.

"I need to return to the river Ebina in Marlosa."

Of course. Take my hand.

Never stepped into the cold water and reached out.

The moment their hands touched, he was drawn down and into the torrent of darkness streaked by coloured lights.

When the journey ended he climbed free of the Ebina and glanced at the sky as water pooled in the grass at his feet. The afternoon was wearing on, despite the speed at which he'd travelled, light growing dull beneath the cloudbanks. To the east, lost in the distance, would lie Disan, the ruins of Oraluca and then the farmhouse where Luis and Tsolde waited.

If they waited still.

He dismissed the guide and made for the nearest stand of trees, dry before he reached them. Once within, shielded from the not-too distant road, Never eased his wings out, letting them nudge his cloak between his shoulders as they unfurled. The span was too great for the space, so he kept them close to his body. They blocked part of his vision but the comforting black was welcome.

"Perhaps I won't kill myself," he said.

Never moved to the edge of the stand and a little way into the razed fields, keeping the trees between he and the road. Then he stretched his wings and beat them once, trying to keep his feet. He wobbled, but managed to stay upright. Then he took a few running steps with his wings held slightly back, again, holding his balance. He grinned. Maybe Cog had been right, Amouni blood seemed to be keeping Never from making a fool of himself. And it did feel unnervingly natural to bear wings. As if he'd always meant to have them.

He came to a halt, then leapt into the air, beating his wings.

The ground lifted... and then rushed up to meet him as he stumbled back to earth. Never grunted. "Timing's still a little off."

He bent his knees and thrust himself up, beating his wings – this time without trying to jump. He rose more smoothly and the fields of grain spread beneath him as he pumped his wings, air rushing over his face. He kept beating his wings, then circled the area, gradually falling lower, before spreading his wings to try and slow his descent before landing.

Still, he hit hard, a puff of dust rising.

Never spat grit and growled. This was proving to be more difficult than he'd hoped. While his wings were strong, far, far stronger than he'd expected, he had no grace. And landing was obviously going to be a problem.

Whatever progress he'd made would have to be enough, Luis couldn't wait forever. Nightfall would be the third day since Never left, who knew if his friend had survived? If Never's own selfishness had cost a friend his life... Never ran for the nearest tree and leapt up to catch the lowest branch. Pulling his wings in, he dragged himself higher and climbed the juniper until he'd reached the last branch able to bear his weight.

The extra height for his starting point would either be a helping hand or a sure way to break his bones when he crashed back down to the ground.

Never slapped his thighs. "Come on, fool. Enough hesitation."

He took a breath and launched himself into the air,

beating his wings hard, clawing higher and higher into the sky. The ground grew smaller and smaller below as each wing-beat lifted him higher. Never almost let himself smile – until a gust of wind pulled him off-course. The world tilted and he swore, angling his wings in time to catch the rising current, soaring up so high that his stomach lurched when he looked down.

He had enough height now that he was able to drive himself forward, making a few tentative adjustments to eventually head toward the east. Far below, the yellow and brown of field and muddy road rolled by, broken by patches of green. The few people he saw were small figures. None stopped to point, at least, none he saw.

As Never flew, he still found himself buffeted by unpredictable gusts, but each time he managed a little better. Yet it wasn't until well after his joints had began to burn from the effort that he realised he could lock his wings and simply ride a wind-current. It was almost effortless, and the slight dives and climbs were thrilling – he laughed at himself for being so stupid. How many birds had he seen in his lifetime and still he hadn't thought to emulate them?

The fields of Marlosa continued to flow beneath him in a dull, yellow stream marred by the road. He would beat the sunset, he knew that now, he was making incredible time. Did he fly faster than most birds? Perhaps. The sight of the charred ruin of Oroluca flashed by and even though his pulse quickened, knowing he was nearing the farmstead, there was still the not insignificant matter of landing safely.

Light still clung to the sky when the farmhouse appeared before him. Never swooped lower as he approached, taking a deep breath. Carefully, carefully. He circled several times, dipping with each arc, and once he judged he was low enough, he drew his knees up and extended them, ready to strike the ground. The shift in weight threw him off-balance and he panicked, beating hard against the earth.

Impact with the ground still sent shockwaves of pain along his legs. He stumbled forward, his momentum nearly enough to slam him headfirst into the mud but he fanned his wings and kept his feet somehow.

Gods be damned, how simple Snow made it seem. Just how long had he been flying, anyway?

Never spun to scrutinise the fields and the road. Empty. He pulled his wings close but did not retract them just yet, approaching the silent house. No movement from within, which meant nothing. Tsolde wouldn't be strolling around before the windows in any event. He circled the place and slowed before the stable. Footprints, gouges from hooves. A good many of them, too muddled to count. Not fresh, perhaps half a day at a guess.

"Pacela!"

He ran to the door and pressed an ear against it, though he didn't know why he bothered. He was too late. No sounds from within – Never pushed his way inside. Nothing out of place, table and chairs set comfortably. Mud tracked through the house however, leading to the room where Tsolde had kept Luis.

Only an empty cot, sheets twisted.

Never thumped the heel of his hand into the doorframe. "Fool!" His selfishness – whatever he'd told himself about following Cog for medicine had been tainted by his desire for the secrets of his ancestors. It might have cost Luis and Tsolde their lives. If he'd instead risked fighting Cog and ridden back, could he have beaten the soldiers?

Could he have defeated Cog at all?

He searched the rest of the house, calling their names, before spinning to charge into the yard. There he picked up the trail of whoever had taken them – if that was indeed what happened – and followed it to the road. Northeast along the King's Highway – which suggested Vadiya. Who else would be so confident to use such an obvious path? Not even Sirgeto, surely?

But there was a chance they were alive, if the Vadiya had known to take Luis and Tsolde captive.

Never glanced to the sky once more. Darkness was falling, but he would have enough light to fly for a little longer at least, and the Vadiya had at least half a day's lead; he had to make up some ground. Returning to the homestead, Never climbed the stable and spread his wings. It wasn't as high as the tree near the river but it would have to do.

A sharp swish cut the air.

Pain tore through his wing and he wheeled with a snarl.

Vadiya scouts were rushing the stable. One man held a horse-bow, arrow cocked for another shot and the other was fumbling with his hand axe, eyes wide. Never collapsed to the roof as the second arrow flew over his head. He checked his wing with a wince; the arrow had sliced his tendon, luckily not severing it. Enough to stop him flying? Maybe not – but enough to give him second thoughts about making himself such a clear target once more.

"Around, around," cried one of the men.

Never rolled his shoulders, retracting his wings before crawling to the far edge of the stable. He gripped the roof's edge and swung his legs over and into a window, slipping into the stable and landing with a grunt.

Stale hay and horse manure filled the dim space. He crept from the stall and across the floor to the entry. Footsteps pounded across the earth, nearing his position. Gardening tools leant against the wall nearby – he took the hoe and hefted it. Heavy. Perfect for de-shelling Steelhawks.

The Vadiya strode into the stable, short sword in hand.

Never swung the hoe. It pierced the man's breastplate and the fellow gripped the haft, gurgling and coughing as he toppled to the ground. Never drew his knives as he leapt over the body. He was too weary to try and outrun the second man or his arrows, and the throbbing in his wing, even retracted, told him he wasn't flying anywhere either.

He slowed before he rounded the edge of the stable. Where was the blasted Steelhawk? Never peered around the corner – empty.

A cry of rage broke the hush.

Never spun back, heading toward the front of the stable. There he found the second Steelhawk rising from where the man had crouched over the body of the first. The Vadiya bore a First Ranger's insignia and beneath it, the Red Talon of the Isajan family. Which meant Sacha was closing in.

"Freak," the man shouted as he raised his bow.

Never cast one of his knives, forcing the man to dodge. The Vadiya's shot flew wide and Never charged. With his second knife he whipped an edge across hand as he closed the distance, slashing at the Steelhawk's own exposed wrist, but the fellow leapt back. He tore an axe free and Never hesitated. There wasn't much skin vulnerable – just the hands and face, seeing as the soldier wore no helm.

"Give up," Never told him in Vadiyem. "Flee and you

don't have to die."

"Shut your filthy mouth, jenaek," the Steelhawk snapped. He raised his weapon to attack, swinging a wide arc. Never fell back. Another blow whistled through the air, this one nicking his arm. Never bit off a curse. The man's swings were fuelled by rage but he wasn't moving wildly. There was still control.

If Never could get inside the man's guard...

Never twisted away from another axe-blow then stepped close, ducking low before the man could launch a backswing – only for white light to explode as the man's knee crunched into Never's head. Never crashed to the ground and rolled, still in a daze.

Something splattered beside him – the axe!

He rolled again, reaching his knees as the Vadiya cursed. The man ripped his weapon free from the wet earth and strode forward. Never threw another knife but the Vadiya knocked it aside with his axe and reared up, swinging down for a killing blow.

Still bleary-eyed, Never threw his hands up and caught the haft below the axe head.

The force drove him back into the muddy earth. His head struck the ground but he did not release his grip despite the pain. The Vadiya brought his body weight, enhanced by armour, to bear on the task of driving the axe head into Never's face.

"Die," the man growled between grunts of effort.

Never ground his teeth; he was no match for the man's weight.

A creaking grew audible beneath the rasping of their breathing. Never frowned. Where did the sound come from? The blade took up most of his vision, along with the shape of the Steelhawk looming above him but Never's pale, birch-coloured hand was visible too – was it possible... Never tightened his grip, twisting, and the creak grew.

He squeezed harder.

The haft snapped in a hail of splinters.

Never flinched but the axe-head merely flew off to one side, thudding into grass. The Vadiya now held naught but a length of wood, his eyes wide. Never shot forward and caught the man by the throat with his birch-hand. He squeezed, crushing the man's windpipe, then shoved the scout aside.

He rose to his feet and looked down on the Steelhawk, whose struggling was already growing weaker.

"Looks like you were only half right," he said with a sneer which was directed at himself as much as his enemy. "I'm more of a freak than I first thought."

Chapter 8.

Never walked into the night, the cold air having long-since turned his hands, feet and face to ice. The muddy road bore no other travellers and despite the scent of wood smoke as he travelled, he saw no lights in the fields. But the moon was bright enough that he was able to follow the tracks of his quarry up until full dark.

After robbing the Vadiya and restoring a fraction of his supplies, he had set off in the direction of whoever had taken Tsolde and Luis. If they lived – and they had to. He couldn't be responsible for their deaths. Not after Zia – he'd sworn it all those years ago. No friend would ever die because of his curse. And while learning he had wings was a wondrous secret indeed, it was hardly worth the lives of his friends. Nor was he flying just yet. His wing had already healed – typical of his body – but he wasn't going to fly at night.

Sometime after midnight, Never found an abandoned barn and slept, shivering within the remnants of hay.

At dawn, he rose to orange light glinting on a frost that climbed the walls.

Luis' fourth day, was he still alive? Tsolde too?

If the Vadiya who'd captured them had done so upon Snow's command, they would have attempted to heal Luis, surely. Of course, there was every chance the messenger Never had intercepted had been carrying the only message with such orders. Yet there were the other men at the farm. Never sighed. There was no way to know. He had to follow the trail and hope.

And somehow, catch up too, which meant flying sooner or later. And flying might be too risky; he'd lose the trail if he flew too high. Too low and he'd be easily visible, another target for stray Steelhawks. "Nothing like being tested by the Gods," he muttered as he slipped from the barn.

Time to decide.

Fly or walk.

The trail was easy to mark, the road had been churned and it looked as though a large force had passed along it. He'd probably see it from a fair distance up. For now, the Vadiya were travelling west, toward Ficcepa. Or perhaps they planned to change course where the Northern Highway reached down to intersect the Eastern Highway, and turn toward the ancient city of Olecsa? There was a substantial inn at the crossroads, the Golden Plains Inn, or the 'Wheat-Bag' as it was affectionately called by most travellers. An important staging point for any force, and no doubt it would have been in Vadiya hands for some time already.

Were they heading there? Impossible to say.

"Follow the trail."

He strode along the highway then broke into a jog. He had to make up the distance somehow, but one leg at a time. His boots thudded along the empty road, earth stretching before him and mud-splattered wheat stalks beside him. More than once he was tempted to try flying again but instead he ran on, ignoring the gnawing pain within his stomach. His pack, along with the supplies, were long gone, either with Luis and Tsolde or taken by Vadiya. If only he still had his mare, though she was probably safer wherever she was.

Another concern had crept to the forefront of his mind, something that had been swept away with the shock of gaining wings, and the fear that replaced shock when he found the empty farm. Cog had claimed that only the blood of an Ascended Amouni could awaken the wings of another – if that were true, who had given Snow his wings?

The thought left Never shivering.

Was there another Amouni out there, and was Snow a pawn? It hardly seemed his style. More likely Snow had an ally. Or someone he'd duped.

Or perhaps Cog had fed Never misinformation and another Amouni's blood was not in fact required for the ceremony. Perhaps that was simply a ploy to allow some of Snow's blood into Never's veins. But to what end? Control? So far, Never felt no different, felt no unwelcome presence within him.

The possibilities swirled within his mind as he ran along the cold road.

Rain swept in by noon. He came to a halt, tilted his head back and opened his mouth to drink. And then he was running again, more of a stumble really. Only once did he see another person – ahead, a man with a long staff approached, only to turn down a narrow trail running between the fields.

Up until spotting Never, he'd been heading in a straight

line.

When the rain finally cleared, late in the afternoon, Never caught the scent of smoke and slowed. Meat... and garlic, something else too. Not, thankfully, human flesh but nothing he could recognise either.

He approached the direction of the smoke; a trail twisting between the giant stalks, many drooping, near rotting in the field. Slippery, dead stalks and husks squelched beneath his boots. Dew from the rain dripped around him, not loud enough to mask his approach so he slowed yet further and listened.

Very faint.

Steel on steel. Voices, hushed. Vadiya? A scouting party?

Never drew a blade and then another, crouching. The smoke had already faded, caught in a changing wind perhaps, and the sounds from what was doubtless a camp had faded. The sharp whisper of steel too, had ceased.

Stalks rustled.

The furry shape of a grain-hog bounded across the path.

Never rolled into the wheat. Something thudded into the wet earth where he'd stood. He twisted around to run along a row, glancing between the stalks. Two soldiers appeared on the trail, one pulled an arrow from the ground with a curse. When the man spun to give chase with his fellow, Never stumbled.

Fool, watch where you're going.

Both men wore leather jackets studded with glass buttons, arranged like constellations. They carried bone-handled weapons; their dark hair was cut close, as were thin beards.

Quisoa.

Never came to a halt. "Huna oc bolate." I am a friend.

The two warriors stopped but did not lower their weapons. Had the words registered? Both men bore bows, each with a nocked arrow. Heavy throwing knives hung from their belts and they were breathing a little hard. Adrenaline was no doubt pumping through their veins – as it was for Never.

He spoke Quisoan again. "I am from the village of Pirchys; I know you, you are men who follow the Evache constellation. When I was young you visited the plains above us each summer and we would travel up to trade batena plants for horses... until a great fire came and swept the plains clean, burning everything to the ground. The next summer you didn't come."

Now the men lowered their bows. The older one stepped forward. "You sound as though you've been away from home a long time."

Never rejoined the path, replacing his knives as he did. Hearing the language of his youth seemed to cut the chill in the air. "It has been. But I can remember most of the words, it seems. I am Never; we followed the Twin Blade constellation." No more, he had not been to his village for many years now.

"An unusual name," the older man said. "I am Bihola and this is Chadya, of the Evache Constellation, as you know. Have you come from the south?"

"Hanik – my companions and I recently escaped the Vadiya. They follow, a significant force, but slowly no doubt."

"They are already everywhere," Bihola nodded.

"I'm searching for my friends now, I fear they've been taken. A young lady, Hanik and a tall spearman, Marlosi. He'd have been running a serious fever."

Bihola shook his head. "We have seen none who match

your description, either alone or with the Vadiya. Come, we can speak more in the camp." Bihola glanced to Chadya and the younger man nodded, taking a position back within the stalks.

Bihola led Never deeper into the field, his bow still held ready. Carvings of the same constellation that he bore on his chest ran along the arms of the weapon.

"Have they driven into Quisoa?" Never asked.

"Not truly. Some of the northern villages – perhaps yours even, are occupied but we spend most of our time leading them a merry chase. The tribes gathered when first we learned of the invasion and decided many small groups were harder to subdue than a single force. They tire easily to be honest, in their foolish armour, and more often than not give up the chase and instead try setting ambushes. Most seem concentrated north or around Isacina. Have you been away long?"

"Yes. And news has been scarce."

"Then let us talk as we eat – our camp is not far," the older man said.

"I have little to share, since hospitality has been lacking of late."

Bihola chuckled. "Not to worry, Never. We have set aside the proper customs for now."

"I hope there will be a time when they return."

"As do I," he said, though his voice seemed to hold little confidence.

Chapter 9.

Bihola's camp was sparse. Within a hollow shrouded by dense wheat stalks, half a dozen Quisoa sat around a single fire, which burned clean. A pot simmered over the flames, perhaps the scent of meat he'd caught on the breeze. A risk, truly, but the sentries seemed vigilant enough if Bihola was any indicator. Horses were picketed nearby, chewing on grass growing between the untended grains.

When Bihola entered, half the figures stood, hands on throwing knives. One woman's face remained cold until Bihola introduced Never. After another glance, she sat back down and returned her attention to creating a new hole in the belt she worked on – times were clearly lean. Had she been wary of him being introduced as Quisoa due to his Marlosi heritage? Never noted the constellation on her tunic was different to Bihola's; seemed she was from the south of Quisoa by the vague horse-shoe shape to the buttons. Lenali?

It put him in mind of Zianna – weren't the Lenali neighbours to her tribe? Gods, how much had he forgotten?

Or forced himself to forget.

"Never brings news from the mountains," Bihola explained. "Though I'm sure you can guess it."

"There is another sizeable force heading down into Marlosa, eager to add their might to the many other forces. I surprised a messenger, they will probably head north to the capital though scouts are wide ranging."

"Still they spread," one of the men said.

"If they keep piling in there will be no-where left to hide," another rasped.

"Perhaps not," the woman said. "They spread themselves too thin – otherwise we'd all be dead."

Bihola exhaled. "That may be the truth of it but it doesn't change anything. We do as we have decided."

"Where will you go next?" Never asked.

"Further south – we hunt a scouting party."

"Could I ask for you to look out for my friends?" Never asked.

"Of course. And where will you travel?"

"I will rejoin the trail heading north and hope that it is the right one. Have you seen other Vadiya forces heading that way?"

"No, but Chadya reported a strong force last night. Scores of Marlosa soldiers."

Captain Sirgeto? Could the man have stumbled across Luis and Tsolde? "Then I will chase them and see what fortune follows."

"But not before you eat," Bihola insisted.

Never accepted a bowl of stew, biting into rabbit meat and peppers, the garlic strong but welcome. In exchange, he offered some of his precious batena, which drew thanks from those gathered, and then he was offering his goodbyes.

As he headed for the edge of the camp a voice stopped him within the stalks.

The Lenali woman stood before him. Her hair had been cut close, as was typical of Quisoa women. A warm blonde, the colour was marred by flakes of dried blood.

"Take this," she said, holding out a throwing knife. Its edges were carved with tiny interlocking triangles that represented a union – such a weapon would have once belonged to her husband.

"I cannot," he said.

"You can. Melid needs it no longer," she said with a trace of bitterness. She paused. "I see something when I look at you, stranger. You are heading into danger, just as we do, but I think perhaps you need the extra knife more than we."

Never couldn't prevent a shiver. "What do you see?"

"Blood-covered feathers – I see you holding them. It makes no sense, I admit."

"Yet I will take it as a warning nonetheless." He accepted the blade. Balanced beautifully.

"Stars shine upon you."

"And you."

He slipped back along the twisting path and headed for the main road, where he broke into a jog. The cold sky shed more than enough light to follow the trail. The hot meal had helped with a burst of strength though he couldn't shake the image of his hands covered in bloody black feathers.

Had he been given an image of his own death?

Or 'mere' injury? Never came to a halt and growled at himself. He had to put it aside. Had to keep moving, vision or no.

Dusk was falling when he once again found himself approaching a camp, this one bolder than Bihola's. Here, set off the road but close enough for easy access, were scores of men and dozens of fires set between scattered tents. The scent of some manner of roasting meat rose on the evening breeze. Nickering from a not too distant picket line reached him when he paused to catch his breath.

Voices called to each other in the dark – speaking Marlosi.

He exhaled. At the worst, another hot meal. At best, a hot meal and welcome news. Never frowned. No. Worst would be once again being responsible for the death of a friend; he could easily be wrong about everything – about the camp before him and about Luis and Tsolde's fate.

Never continued along a little further, scrutinising the shadows beside the road as he did, finally coming to a halt. Armour flashed orange and red in the firelight, markings obscured. Any guards posted around the camp would still be some distance away. Even if he was right about who waited before him, he'd still do well to announce himself to them.

"Ho the camp," he called.

Those nearest stopped, looking into the darkness, doubtless unable to see him yet. Nonetheless, footsteps rushed forward and he soon found himself facing a Marlosa man who studied him over a drawn arrow. Another figure stopped behind Never but he didn't turn.

"I am seeking Captain Sirgeto," he announced. "My name is Never, he knows me."

"Is that so?" said the guard Never could see, tone not disbelieving exactly, but not friendly either. And his reaction suggested that Never's guess was correct – it was Sirgeto's camp.

"It is indeed so," Never replied. "I can describe him and his mercenary friend Vantinio if that helps? Or perhaps young Mondesa?"

The other guard grunted from behind. "Maybe you can, stranger, but we'll let the captain decide what to do with you."

"Do I look that much like a spy?"

The second man chuckled. "Let's just say you look a little unsavoury, whatever you are."

"Unsavoury?" Never objected.

"Just throw down your weapons and hold out your hands," the first snapped.

Never did as ordered, taking his time. A pile of half a dozen knives rested at his feet when he was done. The blade from the Lenali woman rested atop, triangles catching the light.

The second man bound Never with rope, moving with efficiency, then collected the knives. The first fellow kept his arrow trained on Never's chest. A good lad, really – taking his post seriously – but it was still a little disconcerting to be on the other end of the aim. Still, Never couldn't deny that it would be useful to know whether his body could now recover from a fatal arrow-wound.

Why not? He'd re-grown a hand.

Not the best time to find out, however. Instead, Never followed the man who'd bound him. The bowman ghosted Never in turn, as they walked between a palisade which had angled its spikes outward, and through a bustling camp. Evening meals were being prepared, some men ate alone, others at small fires. These were mostly Marlosa folk who had the look of untrained men. Their weapons were mismatched and they often wore little or no armour.

Yet their faces were determined.

Never had to admit it was a welcome change – though he knew with certainty that few would survive the coming weeks. Or days, for that matter.

And the ex-imperial soldiers, those who still bore breastplates and helms, who carried their longswords and spears, would be doomed to the same fate if the fighting went on long enough. And no doubt Snow would ensure it did; if he was to have his new empire. But the Marlosi soldiers did not wear downcast expressions. They were confident; hope seemed to grow in their bearing. The younger boasted of their bandages and the older did not seem inclined to chaste them for it.

Few paid much attention to Never and his escort, not so near meal time, but as he closed upon a line of tents before a squat, flag-less pavilion, a voice rang out.

"Never?"

A young woman pushed her way between soldiers, her curls bouncing as she slid to a halt before his escort. He blinked – Tsolde.

Pacela's Luck!

She had her hands on her hips as she berated the guard, and Never had to laugh –part relief and part amusement. The poor fellow who'd tied the ropes bore a look of shock, yet he untied Never as she demanded, muttering an apology as he dragged his friend back toward the road.

Never grinned at Tsolde. "So who's running this camp? You or Sirgeto?"

Chapter 10.

Tsolde leapt into his arms and squeezed him around the middle, cutting off his air supply. "Gods, where have you been, Never?"

"It's a long story – why don't you go first?" he said when he could breathe. He set her down. "Luis?"

"He's alive," she said, but her joyful expression wavered. "I'll show you. This way." She led him away, toward one of the scuffed tents, its dome sagging a little – yet one of the flaps had been pulled back, presumably to let cool air within – a guess confirmed when Never saw Luis.

Luis lay upon twisted blankets, sweating heavily, his dark hair plastered to his head.

Yet he did appear slightly better. Never frowned as he knelt. Was he only imagining improvement, encouraged by the fact that Luis was still alive? The fact that he hadn't been responsible for his friend's death?

"What do the healers say?" Never asked.

"That without something stronger he won't survive the week. They've done everything they can with what they have,

Never. They saved him at the farmhouse."

Had there been a hint of reproach in her voice or was he imagining that too? "I'm sorry, Tsolde. The first village was decimated. But I have this," he produced the chila powder, "it will save him."

"Can you be sure?"

"It must."

She stood. "I'll bring the healer."

Never nodded and sat back against a half-empty pack, closing his eyes a moment. How long had he been chasing them now? Days but it seemed much longer – from his shoulders to the soles of his feet he ached. All he really needed was a warm fire to take the edge off the night air...

"Never, wake up."

Never blinked. Light had bloomed in the tent and Tsolde rested a hand on his shoulder. "Sirgeto wants to see you," she said. Behind her, a small man muttered away to himself as he worked with steaming cups.

"Luis?"

The healer glanced over his shoulder, revealing a cheery face. "He'll be fine now, thanks to you. Where did you find the chila?"

Never stood. "In –"

"No matter, really, you've saved your friend but only if I stop blathering on. Off you go, he's in good hands," the healer said, pushing Never outside.

"Thank you," Never said. He rubbed his eyes, shivering in the cold. How long had he slept? And how deeply? His limbs moved slowly – as if someone else owned them. "It seems Sirgeto is rallying the people," he said as Tsolde led him between the lines of tents or, sometimes, men rolled in blankets.

"He is," Tsolde said, a note of worry in her words as they approached the men guarding Sirgeto's pavilion.

"Is something wrong?"

"You remember those swords we found in the mountain?"

"Of course."

"Well, they can cut through anything and so as long as Sirgeto and Mondesa are leading, it seems victory follows. It's like the swords are even improving their skills, I don't know how to explain it. And they treat me differently, because... I don't know, maybe because I helped find the swords? It doesn't make sense."

Perhaps not surprising the swords were so powerful. "But that's not what worries you?"

"No. I think the swords are... infecting them. They're changing, Never. You can see it – but no-one talks about it because we're winning. No-one wants to admit it."

Now a chill settled over him. "Changing how?"

"You'll see when you speak to Sirgeto."

He stopped. "Are we in danger here?"

She hesitated, glancing around. "I don't know."

"All right."

They came to a halt before the pavilion, where one of the guards raised a hand. "Just a moment." He ducked inside. A short, muffled conversation followed. When he returned, he held the tent flap open.

Never stepped into a war room.

The walls were lined with maps pinned to the canvas, many criss-crossed with lines. Water barrels stood beside bundles of crossbow bolts and heavy fur-lined coats in various stages of repair. Men were crowded around a wide table but one looked up when they entered.

Captain Sirgeto.

His eyes flashed blue – the barest glimmer, as if it had not occurred. Yet it had; there was something happening to him, it seemed. "Continue," he told those gathered and moved around the group to greet Never.

Up close, Sirgeto's cheeks had taken on a gaunt look, the grey streak in his hacked-off hair widened. The Amouni sword swung at his side, the barest hint of blue escaping from the scabbard. "Welcome back, Never." The man's grin was triumphant. "You appear a little startled."

"You have achieved much since we last spoke," Never said.

"And more to follow," he replied. "I admit I was surprised to find Tsolde and Luis in that farm. They have told me what little they know about Lady Isajan's forces but could not explain the swords you found. I want to know if you can."

"Sadly, no," Never said. "They are a mystery to me."

Sirgeto narrowed his eyes a moment before smiling again. "A shame. Well, stay as you wish or not, Never, but know that I expect you to fight if you do." He looked to Tsolde. "And you, young lady – they are your enemy too."

"Yes," Tsolde replied.

"Do you have a target, Captain?" Never asked.

He nodded. "North. Others will rally to Empress Crisina and I intend to bring her a force worthy of striking back at the Vadiya scum."

"Weeks to the Monasema Mountains, will you reach them?"

"Of course."

"It's a lot of ground to cover and a lot of Vadiya between, you'll be drawing them as word spreads."

Sirgeto grinned again, his lips straining, and the blue flashed in his eyes once more. "True. It saves me chasing them down."

Never frowned. Just as Tsolde said; there was something disconcerting about Sirgeto beyond the blue glow. Did he relish the chance of revenge too much? "Prince Tendov will not stop."

"Yes, we've heard of him. That one, I'll chase home. Sack his whole damn city."

"Ambitious."

Sirgeto laughed, a rasping laugh. "You will see. Now, why don't you get some rest. Tomorrow, we're planning on liberating Ficcepa. It'll be a long march."

Never let Tsolde pull him from the tent, then back to Luis. The healer was gone and Luis slept easy now – no longer sweating at least – though it was a deep slumber. And while Never couldn't deny a stirring of relief; it was marred by concern. Everywhere he turned, he was surrounded by obstacles.

In a way it was nothing new… but with Luis and Tsolde to consider everything was different. The fear was sharper. Gods, had he made a mistake? It was one thing to risk his own life… Was it time to find a safe place for Tsolde and Luis? Did such a thing even exist? Or was Snow taking that away from the world?

"We are in danger," Never said once they'd finished checking on Luis, keeping his voice low. "As soon as Luis is able, we leave."

Tsolde nodded. "And in the meantime?"

"We keep quiet, do as we're told."

"Never, why is the sword twisting them?"

He sighed. "I don't know. Such things were not meant for human hands, it seems. I would take them away, if I could."

"Shouldn't we try?"

He shook his head. "Snow must remain my first concern – and not before dawn in any event. Let's get some rest."

"Good idea," she said. "I'll take the other tent."

Never lay back with a soft groan, stretching his limbs. How quickly the weariness returned now that he'd mentioned sleep aloud. If only he could rest with one eye open...

*

Cold.

Never jerked upright. Darkness surrounded him, but his face was wet. Why?

Light bloomed, revealing a young man with an intense gaze. "Join us outside, Never."

"Mondesa?" Never wiped water from his face and beard.

The man set a pale aside. "Quietly."

Never glanced at Luis. His friend still slept soundly. The tent flap was already closed; Never pushed it open and found Mondesa standing outside, his face calm beneath the moonlight. Trouble? It didn't seem so. The younger man gestured for Never to follow, picking his way through the camp to a position beyond the sentries.

"What's wrong?" Never asked.

"We need to speak to you, Never," he said. "Out of the hearing of the camp."

Wheat rustled. Never spun, a hand on a knife but only Sirgeto appeared. No-one else. He too, wore his Amouni sword and oddly enough, each man kept some distance from the other. Wary?

Never tensed. Tread carefully.

Sirgeto pointed at Never. "The Ladies have told us you know something."

Never blinked. Ladies? Did Sirgeto mean the swords? "I have to admit, Captain. That's not what I expected you to say."

Mondesa shook his head. "She isn't so sure."

The Captain frowned. "He knows something. I can feel her responding to him – like a faint humming, surely you feel it too?"

"I do, but that doesn't mean anything. She hums often. Like yesterday, near that stream – does that mean the stream knows something it did not tell us?"

"Bah." Sirgeto drew his blade and raised it to his face, closing his eyes. The glow lit the tiny clearing and cast his cheekbones into sharp relief. Mondesa stood with his arms folded, watching Sirgeto, tension lingering in the clearing.

Never shifted his feet as the quiet dragged on.

Finally Sirgeto lowered the Amouni blade and his eyes became dark shadows, looking to his subordinate. "She does not know. I only get a sense of curiosity."

"Curiosity?" Never asked. "The sword is curious about me?"

"Yes." Sirgeto sheathed his blade. "What do you know of them?"

"Only what I told you before, we found them beneath the mountains. That is all. They are a mystery to me."

"Yet it seems not you to they."

Never shrugged.

"You must stay with us, Never, until we can discover why."

"And if circumstances arose that required me to be

elsewhere, what would you say then?" Never kept his voice neutral.

"We would not care for that," Mondesa said.

"How very disappointing," Never replied.

"You have no choice," Sirgeto growled as he pointed a finger at Never. "You will go where we go or your friend and the young woman will be killed, understood?"

Never clenched his jaw. "I see."

Chapter 11.

"And so we are prisoners," Never said, finishing his explanation.

Luis set his bowl of broth aside and shook his head. His colour was much better and the glazed look now absent from his eyes. "It seems like each time I awaken lately, you're giving me bad news."

Never chuckled. "At least you're alive."

"True," he said as he glanced over Never's shoulder to the camp beyond. Never followed his gaze. Pale light fell into the tent, bringing the sound of men grumbling as they queued for food at nearby fires. Complaining about the 'same old fare' but it didn't seem bitter, but rather, good-natured. Never wondered how long the cheer would last – as far as he could tell, Sirgeto's men were yet to face a truly large Vadiya force.

A man leant against a stack of crates, arms folded. His armour was still mismatched, only now he'd added burnished greaves that bore the look of Vadiya work. He scratched at his beard as he watched them. Vantinio, the mercenary – obviously given the duty of ensuring that no escape was attempted.

"He's our babysitter," Never told Luis.

"Not him; I'm looking for Tsolde," Luis said.

Never laughed. "Be patient. She'll be here soon enough."

"Well, isn't a returning appetite a good sign?"

"Not if you plan to eat half the stores yourself."

Tsolde returned with another steaming bowl. "This is it, you know," she said with a grin. "The quartermaster's frown was dark enough to put out the sun."

"So be it," Luis said, reaching for the food.

Tsolde sat beside Luis with a sigh. She glanced to Never. "So how do we get out of here? Can we afford to wait for Sirgeto to run into more Vadiya and try and slip away during the fighting?"

"I'd say that's our best chance," Never said. "Vantinio won't be able to keep an eye on us during a battle."

"Then we're going to follow along and hope for a fight?" Luis asked around mouthfuls.

"Until we can come up with something better, yes," Never said.

*

As Sirgeto promised, the day contained little more than a long march beneath the cold sky. Luis rode most of the journey, walking as much as he could. His strength was returning quickly, though he still took regular doses of the chila powder at the healer's insistence.

"We need to be certain," the short man had said.

A philosophy Never was happy to follow.

And so when smoke rose from the plains from where Ficcepa lay, Never hoped Sirgeto would be following the same thought; caution and certainty – even as Never knew the captain wouldn't. And when they crested a hill in time to catch the sun's descent upon the blackened buildings, the rubble and smouldering flames, Never clamped his mouth shut.

Ficcepa would not be liberated.

But worse, it seemed, was the effect the broken town had on Sirgeto and Mondesa. Working from opposite ends of the line of soldiers and ex-farmers, they waved their blazing-blue Amouni swords and screamed into the air, breath steaming. And whether it was racial insults or cries for vengeance, each man drew forth cheers and bloodthirsty roars. And why not – the Marlosi had seen their homes destroyed, friends killed, their very land taken away. The fury was there and Never couldn't blame them for wanting to unleash it.

Yet there remained something unnerving about Sirgeto and Mondesa.

Never glanced back at Vantinio, who rode close behind them, and even the man's usual dispassionate expression was marred by a slight frown as the mercenary watched his commanders.

Sirgeto's gruff voice echoed down the line. At the same time, Mondesa shouted his own commands from the rear.

"...form into squads. Two Imperial, three infantry," Sirgeto was rasping.

"...search for survivors and be methodical about it," Mondesa's voice continued. "Kill any Vadiya on sight..."

"...do not hesitate to..."

"...punish them for what they did..."

"...to your families, your homes, our very nation..."

The leaders went on, voices matching, right down to the inflection of words. Never exchanged a glance with Luis and Tsolde, whose eyes were a little wide. Neither Sirgeto nor Mondesa appeared to hear the other and yet their words aligned perfectly.

"Does no-one else hear it?" Tsolde asked.

"I suspect Vantinio does," Never said.

Luis held his spear, clenching and unclenching his fist around the haft. "They've done this before, right? It's probably their standard speech."

"How likely is that?"

"Not very," Luis said.

Mondesa approached, waving an imperial soldier over as he did. "Yolan, join Vantinio. Go!"

"Yes, sir," Yolan barked. He was a heavier fellow whose bald head was covered in scars. He and Vantinio conferred before the mercenary drew his blade and nudged his mount forward.

"Down we go, and keep your eyes open. I'm not going to end up on the end of some pale-face's sword because you three have your minds on something else," he snapped. His jaw was clenched and his eyes roved the landscape.

The last part seemed to be a warning; he was waiting for them to try an escape. Still, Never followed the man's lead as they approached the still-smouldering town, tension building as he searched the area.

The fields were quiet. A deep orange glow crept over the wheat as the sun set, splashing a bloody light across the remains of homes and inns, across the smoking piles and along the paths leading into the town. The charred remains of small fences around gardens still smouldered. A withered tomato vine had crumbled to the earth. How long since the Vadiya had left?

Small groups of men moved between the ruins, swords drawn. A call for help soon rose – had they found survivors? The call lacked the urgency of battle.

"Focus on our part of town," Yolan told Tsolde, who'd turned to the calls.

She nodded as she followed Vantinio between smoking stone. She kept her blade raised in a guard position, but her grip was too tight. Never could see the line of tension run up her arms to her shoulders. Someone had been trying to teach her basic swordplay but she was simply too tense. It wasn't terror so much as over-vigilance, it seemed. He opened his mouth to give her some direction but Luis beat him to it, his voice soft as he neared her, a fond smile on his lips.

"Well done," Never murmured.

He stepped over a fallen beam and glanced into the half-broken home. Little but shadow and ash. A hint of cloth too, peering from beneath another pile of beams and roofing tiles.

Little chance of survival but he still waved Yolan inside, where the two paused to allow their eyesight to adjust. "Does anyone live?" Never crept forward, knowing his question was a mere formality. Shards of earthenware crossed the floorboards. Only yesterday it had been a bowl; it had been something useful. Today, naught but rubble. Never bent by the cloth, the edge of a dress, the bands of yellow stained black and red with blood. He turned back to shake his head at Yolan.

The man exhaled through his nose but nodded.

The others waited in the narrow street, smoke drifting across them. No survivors as yet. They moved deeper into the ruins of Ficcepa, finding only more dead. Some houses were intact but these were empty. Some showed signs of violence, scuffed floors or bloody footprints, smashed windows.

Vantinio hauled the body of a Vadiya Steelhawk from one home and into the dirt. The man was riddled with arrows. The mercenary gestured. "Quisoan fletching."

Never nodded. "They were too late, it seems."

"Captain and Mondesa will avenge them," Yolan said, his jaw set.

On they searched. The deeper they moved into town the more bodies they came across in the street, some alone or crumpled in small groups but none dead so long that the blood had dried, black though it looked in the failing light. In the cold air the scent of death was not overpowering, a tiny mercy. Most of the dead were unarmed but a few held weapons – town guard no doubt quickly overwhelmed by the Vadiya.

And always none had survived.

In the streets ahead, movement flashed between homes and Never reached for a knife but it was only a dog. One question remained – what had caused the people of the town to rise up against the occupiers? They had to have known the odds were overwhelmingly set against them. Unless something far more vicious had occurred?

He found his answer in the town square.

A mountain of bodies rose before him, topped by the last slashes of orange from the setting sun.

Taller than three men standing end on end, it grew to something of a point, the mess of shattered limbs and blackened faces obscured by the swiftly-falling dark. Some spots in the pile of victims smouldered, as if the Vadiya had attempted to set fires but, for whatever reason, had failed.

The stench here was strong enough that Never heard retching from other parts of town, as more and more squads came across the square. The faces of his own companions were set; tears stood in Yolan's eyes and Tsolde gripped Luis's hand. Vantinio's eyes were narrowed as they roved the square.

It seemed as though the Vadiya had brought in people from outlying villages and homes to add to the monstrous pile, for Ficcepa was not so populous, surely. The killing spoke of cruelty rather than discipline.

Cruelty or revenge?

A rage began to simmer and Never fought it down; he had to keep his wits about him. Yet the folly was too clear, too close – Sirgeto's company. Resistance was fine, but perhaps if the man had not been so bloodthirsty, making his own smoking piles of Vadiya men all over the country, perhaps such a similar fate wouldn't have been visited upon the poor men, women and children of Ficcepa. Equally, there was a chance some ravenous pig of a Vadiya commander was responsible. War forged heroes but it also drew forth scum.

But did it matter, in the end, how or why? Was Snow really wrong if this is what people were capable of? The rage was rising again, quickly now. Warfare was becoming more than an old impediment to his search; it was a stark reminder of humanity's faults and it was growing ever-more difficult to disagree with Snow.

Even if his brother was mad.

Shouts of shock echoed from the opposite side of the

square, joined by the snapping of crossbow bolts and Vadiya war cries.

Ambush!

Chapter 12.

Never spun, even as Vantinio shoved Luis and Tsolde aside with a curse.

Too slow.

Blood exploded and Yolan toppled to the ground, a bolt protruding from his throat. Vadiya were pouring into the ends of the street, between the shells of homes. Never threw a knife at the nearest enemy, who ducked behind rubble. Vantinio leapt to meet a pair of infantry, sword a blur as he drove them back.

Louis stood before Tsolde, jabbing at the nearest Steelhawk, keeping the man wary. More appeared in the alley behind the Vadiya, closing off avenues of escape. But in such a narrow space, Luis was able to keep them at bay. There was still a chance of Luis being outflanked however and how long would his newly recovering strength last? "We have to push through," Never called to Luis. "Somewhere else."

Had his friend heard? It seemed so, as he gave a nod. Never flipped another knife into his hand, slashed the back of his wrist with a snarl. He welcomed the stinging cut, letting it fuel his anger as he charged the line of men opposite Vantinio.

Never cast a blade as he crossed the hard earth, felling one man then deflecting a sword blow, following up by driving his shoulder into another fellow, who was sent sprawling. Never's fury had not abated and he barely kept his own feet, stumbling after the fallen soldier to ram a blade into the space between the man's helm and breastplate.

A shadow loomed.

Never rolled, slashing out at whoever had kept their feet. His knife met only air but the Vadiya screamed and slumped to the ground. Nearby, the crossbowman stood with mouth agape. The horror in his eyes was clear where the embers of a still-crumbling home lit his face. Never lifted his bloody knife but Tsolde leapt across the space, swinging her sword. The weapon bit into the man's exposed face and he screamed. His movement jerked the weapon from her hands. Tsolde flinched but bent to retrieve the sword, trembling as she did.

Never ran to her but she shook her head. "Don't worry about me. We have to help Luis."

A curse crossed the street. Vantinio cut another man down then spun, a wide grin on his face. No more soldiers faced him. Shouts from other battles, distant and dimmed by the mountain of bodies, entered the lull. But it was not a lull for Luis, who still managed to hold back the tide. Never cast another knife, hilt-first, and the hard pommel felled one of the Steelhawks. More Vadiya would be circling already, perhaps leaving just enough in the alley in an attempt to pin Luis down.

"Rest," Vantinio cried, stepping before Luis and catching

a sword on his own, plugging the alley.

Luis fell back, chest-heaving. His jaw was clenched but he seemed well enough. Never caught his friend, looking to Tsolde. "This is our chance. Go," he hissed.

"But..." Tsolde looked to Vantinio.

Never gave her a push. "We may not get another. West, toward the foothills."

Luis set off and Never followed, glancing over his shoulder when they paused to climb through a ruin. Vantinio held his own, using the narrow confines well, but how long would he last?

"Not my problem," Never growled to himself.

Yet it wasn't so simple.

Running now wasn't just an escape; it was sacrificing another to do so. Such a thing wouldn't have mattered before. And it shouldn't have mattered now – he had to escape, had to protect Luis and Tsolde. Vantinio was no-one; he was half a step removed from enemy, really. Never thumped a charred wall. Gods, was he no better than those who slaughtered and piled broken bodies into great heaps of death?

No better than his brother?

"Keep going, I'll find you," Never said as he turned back.

"Wait," Tsolde hissed.

He charged toward Vantinio, urging his blood to pool in one hand. A soldier stepped into view but Never backhanded the fellow aside, his birch hand barely registering the blow. Heat was building in his other palm.

Vantinio fought on but he was being driven back, step by step.

Red light bathed the street and Never faltered.

A globe of fiery blood had enveloped his hand. Just like Snow in the temple. Crimson-fire – Never had its name now. But how? And then he knew. The knowledge had been passed on to Never during the ceremony in the preparation chamber, that was what he'd almost understood. In the past, no incidental exchange of their blood had offered any such knowledge.

The Ascension was clearly different – and for now, it didn't matter.

When Never closed with the mercenary, the lead Steelhawk fell back, eyes wide in the blood-light. Yet there was nowhere to go; the man stumbled into his fellows.

"Back," Never shouted, flinging his hand at them.

Blood shot forward.

Crimson light buried the faces, seared through steel, flesh and bone alike. Screeches of pain rose – only to be cut short. The very walls of the alley shuddered. Stone melted and blocks fell free, hissing against the chill earth.

The stream of burning blood eased. Never fell to his knees, breath rasping in his throat. His vision was a blur of red and black, and an ache spread through his body, swift as poison. He could barely lift his arms, but he had to stand, had to flee. His fiery display would draw attention, if not now, then certainly later when the melted remains of the Vadiya were discovered. Yet the rage and power that had flowed through him, it was all gone, leaving him empty and weak; it was hard to move. To even think about moving.

"Never, quickly." A tall shape stood before him, reaching out. Hands gripped his shoulders. Never blinked his vision clear. It was Luis, his head darting from side to side. "Where's Vantinio?" Never asked.

"He fell back when he saw what you did," Luis replied, traces of awe in his own voice. "I don't know where he went."

"Then he's on his own now," Never said. "I've done what I can."

Luis hauled him up with a grunt. Tsolde appeared at his side and helped Never back to the ruined building where they paused to listen, the scent of burnt timber strong where he slumped against the wall. No sounds of pursuit, but from all across the town the clash of steel and shouting – Marlosi and Vadiya words meshing into a din of meaninglessness.

The last lingering effects of the crimson-fire cleared from his vision and he pushed himself up. His body still ached but at least he could walk unaided. His strength was returning, slowly perhaps, but returning still. "Let's keep moving."

Never led them between more ruins, heading toward the edge of town, angling away from the site of his bloody attack. His vigour returned with each step. Was it determination or his enhanced healing that kept his strength flowing back? He raised a hand at the thud of footsteps, leaning back into the shadows as Luis and Tsolde mirrored his action. A single Vadiya scout ran in the direction of their last position. He did not turn his head. Once the man was gone, Never resumed their flight, finally reaching the thin strip of earth that waited before the half-harvested field of grain.

Beneath the swishing grain the faint light from Ficcepa's sad glow did not penetrate far and Never slowed. It wouldn't do any good to crash through the field and give their position away. Within the deeper shadow, some of the tension slipped from his muscles but he didn't sheath his knife. Too early to feel secure in their escape.

"What now?" Tsolde asked, her face no more than a blur.

"We're going to Isacina to find my brother," he said. "And that means we need to rejoin the road on the other side of Ficcepa or find another way. All roads will be dangerous."

"I know one," Luis said.

"Yes?"

"There's a path east of here, where the land is cracked and no grains will grow. You must know it."

Never nodded slowly. "I do." The Broken Plains were dangerous, especially without a guide – nowhere the Vadiya would want to venture since there were no resources within, no people to conquer.

"Well I don't know it," Tsolde hissed.

"A long series of gorges and splits in the very earth," Luis said. "Legend holds that it was once a fertile place but it's dry and empty now. Some of the paths are dangerous, but if we can reach it, it would allow us to stay out of sight for a good deal of the journey," he said. "We'd be within two days of the city when we left it."

"Then let's go there," Tsolde said.

"It's not without its own dangers," Never warned. "Bandits least among them – there's treacherous footing, cruel beasts, the ghosts of the criminals once cast into its depths by the city – if you believe the rumours."

Raised voices broke the hush, one clear above the rest – Vadiya organising a search party. Never straightened. "They're looking for us, keep moving."

Never increased his pace, using the grain as a guide, his birch hand trailing them, tripping only occasionally on uneven ground between the rows. The voices soon faded; they'd chosen a different direction. For now. Moonlight broke momentarily from the clouds, the fields finally opening to a road that stretched north to south, not west as he wanted, but it would have to do.

"Let's put some distance between us and Ficcepa before we find a camp," he said.

Several times during their march he'd paused to strain his ears in the dark, unsure of whether pursuit was closing in, unsure if he'd caught muffled hoof beats but always the sound faded and he had to move on. The moon had climbed higher, clouds driven away courtesy of the newly risen wind by the time they found a copse of trees. It climbed up and around a dry riverbed, and while it bore no cave or true shelter, the trunks and an outcropping of rock – a huge slab, really – were better than nothing.

They carried food and water in their packs, but making a fire was too great a risk. Food was a problem for the morrow. Never could only keep his head upright long enough to sweep some rocks from the ground and organise a watch – Luis, who seemed most alert after taking another draught of chila powder, was given first shift. So far, no sounds of pursuit. It seemed they were safe enough.

Arranging his cloak for a pillow, Never lay beside Tsolde, who was muttering about the cold earth, and closed his eyes with a sigh. He slowed his breathing, focusing on the simple pattern and trying his best to ignore the way the earth seemed to dig into his shoulder and hips despite the bedroll. At least his wings weren't bothered, a small mercy.

Stone clacked against stone.

He sat upright – only to be blinded by a blue glow filling the camp. "What?"

"Never, stay calm." A woman's voice spoke softly. "No quick movements – you either, Luis."

Never raised a hand, squinting until his eyes adjusted to the light.

Elina stood beside one of the trees, an arrow drawn, her hands steady. Her face was awfully pale and her expression wary. A hood concealed her hair and her cloak was torn in several places. An old bandage wrapped her thigh, dried blood staining her pant leg. Not the first time she'd pointed an arrow at him.

"I feel like we've been here before," he said. "I'm glad to see that you're alive."

"You're coming with me," she said, trying to sound stern but weariness betrayed her; her voice broke.

Never glanced to Tsolde, who frowned beside him, then to Luis, who stood with his spear held ready. The man's expression was torn between a resolve that seemed to suggest he would defend Never and reluctance to hurt their old companion.

"Elina, you don't owe him anything," Never said.

Her eyes flashed. "Do you think so? How easy it must be to live without ties."

"There are downsides."

"Tell me all about them on our way back to the palace." The arrow dipped and she brought it back level with his chest, frowning as she did.

"No. You're exhausted. You need to rest and I have a brother to chase down."

Elina stared at him.

"Think it through," he urged her. "You have to capture and bind me, Luis and Tsolde. Then you have to kill them or force us all to march back across the plains and over a mountain. You have to stay awake the whole time, because we will escape if you fall asleep, for Snow must be stopped, no matter the petty concerns of one King. More, you have to bypass thousands of Vadiya with three hostile hostages. Think you can manage all of that by yourself?"

"Why are you so sure I'm alone?"

"Because you would have called them by now had any of your men survived." He paused. "I'm sorry, Elina."

She swallowed. "I cannot break my oaths."

"I wouldn't ask you to."

Elina's grip on her bow tightened. "One of us must yield. It is the only way to avoid bloodshed."

"There is another way," a new voice announced.

A figure loomed from the shadows behind Elina – an impassive expression on an unshaven face.

Vantinio.

Chapter 13.

"My knife will be swifter than any move you make," Vantinio said.

Tears glistened in Elina's eyes. Her despair crossed the camp, settling onto Never's shoulders. She'd come so close to her goal, or so she must have believed. Never stood, moving slowly, keeping his hands raised. Vantinio watched, apparently content to see what would happen next. "Unless you wish for us to be found by the Vadiya," Never said, "I think we should continue this conversation in the dark."

Vantinio grinned now. "So you can slip away again, I take it? Give me a little credit, will you?"

"Then what do you want?" Never asked.

Vantinio's grin faded. "Escape from the creatures which now possess Sirgeto and Mondesa, and which threaten to swallow the entire company."

Never met the man's unwavering gaze. The mercenary did not appear to bear any guile... which was no guarantee. Vantinio was difficult to read. He had not released Elina either, who now wore a deep frown.

"How can we trust you?" Tsolde asked.

"Because I fear I will only be safe with your unusual friend," Vantinio said. "And surely you can believe that a mercenary would switch alliances when the benefit was great enough?"

Luis narrowed his eyes. "So they might switch again and again."

"True. But the benefit is great now." His voice softened, an undercurrent of discomfort clear. "It is not just my life that I fear for, Luis, but my very spirit. The blades would take the whole of me; I have seen it in the eyes of my Captain."

"You could have two dozen men beyond," Never said.

"Or horses enough for you all to outrun both the Vadiya and Sirgeto, who search for you still."

If true, doubtless that was the sound Never had heard. He folded his arms. "Let her go."

"Very well." Vantinio stepped away and Elina stumbled forward. Her eyes glazed over as she collapsed, bow clattering when it hit the hard dirt.

Never ran to her side, crouching to give her cheek a gentle slap. "Elina?" No response. She was breathing, but up close, the exhaustion was clearer. A bruise had faded near her temple and her lips were cracked too. Another wound on her upper arm had been bound not long ago, blood just beginning to seep through.

He lifted her and called for Tsolde to conceal the light, which she did by wrapping it in her cloak. She left a slither of the light exposed in order to shine it on Elina, whom Never laid across the space where he'd planned to sleep. "She's beyond exhaustion. She might not survive the night or she might recover with rest – I can't be sure." Adrenaline surged through his veins; his weariness was banished. "Luis keep watch. Tsolde, water," he said, then pointed to Vantinio. "Are those horses nearby?"

"Near enough."

"Bring them – we need real shelter."

Vantinio nodded and slipped away.

Tsolde provided a flask, which Never used to dribble water across Elina's cracked lips. He poured a little more and she swallowed reflexively. He stopped. Too much would be dangerous.

"Do we trust Vantinio?" Luis asked from where he stood nearby, facing the darkness.

"For a time," Never said.

"We'll have to rearrange our watch," Tsolde observed.

"True. But I think we can rely on Vantinio to help us stay clear of Sirgeto at the least – those horses will be quite the boon."

Elina did not seem to improve but nor did she get worse and when Vantinio returned with several horses in tow, Never lifted her into a saddle and climbed behind her, taking the reins and resting her head against his chest.

"She had this weary nag," Vantinio said, gesturing to the horse bearing a Hanik-fashioned saddle. "Tsolde, why don't you take her, seeing as you're the lightest."

Luis climbed onto another horse and then they were filing from the copse and returning to the road. Little but starlight guided them but at least they were moving. The night wore on and Elina did not stir save to shiver in her exhausted slumber. He kept her close, wrapping his cloak around them both and eventually the shivering eased but she did not wake.

Elina was likely to cause trouble... but that was no

different to before. On the other hand, she was dependable, a great archer and a member of the Order of Clera; there was a chance she'd held back knowledge that would help him in his quest too.

But beneath all of his reasoning was something simple; she was alive and he was glad.

Dawn bloomed in steel, the new light revealing several mist-shrouded homes set back from the road. Some bore the glow of lights in a single room, others had smoke drifting from the chimney but no-one was willing to offer them shelter. The few who even answered their doors were quick to slam them shut, expressions fearful.

"We don't want that kind of attention," an older farmer had said. "They'll kill us all if you're found."

Hard to blame them, yet Never found himself ready to kick a door open at the next house – but he did not have to. The windows were broken, the door ajar. Empty rooms, a bare kitchen; not dissimilar to the farmhouse he'd left Tsolde and Luis in before finding his wings. How long ago that seemed now, yet the winter was not even half gone.

"This will have to do," Never announced from where he knelt beside the cot he'd dragged into the kitchen for Elina. "We need sleep."

"I can take the first watch," Vantinio said as he returned from concealing the horses in the tiny stable.

"We'll share it," Never said, glancing at Luis and Tsolde.

The mercenary grinned. "Still you doubt me."

"Give me ten years," Never replied.

"Then share with me first," Vantinio said, leaving the room, floorboards creaking.

"I'll wake one of you in a few hours," Never told the

others as he followed Vantinio.

Outside, light was spreading across the damp fields, catching in the collected dew. It sparkled through the morning mist and it ought to have been beautiful but there was little joy to the sight. A cold elegance; prelude to a funeral perhaps.

Never leant against the home's outer wall. Vantinio stood nearby, hands busy with a pouch where he'd concealed himself behind the branches of a juniper growing in the yard. It offered the man a clear view of the road in either direction.

"What is that?" Never asked.

"Dried batena, crushed to a powder," Vantinio said, placing a small pile onto his tongue. He swallowed and gave a shiver. "Keeps me alert, keeps me focused."

"Dangerous in that form though," Never said. Too much in a short space tended to cause convulsions and paralysis, black-outs or death.

"True," Vantinio said.

Never raised an eyebrow. "See anything on the road?"

"Nothing."

"So what happened to Sirgeto and Mondesa?" Never asked after a moment of silence.

Vantinio sighed. "Those bloody swords you found. At first they were just weapons – powerful weapons. Made Captain and Mondesa faster, stronger. Gave them better reflexes. They were unstoppable in a fight – and those blue blades cut through Steelhawk armour like it was made of nothing stronger than mud. We were winning and everyone was happy."

"It didn't last."

"No, Pacela, it didn't." Vantinio took another mouthful of

powder before tying the string on the pouch and returning it to his belt. "After a while they started competing whenever we came across Vadiya, tallying their kills. They became secretive about the swords too, no-one else was allowed to touch 'em. I'd see them holding the blades, eye closed, lips moving. Sometimes, when I spoke to either, I thought I caught a glimpse of blue, flashing in their eyes – usually when we argued about chasing down survivors. I felt we should let them free, to spread word – and fear – of our coming."

"But Sirgeto wanted to kill each and every one."

"Right."

"When did they start sharing thoughts?"

Vantinio nodded. "You heard that too? First time it'd happened was yesterday. And the first time I saw the blue light in some of the other men."

Never frowned. "Other men?"

"A few of the ex-Imperial. Lads who've been with us the longest." He spat. "Like I said, I had to get out before those cursed swords took me too."

Perhaps the swords were a bigger danger than he first reckoned.

But Snow was more of a threat. If the swords remained a problem once Snow was stopped, then Never could worry about them then. If he stopped Snow. In the meantime, Sirgeto and Mondesa would slow the Vadiya at least. Pacela let it stay at that.

The rest of the watch passed with few words. When Never traded places with Luis, Vantinio appeared just as alert as when he started. In the quiet of the kitchen, with only soft breathing from Tsolde and Elina, he arranged himself on the borrowed blankets and sighed.

Finally.

Sweet sleep awaited.

"I'm still taking you back as soon as my strength returns."

Never groaned. "Elina, go back to sleep. Rest."

"I'm serious."

"So am I," he said, keeping his voice low. "I'm more than happy to argue with you some more – but only after I've slept, do you understand?"

But she didn't answer.

"Elina?"

Still nothing. He rose onto one arm – her chest rose and fell, she breathed yet.

Good. She'd either lapsed back into unconsciousness or sleep, giving her body more much-needed rest. At least she was alive. Never stretched out a kink in his neck and lay back once more.

Chapter 14.

It was late afternoon when they set out again, hooves clapping on the hard-packed ground. The sun was once more obscured by dark clouds that threatened rain but didn't seem to ever fall. Twice they took quieter trails to avoid large troop movements; Vadiya heading north, but according to Luis, the stretch of Marlosa known as the Broken Plains lay less than a day away.

Not a place Never was keen to revisit. He'd skirted its edges once, chasing down another fruitless rumour of buried secrets. This time a horn that was said to roll back the mists of the Black Sea. Aside from old bones, both animal and human, he'd found nothing. Twice he'd nearly fallen into a black hole, bottomless as far as he was concerned, and an especially nasty bark lizard had nearly taken out his eye.

Still, Luis seemed confident. "I can guide us through. I've travelled most parts. It is near my old home," he explained.

Vantinio had not argued and neither the seemingly cooperative Elina nor Tsolde knew the land, so they had little to add. And no-one wanted to risk running into more Vadiya. Since leaving the abandoned home, Elina and Tsolde spoke often where they now rode together. They usually conversed in Hanik and Never caught little of what they discussed.

Thankfully, he didn't seem to be the topic.

But Elina had again expressed her determination to take him back to Hanik once she was able. Never had no trouble convincing her to wait until they were in less danger before discussing it again. Of course, he had no intention of going with her. But what to do about her persistence?

He'd already told her; Snow came before the concerns of King Jenisan.

Night seemed to rush in around them before Never grew hungry, yet everyone else was ready to eat. They stopped and made a shielded fire in a clearing within the grain, where Elina ate his share of the dried fruit and hard bread. Like Luis before her, her appetite returned with her strength. Or perhaps it was the other way around?

Once more he shared the early watch with Vantinio.

"Still think I need someone to hold my hand through the watch, Never?"

"For now."

The mercenary chuckled. "So, will you tell me what happened back in Ficcepa?"

"No."

"Come now, I know about your curse already – or thought I did. I didn't think what you did back there was possible."

"It is."

He shrugged but his expression remained even. "Then tell me why? You put your escape at risk."

"You protected us, isn't that enough?"

Vantinio gave a short nod and asked no more questions, and when Elina replaced him, Never couldn't hold back a sigh.

She raised an eyebrow. "I haven't said anything yet."

"And nor do you need to," he replied, heading for his bedroll.

She caught his arm and when he faced her, he found her expression to be one of weariness where he'd expected hardness. "I am doing what I believe I must, Never. Are you so different?"

He offered no answer.

"Surely you can see that he rules your every decision."

Never held her gaze. "Maybe so, but I will change that, Elina. When next my brother and I meet, only one shall walk away."

"And if someone stands between you and he?"

"Like you?"

"Yes. Me, Luis, young Tsolde? What then?"

Never traced one of the scars on his wrist, newly healed and already fading, but could not find an answer, for it was a question he hadn't dared face.

She released him to fold her arms. "Well?"

He turned away. "It's simple enough, My Lady. Do not come between us."

*

Luis led them off the North Road and to a lesser, poorly-kept trail that seemed to fade away into the plains, their pale grasses rippling in the wind. A sleet came with the wind, dampening everything, dulling conversation and fraying tempers. Never did not wish to share many words with Elina in any event, but Tsolde was first to snap – giving Vantinio an earful when he accidently knocked an apple from her hand.

Yet by the time they'd reached the Broken Plains, only Vantinio had managed to keep his calm. Was it his natural indifference, or a strange side-effect of the batena powder? The ground stretched before them in uneven shapes with sudden shelves and jagged lines of darkness, the holes infrequent at first. Further on, much deeper gorges appeared, snaking along the plain. Small shrubs sometimes grew, but they appeared skeletal and grey. Footing was already uneven and the horses had to be walked in places until Luis paused before a deep chasm.

"Do we descend here?" Vantinio asked.

"Not this one," Luis said. He pointed ahead to a variety of thin, ash-coloured trees clinging to the sides of a different opening. "There is the better choice. It will take us further before we have to climb out again. There were five trees last time," he added.

The mercenary nodded. "And inside?"

"Just follow me, I'll warn you about any dangerous ground. There may be bark lizards, but they prefer sunlight. I doubt we'll see any."

"And if we do?" Elina asked.

"They're fast but you can swat them aside if they leap at you. They'll usually give up then."

"What about the bandits you and Never mentioned?" Tsolde asked.

"We simply have to be watchful," Luis said. "I imagine they will have gone deeper since the invasion."

They skirted the first opening to reach the trees and the deeper gorge. A worn series of uneven steps, mostly natural, many quite sheer, led down into shadow. The floor of the gorge was visible, grey stone stretching into black. Impossible for the horses to descend, which would slow them but it was unavoidable.

Never and Vantinio cut their harnesses and spread their dwindling supplies before setting the horses free.

Ready to resume their descent, Luis paused at the first step. Never placed a hand on his friend's shoulder.

"Is something amiss?"

Luis shook his head, though his voice was not entirely convincing. "Nothing, just taking a moment to recall the first turn. It's like a maze down here in places."

Down they climbed. Some steps were simply the result of water and time, others were fashioned, widened by those who used the Broken Plains. Still, it was easy to slip, as Never found halfway down, catching the wall in time to save himself a few broken limbs.

A deep chill filled the bottom of the gorge, yet it was light enough. Most of the sleet could not reach them as they started along a dim trail. The constant trickle of water followed them along, dripping from overhangs, or from more of Luis' tortured-looking trees.

Ahead, shapes loomed from the shadows, mostly twisted pillars of stone or old rockslides. In a way, not unlike the ruins of Sarann. But here there was only the damp echo from their tread and no sense of ancient life, of history waiting to be discovered. Never followed Luis, who led with his spear. Behind Never, Elina and Tsolde and Vantinio in turn. All carried their weapons, or at least had a hand near a hilt.

Was it the apparent emptiness that set them on edge? Or

the promise of bandits and ghosts?

High above, the light faded as the day wore on yet they encountered naught but winding trails and the occasional fork, where the earth rose up. At times, the light fell in strips or from odd openings, pale beams tunnelling down when the gorge narrowed overhead. At such times, anyone walking above would have had an ankle trapped within such a hole, or simply fallen through if the earth was weak.

And it was; sometime after they stopped for a meal, stones had crumbled down to shatter before them. Still far enough that no-one was hurt, but Luis had exhaled. "Don't forget to keep an eye on the roof, too," he said.

Before nightfall they climbed free again. The rain had eased to a mere mist, which concealed anything in the distance. Beyond it, however, would loom the Folhan Mountains and Isacina. And hopefully Snow. The next landmark Luis found near darkness, twin columns of stone shards had been gathered, marking a gentle slope that led into shadow once more. Luis paused before starting down. "It will be drier below, but I feel like a double watch is still in order." He spoke a little absent-mindedly, still seeming preoccupied.

"Agreed," Never said. "We've had a quiet journey so far but that doesn't mean it will stay so."

Within, they found a clear place to camp; it even came with a fire pit courtesy of other travellers, and each set to work on their tasks. Food was running quite low but everyone wanted a fire first. Never joined Luis in scavenging for dry wood, which would be quite a feat despite the occasional tree above.

Yet their luck held; in the failing light they found a

twisted heap from another collapse, clumps of dirt and stone concealing one of the dead trees. Never dug out a few pieces and set them in a pile while Luis worked on another.

"What troubles you, Luis?" Never asked as he worked on a heavy piece of stone.

Luis paused to sigh, then he sat on the pile. "You remember what I said about my father? My home?"

"A violent silversmith. You left."

"I did." He stared into the darkness of the trail. "He's down here somewhere, Never. I heard about it years later. He was drunk and brawling in the inn. He killed an Imperial Guard when they came to put a stop to it. Afterwards, my father was executed and cast into the gorge. Imperial orders."

Never blinked. "Luis..."

"Somehow, my mother still loved him and it broke her heart... I still haven't been home. I can't face her."

"Why?"

"Because if I hadn't left, maybe I could have stopped it all somehow."

Never took a seat beside his friend. "Do you really think so?"

"I don't know," he said with a shrug. "Yes. Sometimes."

"You knew your father... so ask yourself, do you think he could have changed? Could you have changed him?"

Luis nodded but didn't answer. Never gave him a smile and returned to work, adding more to his pile before heading back toward the camp.

Tsolde met him, her voice soft. "Is Luis all right?"

"Yes. I'm sure he'll join us in a moment," Never said.

She frowned. "What did you talk about? Is there something you two aren't telling the rest of us about this place?"

"No, nothing like that," Never said. "Ask him; he'll probably confide in you too, Tsolde."

She blinked. "Oh. Do you think so?"

"You're important to him, of course."

"You mean..."

Never grinned as he handed over the wood. "Yes. I mean he cares about you, why wouldn't he? Just as I do. We've been through a lot together, don't you think?"

"Yes, of course we have, you're right, Never," she said and turned back to Elina and Vantinio to begin work on the fire. Never had to fight another grin. Of course he'd seen the small signs of something growing between them but it wasn't his place to give either of them a push. That would only spoil their fun.

Patience in matters of the heart – if only he'd realised that with Zia.

Chapter 15.

Once again Never trailed Luis along the dim paths. The sky above remained cold and while the rain had eased, wind tore howling through the gorge. It moaned and whistled, a tortured sound of loneliness. After an uneventful watch and quiet night, it was a most unwelcome change.

"Behold the ghosts of the Broken Plains," Never announced.

"How long is that likely to last?" Elina asked.

He shrugged. "As long as the wind is up. Luis?"

"Right. It won't last."

Two walls converged ahead, like the point of a triangle, but Luis merely twisted his body and slipped between a barely discernible gap – not until he was closer could Never see where the two walls did not align. He squeezed through into true darkness and followed Luis' footfalls. "It's not far," Luis said. His voice echoed in the darkness. "There's only one path."

Never waited a moment for Tsolde, passing the message along, and then resumed his walk, one hand raised before him just in case. Yet he did not fall or even stumble and when light appeared ahead, Luis' silhouette leading, Never had to squint. Upon exiting, the light was blinding. He had to stop to let his vision adjust, shifting away from the opening.

To one side of the path waited a deep chasm that stretched far and wide, only impenetrable shadow at its bottom. Opposite, the walls of the gorge soared up in a sheer face – and at its top rested some manner of platform, steel catching the wintry sun. Luis did not stare up at it, he bent by the ground beneath.

There, dark stains covered the stone.

Never joined him. "What do you see?"

"Nothing. I just wondered… did he shatter his bones here?" He turned and gestured to the chasm. "Or fall below?"

Never glanced back up to the top of the cliff. A deadly drop but there was a chance, perhaps, that someone might survive if very lucky.

Luis stood with a small smile, as if he knew what Never had been wondering. Luis held his hand out. "Here. In case any did survive the fall."

A rusted arrowhead rested in his palm. Nearby, Vantinio explained to Elina where they were.

Never took the relic with a frown. "Bandits?"

"No, turn it over. See the mark."

On the opposite side of the arrowhead, half-obscured by rust and grime, lay the stallion of the Marlosa Empire. "Thorough."

"Right," Luis said. "We'd better keep moving. I doubt the Vadiya will be here but from this point onward, parts of the gorges tend to be more occupied."

Again they resumed their cold trek through shadows. Whenever the paths multiplied Luis chose without hesitation but there was little sign of others. The wind had died down – Never hadn't even noticed.

"There. A camp," Luis said.

Structures had been built between and within the open spaces. Mostly with foraged wood but there were low brick walls and oiled tents stretched across steel frames in places. A cold hearth sat in a central location, a black grill beside it. But no lights and no sounds from inside, not even a hint of movement.

Luis called and received no answer. "We wish to pass through. We are hiding from the Vadiya."

Never drew a blade – the heavy throwing-knife given to him by the Quisoan woman. Had he gone through so many, so fast? He had two left, aside from the beautifully crafted weapon he now held.

Would he even need to use it?

A deep silence exuded from the camp. The kind of silence that was assured of lingering – whoever had lived in the camp did not intend to return. "Spread out, but not too far," Never said. "See what you can find."

Within the first structure a narrow cot and a small chest only, empty blankets and a chipped statue of Pacela. She was missing an eye, but her serene smile seemed somehow unaffected. "Are you watching over this place, Lady?"

Similar scenes in the other places he searched, meagre possessions left untouched. No scraps of food, no weapons, no gold. No clues as to what happened. He removed his marble figure and the little man was at rest. Never returned to the hearth to hear similar stories from the others, no signs of recent life.

"Something happened to make them leave, but was it sinister?" Elina asked. "I don't think it so, I don't get that impression."

Vantinio shook his head. "No. We have to think like bandits – this is a trap, surely."

"They're waiting a long time to spring it," Never said.

"Well, I'll be watching in any event."

"We have the chance to climb out again before nightfall if we want," Luis said. "Or we can stay down here one more night and start up with the dawn. By the time we camp, we'll be less than two days from the city."

"We'll be out of sight down here; it's probably safest."

"And if all of this," Vantinio waved a hand at the empty dwellings, "is some manner of a trap, what then?"

"Then whoever takes watch had better be prepared," Never said.

*

Never woke to the usual chill of morning, only the faint taste of ash on the air as the fire continued to die out. The first morning without food too, which meant they would have to hunt or forage. Water wasn't so much of a problem, they'd filled their flasks at a rivulet but it wasn't a pure mountain stream. Nor was it ale or even the thin wine he might have had at an inn.

Still, it kept him alive – hard to argue with that flavour.

"Did you see anything?" Vantinio was asking Luis where they stood before the large room chosen for their camp.

"Nothing. I don't understand where everyone has gone."

"Hmmm."

"Whatever has happened works to our favour at least," Never said, standing and stretching. His muscles were stiff, typical after a cold night but a cramp was building between his shoulders – he needed to stretch his wings. Which meant privacy, for he did not wish to instil any fear or unease in the others. Nor, if he was honest, answer all their questions. Half he didn't have answers to himself.

"Is everyone ready?"

Nods.

Never looked to Vantinio. The mercenary was dusting his tongue with a little of his crushed batena. "Vantinio. What have you heard about the occupation of the Imperial City?"

"A little. Reports are vague. I hear they control it completely and have driven out the ruling class but allow trade." He finished with his powder. "Are you still set on infiltrating the city?"

Never raised an eyebrow. "Thinking you've made the wrong choice?"

"Not truly. I wouldn't have survived those swords – that I know. I used to dream about them. They called to me all the time. I knew if I answered that it would be the end. But that's finally stopped. I'll go where you go if I think we have a chance."

"And do you?" Never turned to the others. Luis's expression was determined, as was Tsolde, but Elina's brow was furrowed. "My Lady?"

"If your brother is what you say he is... and I don't doubt that he is a poison, there must be another way, something better than storming the city. Half the Vadiya forces are said to be there, Never."

"Maybe less," Vantinio said. "Half further north, pinning

down the Empress around Monasema."

"That's still thousands against five."

Never grinned. "I never intended to simply walk up to the gates and demand to have my brother brought forth in chains. In fact, I'm not even sure he's there. Still want to follow me?"

A moment of quiet followed.

"You know I will," Luis said.

"And I," Tsolde added.

Elina folded her arms. "You don't leave me with any choice."

"Then we have to start planning," Never said. "If you don't want to impersonate Vadiya, then we have to think of something else."

"Something else," Luis and Tsolde said together.

He laughed. "Very well, lavish your ideas upon me."

Chapter 16.

When at last Never found himself concealed in a cove within sight of Isacina's gates, he breathed a sigh of relief... and a twinge of despair, for not only were the gates buried in Vadiya tents, but the Imperial City had changed.

No longer the pale jewel of Marlosa's crown; the torchlight was enough to reveal the Royal Wolf flying on banners above the grey and white walls. And still with no plan... it was always going to be hideously difficult to achieve but being confronted with the city as it stood... it was like a broken dagger jammed into his side. Yet he did not turn away.

Luis sighed from where he lay beside Never. "Even if you sneak in alone, what's to say you'll come up with something? You know the Vadiya, you know what might work, your idea isn't so bad."

"It might not be enough. I think I could bluff my way inside, posing as a turncoat working for Lady Isajan but that wouldn't work for everyone. It's unlikely they'd believe you're all my prisoners, not with Elina and Tsolde."

"There was that caravan guard who mentioned the travelling performers. He thinks they were allowed in the city."

"But were they allowed out?"

"One thing at a time. I think we could manage it. Find me a flute and I'll outplay anyone, you know. We could find other talents if we tried."

"Perhaps. There's still the Brotherhood, if I can make contact we might have an ally there."

"So how do you contact them?"

"That's the question," he said. "Let's go back to the others a moment."

Deeper in the stand of trees, Never gathered everyone around the minuscule glow of the blue-stone where it slipped between Tsolde's fingers. Vantinio sat with his back to them, watching the trees, but he cocked his head as he listened.

"Bluffing my way might still be the best chance, especially if we can't get through the gate. There's half an army camped beyond the city."

Elina frowned. "There's still Tsolde's idea of merchants; we all saw them enter earlier. We just need something to sell."

"Travelling performers might better explain you two Hanik girls," Vantinio said.

"And what talents do you have, then?" Elina asked.

"Plenty," he grunted.

"We still need to know who is allowed to move freely through the city and under what conditions," Never said. "So we're back to me sneaking in first."

"Then how?" Tsolde asked.

"Bluff my way inside."

Tsolde shook her head. "I don't know. You said Isajan was spreading the word to look for us. That would include descriptions of you, Never."

"True." He'd forgotten about that – highly inconvenient. There was another way of course… but was he ready to share it? Did he have a choice? The Brotherhood, who controlled the largely forgotten Fire-Gate, were hardly easy to contact from the wrong side of the city. "There is a way – if the moon is hidden – that no-one will see me."

"How?" Elina asked.

He hesitated. "I'll show you under one condition. No questions, because I don't know the whole of the truth. Agreed?"

"Cryptic," Vantinio murmured as he turned.

"If it's the only way," Tsolde said with a shrug. "Show us."

Never stood back, glancing side to side. There was enough room but still he did not make a move. Luis would accept him, and Tsolde no doubt. Vantinio, well, it was hard to say. And Elina… she probably still hadn't shared all she knew about the Amouni. But what other option did he have? Never pushed his cloak free and rolled his shoulders. Muted pops followed as his wings unfurled and he sighed as they stretched to their full span. Finally! After so long retracted, allowing his wings some freedom was most welcome.

Open mouths and wide eyes were clear in the blue light.

Silence stretched.

Finally Vantinio whistled. "See. I made the right choice."

"How?" Luis asked.

"And when?" Tsolde added after swallowing. She moved a little closer. "Can I touch them?"

He angled a wingtip to her as she passed off the blue-stone. "Forgetting my request, aren't we all?" he said with mock-sternness.

Tsolde took his feathers in shaking hands. "Aren't they soft? Come, Elina," she said.

But Elina had folded her arms, though she still seemed awed, as if she could not focus fully upon her disapproval. Was she thinking of her order's hopes and dreams? That he truly was going to end up being a help to the world? "Why did you hide this from us, Never?"

"Us? You've not long returned, I'd remind you."

"You know what I mean."

"Various reasons. It was nothing I wanted Sirgeto to learn of, for one." He looked to Luis. "Somehow, Cog knew my wings were dormant. And by somehow, I mean Snow knew. It's merely another of the mysteries surrounding my heritage for now. Like I said, I cannot explain it. I don't know myself."

"You saw Cog?"

"Yes. He was waiting for me in Disan; he took the last of the chila powder and then blackmailed me into awakening my wings."

Luis frowned. "But why? What reason would Snow have to help you?" he said, then apologised. "I know he is your brother. But I don't trust him. And my ribs still trouble me at times."

"I don't trust him either, Luis," Never said. "And that is my own concern. Snow would only awaken my wings if it served him somehow."

Vantinio cleared his throat. "You know, none of this is making much sense."

"Ah, you wouldn't know, of course." He outlined the bare facts and finished with his question from the Broken Plain. "Still happy to play along with us?"

Vantinio's usual neutral expression appeared a little shaken but he shook his head. "Despite all of what I've heard, I haven't changed my mind. Like I said, I made the right choice. If anyone can protect me it's you."

"Never, can you be sure you're not playing into his hands by coming here?" Elina asked.

"I cannot simply let him do as he wishes."

"Nor should you, but if you're captured –"

"I know, Elina," he said, softening his tone. "It's dangerous. We all know that. But this is the best way since I don't want to risk your lives too. I will fly over the walls, learn what is afoot in the city – if Snow is even here – and then we will enter if needed. Otherwise, north to the Empress, perhaps that is where 'Tendov' is at work." He flexed his wings, stirring the hair and clothing of his friends. "If I'm not back by dawn – return to the Broken Plains and wait for me there."

"And how long should we wait?" Luis asked.

"If I don't return, flee to Jenisan or even Sirgeto. You'll know if it's been too long – I'm a fast flyer," he said with a grin, but he couldn't hold it. "Watch over each other."

Never slipped into the trees then angled away from the camp, stumbling once before he found clear ground – one of the many trails leading toward the city. He sprinted along it, spreading his wings then leaping up into the night.

He beat his wings hard, driving his body higher. Cold air rushed across his face and hands as he spiralled up, breathing deeply. His muscles seemed to groan at the effort after long disuse, but everything came back quickly. He caught a wind-current and climbing was suddenly swifter. The ground receded until it became a dark, featureless sea broken by dwindling lights from the Vadiya camp. A camp mostly of tents. There was little in the way of war machines; no catapults or wheeled rams, instead, just rows and rows of soldiers. And why not? They hadn't needed them to take Isacina by surprise, sliding down from the mountains. Such machines would be further north. And so it was only tents that spread before the huge, closed gates and the towering wall, some forty feet high.

Yet Never was already well above it, looking down on the small shapes of guards that paced its length. None saw him as he angled away from the walls to fly across the city, rooves and squares flowing below, street lanterns casting a scant glow.

Pacela's Spire loomed ahead, the white wings like charcoal in the night. Yet yellow lights dotted its surface, along with the tower itself, rising in a beautiful spiral. Candles from within, their light somehow enhanced by the special glass used by Pacela's faithful.

Never banked, slowing his flight. A fine vantage point.

A walkway ringed the spire's peak, guarded by a stone rail. If he was careful, it would make a fine landing point. Never circled the tower, lowering himself until he was close enough to judge his landing, then pumped his wings in a sharp flurry, slowing to thump onto the walkway. Excess momentum from his landing sent his outstretched hands slapping against the stone wall.

He grunted at the shock that ran along his arms. Not too bad, overall.

Never turned to the rail and leant against it to stare down on the city. Shadow obscured much and activity was limited below. The broad thoroughfare that led up toward the huge, gleaming dome of the palace appeared to be guarded by checkpoints at several intersections, otherwise he saw little of use.

There was some activity from inns nearer the gate, light flashing on steel, but this high up, the wind still swirling, he heard no voices. Daylight probably would have helped; he'd see merchant trains or even who and how many people could move around un-accosted. Of course, daylight meant he'd be just as visible and wings or no, the Vadiya were doubtless still looking for him.

If he swooped down lower, maybe to the next largest building –

"Pacela!"

Never spun, hand going for a knife hilt.

A Priestess had fallen against the spire wall beside an open doorway, where there had been no door before. Her whole body trembled and she was mouthing something to herself. A prayer? Her pale yellow robe was adorned by a single sprig of juniper sewn over the breast. Which made her an acolyte, if he recalled correctly. It had been so long since he'd actually seen a Priestess. How long had they been hiding themselves away now?

He raised empty hands. "I mean no harm, Lady."

She swallowed. Her eyes were so large, it was like staring at a doe. A stab of guilt ran through him. He'd terrified the young woman with his carelessness.

"You..." she trailed off.

Never did not approach, instead he leant against the rail,

drawing his wings closer to his body. "Forgive me, I know I've frightened you but I will leave soon. But if you could help me first, that would be wonderful."

Her trembling eased and she seemed to regain control of her voice. "Who are you?"

"My name is Never and I am someone who wants to help the city, that is all."

"You've come to help us?"

"Yes."

Her eyes lit up. "Then you are Her messenger? I must tell the High Priestess Jardila." The acolyte turned for the door.

"Wait, no," Never said, unable to keep alarm from his voice.

The young woman fell to her knees. "Forgive me, Messenger."

He approached. "What is your name?"

"Lina." She did not rise.

"Lina, you can stand. Please, I'm not one for ceremony and nor am I a messenger from Pacela but I do need your help. Please stand."

She rose, keeping her eyes downcast. "Thank you, Messenger."

He sighed. "Lina, you shouldn't call me that because you'll only be disappointed. Now, I need to ask you a few questions, can you help me?"

"Yes."

"Good. Now, what of the Vadiya. Are the people of Isacina free to go about their lives?"

She nodded. "Yes. For the most part. Only, none may bear arms and the palace is closed... at least, that is what Father Gelvi has said."

Good, that made things a little easier. "And what of the gates?"

"Open in the day but sealed at night. I feel the boom in the walls of my room," she said, raising her head a little.

"Thank you, Lina. Now, what about trade? Merchants?"

"I'm not sure." She looked down again. "We do not leave the Lady's Spire much, even less so now that the Vadiya are here. They tend not to trouble us... they allow us to leave for supplies but that is all."

"Hmmm." Any wares brought into the city would be searched, that was simply standard practice for an occupying force. And it did seem as though merchants were free to move around the city, only not the palace. But with no cart or goods... no, it was not the best option.

But something Lina said bore real possibilities.

"Lina, do you have access to more robes?"

A slight frown crossed her brow. "Of course, Messenger. Do you need clothing?"

He grinned. "I and others, Lina."

Chapter 17.

"Am I covered?" Tsolde asked.

She stood in the morning light where it streamed through the trees, arms outstretched, draped in pale yellow robes of a Pacela acolyte. Her hands, forearms and face had been wrapped in bandages, leaving only her eyes visible. Close scrutiny would probably reveal her Hanik heritage but Never hoped that his story of a 'serious illness' would deter the gate guards from any such examination.

"Well enough," Never said as he fastened the bandage on his birch hand.

"What if they don't buy this?" Elina asked. She stood between Luis and Vantinio, who were each working on wrapping an arm.

"Since we'll be surrounded by half an army, I think surrender is the best option."

Vantinio paused. "That's not much of a plan."

"Then let's make this one work," Never said as he checked on the sprig sewn into his own robe – this had three branches as befitting a senior priest. Lina had been able to find sizes suitable for all, though Luis' was a little short at the hem, showing his boots. Perhaps a little unusual for a Priest of Pacela, but hopefully not for a group of missionaries returning from the Ramakki Islands. To further complete the illusion, Never had trimmed his beard and had Luis and Vantinio shave their stubble. Once finished, he bundled up the implements ready to return to Lina. Shaving had been her idea too, and a good one at that.

Finally came the stretcher, for which he'd had to rely on Lina for materials once more. Flying them back to the cove had been a feat in itself, the way the poles threw off his balance. But once all was assembled, the illusion was complete.

"There. We're merely a small group of priests returning sick brethren home," he said.

"I don't feel any closer to Pacela," Vantinio said.

Never grinned. "It'd take more than robes."

The mercenary chuckled before lifting his stretcher and beckoning for Tsolde to arrange herself on it. Luis and Never took Elina's and they set off, breaking free of the cover of trees and starting for the road.

Never scrutinised the trail ahead, the weight of the stretcher pulling on his arms, filtering out Tsolde's grumbling. Her ride would become less bumpy on the road, before which he hoped she'd stop. Still some distance yet, waited Isacina. Beneath scuffed walls and the monstrous, open gate, stretched the Vadiya tents – a dark wave of blue across a muted plain. Smoke rose from various cook-fires and the din of many voices crossed the field. Like a makeshift town.

On the road they travelled more swiftly, eventually joining other travellers, who rarely spoke. One woman, tools swinging from her belt, offered a single coin to Never. "Pacela's Blessing upon us all," she said. He did not know how to return the money.

After a merchant train had passed, Elina muttered something in Hanik before switching to Marlosi. "What's happening? All I can really see is the sky."

"We're closing in on the camp," Never said. "Best to stay quiet."

The tents rose around them, uniform in their dark blue. Steelhawks and regular soldiers moved between them, meeting in small groups, sitting atop crates to work on their armour or weapons; the hiss of whetstones brought a constant sibilance.

But no-one stopped them, few even glanced their way.

Conversations drifted to him – men arguing over dice, others complaining about being 'stuck outside in the bloody mud while the Firsts got it better in the city', and even one man explaining sword techniques to another.

Unlike the walk through Sacha's camp, the more tents he passed the more the tension fell away. Lina was right; it seemed the Vadiya did not care what Pacela's Priests did. Of course, the gate would be the true test but something urged him on. A feeling – Pacela watching over him? He sent a wry smile to the dirt road; why not? Such help couldn't come soon enough.

When the gates finally did appear before him, towering high enough to block the thin sun and cast the guard post in shadow, he shivered. A farmer's cart was being searched by half a dozen Steelhawks, their striped insignia revealing high ranking officers. They climbed into the wagon and began removing crates of pomegranate, commencing a thorough search – which didn't bode well for Never's disguises.

Doubt crept forth.

"Let's rest a moment," he said, angling his head to Luis.

Together they lowered Elina to the earth, closer to Tsolde. No-one spoke while they waited and when the Steelhawks finally waved them over, Never nodded before lifting Elina and starting forward, Vantinio beside him. Now for the test of their disguise.

The lead Steelhawk, who bore markings of the Falcon, raised a gauntleted hand, speaking fair Marlosi. "Your business, Priest?"

"We are returning home from a missionary trip to the Ramakki Islands," Never explained.

"And your fellows?" He gestured to the stretchers.

"A serious illness," Never replied. "We hope to complete treatment here in Isacina."

"Illness?" The Falcon grunted. "Find another place, Priest. We don't need whatever pestilence you bring with you."

"We would confine ourselves immediately to the Goddess' Spire, My Lord," Never added.

The Steelhawk backhanded Never. "Fool."

The blow split Never's lip but he didn't retaliate, save to go to one knee. "Forgive me."

A second Steelhawk approached, taking the Falcon aside and speaking softly – too softly to be heard, despite Never's skill with the Vadiyem language. The second Steelhawk, whose breastplate bore no family markings, released the Falcon once the man gave what appeared to be a grudging nod.

"You will be escorted to the spire and there you will remain, understood?"

Never nodded. "You have our and the Goddess' thanks." He motioned to Luis, who took his end of Elina's stretcher. Another member of the Falcon family assisted Vantinio with Tsolde.

"Be quick about it," the first man said, a sneer on his lips.

Two Steelhawks led them, but none were the man with no markings on his breastplate. Such a man ought not to have been in a position of power in Vadiya society, given his seeming lack of family. Never resisted the urge to look back; drawing any more attention from that particular Steelhawk would not be wise.

There was always a chance the man was simply displaying a kindness... but it was hard not to see Snow's hand in every act. And mere moments ago he'd been wondering about Pacela's hand.

In any event, the fellow would bear watching.

The streets were quiet but not empty. Few people went about their usual business, but Never barely noticed them – for their path took him near Ashina's giant oaks.

The trees were broken, blackened.

The soft green lawn that once caught the falling leaves was now nothing more than a mess of mud and broken branches. Vadiya soldiers formed a line, carrying away lumber from where several groups of shirtless men worked at hacking into the mighty trunks. How long had they been working on the great trees?

He gripped Elina's stretcher hard.

Further into the city waited more signs of occupation, stone carvings of the Vadiya God, Sovant with his broadsword, resting on newly constructed platforms. Taverns were announcing that they now sold the dark, mint-flavoured liquor favoured by the Vadiya. A desperate attempt to appease the occupying force? The drink had always been available but it simply wasn't popular in Marlosa before.

And while the streets were not empty, they were hardly bustling. Those Marlosi citizens moved quickly, a pair of women carrying linen baskets barely looked up to see where they walked. Even the yellow and red stripes on their clothing seemed flat and muted.

Vadiya swaggered wherever they went.

When Pacela's Spire finally came into view Never's arms were burning from the stretcher but he didn't bother calling a halt, better to reach the comparative safety of the spire sooner. The square resting beneath the Spire lay empty. Silver figures of Pacela in her flowing robe stood at each corner though naught but new weeds crept between the flagstones.

"Go," one of the Steelhawks said, waving with his sword.

Never and Luis took Elina to the great, banded door, pausing a moment for Vantinio and Tsolde to join them. Then Never thumped upon the wood with the ornate knocker and waited.

"Will they let us in?" Elina asked from where she lay on the stone.

"Lina was confident," Never said, turning to face the Vadiya as he waited. The Steelhawks were watching, one with hands on hips, two holding loaded crossbows. It was clear what would happen if the door did not open. "But I do hope she hurries."

Never knocked again. Still no response from within.

The Steelhawks remained in place, their weapons ready but not aimed. Yet.

"This isn't looking good," Luis said.

"She'll be here," Never replied. She had to, or else events were going to take a turn toward disaster. Running across an open square under fire – or trying to outrun the bolts – was not something he wanted to experience. And it would be worse for Elina and Tsolde, who had to stand even before they could run.

They would be no more than target practice for the Steelhawks, no more than a story the Vadiya could later tell with much mirth around their fires as they gouged themselves on the fruit of Marlosa.

A wooden panel snapped open.

Lina's large eyes appeared in the shadowy recess. "Messenger?"

"I prefer 'Never' if you could, Lina. And I'd like it even more if you'd open the door."

"Of course," she said, then closed the panel. The sound of a heavy bar being slid free followed and the creak of wood as the door swung inward to reveal Lina in her acolyte's robe, lit by the warm glow of lantern-light.

"Welcome to the Goddess' Spire, the Light of Isacina," she said.

Chapter 18.

Never waited, the trickle of water from a fountain filling the hush.

The High Priestess Jardila regarded him with some concern, her four braids glistening black in the lamps that filled her chamber. They cast warmth across carvings on the walls too; images of Pacela working in hewn earth or tending saplings deep in forest glades – though there were images that revealed her displeasure too, where she cast forth a fierce golden light to eradicate unidentifiable shades that were devouring the very fields of Marlosa.

Jardila sat at a tear-shaped table, or, more likely for Pacela, it was to represent a seed. The High Priestess sat in a half circle that had been cut free of the point, attended by two priests and Lina, who knelt near the woman.

Never and his friends spread around the bulb of the seed, robes removed and cool fruit juice and wine in glasses before them. The juice was tart against Never's tongue, but welcome. Yet he could not relax fully, not yet. Jardila's expression gave him pause. While she'd welcomed everyone and offered Pacela's protection, she did not seem to have decided how long that might extend.

"You may, of course, stay here in peace so long as the Vadiya allow us such leeway, but who knows how long that may be?" she said. Her voice was quite musical to Never's ear, there was a slight inflection that he could not place. "We have perhaps kept ourselves locked away too often over the years, focused too inwardly, too deeply on our search for Pacela, done too little to spread her wisdom."

One of the priests leant down. "My Lady, we cannot blame ourselves for what has happened to the city."

"But it is our home, Gelvi, shouldn't we be a part of protecting it?"

"Where possible only," he replied.

"Perhaps," she said, then stood and turned to Lina. "Will you take our guests down to their rooms, Lina? Arrange for baths and whatever else they require."

"Yes, High Priestess."

Lina motioned for everyone to follow. Never stood and joined the group as they filed toward the arched exit. Before he reached the door, Jardila's voice stopped him. "Never, I would speak with you a moment."

He stopped. "Of course."

Luis had paused but Never gave him a nod and his friend continued on, just as one of the Priests was no doubt offered a similar gesture from Jardila, but when Never turned back, she was facing one of the carvings on the wall.

Never approached.

Jardila was tall, yet her robe still brushed against the floor, as if it had been cut so. Unlike the acolytes and priests, her arms were left bare. Each shoulder was adorned by a tattooed pattern resembling a tree within a circle.

She faced him and her expression was a hard one. "You are not a messenger from my Goddess."

"That's true"

His answer gave her slight pause, as if she'd expected something else. "Yet you have wings – Lina would not lie to me."

"Would you like to see them?" he asked.

She raised an eyebrow, as if she had already made the request.

He chuckled. "Very well, My Lady. Here they are." Never stepped away from the wall then flicked his cloak back and rolled his shoulders, letting his wings unfurl. Black feathers stretched to the carving on one side and he pulled them in a little.

Jardila's eyes had widened, but she controlled her face better than Lina had. She circled him slowly. "May I see?"

"There is a tear in my clothing."

She lifted the tunic and gave a gasp. "They are... a part of you."

"I thought you believed Lina?"

Jardila returned to face him. Her expression was more uncertain now. "I said she would not lie to me. She may have believed that you truly had wings and yet been mistaken. Follow me, I must show you something."

She led him to a carving of Pacela where the Goddess was speaking with a boy, her face serene and his awed. Jardila produced a pendant from her robe and held it up against the carving, aligning it with corresponding jewellery in the artwork.

Stone rumbled and part of the wall slid open.

The High Priestess entered the dim passage and Never paused. "Do we need light?"

"It is not far." Her voice echoed.

Never followed the sound of her footsteps. The passage was smooth but narrow. Natural light soon appeared ahead and he joined Jardila in a small room that held a single podium lit by a skylight. A heavy tome rested atop. Beyond waited a closed door, but no indication of what might lie behind.

The High Priestess gestured to the book. "There is something within that I wish for you to see."

"Is there a particular page?" he asked as he reached for the cover.

"Yes. Three pages marked by yellow ribbon – gently now."

"Of course." Taking care, he opened to the first yellow ribbon, pages settling with a crackling.

Before him, a winged man appeared to have burst from a stormy sea, a young child in his arms. Ancient text, so Never supposed, lined the bottom of the image. The words were not Amouni... but what of the picture itself? Never glanced at Jardila, who merely indicated that he should view the next page.

He took the next ribbon and revealed a winged woman. By her stern expression, she was pronouncing judgement upon people who had gathered. Some of the folk wept, and others clung to one another in despair, their bodies slumped.

"And the third?" Never asked.

"Can you not guess, considering what you are?" she said, steel entering her voice.

"Considering what I am?"

"Amouni. Old Masters here. Or tyrants."

Never turned to the final page and shook his head. A winged man, this time a man standing atop a pile of corpses, blood streaming from his hands and flying into the air. The writing beneath this image had been written taller, with a more forceful hand.

Snow – it didn't have to look like his brother to remind Never. Or even his own actions in Ficcepa.

His every fear summed up in one image.

"And you show me this why?" Never asked, his voice heavy.

The High Priestess was watching him. "To gauge your reaction, for one."

"And have I passed your clever test?"

"Perhaps."

"What do the words say?"

"The first page speaks of the Amouni as arriving to save us, as messengers from the very Gods." She closed the book. "The second describes the onset of their overwhelming arrogance as they began to decide what was best for the world. The final was a warning, urging us to prevent the return of the Amouni at all costs, lest humanity become utterly enslaved, utterly lacking free will, purpose, hope."

Never folded his arms. "Do not paint me with such a brush."

"I am giving you a chance to convince me that the warnings were false."

"You are most generous."

Her eyes flashed. "Don't mock me, Never. It is not outside my capabilities to stop you now."

"Are you sure of that?"

She hesitated, barely a moment, but it was enough. She could not stop him, or at least it seemed, not if he was ready for any such attempt. "You are here as a show of mercy, do you understand?"

"I understand. Can you also explain how our squabbling helps Isacina?"

Jardila rapped her fingers across the cover of the book. "Your point is well made."

"Then what do you want from me?"

"Proof that you are better than your ancestors – I want you to be the Amouni in the first image, to fulfil the promise of the Gods, that which we have been taught through the generations."

"And you believe it?" Never asked.

"I must."

Chapter 19.

Never paced the thick rug of his room, glaring at the bed. "And those tassels, they don't serve any purpose that I can see."

His room was comfortable and pleasant, spacious too. And yet somehow even that offended him. The soothing pale yellows and greens, it was all too much after his interrogation. Or was it the reminder of his cursed heritage that had gotten beneath his skin? The reminder that Snow was forging a path that would see him upon a throne of corpses.

"I think they're nice," Tsolde said from where she sat on Never's bed. Like the others, she had bathed, washing the grime of travel from her face and coppery hair. She lifted the blanket and ran a tassel between her fingers. "Such soft thread."

"Never, that can't be all she said," Elina interrupted from where she sat at the small table. Luis stood nearby, still eating cold meat from a plate, while Vantinio leant against the window, staring down onto the city. Only halfway up the Spire, it had still been a serious climb.

"I've told you it all," he said. "She expects me to save Isacina. All of it."

"Aren't you trying to do that anyway?" Vantinio said without turning.

"Not truly," Never replied. "It would be more of a welcome after-effect to stopping my brother."

"Splitting hairs, I see."

"Can't we simply enjoy this respite?" Elina asked. "I don't imagine a place this secure or well-provisioned is going to be usual in the middle of an occupied city."

Never slumped into a chair and threw a leg over the arm. "Truly spoken, Lady Elina."

"Then we plan our next step during the morning meal," she said. "We all need to rest now."

Murmurs of agreement as his companions sought their own rooms but Elina paused at the door; he felt her eyes upon him as he rose and dragged his weary limbs toward the next room where his bath still steamed. "Yes?" he asked.

"You know I have doubted it in the past... but I do believe you can make our lives better, Never. And not only I, but my grandfather and the Order of Clera believe it too. Don't let Jardila's fear convince you otherwise."

Never leant against the doorframe. To exist simply to make the lives of others better, to be a tool only, to have no fate of his own, no name even, it was hardly of comfort. It might have enraged him. Might have set him off again, railing at Elina until he was hoarse.

But it did not.

Unlike the High Priestess, Elina was telling him something few dared, Elina was saying he was not a force for death and destruction.

How rare, such words. How welcome.

"Thank you," he managed.

She closed the door and he continued on, removing his cloak and tunic, pausing at the glow on his chest. The five-pointed leaf symbol blazed and pulsed in time with the blood in his veins, yet as before, the light did not last. Why? What did it mean? He had no answers, of course, and so he started on his boots and continued, remembering to retract his wings, until he could finally slip into the still-hot water with a deep sigh.

Tomorrow. Everything could wait until tomorrow.

*

Lina and several other acolytes brought sliced fruit with tall glasses of milk on trays, arranging them on the table in Never's room. The others did not seem to care for Lina if their dark glances were any indication, or the way they laughed when Lina fumbled with the knives and forks. But they all bowed to him and scurried out to the hall, something he could have done without. He called Lina back while his friends started the breakfast, cutlery clinking behind him.

"Lina, will you send for the High Priestess?"

She swallowed. "Send for?"

He grinned. "You can phrase it however you wish, but I need to speak with her this morning."

"Of course, Mess – ah, My Lord. I will request a meeting on your behalf. If that is all?"

"No," he said. "I noticed the others did not act kindly toward you."

Tears built in her eyes but she dashed them away. "It is nothing."

"Lina."

"They do not believe me, that I saw you on the roof, that you have wings or that you are a Messenger."

The childishness of youth. "I see. Don't let them trouble you, Lina. I have a feeling they will change their tune soon enough."

"Thank you," she said as she left, though the tone of her voice suggested she did not believe him.

Never returned to the patch of light provided by the window, where his companions were devouring the fruit. "What have you left me then, you wonderful pigs?" he asked.

Vantinio laughed and Luis grinned around his apple, while Tsolde gave him a mock-frown.

"You seem in higher spirits today," Elina observed. She, like the others, appeared much better after bathing, a good meal, and a deep sleep in a secure place. The bruises were well and truly faded now and her skin no longer bore additional paleness.

"Let's see if it lasts until the High Priestess arrives," he said.

"You don't expect her now, surely?" she asked.

"Not truly." He drank his milk – cool and clean against his tongue. "But while we wait, let's talk about the next step."

"We have to discover if Snow is even here," Luis said.

"Which means sneaking into the palace, doesn't it?" Tsolde asked. "Rumours on the street won't be enough."

"Don't like our chances of sneaking in there," Vantinio said.

"I'm not worried about that, I know a way in. Even if I have to fly you over the wall one at a time – I'm worried about how to move around once we're inside," Never said.

"Snow first, remember?" Luis took a sip from his own milk.

"What if we cannot gain entry to the palace?" Elina posed.

Silence around the table. Never drummed his fingers on the wood, the gesture bringing Jardila to mind.

"Take a high ranking officer," Vantinio said. "A First or a Commander."

"That has possibilities," Never mused.

"Assuming you can force them to speak." Elina put her glass aside and stood, pacing across the rug. "Let's set aside the matter of whether Snow is in the palace for a moment, either as Tendov or in a more secretive presence. How will you find him and what exactly are you planning to do then?"

"We can assume our disguises won't hold up within the palace," Luis added.

"I doubt any disguise would work," Never agreed. "Boldness, speed and stealth, perhaps," he said. "There are places we may be able to hide for a short time. But I fear this will be another of those times when I may have to take the final step alone."

More silence.

Tsolde finally broke the hush. "How will you stop him, Never?"

He did not answer at first. "I fear I won't know until we meet again. The last thing he would accept... is that I would seek to kill him."

A knocking came from the door.

"Enter," Never called.

A Priest opened the door and approached, his stern face seeking Never. "The High Priestess requests you join her in her private altar room, once you have had a chance to prepare for the day."

"Certainly." Never stood. He looked to the others. "See if you can discover whether the Steelhawks are watching us."

He followed the priest outside and into a nearby stairwell where he started up, boots echoing. The priest climbed without comment and after a time, Never found himself glad of the silence, concentrating on his breathing instead.

Jardila's altar room was not so high as the roof, but when he was finally admitted, it was with no small amount of relief. The altar room was as sparse as the hidden chamber with the old tome, yet the statue of Pacela that filled it was unlike any Never had witnessed anywhere in Marlosa. The silver figure was female in suggestion only, via the graceful lines perhaps, but she appeared more a frozen flame here.

The High Priestess stood before it, hands clasped before her.

"The Goddess appears unlike herself," Never said after a moment.

Jardila turned, braids swinging. "Perhaps, though this is merely one of several representations created over the centuries. Pacela, Light of Marlosa. Now, why did you wish to see me, Never? You are leaving already?"

"Perhaps. But I have come to make provision for my friends."

"I see."

"Is there a secret way from the spire? If you were attacked?"

She lifted a thin eyebrow. "You mean, if your activities brought the Vadiya down upon us?"

"Yes." He saw no reason to lie and Jardila herself had claimed to want him to do something to save the city. And that meant taking risks. Yet if he could negate enough of them...

"There is such a way."

"I would ask that you take my companions if it comes to such a time."

She sighed. "Perhaps when, Never, not if. And of course, we will offer such temporary respite if you are to fail."

"Thank you, My Lady."

"You have chosen a path of action then?"

"Chosen first steps, at least. Much hinges upon whether Prince Tendov is in the city," he said. No need to let her know who or what Snow was.

"He is said to be in the palace often," Jardila said, turning back to the statue. "Though I cannot confirm such a thing one way or another."

"You have no-one watching?"

"Of course we watch, but we have no eyes in the palace, Never."

"Few would, I imagine. I'll take my leave then."

She did not answer, as if deep in prayer once again.

Outside, Never found no attendant and so descended alone. When he reached his room, passing no acolytes or priests, he found it empty. He searched the other guest rooms but it wasn't until he found an alcove set off another flight of stairs that he heard voices – giggling.

He peered around the alcove.

Two acolytes sat beneath a window, heads together over a book.

Never cleared his throat.

Both looked up, faces covered in guilt. One girl hid the book, but not before he saw the title – The Songs of Sondella. Common fare, even in reputable taverns, but hardly forbidden material, surely? But then, he was in a sacred place.

"Can we help, My Lord?" One girl asked quickly.

"I'm searching for my friends," he said, pretending he had not seen the book.

"They're in the Eyes," the other replied.

"Eyes?"

"Patrina will show you," the first girl said, keeping her hands in her lap, Sondella's book hidden in the folds of her robe.

"Yes, of course," Patrina said, bounding up.

"That's kind of you."

He followed her through an open doorway and a long passage, lit by a lamp that Patrina paused to refill from a canister of oil placed within an alcove. Next a set of stairs, leading up once more and passing a series of doors, curving around the spire until she stopped at a broad, double-door marked with the old rune for 'seeing'.

"You'll find them within, My Lord."

He gave her a smile then pushed on the doors.

A dim chamber was revealed, lit by a thin horizontal window. It took up half the curving wall, broken only by silhouettes. One moved closer as Never's eyes adjusted – Luis. "Never, you have to see this." He was grinning. "It might have been made by the Amouni, the priests don't know, they say it's always been here."

Tsolde stepped away from an odd contraption, a set of steel cylinders and a stool mounted on a steel rail. The cylinders were pointed out to the city and the rail followed the curve of the room. "You look through them and the city seems closer," she said.

"It is impressive," Vantinio added. "They've all been fighting over it since we got here."

Never took the seat and used his legs to move along the rail a little, pressing his eye against the metal to peer through the cylinder. Glass or quartz distorted his vision, revealing a dark blur only, until Tsolde tapped a tiny lever. "Pull this down or up if you cannot see," she said. "I was looking at one of the buildings, it's closer than where you've moved to."

He pulled the lever and a dark mass of a building resolved, an inn with an extravagant garden on its upper story. He could see directly into the windows on the top floor; the foot of a bed, its blankets rumpled.

"Impressive is an understatement," he said softly.

Elina used her boot to slide him further along. "Tilt the cylinder with that handle," she said. "Tell us if he's still there, by the pile of crates near the tailor."

"Very well." Never reached up and wound the handle, a deep clicking following. The cylinder eye showed the street in clear detail, close as if he were mere feet away from the cobblestones. The needle and thread painted on a sign revealed the tailor, but he saw no crates. Never slid the contraction further and paused.

There.

A Steelhawk sat atop one of the crates, facing the Spire. Watching?

"I see him."

"Now switch to this cylinder." Tsolde tapped on the second.

The Steelhawk was so close that Never could see the apple core the man nibbled upon. The fellow cast it aside then folded his arms. As he did so, his breastplate was revealed – and the lack of Family insignia or rank.

"My my," Never breathed. The same man who'd convinced the gate guards to let them into the city.

"Recognise him?" Luis asked.

"I do," Never said with a grin. "And I believe we just found our high-ranking officer."

Chapter 20.

"Ready?" Never asked.

Nods from everyone gathered in the antechamber before the great doors. It was an exceedingly simple plan. Never would stroll the streets, circling toward an alley chosen from the vantage of the Eyes. Once the mysterious Steelhawk started after Never, Vantinio would follow at a distance. Luis and Elina would, in turn, follow any Steelhawk that might have lingered to trail Vantinio.

Tsolde, much to her frustration, was staying in the Eyes. It was her job to signal with a coloured lantern if she saw something amiss. She'd wanted to help on the ground but Never held back while the others began the descent. "If we're unlucky there will be plenty of chances for you to take risks."

She'd narrowed her eyes. "Don't say that because I'm a young woman, Never. You know I can help."

"You could indeed. But I need Luis focused on the task at hand. If he knows you're safe here, there's less risk."

Tsolde flushed. "You know... how we feel for each other?"

"Of course and I'm happy for you," he said with a grin.

"Just help us here. Next time I'll ask someone else to take watch."

"Fine," she said. "But you know this doesn't stop me worrying about him."

"Don't worry, I know exactly how you feel," Never said. "I worry about you all every day." He shook his head, it was something he hadn't admitted aloud and in a strange way, it was almost a relief. "I won't let anything happen to him."

She nodded. "I know. Go then."

And now it was time to put the plan into action. There wasn't too much that could go wrong, the best thing about simple plans. Of course, if something did go wrong it would likely be a disaster. If, say, the strange Steelhawk was hiding twenty men in a nearby building.

Still... if the man had wanted them captured, he would have done it at the gate.

Never removed the bar and entered the square, crossing steadily beneath the dull sun. He wore no disguise this time, not wanting to be missed. What he did carry was his knives. He kept several belted in plain sight. He was taking no chances in catching the man's eye.

He started up the deserted street where the Steelhawk was waiting but did not search for the fellow. Instead, Never continued on his path, smiling once he heard the tread of boots following. He soon turned into a side street where he bypassed piles of refuse, then back to the broader thoroughfare.

Hooves clacked ahead, the rattling of wheels on stone joining it, and a carriage swung into view. Never stepped to the side, closer to the buildings, as the carriage rumbled by, curtains drawn. No clues as to who it carried. Never resisted the urge to quicken his pace even a little, the steady walk was enough. By now, Vantinio would be following the Steelhawk and Luis and Elina were in turn, keeping an eye on Vantinio.

The pre-arranged alley appeared, marked by the abandoned toymaker, or so Pacela's priests claimed. It certainly bore a look of emptiness – garbage gathered in the doorway and dust darkened windows.

Never glanced back to Pacela's tower, taking a moment to locate Tsolde's window. No coloured lamp, no trouble. Good. He turned into the alley and slowed his tread. Before he reached the opposite end, the Steelhawk entered. Never grinned. A little further, fellow. Never bent, as if to check his boots. Was Vantinio in place? Footsteps halted behind him. Never turned.

A little way into the alley, the dark shape of the Steelhawk stood – and behind the man loomed another figure, who hurled something into the air. The net quickly resolved, weighted ends crashing down over the Steelhawk, who collapsed with a clatter.

Never charged after Vantinio, who was already upon the Steelhawk with a length of rope. "Help me with his hands."

The Steelhawk struggled but was no match for the strength of two, and was soon bound. Together, Never and Vantinio hauled the man to his feet and shoved him through the nearby door – into the darkness of the toymaker.

Deserted, as promised.

Light from the doorway revealed a bench strewn with chisels, a delicate hammer and half-finished toys like abandoned children, all sombre in the dark. One wooden figure seemed connected by tiny chains but was missing its head. Never dragged a stool into the centre of the room. Vantinio set the Steelhawk down and drew his sword, keeping it at the man's throat.

"Don't move," Vantinio said, speaking Vadiyem.

Never closed the door, reducing the light to whatever pushed through dusty window panes, then drew one of his knives. He flipped it into the air, catching it by the handle as he faced the Steelhawk. "You have no family," Never began, also speaking the Vadiya tongue.

"It would seem so," the man replied, an unconcerned expression clear on his delicate features. Yet there remained a gleam of cunning in his eye, each a different colour – green and blue.

"What is your name?"

"I am Andramir."

"You seem to have been assigned an inordinate amount of power."

Now he smiled. "Responsibility, perhaps."

"For what?" Vantinio asked. "And don't think a lie will do."

"I have no need," Andramir replied. He turned back to Never. "Prince Tendov asked me to watch for your appearance and then to ensure you were not still... encumbered by any lingering impediments."

Lingering impediments? Snow's words on the mountain. "Vantinio flee."

"What?"

The Steelhawk only grinned.

Wood creaked and light flowed into the room. Luis and Elina entered the toyshop, weapons drawn. "No-one followed Vantinio," Luis said.

Never shouted. "Run, all of you – it was a trap!"

Andramir stood and Never blinked. The man had simply passed through the net, passed through the sword tip as if it were not at his throat. "Stay," he said, and his voice was soft, sibilant, yet it filled the room.

Never could not move.

Vantinio stood like a statue, sword-arm outstretched. Near the door, Elina and Luis were frozen, expressions of shock clear, though their eyes darted.

Andramir crossed the room, walking directly through Luis and Elina to stand outside a moment, then he returned, pausing by Vantinio. "I count three yet no girl. It should be four, including your new companion here. Never, where is young Tsolde?"

"No."

"It's no trouble to guess – you left her in the Spire, yes? Inconvenient but not insurmountable."

"Tell him I will see him," Never said. "But if something happens to my friends I will make sure Snow fails in all he seeks."

"Will you?"

"With me dead, he will fail – I know he needs me."

Andramir narrowed his eyes. "I think this is a terrible bluff."

"Are you sure you want to take that risk? I don't imagine my brother would react very well to failure."

"He is not fond of mistakes, that's certainly true," Andramir said with a frown. "But we still cannot have your companions getting underfoot." He approached everyone in turn and spoke only a single word 'Slumber' and one by one, they fell to the floorboards and remained, eyes closed, chests rising and falling in sleep. "And so they will remain until I alone wake them."

Never kept his relief on hold. "Fine. Take me to my brother."

Andramir shook his head as he started for the door. "I have other tasks to complete – and you are most capable of finding him."

"Leave her be!"

"I cannot." And then he was gone.

Chapter 21.

Too much time had passed.

The shadows of unfinished toys filled the room, crossing the floor and distorting where they covered the sleeping forms of his friends.

He had failed.

Failed to escape and failed those who depended upon him.

Just as he'd feared. Never clenched his jaw. Too many times, far too many times. The old way was the best – if he hadn't been so arrogant, he might have remembered that. For any who neared him would be dragged into his curse. And maybe they wouldn't die by his blood but it would still be by his hand that they met their fate.

More the fool that he thought he could keep them safe.

Never roared into the empty store.

Only silence answered with its dust and its indifference.

He closed his eyes.

How long now since he'd lost Zia? Years, yet it struck as hard as ever. The deep indigo of the night, interspersed by the glow of lanterns, wind sweeping across the tower, eating all sound, water flying as he splashed his way through the puddles. Sprinting but too slow nonetheless, her body still and Snow shouting for him – even from a distance Never could see he was too late.

But it had made no difference, none of it, not the medicine he carried or the foolish hope he brought with it. How the Gods had mocked him then; he and Snow had already saved her from the group of thugs, only to lose her to the curse.

No, the bitter argument he and Snow had fought after saving her – that was the cause. Blaming each other as they struggled, jealousy fuelling their knives. And Never couldn't say for sure whose blood had stolen so much of hers; he experienced none of her memories and Snow had always claimed the same.

They had only each other to blame in the end, arguing over who would run for help and who would stay and hold her.

Wasting precious moments.

Never hadn't been able to drag himself all the way back, instead stumbling into the shadows and collapsing against the chill stone, struggling to breathe, tears burning.

The last time he'd seen Zia.

The last time he saw Snow until their meeting on the cliffs, years later, where each had vowed the other's death.

And here he was again, seeking an end to Snow, yet for different reasons.

Never staggered forward, limbs free all of a sudden. Had Andramir let him go? Or had the man's magic simply worn off? Never crouched by Vantinio; the mercenary still breathed. Good. Yet he could not be woken. Next, Luis and Elina. The same. Never pushed himself back up, limbs aching, no doubt an unfortunate after-effect of being frozen in place.

Footsteps thundered outside.

He spun, knife in hand.

An arm appeared in the light, pushing on the door, clothed in yellow. "Messenger?"

Lina.

Never lowered his blade. "Yes."

She stepped inside and gasped. "Are they dead?"

"No. Just asleep, yet nothing wakes them," Never said.

"Oh. Like the young Hanik woman."

Never uttered a curse, ignoring the way Lina flushed. "A Steelhawk?"

"Yes. He simply appeared... we couldn't stop him, we couldn't even touch him. Some of the Priests he froze, others he beat."

"I'm sorry," Never said. Tsolde too – not a surprise, but at least Andramir had spared her. The man had taken Never's threat seriously at least. But was it anything more than a threat? No way to know. Not until he faced Snow.

Which would surely be soon.

"No-one has died... yet, though Brother Mil has not woken from his wounds."

"Lina, I need your help, we need to get everyone back to the Spire. Will the Priests come?"

She nodded. "I've been sent to find you, the High Priestess wishes to see you. Others are nearby."

"No doubt she does," he said. "Now hurry, and thank you."

She smiled as she ran back into the street.

Never paced the toyshop. He glanced at the figure in the marble ball and it was standing to attention, arms straight at its sides, fists clenched. Tense. Lina soon returned with the priests, who helped with neither complaint nor cheer. Never helped carry Vantinio and once they were each lain in simple beds on the Spire's ground floor, and once he had checked on the sleeping form of Tsolde himself, he let Lina take him up to the dining hall.

"We eat together with every change of the moon," she explained. "The High Priestess is waiting in the kitchen."

"She prepared the meal? For everyone?"

"Assists," Lina said. "It is tradition."

The dining hall was vast, taking up what had to be half the entire floor, but it was not full. There were many empty seats and whole sections cordoned off. Were the numbers of the priesthood declining? Many of the heads that sat at benches were silvery or bald, easily outnumbering the younger acolytes.

The sounds of spoons in bowls ceased. All eyes followed them as they walked the aisles. Lina seemed to wilt a little but Never stared back, ignoring the muttering. So, they had learnt the truth; he was no Messenger, he was only trouble and danger. Which meant Snow had to be stopped all the more swiftly.

The kitchen bore less resentment, rows of ovens were tended by acolytes with sleeves rolled up and cheerful expressions. The scent of baking sweetbread filled the room. High Priestess Jardila herself was working dough with a worn rolling pin. Her braids had been tied up and her mouth moved as she worked, another prayer no doubt.

"My Lady?" Lina announced herself.

The High Priestess turned, her expression growing weary upon catching sight of Never. "Thank you, Lina. You are free to resume your meal." Jardila raised her voice, turning to the other girls. "And you, quickly now."

Once alone, she gestured that Never should take a stool. He did so. "I hope no-one was killed?"

She sighed. "Brother Mil clings to life. Worse, perhaps, is the straining of faith in the Goddess. Many have questions that I cannot answer, fears I cannot allay."

"Such is life itself," Never said. "Surely they don't blame you?"

"They blame you."

"That is fair," Never said. "If you could be patient even longer, and protect my friends as best you can, I go next to the palace."

She raised a feathery eyebrow. "Where you will single-handily drive the Vadiya away?"

"Where I will draw them away," he said. "Prince Tendov seeks me but he will have to chase me."

"Foolishness. Why would he do that, Never? You may bear Amouni blood but that does not make you a God."

"Because I will kill him if he does not and I will kill him if he does. Either way, I will let the Vadiya know, and they will pursue me."

"Perhaps. Or another will simply take his place. Rage alone won't win this struggle."

"True. But I possess a few surprises, don't worry, My Lady." He stood. "You will continue to care for my companions?"

"Yes. But the Spire will be sealed should you fail."

"Sealed?"

"By my hand; I will invoke the Goddess' Seal and then

none shall enter or leave until I lift it, be they man or... whatever that man truly was. You stir unnatural forces, Never."

"Andramir. Lina said he came."

"Yes, as though no walls stood. No hand touched him and only the inner chambers rebuffed him, though he attempted to breech them nonetheless."

"Inner chambers? What did he seek?" Which was the same as asking, what did Snow seek?

Jardila did not answer at first, instead regarding him for a long moment. "Meet me in my reception room shortly. I will show you."

He bowed. "Thank you for trusting me."

She did not answer as he turned and he was struck by an impulse – perhaps Pacela's faithful needed something to shake their doubts. And even if he was no Messenger, he was the only thing that could stop Snow. Perhaps he could offer some hope?

In the still-hushed dining hall he climbed onto the nearest empty table, eliciting murmuring. Once he was sure he had everyone's attention, he stretched his shoulders and let his wings unfurl, so that they snapped up behind him.

Gasps followed.

An elderly priest collapsed against one of his fellows.

"I regret that darkness has followed me into your home," he said. "But I will go now and drive it back or perish myself. While I do this, I would appreciate anything you might do to help my friends while they are defenceless."

He stepped down, and amongst yet more whispers and hushed exclamations, sought out Lina, who ate with two other acolytes. There, he reached up to his wing and plucked forth a black feather, handing it to her. "Perhaps now they will believe you, Lina," he said.

Her smile beamed back up at him, and he continued along the aisles.

*

Jardila opened the door that stood beyond the tome she had shared with him earlier, again using her pendant. There she paused upon the threshold. "What lies beyond is not of Pacela, but your ancestors. It had been concealed – hidden – within these walls for hundreds upon hundreds of years before I took my role. Each High Priestess or High Priest had passed down its knowledge and been given the responsibility to exercise judgement – to reveal or hide – should a Messenger appear."

"And you would reveal it to me?"

"The infiltration of the man called Andramir has forced my hand. I have no doubt he was seeking this and have to wonder, if he is of the Amouni, like you?"

"If so, wouldn't he have been able to enter?"

"I do not believe so." She paused, expectant. Waiting for an admission, it seemed.

Perhaps it was time to offer her something. "I believe Andramir has been... twisted by another Amouni."

Jardila sighed. "I feared as much. He is known to you, this other descendant?"

"Yes; he is my enemy." And that would be enough.

"And he leads the Vadiya?"

"Prince Tendov."

She nodded. "Then you must stop him. Prevent him coming here."

"I will."

Jardila stepped into the room and Never joined her in a dim chamber, vague shapes only, visible until she raised a hand to the wall.

Blue light grew, soon surging across the walls like a river. Yet it was not so bright as to blind him when Jardila stepped back to reveal the Amouni artefact.

In the very centre of the room stood a man of silver.

He was as tall as Never and as broad shouldered but his features were vague, a smooth head and indents only for eyes and mouth, a slight protrusion for a nose. The figure stood naked but once again, only the most general features had been moulded. Despite the age Jardila claimed – which he did not doubt – the silver bore no trace of tarnish, it gleamed, a thing of beauty. And more, it responded to his mere presence, nothing beyond an awareness perhaps, yet had it eyes, Never imagined they would have turned to him.

"It is written that in the time after the Amouni disappeared that the ancient peoples gathered all artefacts and items, some to use, some to destroy and others to hold over, in case of a return. This is one such item, my predecessor said that despite years of study it has never revealed its purpose or function, never moved, never responded in any form."

Whatever its use, Never could feel the potential.

And he knew that Snow should not have access to it, not under any conditions.

Never reached out to touch it – the surface was cold but something pulsed beneath it, just below his senses, as if he was close to understanding it... but the feeling passed and he sighed. "Prince Tendov must not ever see this."

"Agreed," Jardila said. "Do you know what it is? You sense something about it, don't you?"

"Only that it has responded to me as Amouni. And that it must be kept safe."

"So it shall be."

Chapter 22.

Never completed his preparations as darkness fell, settling over the city without a shred of warmth. A cold wind ruffled his wings and a light rain beaded on the stone around him. When he lifted his hands from the Spire rail the stone was dry.

He vaulted onto the rail then launched himself into the night.

With only a few pumps he was high enough to simply swoop down in a long line toward the circular palace towers, all dark. The central dome itself bore light however, its windows aglow all over. Within, no doubt the Vadiya enjoyed the luxuries of the palace and for the servants, perhaps nothing had changed in their daily toil.

For a moment no more, Never hesitated in his approach.

There was hardly a need for stealth.

Diving, he hurled a knife at the glass ceiling of the Grand Hall. Glass shattered and mere moments after, he crashed through feet first, stained glass flying. Stinging cuts appeared on his hands and face as hot blood trickled down his skin. He flared his wings and beat them with enough time to thump into the heavily-carpeted room amidst cries of shock.

Steelhawks and Vadiya nobility in their blues and whites, cowered around gilded furniture. One man was even clawing at a wall-hanging of the Marlosa Stallion, tearing the rich fabric. Glass still trickled down from the dome. A shard smashed into a server's trolley, splattering a dish of custard.

Never folded his arms and flared his wings. "Bring me Prince Tendov, immediately," he roared. When no-one moved he took a step toward the nearest soldier. "Now, imbecile, lest I tear you to pieces where you stand!"

The man fled, feet scrambling, as did several of the nobility but other Steelhawks lifted their crossbows and trained the weapons on him. None fired but their trembling limbs were much in Never's awareness as he walked to the dais and waited. One man was breathing hard.

Never turned his gaze upon the fellow. "Careful with that; I don't take kindly to being shot."

The man flinched, getting a firmer grip on the weapon. Yet he did not lower it, nor did any of the others. Trained too well, of course, but they'd not make a whit of difference. If Snow didn't send them away, Never would burn them to smoking piles of steel if needed.

As he stood, he became aware of the Empress' throne lurking behind him. He glanced at it – the seat was oversized, an ornament in and of itself, the rich red colour supposedly achieved by mixing gold and the blood of the first emperor. What would Cirsina think of him bursting through her ceiling?

Possibly nothing, if it meant being restored to the throne.

Finally the muted thunder of boots on carpet came and a small squad of Steelhawks skidded into the hall. Each bore the Red Talon of House Isajan.

"Never?"

Sacha.

She tore off her helm, waving her guards back as she strode forward, her eyes wide. She was just as he'd seen her last, beautiful and fierce, her short, pale hair dark with sweat at the temples. She bore her usual longsword but her blue eyes burned with shock, curiosity and even fear, he saw when she stopped before him.

"Where is he, Sacha?"

She reached up as if to touch his wings but dropped her hand. "How can this be?"

He lowered his voice. "I'm cursed, Sacha, you know that. And I am asking you to send for the Prince and then I want you to leave, for I do not wish to hurt you."

Sacha frowned. "Hurt me? Never, what madness is this? The Prince is not here."

"What?"

"He comes and goes – and I would not let you attack him, or me, in any event. You had better explain or I will have my men fire."

"Send them away and I will tell you everything."

She put a hand on her hilt. "Tell me now."

"He is my brother. Now do as I ask," he hissed.

Sacha gaped, her confusion evident as she struggled to speak. Still she could not answer and her grip faltered. There was such turmoil in her eyes; he repressed a stirring of guilt. Causing her pain was not part of his plan, but even his onetime lover could not stand between he and Snow.

"Lady Isajan?" One of her Steelhawks raised his voice.

She spun on him. "Empty this room."

"My Lady?"

"Do so or lose your rank and then your head, understood?"

He went to one knee then issued orders. The Steelhawks filed from the Grand Hall, several of them hauling babbling courtiers from where they were still curled beneath the furniture.

When the room was finally quiet Never examined Sacha once more. Tension rippled in the muscles of her neck and throat, but she was still able to maintain composure. Gods, she was still beautiful – her strength already beginning to overcome the shock. "Your King is known for adopting sons, if not daughters," he said.

"All know that," she snapped.

"Indeed. The man you know as Tendov is my brother, Snow. He and I parted ways many years ago, over something that came between us. We were both fools," he said. "And now I have come to put an end to his madness."

"That makes no sense," Sacha said. "Why, Never? Are you angry with me for choosing another? For invading your country? That I could understand, but not this strange lie. He is Vadiyem by Sovant!"

"You yourself said we were similar."

Sacha stalked closer. "Leave and I will spare you, Never."

"No."

"Leave. That is my only offer. I will not let you take what I have now, Never. I told you; he made me who I am."

Never softened his voice. "You did that yourself, Sacha."

She stepped back and pulled her sword free. "Do not overestimate what our past means to me."

Never drew his knives, though with her words she had landed the first blow. Yet he'd already decided as much for himself. No matter what he and Sacha had shared in the past, Snow had to be stopped. "He has too much to answer for, Sacha."

"Then you've chosen?"

"I have."

Sacha swung her sword. He leapt back and buffeted her with his wings. She stumbled and he circled away. Could he hurt her? His rage was fading; there was no reason to kill Sacha. Landing even a single cut would be a risk, considering his own wounds courtesy of the roof. Could he control his blood? More, could he even best her? Sacha was near unmatched with a sword and she had much longer reach...

But she stood between he and Snow.

Sacha closed, slashing high and low. He deflected the first blow and dodged the second, slashing back at her – but didn't commit to his attack. She knocked a blade from his grip with her free hand and frowned at him. "Why are you holding back?"

Taking a new knife, he drove her back with a quick succession of slices, none of which made contact. He leapt away again, wings aiding him, creating extra distance. "Because I have no quarrel with you," he said as he landed, boots grinding broken glass into the carpet.

"Don't insult me." She pointed with her sword, shouting across the dais. "One of us will die, Never. Do you understand? That's what you've chosen."

"Perhaps neither ought to die," a new voice announced.

Snow.

Chapter 23.

Snow approached, dressed in Vadiya armour and clothing, his blue and white tunic bearing the golden wolf's head of the royal family. He carried an ornate helm beneath his arm and his gauntlets in one hand. At his belt swung a longsword, his preferred weapon when he bothered.

Sacha lowered her blade. "Then it's true?"

"Of course. He is my brother."

"Why didn't you ever say anything?"

"I did not know how," Snow said, and there was pain in his eyes. He truly hadn't wanted to hurt her. Never realised he was surprised – how easy it was to think of Snow as a monster, it made evidence to the contrary unnerving.

Still, Snow was hardly to be trusted.

"Why don't you tell her your vision for the future, brother." Never folded his arms. "Or show her your wings."

Sacha's head swivelled between Never and Snow.

Snow's frown was swiftly replaced by a smile. "I know why you are here, Never."

"Do you?"

Sacha strode across to Snow. "What is Never talking about? Your vision? You have wings too – how can that be? What are you both?" Her voice had grown hard, harder than Never had ever heard it.

"My wings are easily hidden." He took her free hand. "Sacha, we will talk and I will tell you all that I've been meaning to share but Never and I have unfinished business."

After a long moment of regarding him she spoke. "Then do so, but I am not leaving and don't expect me to watch you two fools kill each other either." Sacha stood back but watched Snow, her sword still free.

Snow thanked her, then turned to Never. "Brother, I do know why you are here. I have spoken to Andramir and he informed me of his... adequate improvisations."

"If you try to hurt them again –"

"That's up to you, isn't it?" Snow snapped, his anger rushing forth. And it was clear why he'd lost his temper, seeing as Never had ruined whatever schedule Snow had for revealing the truth to Sacha. "Enough of this time wasting. It is wearying. You have your wings, you know our history and you know our birthright. You can see that we are chosen, even among the Amouni we come from a rare line – Chosen of the Gods, Never! Take your birthright with me, finally, now that we are together again."

"No."

"No?" Snow spat out a curse, tossing his helmet at the throne. It clattered to the dais. "Still I cannot understand your dogged refusal. You ought to be overjoyed – your life means something, something noble, something world-changing. Why aren't you happy? Why aren't you at least relieved – you always feared that the lies humans told us were true. And now you have proof but you refuse it? Why?"

Never ground his teeth. "What is it you do here in Marlosa, in the palace? What is here? This is where the invasion started. This has always been your goal, hasn't it?"

Snow shook his head, anger still evident but he exhaled before he answered. "Not precisely. There is something here, something only you can help me with. But the city is only the first step in the Empire, that you already know."

"What is here?"

"Are you saying you want to help me now?"

Never hesitated. For the first time, it seemed he had some power in the game between them. Perhaps not much and there was still the very real risk Snow was continuing to manipulate him... but he had no choice. Luis, Tsolde and Elina, even Vantinio deserved better. Finally, he spoke. "Call Andramir here. Have him restore my friends."

"That is what it will take?" Snow raised an eyebrow, a trace of disappointment in his voice. "So be it. I will do as you ask and then you will join me in unlocking the last secret of the Amouni, the Memory Seeds. Do we have an agreement?"

"The Memory Seeds?"

"The final piece, as I told you. Do we have an agreement, Never?"

He nodded. "Call Andramir."

Snow turned to Sacha. "My dear, would you find a Hawk to run my little errand?"

"And then it's my turn to ask the questions," she said, still frowning.

"Yes."

Sacha sent Never a warning look as she left. The meaning was very clear; he was not to attack his brother.

"There is no-one else like her, Never. No-one who could possibly stand beside me." Snow said, fondness in his voice. "So strong-willed."

Now it was Never's turn to raise his eyebrow. "You think I'm going to reminisce with you, about Sacha?"

He shrugged. "Why not? She's not the first woman we've both loved."

"This isn't about Zianna."

"I suppose it's about you and I." Snow sighed as he began to pace. "Don't you miss having a brother? I do, Never."

Never closed his mouth, cutting off whatever retort he'd been about to deliver. Snow.... And then Never kicked a nearby footstool. The side crunched; a deeply satisfying sound. "No. Don't try and manipulate me."

"I am not trying to do that."

"Of course you are! You are always trying to have me dance to your tune. I cannot trust you, brother."

"Yet you must."

The frantic ringing of a bell cut through the room. An alarm? The bell on the city wall, the bell that should have rang when the Vadiya first invaded. And now its cry tore across the darkness.

Never ran for the window, joined by Snow.

Down beyond the walls, the orange glow of fire rose, colouring the underside of climbing smoke. It came from the tent city before the gates. An attack? But who? "Trouble afoot," he said.

Snow did not answer; his eyes were closed. "Confirm it for me, I want to know if it's really him."

Never frowned. "Who are you talking to?"

Snow waved a hand, eyes still shut, as if listening. Finally he growled. "I know that, don't tell me we're stretched thin. Just be ready." And then, after another wait, his voice changed, a note of weariness entering. "So be it. I will deal with Sirgeto – just hold your ground until I send someone." His eyes snapped open.

"Captain Sirgeto is here?" Never asked.

"Yes." Snow rubbed his temples. "He's here with a thousand men, nearly half of them infected by those damnable swords of yours!"

Never repressed his own concern at such news. "Isn't that your problem?"

"No, brother. It's yours, since Andramir is down there protecting his men – and you're going to save him, if you want him to wake your friends."

"What?"

"Find a way and be quick about it – Andramir is my greatest creation, Never, I will not lose him."

Never couldn't stop a shiver at the words: greatest creation. "No-one can touch him, I fail to see how you'd lose him."

"His abilities are finite, he cannot always walk between flesh and spirit. If he exhausts himself he will be killed."

Still Never did not move. "Surely you could save my friends?"

"No, what Andramir has done I cannot undo. Stop stalling, Never."

Was Snow telling the truth? Even if he was lying, would he even want to save Luis and the others? At least Andramir would follow Snow's orders. "And just what will you be doing?"

"Everything else, it seems," he said, throwing his hands into the air. "Even we Amouni have limits, Never, and you don't know the half of what I am currently tending to."

"The half of what you tend to? Don't feed me such –"

Snow pointed at Never. "Be Amouni for a moment, will you? Can't you sense it? There's another force attacking via the mountains – I must put a stop to them."

"Who?"

"That imbecile Jenisan – now get moving, Never. You want to save your friends? Then do your part to save my city."

And then he was striding from the room, Never staring after.

So, Jenisan had rolled the dice. A bold move indeed. Or was he somehow in communication with Sirgeto?

Never shook his head, time was wasting.

He lifted the pouch of batena powder, taken from Vantinio, and swallowed two great mouthfuls.

The sour flavour exploded in his mouth.

His heart thumped and his body trembled but it banished the effects of his weariness, a tiredness he hadn't even noticed until now. The powder gave him new strength with the alertness, as if he had rested a week.

If that's what it took.

Never leapt into the air, driving himself up with his wings. At the broken section of roof, he knocked a few jagged shards free then slipped out of the dome, where he worked to gain altitude. Smoke beyond the walls was now tinted blue. "Gods be damned," he cried. Mere moments ago and he'd have welcomed an attack! With Jenisan in the mountains there was a chance the city could be retaken – but now he couldn't simply let Sirgeto into the city to wipe out the Vadiya.

From his vantage point it was easy to see Sirgeto's force,

their blue swords flashing. The greater glows came from two positions before the gates, Sirgeto and Mondesa. Yet other fighters bore their own tinted weapons. The Steelhawks and infantry who faced them were cut down quickly – though crossbow bolts from those lucky enough to get off a shot felled their targets, blue weapons or not. Never swooped lower. Andramir was a pale shadow, leading a counter-charge, nearing Mondesa – which meant Never was headed in the same direction.

He dived, streaking down to crash feet-first into a Marlosi farmer, sending the man sprawling. Never barely kept his feet, spinning to blast a pair of ex-Imperial soldiers with his wings. They were thrown off balance and engaged by a Steelhawk. The shouts, screams and crackle of flames washed over Never as he faced his first opponent with a glowing weapon – a wide-eyed man with the look of someone who had once wielded a quill rather than an axe.

The blade glowed blue as it moved. Never ducked and slashed at the man's knee. Steel bit into flesh and the man crumbled to one leg – yet his axe leapt forth of its own accord. Never swung one of his knives, a mere reflex.

Sparks flashed when the weapons met, pain shooting up his arm.

He swore, dropping the suddenly-hot knife.

Both blades hit the ground, in a heap of twisted steel, the axe still aglow.

The Marlosi man was frothing at the mouth as he clawed the hewn earth, dragging himself toward the weapon. Never kicked him aside and snatched the handle of the axe. A blue screen dropped over his vision – and in an instant he knew what to do. His connection to the other weapons was so strong. Every sword thrust and swing, every jab from spear or crushing overhand blow from a blacksmith's hammer was clear to him.

Above all, the director – the Amouni sword.

It was alive. Or if not, it was terrifyingly close. It drove Mondesa's body tirelessly on, the man's personality now no more than a tiny thing that clung to the blade, a mere spark, and Mondesa's hatred for the Vadiya linking man and sword, feeding the sword. Never understood now. Amouni blades took on personality traits of the wielder but with humans the exchange would start even but quickly turn in favour of the blade.

A figure rushed toward Never, breaking his concentration.

This imperial soldier bore no special weapon but swung his blows with precision, despite appearing momentarily distracted by Never's wings. Never caught each blow with the axe but did not fight back – there was no need. His opponent's sword was melting, deep gouges appearing in the blade. The man fell back in frustration. Never pressed his advantage, backhanding the fellow with his birch hand and felling him instantly.

If the man survived the blow, he just might survive the battle, so long as no Steelhawk stumbled across the fellow. There was every chance the imperial soldier would be mistaken for dead and wake up later.

But it wasn't Never's concern – that had to be Andramir.

The man was slipping through the fighting, untouchable but still helping his men by dropping each enemy with a word or silent blows from his transparent hands. He was closing on Mondesa and the young man's beacon-like sword.

Never focused on the weapon again – the link was there.

Between every weapon and between every man and his own weapon. All Never had to do was sever it – he could feel its tenuousness. Or maybe it was only tenuous to someone with his blood. The link, the weapons, they all responded to him, expectant – even Mondesa's sword. Was it so simple? Never took the axe and lifted it over his head.

"Break," he cried, swinging down and snapping the handle over his knee.

The blue glow died all around him.

Cries of despair rose, followed swiftly by screams of pain. A little stab of guilt ran through him, but if the axeman was any indication, the men were better off dead, rather than enslaved by an unnatural grief.

The Marlosi force faltered. Crossbow bolts snapped and conflicting orders rose from different quarters as Sirgeto's forces continued to take heavy losses under the Vadiya counter-attack. "Retreat, fall back," Never roared in Marlosi.

Would it make any difference? Mondesa might be able...

Never whirled.

Andramir had paused, shock evident even in his see-through face. Once he saw Never, he seemed to understand and offered a salute with a hand before fighting on. Nearby, standing stock still, a deep frown of confusion on his face, was Mondesa. He looked as if he was waking from a dream. Andramir bore down on the unsuspecting man.

Never charged. "No!"

But Andramir was already upon the young man, pale hands flashing.

And Mondesa crumbled to the earth.

Never thundered over the ground, leaping over dead bodies, using his wings to cover the distance. He landed before Andramir, who was breathing hard.

"Thank you for that. Your brother told me you'd be coming. And that I'm to help you – so let's finish up here, yes?"

"The sword's grip was broken, there was no need –"

"He is still my enemy," Andramir said, his different-coloured eyes hard. "Help me put a stop to this attack and then we'll go to the Spire. Not before." He bent, as if to retrieve the Amouni blade.

Never snatched up the sword first, muttering a curse. "You might not like what this does to humans," he said. "If that's what you are."

Andramir grinned, an echo of Snow. "Coming to accept your heritage?"

"Just move."

Sirgeto's force fought nearby, cutting through the Vadiya camp with relative ease. Yet reinforcements were soon to outflank his force thanks to the crumbling of Mondesa's men. Thanks to Never. "I need one of their weapons," he said. "Something with a wooden haft."

Andramir nodded and shot forward.

Never slowed to help a Marlosi soldier to his feet. "Flee," he said, shoving the man toward the dark beyond the still-burning camp. The man took one look at Never's wings – or maybe his expression – and ran.

Andramir was returning, a spear in hand. "Here."

"Keep everyone away from me," Never said.

"Done."

Already the blue had enveloped Never. Movement of the weapons washed over him like a furious tide. Yet one sword stood brighter than the others – Sirgeto's. While the unfortunate Mondesa's sense of self had survived, in a small way, Sirgeto did not exist any longer. The Amouni sword had taken on his hatred and desire to recruit men, his need to reclaim his nation, and then overwhelmed him.

Yet as before, all weapons and their tiny awareness's seemed to turn to him – a true master, Amouni.

Never brought the spear down across his other knee. "Enough!"

And the glow disappeared – every sword, axe and knife, all but Sirgeto's sword. Never swore, his voice lost in the fresh cries of anguish. The link between Sirgeto and blade was no longer in place, it was as if there was no link anymore. As if the two were simply one.

"Well?" Andramir was staring after Sirgeto, whose blade was a blue blur, cutting his way free of the press, even as all around him his men faltered – and then it seemed to Never that Sirgeto was slaughtering even his own troops in his mad flight.

"He is no more, there's no link to break. I have to face him," Never said. It had been a mistake, ignoring the threat posed by such blades but that mistake was in the past. He had a chance to do something about it now.

Never leapt into the air, wings beating hard.

He climbed enough to see where Sirgeto now fled into the darkness and angled after the man, only to have a Vadiya soldier below lift a crossbow. Never banked sharply and the bolt flew wide. Below, Andramir was shouting for his men to cease firing but another bolt hissed by Never's arm. He twisted again, swooping low and cursing. He was a fool; he'd been lucky to get away without being shot at as long as he had.

But at least there was no more steel flying forth.

He landed with a thump and strode to Andramir, ignoring the awed murmurs from the Vadiya. Never pointed to the darkness. "He's escaping. Who knows where he'll end up."

"I'm sure your brother will have an idea of what to do, after he deals with the Hanik," Andramir said.

Never turned back to the palace.

"Once I organise my men, we'll head to the Spire," he said. "After which, your brother is expecting you in the palace. I hope you will not be tardy."

Chapter 24.

Andramir simply stood over each sleeping figure in the lamplight and spoke a single word 'wake' and their eyelids fluttered. After which, he gave Never a look which suggested Snow was waiting, and passed through the wall, leaving the same way he had arrived, something Never thought best.

"Thank you, Pacela," Never said as he slumped against the wall with a long sigh. He'd come close – too close to failing them. And his relief was further marred by another thought. Just what had Snow done to Andramir to give him such abilities?

Tsolde was first to come fully awake, sitting with a frown, rubbing at her temples. Relief crossed over her face when she caught sight of Never. "What happened? I... I was in the Eyes and then nothing." She glanced at the others who were also rising, but her gaze lingered on Luis. "Were they hurt?"

"I don't believe so." He took her hand. "Tsolde, I'm sorry. I was a fool."

"We seem to be safe enough now, Never. Forget it, just tell me what happened."

Once everyone was awake Never explained the chaos that had followed their failed attempt as best he could, finishing by raising the Amouni weapon. The blue glow was soft. "And now I bear Mondesa's sword but Sirgeto has escaped. Whoever the Vadiya sends after, I could almost pity them. The Captain has been completely devoured by the sword." He looked to Elina. "There is more."

"What has happened?" she asked, voice wary.

"Jenisan is trying to break into the palace via whatever mountain path the Vadiya themselves used. Snow promised to stop him."

She shot to her feet. "Take me there."

"He will kill you, Elina."

"You can protect me from your brother. I must go, Never. Jenisan is my King, whatever our differences."

Never shook his head. There was no guarantee that he could protect anyone, he had accepted that once more. Luck had been on his side, luck of the Gods, perhaps. After walking blindly into Snow's trap, he'd been offered a second chance to keep his friends from danger. At least if they stayed in the Spire, they'd be out of harm's way for the most part. Of course, Andramir could leave and enter at will – in all places except the inner chamber.

But if Never had his way, Andramir would perish along with Snow.

Somehow.

"I will go alone."

Protests from all quarters, but he only raised a hand, refusing to speak until they quieted.

"Snow sent Andramir to kill you all, you know this. He sees you as impeding my Ascension. He will kill you if you follow me, swiftly this time and without remorse. Somehow, despite my mistakes you survived his last attempt but I would be a fool to believe my luck is boundless. I will not take you knowingly to your deaths."

Tsolde opened her mouth but only swallowed, as if she could find no words.

Luis put a hand on Never's shoulder. "We are not safe anywhere, Never."

"But if you come with me your deaths are certain," he said. "If you stay here, the High Priestess may be able to protect you."

"Even from Andramir?" Vantinio said.

"Perhaps. Jardila has her own secrets. If motivated, I believe she could defend this place," he said. He paced as he spoke. "And I may need you to stay for another reason."

"What?" Tsolde asked.

"Jardila showed me something that her predecessors have long protected and I fear Snow seeks it. It must be protected if I fail." Never explained about the silver man. "And so if you wish to help me, stay and pledge to defend this place. Andramir cannot enter the inner chamber but Snow might. Help Jardila flee with the silver man if it becomes necessary. It may be the only thing that can stop Snow if I cannot. Take it to Elina's grandfather, perhaps he can unlock its secrets."

Elina spoke. "When I leave, I am heading for the palace. It is my duty."

"It is not your duty to throw your life away."

"Nor is it yours." She folded her arms. "Do you know how to stop your brother?"

Never stopped pacing. "There will come a time when he lets his guard down, when he needs me most, I can feel it.

Then I will strike." He looked to each face. "Please, can you understand why I must go alone? It may be hard to believe but I am not truly a gambler. I won't risk everything on one throw – I need to know that if I fall, you will still be working to stop Snow. There is no one else."

Silence.

Hurry along now, Never – I am waiting. Snow's voice rang out in his mind, and he nearly jumped. Had Snow been listening to everything? Or could his brother only send thoughts? Never waited, but no other command came and no confirmation one way or another whether Snow was able to eavesdrop.

No choice but to continue on as if Snow was ignorant of what was said.

Luis spoke first, his voice weary. "I don't know what's right anymore, Never. I promised I would help you, no matter the odds."

"Then help me now. Protect Tsolde and help Jardila."

Luis nodded, despite the conflicting emotions on his face.

"Vantinio?" Never asked. "Would you stay, also? There may be greener fields elsewhere, you know."

He grinned. "Or no fields, if Snow has his way. That's not a world I want to see, Never."

"Thank you." Finally Elina. "My Lady?"

"Take me as far as you will or not at all, Never. I will walk if I must."

He sighed. He could not stop her without force. Just as she'd told him before – they were similar; neither willing to turn from their duty. "Very well, do what you think is best."

Tsolde, her eyes full, ran to Elina and hugged her. They exchanged words in Hanik, Elina stroking Tsolde's coppery hair, and he recognised a farewell, and then the young woman was hugging him around the middle. "I won't forgive you if you die, Never. You owe me, just remember that when you're going to take a stupid chance."

He swallowed, lifting his arms to take her by the shoulders. "I will."

Snow's voice cut into his mind. *Now, brother!*

Chapter 25.

At first, Elina remained tense – and he couldn't blame her.

She'd trusted him upon his leap from the Spire and after the way they'd plummeted at first, he must have given her the fright of her life. Once he'd adjusted to the extra weight, angling his wings accordingly and keeping a firm hold on her wrists, his own wrists straining under her iron grip, she seemed to enjoy the flight.

"The air is so cold," she shouted as they approached the palace. "But it's still beautiful."

"Just wait until you experience a landing."

Dawn was simmering in the eastern sky, the colour of newly-forged steel. Would it be his last? He did not shiver at the thought but a flash of regret followed. To know his true name, to finally know if he was cursed or gifted. To finally have a chance to... a sinking feeling overcame him.

Was there even anything beyond his quest?

"Never!"

The palace loomed ahead. He banked, wind rushing as

he turned from the gleaming central dome and toward the parapet nearer its base, a long wall that curved around and stretched back, back to meet the distant mountain range. Not unlike a small road. It would provide Elina access to the passages within the mountain, but from a different position to where Never suspected Snow was waiting.

"I'll release you when we're closer," he said. Distant torchlight was enough to judge the ground, since it was still quite dark. But he managed, beating hard to hover, not unlike a hummingbird, and released Elina. She landed and fell into a crouch before darting to the shadows where the wall met a watchtower. Hopefully it was empty.

Or perhaps Snow had simply asked his men not to bother Never. The same courtesy would not likely extend to Elina.

Never swooped after, landing beside her.

"What now?" she asked, rubbing at her wrists.

Never glanced back to the glow of the central palace dome then to the lawns between them, broken by evenly spaced statues and benches in tiny garden plots. The scent of rain and damp earth was strong but he saw no movement. "Now run along the wall and into that watchtower," Never said as he pointed. "It should take you eventually to the Folhan Passages; there are two I know of. One is quite small and another is the old Royal Merchant's way. That is where Jenisan will have struck."

"I'd always thought the Merchant's Passage was closed? Caved in centuries past."

"So did I," Never said. "But Snow and the Vadiya found a way and Jenisan did the same, it seems. As I understand it, the Vadiya even scaled down the very mountains themselves."

"I'll find out soon enough, I suppose," she said.

Never glanced at her. Her mouth was set in a firm line and her eyes caught light from the still-distant torches. "Do you still want to do this? It's madness, you know."

She gripped his arm. "I keep telling you, Never. We share that madness. Do you tell yourself that what you do is madness?"

"I tell myself there is no-one else."

"And who will help Jenisan from inside the city? You?"

He sighed. "Very well. Can I take you closer?"

"No, this will be fine." She released him and pulled her quiver into her lap where she began counting arrows, checking fletching by feel only, it seemed.

He stood. "Fare you well, My Lady. May Jyan bring you another spring."

"Never, wait. I would tell you something, before you go."

"Yes?"

"Do you remember when you asked me about my tally, in the White Woods?"

"You had twenty-one I think."

"I did." She shrugged. "I have not told this story – I did not even tell it all to my parents before they died; they thought him lost."

"Who?"

"My brother," she said. "And in a way he was lost – you know that there are those who would abuse things like the honey stick?"

"Like all things."

"Well, Hendryl used it like any other, at first, mostly on hunts. But he was younger than I and would not listen to any warning. I tried to make him see, Never. It was killing him, changing who he was. His mood turned dark, always.

He stole gold from mother and father, from any he could manage – at first to buy more and then to cover gambling losses." She looked up at him. "Can you see where this is going?"

"I believe I can."

"He fled into the forests, chased by those he owed money to. Hunted." She gripped her bow. "When I found them… they'd tied him to a tree. But I saved him. I shot each one, many around their fire. Those who ran I stalked and feathered them too," she said. "When I freed Hendryl both his eyes and mind had grown blind, he did not know me. In his broken state of fear he lashed out, scarring my arm, and fled, stumbling and crashing through the trees until he fell into the lake."

Never waited while she took a shuddering breath, shaking her head at herself, it seemed.

"I should not feel it so, not now, after years."

"Elina –"

"Let me finish," she said, but she was not angry. "I reached him in time. I could have pulled him ashore but I did not. He called for me as he struggled to keep his head above water, he called for mother and father too. For anyone. His cries were so loud, it was like they were searing the very trees but I stood on dry land and watched until he did not rise again."

Never could not speak, instead he placed a hand on her shoulder.

"It was not my brother that died there, Never. Hendryl was lost the moment the resin took hold – yet every day I fear I made the wrong decision."

"You made a choice. Perhaps the merciful one?"

"Perhaps." She met his eyes. "But I wanted to warn you that no matter what has come between you and Snow, to take the life of kin is not without cost."

"I fear it, Elina," he said. "But I will stop him no matter what."

"I know. Go – maybe we will meet at the passage."

She did not believe it and Never doubted his gaze offered her any more certainty. He turned and ran across the lawns, moving from statue to statue, then found a garden with a quiet fountain. He leapt onto it and spread his wings, launching himself into the air.

He flew toward the old barracks, those built around the Royal Merchant's Passage, where it once would have allowed official convoys between Marlosa and Hanik, but which now would have been jammed with soldiers. Torch and lantern light filled the windows and the nearer he drew, the clearer the shouting in Vadiya became.

I need you at the front.

Snow's voice again.

Never swooped low and landed within the barracks courtyard. Steelhawks and infantry filled the yard, faces grim. The wounded were stretched out on one side and across from them, barrels of crossbow bolts and replacement spears. No-one gave him more than a glance as he crossed the yard – it seemed Snow or perhaps Andramir had indeed passed orders to leave Never unaccosted.

Either way, it allowed him to make swift progress through the dim halls and finally to the double doors set in the very mountain, twice as tall as needed for a man on horseback. For now the doors were open but large statues of stone and rusted iron rested nearby, ready to be used as obstructions.

The passage remained as broad and smooth as anything he might have found within the palace itself, even the wagon grooves appeared regular. Just how much in the way of materials had been transported between cities? He hurried on, passing more wounded men. Finally the surface changed – more grit and rubble beneath his boots. Here he also found new support beams and steel frames with thick wire netting – as if it were keeping the mountain from collapsing further.

And perhaps it was.

The Vadiya had taken no half measures in their invasion. How had Jenisan discovered and then reopened the path?

Pale light appeared ahead, turning rows of men into dark outlines. A murmuring filled the passage, but no shouting, no clash of steel. Odd for a battlefront. As he neared the men, eyes slow to adjust, they parted for him after only a glance. Snow had indeed spread word then.

Snow himself stood within an open area, still dressed as Tendov and attended by Andramir. The circular space, not unlike a courtyard, stood open to the slowly lightening sky, high above. Not unlike the 'air hole' cut into the silver mines. Yet this was different, there was purposeful stonework here – a low wall ringed a well, where Snow waited.

"What is this?" Never asked as he approached. "A mime of war? Are you planning to collapse the passage?"

"No. I spent far too much effort clearing it to begin with."

"Then why are you waiting here?"

"This is a Sun Shaft. Its use is long lost but not forgotten. It was to aid Amouni machines that once travelled this passage and I will restore it in time. The Hanik have taken heavy losses and have withdrawn for now – they wait beyond the last blockage, not too distant."

More Amouni secrets. "And you're waiting for them to return?"

"No, I have sent a guide to harry them."

Never frowned. "A guide? How?"

"I will show you, since I require your help for the other," he said before turning to Andramir. "Check on its progress, will you?"

Andramir bowed and ran into the shadows, no hesitation in his bearing. Why would there be? No arrow or blade would find him. Snow gestured to the low wall. It was no well, but more of a barrier for the tarnished mirror within. Several pieces of quartz lay atop it.

"It is from these that I can alter the guides, but it will take your blood, for it seems I am only permitted to create but one, a most vexing outcome."

"Create what?" Never asked.

"A quartz soldier."

Never exhaled slowly. He would have to go along with it; if not, who knew how Snow would retaliate? There was always a chance he'd seek to kill Luis and the others even if Never helped – but for now Never had to become a party to more of his brother's plans.

He drew the Quisoan blade and nicked his hand, blood welling.

"Good." Snow raised his voice a little. "Guide, attend to me."

A figure appeared, rising from the mirror, long white robes and bare shoulders typical, but bearing a blank oval for a head, like another mirror. *Master, do you wish the sun?*

"No, Guide. I invoke Protection – prevent the army

beyond the shaft advancing any further."

Understood. I require assistance. The figure held out its hand, palm up.

"You shall have it. Wait." Snow tossed a hunk of quartz to Never. "Cover this in blood and hand it to the guide."

"That's all?"

Snow chuckled. "I will arrange the rest; I only need your raw blood to initiate the exchange. I doubt this is how our forebears worked, I am improvising as best I can."

Never took the quartz and smeared his blood across every facet then handed it to the guide. The bloody quartz seemed as though it would fall through the outstretched palm, but instead the guide seemed to shrink into the quartz and there it stayed, hovering in air.

The rows of men behind did not gasp – perhaps their shock was spent on the first creation of Snow's quartz soldier. Never glanced at them, noting the lack of family marking on their armour. Men loyal directly to Snow, rather than Tendov?

Snow then moved around the quartz, speaking firmly, words of command it seemed. The language tugged at Never's awareness – Amouni. While nearly all the words were unfamiliar, he understood one: lefr, the word for Rise.

The quartz shimmered and grew bright, a light blossoming from within. It became so strong that he had to shield his face but when the comparative dullness of daylight returned, a hulking figure of quartz stood in the guide's place. Its chest was a huge block and a flat, featureless head faced forward as it turned to do Snow's bidding. Each step scraped on stone as it disappeared into the darkness.

"Shall we watch?" Snow asked. He removed the quartz

from the mirror then wiped at the dust. "I will show you what Andramir sees. Look."

An image resolved on the mirror's surface. Torchlight illuminated the broad passage, gleaming on the surface of a quartz soldier. An arrow bounced from the surface – Never squinted. Harder to see were Hanik men in forest greens, one man was waving a hand at an archer, the message clear: don't waste arrows.

Yet the quartz soldier was not attacking, it had arranged itself in such a way as to plug one half of the Royal Passage and its fellow was not far behind. When the second soldier reached the first, they aligned perfectly, sealing the tunnel.

The image faded.

"And there, all is well," Snow said. "The way is sealed without collapsing the passage and ruining all my previous work."

Never looked to his brother. "This is more merciful than I expected."

"I have also sent a large force to scale the mountains in order to trap and slaughter Jenisan and his men. It will take some time but rest assured, Never, my resolve has not wavered."

Chapter 26.

"What now then? How do we find these Memory Seeds?" Never asked his brother as they started back toward the palace. They crossed the lawns alone, morning light continuing to grow, thinning out the shadows as it did.

"Now I must show you something before we rest; it will be difficult to locate the Seed."

"Show me what?"

"That which I promised in the temple. Father."

Never stopped.

Snow carried on several paces before turning back. "Isn't this what you've been seeking?"

"If you are lying once more..."

"No, no lies – this is our heritage, brother. Come."

Snow led them back into the palace via a modest door. He took a lantern and started along an unadorned passage, the light swinging in his grip and casting restless shadows. The corridor ended in a narrow stairwell. At the bottom they passed through a storeroom and Never was struck by a memory of Harstas, though it was a different room.

Snow walked to the rear wall and slid a stack of empty crates aside, revealing blank stone. Then he produced a small blade, pricked the tip of his finger and touched the wall. A silver glow appeared in the shape of a doorway.

"Have the Amouni been everywhere then?" Never asked.

Snow smiled. "Of course. They were custodians – everywhere they went they improved the lives of people with their knowledge."

"Yet it ended in bloodshed."

"Sadly, yes." Snow stepped through the doorway and Never followed his brother into a long hallway lined with stone doors. Each door bore an Amouni symbol, he saw the three fingers, the coil, the lightning bolt hitting the V, the mountain ridge and others from Snow's die, but many he did not recognise.

They came to a halt at a door bearing two circles, one off-set within the other. Again, his brother brushed the stone with a blood-stained finger and a silver light admitted them. Snow lifted the lantern, setting it on a hook, then stepped aside.

An unfinished skeleton of silver and bone had been tied to a chair.

The skull was intact, its eyeless gaze brimming with shadow, but several teeth were missing. It bore one collar bone only, several ribs were absent and an entire arm gleamed with silver. So much of the man was forged of silver that Never hesitated to call it a skeleton. Was Snow attempting to create his own silver man, like the one hidden in Pacela's Spire?

"Never, meet our father."

The words did not at first sink in.

Father? How could that be? Was it another trick – this one cruel even for Snow?

Finally, Never glared at his brother. "What is this?"

Snow moved to the skeleton, lifting a silver rib free. "It is my recreation – unfinished. These bones replace those that were missing when I dug him up." He placed the rib on a nearby bench, which stood covered in shadowy objects.

"The Gates of Ju-Anna," Never breathed. Just as Peat had told him, on their way to the Amber Isle. "You were there."

"Yes, I searched the entire Imperial Cemetery. I pieced together the fragments of his life over years of searching, Never. And when I found his resting place there was only these."

Never drew in a shuddering breath. Had his father truly been dead for... who knew how many years? And why? How? And more importantly, could he even trust Snow's claims? "How can you know? How can you be certain?"

"I found records, sealed within the Empress's chambers that spoke of a criminal who had been buried with no marker. A man who had been hunted all through the world – here, Hanik, Vadiya and even Kiymako. In all reports, written in all the languages, bearing all seals, this man was described as a vampire, one who stole the blood of his victims." Snow paused. "Does not such an affliction sound familiar?"

"It does," Never admitted with a frown.

"This man killed many in his search – mostly women. I found a reluctance within the reports, to commit his acts to writing. When he was finally captured here, he was drawn and quartered then spread across the cemetery and other places. It seemed the old Empress was advised that spreading his bones would prevent his return... but that if another like him was found, having at least parts of his skeleton on hand would help in destroying any such new creature."

"So some of his bones were kept in an unmarked grave, here in the city," Never said, his voice flat. Had Father truly been a murdering coward, fleeing from land to land? It would explain why the man featured so rarely in Never's memories.

"Yes. When I found them, I hid them until such time as I could do further tests."

"Such as?"

"Without blood, I had to see how the guides and other artefacts responded to his skull. I took a femur to the Seers in the Ramakki Islands and half a dozen other things to be sure... all told me that our father was the same treacherous scum I had long suspected. But I did not believe it still."

"But you do now."

"Not until I ground a piece of his bone to powder." Snow paused and the icy blue of his eyes burned. "Once I drank, I knew. I saw, Never."

Never swallowed, even as he shook his head. "Then why this mockery before me? If he is who you say he was."

"Because I need more from him – his body must yield one more secret, Never. But one. He must tell me if we truly have a sister."

Never blinked. A sister? How and where? There were still so many unanswered questions about Father and Mother before adding that of another sibling! Never was almost numb from such revelations – yet he still reached out to grip Snow at the neck of his tunic. "Do not toy with me, Snow. If this is some elaborate web of lies I will throttle you right now."

Snow did not retaliate. "If you doubt me, drink of his bones."

"What?"

"I can hardly blame you, since I could not accept it for myself at first. Yet you will see what you need to see and more – and you will be sorry. Or, you can take my word, allow me to shoulder the burden of truth."

"You would keep me in the dark, as usual," Never said, though he released his brother. Doubt had already nestled itself deep within him; where it seemed most comfortable. Could Never face yet another disappointment confirmed? If Snow was telling the truth for once...

"Shall I send for your vial?"

"You have already prepared it?"

"The base elements, yes."

Never frowned. How endless, Snow's manipulation. But to what end now was still not clear. And Never did want to know what the bones could tell him; this was not knowledge he could turn aside from. Over half his life had been consumed by the search for his true heritage and it was very possible a piece lay before him now.

"I will take the drink."

A touch of sadness passed over Snow's face, but he closed his eyes and spoke – again, to someone unseen. "Bring me the silver vial from my quarters, along with the mortar and pestle."

Never paced while he waited, unable to halt his train of thought, the cycle of doubt, fear and curiosity. He could not look away from the skull's eyes. *Is that you, Father?*

Snow said nothing, only waited in silence.

When someone finally knocked on the door, Snow

opened it at once, exchanging few words with whoever stood outside before returning with a glass vial and mortar and pestle. Within the vial rested a silvery liquid. He handed it to Never. "It will burn a little but the other effects are worse. I would sit." He dragged a second chair from the shadows.

"Other effects?"

Snow grinned. "Your wings are already awoken – I refer to the memories; they will not be pleasant." He snapped one of the human knuckle bones from the skeleton and stood at the bench, where he ground the bone into a powder.

So their father was the Ascended Amouni whose body – not his blood – had awoken Snow's wings. Just how much had Cog been told? Never took the chair then lifted the vial. The silver liquid moved slowly when he tilted it. He pulled the cork free with a tiny pop. "You expect me to see what you saw?"

"I cannot be certain but I have no doubt you bear similar questions within your heart," Snow said as he finished his work. He strode over and added the bone powder, tipping it carefully into the vial. The powder dissolved within a moment.

Just how much would it burn when he drank it?

"It is ready," Snow said.

Never frowned at the vial a moment before lifting his chin and tipping the concoction after. Fiery liquid hit his throat but he swallowed quickly. The mixture of bone and whatever else Snow had used dimmed his vision. Not unlike whatever Cog had used in the Preparation Chamber. Never tried to speak but again, control of his own body was denied him and the whole room was smothered in blackness.

An image resolved – a young man striding along a

forested road. His features were too familiar; like seeing a younger version of Never himself, only with variations. A higher brow, a broader nose. But the eyes. The eyes were his own, the eyes were Snow's eyes too.

Just the man's face was enough to shatter any doubts.

Father.

Never's stomach convulsed, a faint sensation, one he couldn't fully attribute to either knowledge or vial.

Yet the vision was fleeting – now his father sat in a clearing, waving grass all around, two young boys at his feet. By the pale skin of one boy, it was clearly Snow, and the other boy's skin was darker – Never himself. Their father was explaining something, laughing as he did. He wore a ragged cloak and a sword at his belt, his leather armour sported a newly repaired gash.

And then the scene changed again, gone before Never could register any further details.

Father sat in a dark tavern, glaring at someone sitting across from him, lost in shadow. Yet the figure leaned forward enough to reveal golden glowing eyes... somehow unnatural. The pupils appeared non-human. A clawed hand, covered in grey fur turning white, crept across the table. Misshapen, the hand was human-like yet it trembled and could not open properly.

Once again, the image did not linger.

A covered walkway stretched between buildings, the hand-rails made of bamboo. Mist cut across the scene, obscuring the rest of the city. Father walked along one of the walkways, pausing before what appeared to be a temple entrance, flanked by twin statues of the firebird. A tin rested before the door, which he opened, revealing white paint. He dipped his hand within and drew a symbol upon the door.

Another change.

A young woman sat in a kitchen, sewing a shirt. Her foot tapped on a dirt floor, moving to a tune Never could not hear, one that she hummed. Her fair hair was cut close, in the Quisoan way but a single short lock fell over her brow to one side. Her eyes were a startling green that cut into his very heart.

Mother!

Distant still, Never felt hands pressing upon his shoulders.

Father appeared in the kitchen door and Mother jumped up, backing away at the sight of him. She glanced to the window and then to another doorway, then back to Father. His appearance had changed; dishevelled hair, breathing hard, eyes wild as he cast the table aside.

And now the thunder in Never's chest grew strong, his pulse began to race.

Something was terribly wrong.

Again, Mother looked to the window and the shadow of the other room, her mouth open in a scream. Movement stirred beyond the window; a small face peered over the sill, pale, streaked with tears.

A different voice was calling Never, frantic, barely registering at the edges of his awareness, but persistent nonetheless. Never's body convulsed, as if he was no longer in control of it, of anything.

Father leapt upon Mother, tearing at her robe –

"Never!"

The lantern-light of the room snapped back around Never – a figure looming above him, pressing down on his chest, holding him on the floor. Never's breath escaped in ragged gasps and sweat ran down his temples to his throat.

"Let me free," Never shouted. "I will slaughter him!"

Snow himself was straining to keep Never still. "You cannot, brother. You cannot."

Never roared, fighting to pull an arm free but Snow would not budge. Never's throat constricted. Futile! Finally he fell limp, simply lying still to breathe, to try and ease the raging pulse that thumped in his temples.

Snow rose and slumped against a wall.

Never blinked away tears he did not recall weeping. The chair he'd sat upon lay near the door, whereas the silver skeleton remained untouched, illuminated from the lantern above. Its shadows were no longer unfathomable. His father – everything Snow had claimed. Everything Never had feared. Criminal, murderer, rapist.

"You knew. You've always known," Never rasped.

Snow nodded, his jaw clenched.

"Why?"

"You still believed, for a time that Father would return for us. I couldn't take that away from you, brother. If you'd known who was responsible for Mother's death. If you'd known what he had done to her..."

Never squeezed his eyes shut; a new tear had already escaped, running down his cheek. Not only for the mercy his brother had offered but for the vision. "I saw her, Snow. I haven't been able to remember her face clearly, for years now. It's like a gift... but one that he has tainted."

"I know."

"Why?" Now it was another question, but again, Snow knew exactly what he was asking.

"I believe he was trying to sire more Amouni children.

His fear that he was the last drove him insane."

"Were we not enough?"

"I don't know if he ever would have been satisfied," Snow said, his own eyes glittering – but with resentment, not tears. "It seemed he spent most of his life trying to save our bloodline, which is no doubt why Mother cast him out; I doubt he spent more than ten days with us after we'd grown enough to talk. He could hardly have provided much of a life for her. Or us."

"One of the visions," Never said. "Did you see it? He was talking to us, teaching us something on the plains."

"Yes. I recall. You saw the stranger in the inn?"

Never straightened. The pupils had not been human. "A wolf in a man's body."

"I have people searching but have found no trace of such a creature in any land, not history nor legend."

Snow's claim about a sister had not slipped Never's mind, but he would not mention the Kiymako temple in case it was a link. "Did you see anything else?" he asked, not having to work to let the weariness in his voice come to the fore.

"No," Snow said. "And despite my disappointment that your vision yielded nothing new, at least you know the truth at last." He shrugged. "And perhaps you can further imagine why I believe humanity unfit to govern itself."

"But father was not human."

"Human blood ran in his veins, just as Amouni – yet I think we both know which strain was stronger."

"And we're better than he?"

"Assuredly."

Never did not continue, not having the strength to argue. He had been awake for days, eaten little but batena, had flown all over the city, had broken an attack, had helped create a quartz soldier and finally uncovered a terrible, disheartening truth about his past – all he needed now was the oblivion of sleep.

Yet he had strength for one more question. "In my vision I heard nothing – surely Mother called for us to hide or flee. Did you hear her? Do you know our true names?"

"No, brother. That secret eludes us yet."

"Then why did she refuse to name us? Why?"

Snow sighed. "What we could not figure out together I have not discovered alone."

Never hesitated. Knowing what he now knew about his father... "Was it shame? Shame for what our father was?"

"No – I have no answer better than that, Never, but I do not believe it so."

He nodded.

Chapter 27.

Never woke to thunder.

He sat upright with a shiver – a heavy blanket lay across his legs, leaving his chest bare, as though he had thrown it aside in his sleep. But sleep he had, and when he crossed chill tiles to pull aside the heavy curtains, it was to reveal hammering rain and jagged streaks of light in the black sky.

They lit the city, bleak white everywhere for just the blink of an eye.

The streets were empty.

On the second strike he saw wind hurling a rag across the cobblestones and caught a glimpse of the Spire. How did Luis and Tsolde fare? Was Vantinio still with them? And Elina, had she survived? Had she even reached Jenisan and did the Hanik king live still? Pacela would have to watch over them, despite Never's urge to find a way to be sure.

His task remained – but had it changed at all? Could he stop his brother without killing him? All previous encounters suggested no. Yet learning the truth about Father had woken something long-buried; it was as if a brother had been returned to him.

A troubling development.

Never searched for his clothes and found an Amouni robe beside them. He lifted it, the fabric smooth beneath his fingers. Long, flared sleeves and a five-pointed pattern ran along the hem. The same symbol appeared on the chest, spun in silver, just like that which Snow had worn in the mountains. Never set it aside for the moment and sought the bath he'd glimpsed before stumbling into the bed. He washed as best he could in the cold water then took razor and basin to the ornate mirror. He found scissors, needle and thread in a cupboard, but took only the scissors, and began cutting the ragged ends of his hair, keeping it long but neat.

Next he worked on his beard, then switched to the razor.

Sometime later, it was with an odd sense of pride that he ran a hand across his clean-shaven face. Only a single nick at the point of his jaw, near the ear, and already the bleeding was stopping thanks to his usual Amouni healing.

He started to dress, finishing by pulling the Amouni robe over his clothes and weapons. "Why now?" But he had no satisfying answer for himself. Was it acceptance of his heritage? His broken past? Or part of preparation for his fate, whatever that would be. Whatever the reason, he was groomed and attired as he believed his forebears would have been and that was how he would face his brother too.

Never left the room and made his way through dim corridors to the Empress' quarters – only to be redirected to one of the towers by the First Hawk standing guard. "The Master will be within, My Lord."

Never thanked the man and quickened his step.

At the foot of the tower he was rebuffed by a sealed door. He thumped upon it. "Snow," he called.

A moment, Brother.

Never tried the door again and this time it opened, revealing a winding staircase. He started up, wondering how Snow was able to speak into his mind, for no such option was open to Never. Or was it? He paused. He had not tried before. Was it simply a matter of attempting?

Snow.

He directed the thought 'up' or so he hoped, yet there was no response and so he continued walking.

The open door at tower's top revealed a sparse room lit by a blue-stone and ringed by closed windows, lightning spiking beyond. Thunder rattled the jars and pots Snow had surrounded himself with. Dressed in his own Amouni robe, Snow was painting a door on the stone wall between windows.

The painted door was an outline, truly, the blank space inside the line of symbols representing the door. Amouni leaves were interspersed with familiar and unfamiliar symbols, yet all were linked by unbroken lines, some silver, gold and scarlet – even a bright green too. Never paused to admire the work; it was complex but not so much so as to lose its beauty.

Words also lay within, and this time they were familiar - Amouni phrases, formal requests for safe passage?

Snow spoke without looking up from his work. "I have only a few more to complete."

"I forgot how much you loved to paint."

"It clears my mind, Never," he said, and by the sound of his voice he was smiling.

He worked a little longer, dipping his brush into different pots. When he stepped back to admire his work, it was with a critical eye and finally a shrug. "I believe it will work – the final symbol is most important anyway." He smiled at his brother. "I admit I am surprised to see you attired so, appearing so accepting of your heritage; I did not think you would welcome my suggestion."

Never couldn't prevent a little frown. Still Snow saw his own hand in every action. "I am doing this for myself; there are things I would learn."

"Very well," Snow said. "The final symbol – the rune avalepa."

"Open," Never said, recognising another word, no doubt in part, thanks to the Leschnilef. A touch of resentment lingered at the thought; he ought to have learned the Amouni language from someone else. Anyone but those creatures.

"Indeed. And it must be the blood of two of the Prime or it will fail."

"You and I, we are Prime?"

"Of course." Snow opened his robe and drew a small blade, revealing an Amouni sword belted at his waist.

"Wait," Never said, pointing. "Where did you find that?"

"I found it amongst other relics beyond the Preparation Chamber," he said. "All of which have proved very useful in allowing me to reach this point in time. Now, let's not tarry." He cut his hand deep enough that the blood flowed readily into the jar he also held. "Now you."

Snow's answer explained why Never had felt such certainty that there was something at the base of the great chamber. Doubtless Snow had simply flown down to access all that he needed. Never cut his own palm, the birch colour stained by red. He let the flow trickle into the jar, meeting Snow's gaze. His brother looked to the new hand. "You have healed quite beyond what I expected, for which I am glad."

"I believe saving the Bleak Man's birch tree has accelerated our natural ability to heal, even so far as regeneration."

"Like a tree growing a new branch perhaps," Snow said, his eyes glittering. "How curious."

"What did you take from Sarann?"

"Other items that have greatly assisted me in both uncovering the location of The Memory Seeds, and how to open the way, beyond this door." He produced a triangular piece of quartz which caught the light of the blue-stone and spread it in odd directions. "This is required for the final barrier. I found it set in some ridiculous amulet, doubtless crafted by our one-time servants."

"And this door?" Never asked. "Where does it lead?"

"To the Stair of the Wind," he replied.

"Two must climb the Stair of the Wind," Never said softly. Just as King Noak had whispered on his deathbed. How much Amouni lore did the King possess – had he too, been a member of the Order of Clera?

"Yes," Snow said. He stirred their blood together then took the brush from where he'd left it in another pot. He did not seem curious as to where Never had received his knowledge of the stair. Perhaps he simply thought Never offered the obvious response, since it would take two to open the way.

Snow painted the rune for open on the stone where the doorway would appear, drawing bold but deft strokes – a series of curves to make up the symbol. Once he finished, he stepped back. "Do not block the blue-stone's light," he said.

Never stood off to the side.

Light flared in the blood then shimmered across the stone to the symbols, each responding with their own colour – red, green, silver and gold pouring forth, mixing with the blue but somehow still creating a harmonious rainbow. And then stone shimmered and disappeared, replaced by a black rectangle, no light, no movement – yet a soft breeze emanated from the doorway. "That was rather easy," Never said.

Snow bent to collect the blue-stone then raised an eyebrow. "Easy? Finding and then learning to draw the symbols alone took me months of study."

"Time well spent then, brother. Shall we begin?"

Chapter 28.

Winter had been banished. Night too. Even the city of Isacina was gone.

Beneath a sunny sky of blue, the Stair of Winds stretched up, scattered podiums like stepping stones soon lost with the white clouds high above. From their own platform of ancient stone, Never crouched, peering over the edge. Nothing but sky below, lost to yet more clouds. Powerful Amouni magic indeed. "Not much of a stair," he said.

Snow turned from where he peered into the sky, white wings free, feathers twitching in the breeze. "Never. We are, as best I can tell, miles and miles above the city, perhaps even residing in a frozen time, like a memory that none but we two can access – it should not be a simple thing what we do."

"Nor will it be, I suspect."

Snow crossed the stone, pausing in the centre to examine the carven rune.

"Well?"

He shrugged. "It is only the word for stair."

"What do you know of this place?"

"That it must be climbed by two and that it leads to the Memory Seeds, where the Amouni hid their most precious knowledge," Snow said. "It was designed to be a difficult climb, even for Primes."

"Primes. That doesn't sit well with me."

"Well I have become quite accustomed to it," Snow said. He pointed. "The next step is a short flight. Be wary."

Never stood, letting his wings free via the slices in his robe. "Of what exactly?"

"Whatever safeguards our forebears left behind."

"And all your research didn't give you any clues? We might as well be blind – it could be anything. Remember the Sentinels in the Amber Isle? What if some unseen hazard waits out there?"

"Then we face it like any other," Snow said, then leapt into the air, beating his pale wings.

Never muttered a curse as he followed.

The rush of air was pleasant against his skin, alleviating the warmth of the sun, which he had not expected after the winter of the city. His eyes roved the sky as he flew, but nothing appeared and he soon landed beside his brother on the second stone circle.

"That was too easy – an ominous beginning." Never turned a slow circle, still searching the sky.

"Then let's try for the next one, before something happens."

This time they flew together, bursting through several clouds before reaching the third step. It was broader than the rest and bore the same rune in its centre. Yet this offered no clue. Snow paced while Never pulled a wing close and examined his feathers a moment, straightening several.

"There has to be something we are overlooking," Snow said.

"I agree."

"Then help me think, brother."

Never strode to the rune, pressing the toe of his boot into them. Nothing. But then, Amouni secrets tended not to reveal themselves upon first attempt. And there was no guarantee that the rune meant anything. He glanced up to the next step, which appeared little different. "Perhaps the next one will have more or different runes?"

"Let's see."

Again they leapt into the air and flew for the next stop. Never beat his wings, gaining altitude, searching for a current to glide... and found none. He flew on with a frown. While he was not fatigued by any stretch, he was beginning to sweat. How far away would the next podium rest? And what manner of Stair of Wind would bear only such a unreliable winds?

Unless that was part of the trial.

"Never, look," Snow called. He too, was beating hard to climb, without the benefit of any rising currents. "Have you ever swung a blade in the air?"

"No, I haven't." Never squinted into the sun, to where Snow pointed.

Distant yet, twin shapes were hurtling toward them. Slowly they resolved into winged men.

"Then race me to the podium," Snow said.

Never pumped his wings, clawing at the air until the stone circle drew near. He glanced over his shoulder. The figures were closing. Each wore silver robes that left their arms bare to the shoulders. Guides? Never landed with a thud and spun, using his wings to steady himself.

The guides were already landing.

Unlike other guides Never had encountered, these bore human, rather than animal heads. Yet both faces were the same; a clean-shaven man with grey hair and a dark beard. The first charged Never, a sword appearing in its hands. Never threw a knife but the guide deflected the blade. Never drew the Amouni sword and met his opponent's first swing.

Blue sparks exploded around him and he ground his teeth, hurling the guide back. The man used his own wings to keep his balance and strode forward again, making no sounds, not even breathing, as he swung his weapon. Never deflected a series of rapid cuts, unable to prevent himself being driven back.

He gave ground until his foot slipped from stone, finding only air.

Never fell.

A blade whistled over his head, and he twisted in the air. The world spun in a disorienting streak of colour, but he beat his wings and righted himself enough to meet another sword stroke from the guide. The man's attack was relentless; it was clear he would not tire. Never fought simply to keep himself hovering in place but each time their blades met with a splash of blue sparks, Never was driven down or sideways through the air. He caught another overhand blow from his opponent, cross pieces locking, and instead of pushing back, Never tore his birch hand from the hilt and drove it into his enemy's face.

A thunderclap split the air and the guide disappeared.

Breathing hard, Never drove himself back up to the podium where he found Snow running for the stone edge, blade drawn. Snow skidded to a halt. "Never."

Never landed with an explosive breath. "That's our reception, is it? Murderous guides?"

"So it seems." Snow sheathed his sword. "I tried to command mine but it did not respond. They have been given a single order only I believe."

He nodded. "And they'll probably attack every time we fly to another step."

Snow's eyes flicked to a spot behind Never. "Or sooner."

Never spun. Another pair of silver-robed guides were spearing down from the clouds. He lifted his sword. "Good – the last one nearly decapitated me, I can't wait to see what these will try."

Before the guides landed, they split apart, one circling, as if to outflank them. "Back to back," Snow shouted.

Never shifted, the sound of his brother's breathing matching his own. He lifted his sword and then the guide was upon him – the man's face identical to the last pair. This time Never took the offensive, closing quickly and catching the first strike with his own sword, then whipping a knife free and slashing the figure's chest.

Thunder clapped again and the guide was gone.

Never spun. The other guardian was matching Snow blow for blow, but his brother's speed was going to decide the struggle. Before Never could assist, Snow had slipped around the guide's guard and landed a blow.

Thunder rang out again and they were alone.

"Did yours wear the same face as the first?" Never asked.

"Yes. It seems the same image was used for all protectors." Snow shaded his eyes. "Hmmm. Let's see if these are also the same."

Above, the sky was full, twin lines of guides pouring down.

"Only about a dozen each," Snow said with a laugh.

Never grinned. "Like the bandits on the east coast, remember?"

"Let's see if we can't send this lot running too."

The first guide landed and sprinted across the stone. Never dropped into a crouch and waited. The guide simply ran on, sword raised. Never held his breath. A little closer, come on, closer now. The fellow swung but Never sprang up, battering the man's sword aside and driving his knee into the man's jaw. Thunder split the air. Never landed, sword ready – but the next guide was only now running for him. The others, ten more of them, were filing into a standing position, as if waiting their turn.

Never frowned, even as he met the first sword blow with another fountain of blue sparks. The guide attacked again and Never side-stepped, swinging his own downward cut. His opponent spun away and Never followed, slashing hard at the man's body but overextending. The guide flicked a riposte that sliced Never's forearm. His sword clattered to the stone but he dove forward, jamming his knife into the guide's boot.

Thunder.

The next guide charged and Never scrambled for his sword, wiping blood from his hand as he did. He growled as he rose; he was better with knives but didn't like his chances over a protracted struggle against protectors with better reach. As he fought, a strange sense of familiarity fell across him. The guides were the same, silent, expressionless, every detail from face to arm and robe, right down to the rune for

Protection carved into the base of their blades – no detail was different.

And that sameness extended to their swordplay.

The style was old, utilitarian, no flashy strokes that would eventually tire the user, just economical blows and a strong guard. Yet they seemed ill-able to react to unpredictable events, like Never diving and aiming for the feet, or the flying knee he'd used earlier.

And more, each guide had opened with the very same overhand blow.

Those that were given a chance to swing a second, always aimed opposite and followed that with a quick lunge.

And he knew why.

"Snow, they use the same pattern," he shouted, felling another guide.

"I know," Snow called back. "It's a variation on how the Vadiya train. Less reliance on single handed fighting."

"No, I mean everything. They always lead with the same attack, they always follow with the same strike second." He dodged and drove his opponent back. "I don't think they can work outside of a predesigned series of attacks and responses."

Twin thunderclaps rang out as he and Snow defeated their guides. Never let the next one close in, measuring the blows. Overhand, opposite, lunge... feint, backhand, back to overhand blows, twice now and lunge again.

Never beat the guide's sword aside and once again inflicted a minor cut with his knife, enough to destroy the guide with the customary boom. "Do you read the pattern?" Never called.

"I do, brother."

The next guide was upon him. Never defended, dodging the lunge and instead of needlessly defending the feint that followed, he switched to the offensive, hoping his theory was correct.

And it was – his weapon sliced past the man's blade and into the chest.

Thunder.

The next guide met the same fate, and the next, and each one after until none stood before him. He lowered his sword, breathing hard. Even knowing the pattern, he still had to work, still had to concentrate.

Snow too, had finished his line. He turned and gripped Never's shoulder. "Quickly, to the next podium before –"

"Too late," Never pointed with his knife.

Stretching down from above were dozens upon dozens of protectors, their shadowy shapes quickly resolving into silver robes and blue-tinted swords.

Chapter 29.

Sweat slicked Never's hair and ran down his face, stinging his eyes.

It trickled down the back of his neck, along his throat and it coated his hands, threatening his grip. Whenever he had a chance between dispatching guides, Never wiped his hands on his robe. Yet even it was damp from perspiration.

"They're not going to stop," Never cried, defending the first blow from a protector.

Snow gave a roar and thunder clapped. "I'm thinking."

How long had Never been fighting the same man? The grey hair and dark beard, the flat eyes, tiny scar on the cheek, everything about the man was burned into Never's mind. It was as if he had always been fighting the Amouni guardian.

Yet there were short periods of respite. Between each dozen guides, there was enough time to rest his aching arms and catch his breath. Not long, but once he was able to tear the hem of his robe and bind a deep gash received after losing track of the enemy pattern.

It was healing, of course, but that didn't solve the problem.

Never struck down another guide, the final of the current wave, and swore again. There had to be a way to stop them, something they had overlooked. Something only a Prime would know. He snorted, some Prime he was.

"What is it?" Snow asked.

"Only a Prime can solve this, yet I don't feel like a Prime anything."

"It's something we've overlooked," Snow said. "Something we should be able to see."

Never nodded. "Are we focusing too much on the guides?"

"What are you thinking?"

"The steps themselves."

Snow glanced at the stone beneath their feet, eyes narrowed. He flexed his fingers, knuckles cracking. "Perhaps."

"Here comes the next wave," Never said.

Snow turned to face them, lifting his sword. "I have an idea. Between the next wave."

"Good." Never fell back into the rhythm of defending and waiting to strike, the routine now so familiar that the last guide disappeared before he knew it.

Snow had already finished his wave and was rubbing the blue-stone between his hands. Symbols responded, pulsing blue beneath his feet, spread across the entire step, one for each flagstone. "And there you hide," Snow said. He moved the blue-stone away from the centre, glancing at the sky. The next wave was already falling. "It's a map," Snow continued. "And I think I know what it means."

Never was rolling his shoulders. "Hurry."

Snow's head jerked up. "Give me a little more time – draw them in and finish them with crimson-fire, can you manage it?"

"For how long?"

"Two waves."

Never frowned but gave a short nod, slicing both palms with his Quisoan blade. Doubtless he could sear every guide that appeared until his body was drained of blood but how long could he use the fire and still survive the after effects? Crimson-fire didn't use pure blood, else he'd be drained in moments, he knew that much, but it was supplemented with enough that what he was about to do involved no small risk.

The first wave touched down, one charging from his left. Never skipped closer to the second wave, drawing the lead guide's attention where he braced himself over the stone marked for Stair, spreading his arms wide.

Bloody globes sprang to life in his hands, fuelled by heat, blood and even his frustration. "Back," Never cried. Two streams of crimson-fire shot forth, striking both lead guardians. They disappeared in a flash, thunder ringing across the sky. The next guides fared no better and soon the whole place was filled with hissing and thunderclaps.

The first wave was down. Never halted the flow, leaving the globes ready. He was breathing hard, already a little light-headed. Compared to what he'd done in Ficcepa, this was two streams for twice as long. He glanced over his shoulder. Snow was dashing from stone to stone, holding the blue-stone high in one hand and swirling his free hand over the symbols. Did each symbol move as he did so? Yes! A tiny clicking sound followed each movement.

"Is it working?" Never asked.

"I think so – if I can line them all up, we'll be free of the guides."

"Keep going."

The second wave thudded onto the podium. Never lined each up and sent more sprays of crimson-fire forth, narrowing the stream with his hands, evaporating each protector, each strike bringing concussion after concussion, until the second wave too, had been burnt to nothing.

Never halted the flow and opened his mouth to check on Snow's progress, only to find himself unable to speak. Black spots swam before his eyes and his legs grew weak. He groaned, flaring his wings to keep himself upright.

"One more wave, Never," Snow called.

"One more," Never managed. He shook his head, clearing some of the spots, and let the globes simmer while he focused on his breathing, sucking in as much air as he could. The sun seemed to mock him by adding more warmth to his already overheating body.

But by the time the third wave landed, he was ready.

Or at least, more so than before.

Again he flared the globes and sent a stream of crimson-fire slicing into the lines of guides; wiping each from the podium almost before they landed.

Finally the last peal of thunder echoed and Never collapsed.

*

The sun was warm upon his face.

He woke to the sound of Snow's voice and his brother shaking him by the shoulder – yet he couldn't open his eyes, couldn't move. It was as though his body was so empty of strength that it simply refused him even control of his eyelids.

At least his ears were cooperating.

"Brother, drink this," Snow was saying.

Never opened his mouth. Another body part responding, good. Something hard was pressed against his lips and warm liquid splashed over his tongue and down his throat. Coppery, but with something else quite familiar. His eyes snapped open to the blue sky. Batena powder. Never lifted his head.

Snow sat beside him, a look of relief on his face. His pale features were cast in blue from the light that covered the stone. "It worked. Look."

The floating stepping stones were converging upon a point directly above them, flying over from where they had previously been scattered across the sky. Each piece bore a blue-glow in the centre, matching the same light that tinted Snow.

Never tried to stand but could not.

A limit to the wonder of blood and batena powder.

"I will carry you," Snow said, bending to lift Never. He stood with a grunt and glanced up. The stones above were completing their alignment.

"What's happening?" Never said. His head had begun to ache and his limbs trembled lightly; he could not control them.

"The true Stair is opening," Snow said. "If we'd realised it, we could have arranged the stones from the first point. The map beneath us shows the alignment order of the Stair. The protectors are gone."

Above, a pure white light overtook the blue glow, then expanded, falling down in a beam. When it covered them, the sound of the wind disappeared but Never could still see through the beam to a boundless stretch of blue sky and clouds. And then they were rising, drawn up by the light.

The steady climb was broken only by the occasional shadow, when they passed through what he assumed to be more stepping stones.

Never tried to control his limbs but either the batena powder was not enough or the exhaustion from the crimson-fire was too much. "And the precious Memory Seeds wait above?" Never asked.

"I believe so. I could find very little written about the location or even the nature of them but I suspect our ancestors would have fortified it in some way beyond the Stair and protectors."

"And the Seeds themselves? What memories do they hold?"

"Of all Amouni lore that was not destroyed in the Eradication. Once we evolved from the sharing of knowledge through blood, lore was stored in such seeds as a matter of routine. I do not know what percentage was saved, hopefully enough."

Never tried to raise a hand but it did not rise far. "Wait. Our curse, our blood. That is why it drains others? It seeks knowledge?"

Snow shrugged. "I believe so. Over time, the finesse required to complete a mutual, safe transfer was lost. But we need such methods no longer," he said. "With the seeds, I can begin to restore the world to its true state, Never. The marvels we are experiencing now with this stair will become commonplace; the world will see such sweeping changes, such improvements. It will be worth all that I have sacrificed."

"And those that must die for your vision to come to pass?"

"I will not bicker with you now, Never, for I cannot be distracted. I must concentrate, as I said, our ancestors will not have left the Seeds unguarded for simply any fool, even a pair of fools who were lucky enough to Ascend and climb the Stair of Winds."

"You must know I will try and stop you," Never said, well-aware of how ridiculous his claim sounded, drained as he was, supported by his brother.

Snow smiled. "I know that, yes. But I believe you will help me for the good it will do."

"And if you're wrong?"

"Then for the lives of your friends, perhaps," Snow said. "Starting with the lovely Elina."

"You have her?" Never struggled to straighten, glaring up at Snow.

"Of course. I had Cog pick her up not long after you deposited her on the palace grounds. A plucky woman, isn't she? Foolish, but duty is still an admirable trait, I will admit," he said, adjusting his grip on Never. "And her speech was quite touching, wasn't it?"

"How? How did you know where we were, what she said?" Never demanded.

"I always know where you are, brother."

Never gripped Snow's arm, gasping with the effort of moving his limbs. "Tell me."

Snow sighed, removing Never's hand as if a mere child had taken a hold of his sleeve. "Save your strength and I will tell you."

"Fine."

"My gift to you – the Amouni die, Never. I carry its twin with me."

Never closed his eyes. What an idiot he was. Of course the gift had another purpose, of course it was just another way for Snow to exert control. Part of Never had taken it as a gesture of the bond that had once existed between them... the same bond he'd felt re-knitting itself on their journey now. But that was all too naive of him and the bond was as fragile, as tangled, as ever. "I am a fool." He opened his eyes. "Free her."

"Continue to aid me and I will do precisely that. In fact, I will let all of your friends live in the new world I create, despite their flaws."

"It is another lie, another deception – I cannot believe you."

Snow sighed, as if weary of the discussion. "Do you really have any other choice, brother?"

Chapter 30.

A looming shadow waited beyond the light at the top of the stair; large enough to be a hilltop or castle yet Snow did not approach, instead he paused. "What will it be?"

"Let me stand," Never snapped. He had recovered significantly it seemed – no doubt assisted by his rapid healing. When Snow helped him down, Never was able to support his own weight and walk without trouble. Was it the mixture of Snow's blood and the batena powder too?

Or his anger?

Yet Snow had the truth of it – there was nothing Never could do except take the risk of trusting his brother once more.

"Then you agree?"

"You said it yourself – I have no choice."

"Then onward," Snow said, stepping into the light.

Never passed through the beam.

On the other side he found a paved path leading to the huge shadow – a keep. Yet it was like no keep he had ever seen; the stone had been shaped as a giant face, carved from dark granite. It towered over them, the very force of it crushing Never with sudden feelings of insignificance, as though he was naught but a pitiful ant, tiny, useless.

Nothing.

But he fought the sensation. He ground his teeth and lifted his chin in defiance while Snow folded his arms and sneered back at the magnificent, terrible visage.

"Is this another test?" Never asked.

"A trifling one, if so," Snow said.

The sun beat down upon the smooth brow of the keep, the bald dome of the head and glinted in whatever enormous jewels had been used for eyes – each window round as a tower. A straight nose hovered over the mouth, which had been drawn closed in a firm line. The face's chin bore a stone stairway, the steps themselves half the height of the giant Amouni gate.

"How do we enter?" Never asked.

Snow held up the triangular piece of quartz. "I place this within a keyhole."

"And still no final protector?" Never rested a hand on the hilt of his sword.

"I may have been wrong, we shall soon see."

He strode toward the staircase and Never followed more slowly, glancing over his shoulder as he did, checking the sky. No guides were swooping down upon them. Still, he removed the marble and its figurine. The little man was at ease. "Good enough for me," he muttered.

Together they climbed to the top of the stair, where Never paused to catch his breath and Snow examined the wall for the keyhole. When he found it he placed the triangle into the wall and spoke, "Jev cesas a ysom." Open, in my name.

Then he stepped back, letting the light fall upon the quartz.

Stone rumbled. The whole keep shook and with a deafening grinding, the mouth creaked open. It soon slid to a halt, leaving just enough space to walk within. Snow entered and Never hurried after, finding himself in a vast, open chamber.

It spread far and wide, the floor empty of all but patterned flagstones and dust, its emptiness reminding him of the Amouni temple beneath the mountain. The patterned floor directed the eye in toward the centre of the room, where a towering tree of steel stretched up. The trunk was broad as an inn. Its branches were made of silver and they spread high above, catching light from the jewelled windows. Their position almost gave the impression that the branches formed the brain of the keep, filling as they did the top of the head.

"Then this houses the Memory Seeds," Never said.

Snow nodded slowly, his face alight. "Within the branches is stored the knowledge of generations, the power to shape the future. To cleanse the lands of humanity's vileness, to save them from their own mistakes, Never. Mistakes they have made time and time again without us to watch over them."

Never shook his head. "You're too quick to dismiss them."

Snow turned a fierce gaze upon him. "Ah, so it's 'them' now is it?"

"You would see it that way – us and them only."

"We are the only two," Snow said. "Let me show you. Can you fly?"

Never flexed his wings, testing the muscles and joints.

Tender, but he would manage. "Yes."

Snow leapt up, spiralling for the silver branches, catching one and clinging to it with hand and feet. Never followed, finding it less difficult than he'd expected, and joined his brother.

"See here," Snow said, touching a bud growing from the end of a silver branch. It spread like a flower opening and within sat a tiny golden seed. Snow lifted it free, holding it up between thumb and forefinger where it caught light from the window-eyes. "Stare within and tell me what you see."

Never focused on the seed.

Something faint seemed to flicker and move within, not unlike the Living-Memory revealed by the Altar of Stars. The harder he stared, the more the surrounding keep, the branches, Snow's hand, the more it all faded away.

An Amouni man, bald, smiling as he gestured, spoke as if to Never. His words were clear but Never understood too little – the man was explaining complicated healing procedures. Sometimes, he gestured to a body lying upon a steel table, repeating certain phrases and pointing or drawing upon cold skin with a quill-like device, labelling muscles and organs beneath. And for just a moment, Never was inside the room with the Amouni healer – the tenor of the man's voice changed, no longer echoing in the vast keep, but sounding more intimate. The healer lifted a slender tool with a sharp end. "Now you try," he said.

Before he could stop himself, Never reached out.

The vision disappeared and he was suddenly falling; light spinning. He spread his arms and flapped his wings, halting his fall, heart thumping as he returned to grip the tree.

"Forgive me, I did not expect that," Snow said, but his eyes were alight once more. "But can you see now, what could be possible?"

"I can see." And it was wondrous. A way to learn directly from masters of their art; a way to truly better the entire world as Snow claimed, it seemed. Yet Never well knew that was only true if the Seeds were used by the right people.

Snow replaced the seed, the bud closing over it protectively. He breathed a little sigh of relief. "They are most delicate." He swung to another branch, placing a hand over a bud and closing his eyes a moment. "With the knowledge here I could save people from plague and sickness or cure those born without sight or a dozen other miracles."

He hovered a hand over another bud. "And this one, allay maladies of the mind – restore those who can no longer think, those who jump at shadows – the possibilities go on, Never."

Snow flew to another series of branches, higher up. "And here, ways to improve travel – imagine being able to cross to the ends of Marlosa with a single step! There is the lore within these seeds to make it possible."

Never followed his brother and chose another branch, resting a palm gently upon a bud. Within lay something majestic, soaring over the waves... a ship without oar and sail, its decks covered in dazzling panels that caught the sun. His eyes widened.

"You see, don't you, Never?" Snow waved him to another branch. "Here. With this seed alone I could establish a clean slate and with the next, craft future generations, vastly improve upon what I have started with Cog and Andramir."

And there, another reminder of the deadly threat Snow

posed. Never hesitated a moment before reaching for the bud. A sense of blue, fiery light – something so bright and powerful that it would tear people from the ground, suck them into the air and disintegrate them as it did so, and all without direction or purpose, a blind fury. An echo of his vision in the Amouni temple.

If possible, the next bud was worse.

He could not fathom it in full, but within seemed to rest the knowledge that allowed the deliberate, large-scale isolation of certain human traits – either for removal or transfer. Knowledge of the kinds of strengths and weaknesses a child may be born with, before that birth, knowledge of how to encourage or remove such traits.

The total destruction of chance and freedom.

"Even in a few short years we could accomplish so much," Snow said.

"So we could," Never replied, his tone grim.

For it was clear, it had always been clear, that Snow was not the one to drive such change. His vision of the future was still far bleaker than one which did not involve the benefit of Amouni lore; and Snow would never see that.

Chapter 31.

"Turn away, Snow," Never said. He had to make one final attempt, if not for the man Snow was today, then for the brother he had been. The brother who had once protected Never at every turn.

Snow's head turned from examination of a golden seed. "From what?"

"From this path. You can atone for what you've done, there's still a chance with what we've found here."

It was a sad smile his brother gave him. "I know you would like to believe that. But I will not; I have been given an exceedingly rare chance to remake the world, to remake it without the terrible flaws. I cannot waste such good fortune."

"You want to remake it in your own terms – you don't have the wisdom to see so far into the future. Neither of us have that."

Snow swung closer. "Brother, you must realise that you cannot convince me with words. Where does that leave you?"

Never did not answer, though he clenched his jaw.

"That's right. All that is left is for you to kill me and you cannot do that. I know you, Never." He frowned. "You were always weaker; you always hesitated over the important decisions and that is why I had to protect you so."

Still Never could not respond. How could he swing the first blow?

"You are so close to being true Amouni, Never. Join me."

"No."

Snow pushed himself from the tree, into open space where he was transformed into a silhouette by light blazing in through the jewelled eyes. He drew his Amouni blade. "Then stop me now, for I will wait no longer."

Never reached for his own sword but paused. Was there another way? Snow had searched, studied and fought long for the lore within the tree. Two seeds in particular seemed to be of interest... Never tapped the nearest bud, and pulled the golden seed free, along with the next, slipping both into the palm of his birch hand.

Snow pointed with his blade. "No! They are too precious."

"I will crush them, Snow."

His brother exhaled slowly. "Be calm. You risk much."

"As do you."

Snow finally laughed, yet there seemed a hollow note to the sound that echoed within the keep. "Think, brother. There are so many branches here, so many seeds. I do not need those two as much as you think."

"You're trying to bluff me." But if Snow was not lying... there was another path open to Never. He leapt from the tree, diving for the flagstones below. From the corner of his eye, he saw Snow give chase. Never twisted as he plummeted down, the floor rushing up to meet him – and pulled up out of his dive at the last moment, twisting in the air to wheel around the steel trunk.

Snow had matched his move, staying close behind. Never swooped low and this time he hit the ground running, stirring dust as he slid to a halt. He ripped his own Amouni blade free and caught Snow's first blow.

Another explosion of blue sparks as their swords crossed.

Snow's face was a snarling mess, his ice-blue eyes were aglow, a stark contrast to the triumph, and even joy, Never had seen before. "Give them to me."

"I cannot." Never hurled his brother back, but Snow adjusted his wings, keeping his balance.

Snow charged on, unleashing a flurry of sword strokes that tore at the very air. Never struggled to keep up, driven back across the stones. He continued to give ground, grunting at a cut to his shoulder. Never ducked the reverse cut, the point of Snow's sword nicking his cheek.

Hot blood flowed.

Too slow; so soon after the climb and his limbs were tiring, reflexes dulled. Snow was the better swordsman at any rate, all it would take was time and Never would fall. Snow thrust his blade forward and Never batted the sword aside as he scrambled back.

Snow closed and Never deflected another slice, lashing out with his elbow. The blow knocked Snow back. "Give up this madness," Never cried. "Please, you are my brother!"

But Snow only spat blood and charged once more.

Space. And time. He needed room and the time to use it. Never spun and leapt into the air – and something caught his foot. Snow held Never's boot in one hand. Never beat his wings and kicked out at his brother, who dodged the blow and dropped his sword to grip Never with both hands, tensing, straining. Veins in Snow's neck bulged as he sucked in a mighty breath and dragged Never down, roaring as he did.

Never hit the stones and bounced, a crack splitting the air.

He screamed.

White hot pain shot through one of his wings, bent and crushed beneath his body. He rolled, rising to one knee, breathing hard, eyes watering. Every movement sent pain slicing through his back and shoulders. Bloody feathers lingered in the corner of his vision, one drifting to the ground from the ruined wing. He blinked: just as the Evache woman had predicted. Dire injury – would it be the death of him yet?

Snow was retrieving his weapon, no longer rushing. And why would he? He held the upper hand.

But Never finally had what he needed, enough respite to act.

He cut deeply into his hand, the sting a slight distraction from the searing pain in his back, and urged his blood up into a globe of crimson-fire. And then more, he pushed more blood free, the sphere enveloping his whole forearm, the red glow spreading.

Snow froze where he'd lifted the Amouni blade, but Never did not aim at his brother.

He swung his arm at the tree's canopy.

"Not that," Snow shouted. "There are other ways."

Never lifted his birch hand, which still cradled the two seeds. "One or the other. Or maybe both, unless you abandon this place now."

Snow made no move but his wings twitched as he stared

across the stones.

Never dared not look away. His brother would try something, but what? Snow was fast but no-one was that fast. It was a dozen paces, Never would have time to release the crimson-fire before Snow took two steps. Yet who knew just how many Amouni secrets the man had kept to himself?

"Decide," Never commanded.

Snow disappeared.

Never blinked. Where was Snow? There'd been no warning. Never tensed as he spun around, yet Snow was not behind him, nor above. Again, Never turned, only to find emptiness before him, the shuffle of his boots on stone echoing in the quiet keep.

A hint of movement.

Something indistinct – revealed by the red glow of the crimson-fire.

Never flung his birch hand out. It struck something hard and cold. An Amouni sword clattered to the stone as Snow reappeared, diving forward. Never reared back but Snow was too close – his brother hit with a growl, and they crashed into the flagstones.

Never's already injured wing crunched further as his head struck and he shouted – the shock causing him to release the crimson-fire.

It shot forth. The fire was off target, yet it flew true enough to spear into the great trunk, a hissing rising as it bored deep into the steel. Snow had frozen where he lay nearby and Never held his breath. The trunk continued to steam as the fire ate deeper and deeper... and stopped.

The tree stood, unbroken, a black hole in its centre.

And then Snow was upon him, straddling his chest and

clawing at Never's birch hand. Despite the way Snow tore at the flesh of his fingers and palm, there was little pain. Numbness? The extra strength – or was there simply too much agony from Never's other injuries? Yet his hand was stronger than Snow, who could not pry it open.

Snow beat it against the stone but still Never did not release the seeds. "You cannot have them," Never shouted, fumbling for a knife. Snow spun, lashing out. His fist cracked into Never's bloody cheek and he fell back, dazed. New pain shot through his skull and blood pooled in his mouth. Was his cheekbone shattered?

But Never retained enough presence of mind to keep his birch hand sealed.

Snow beat Never's hand against the stones. "Open!" he screamed.

Gripping the Quisoan blade, Never swung blindly. The knife bit deep into something unresisting – Snow's thigh. Yet his brother did not react, continuing to slam Never's fist down, again and again. Flecks of blood appeared on the flagstones as even Never's hardened skin began to fray under Snow's onslaught.

The sharp tang of blood continued to fill Never's mouth. He turned his head, coughing and spitting as best he could, so as not to choke – and caught new movement. The tree was shuddering forward. The hole his crimson-fire made had never stopped eating away at the steel; the tear was now so large that the trunk could no longer support the enormous canopy of silver branches.

And it would crush them.

Never twisted his body, trying to hurl Snow free but only served to send a new flashes of pain lancing through his back. Over Snow's shoulder, the tree continued to tilt. Never beat against his brother's side to no effect.

"Snow," he cried. "The tree!"

Snow did not seem to hear; a crazed fire seemed to blaze in his eyes as he tore at Never's hand with bloody fingernails.

Break the trance of madness.

The knife!

Never gripped the handle and wrenched it as hard as he could. "Brother!"

Snow screamed and gripped Never's hand, thumb digging into his wrist. Never released the handle but caught Snow's own hand, locking eyes with his brother. "The tree is falling," he screamed.

Snow whipped his head around.

Too late, the trunk was screeching as steel bent. The canopy bore down upon them; a silver wall of death.

Snow turned back and his face had changed, the madness replaced by true desperation. Again, their eyes met and the world receded long enough for Never to see – deep within the icy blue of Snow's eyes lay a glimpse of something Never had thought long gone; the boy who had always tried to take the first blow whenever a villager threw a stone, the boy who had been the one to pull Never back to his feet, the boy who had been sure their curse did not have to damn them to a life of loneliness and hate.

His brother, restored for just a heartbeat.

And then Snow was gripping Never beneath the arms, hauling him up and with a roar that filled the keep, casting Never clear with all his strength.

"No!"

Never reached for Snow as he flew through the air, even

as the canopy rushed down. One of its branches pierced Snow's chest... and then the rest of the canopy crushed Never's brother into the stone.

Everything seemed to happen before Never hit the floor, before the rest of the branches shattered around him in a hail of bright silver and glittering golden seeds, exploding when the buds slammed into the ground with a cacophony that battered his ears.

Yet he knew he had landed at some point, for he was alive and once again, he was alive because Snow had saved him

Chapter 32.

A bloody hand snapped around a silver branch, smearing the pristine surface.

In his chest, a terrible new emptiness bore down upon Never as he pulled himself up, the ache from a dozen wounds slowing his every movement, his shattered wing pulling him off balance as he staggered forward.

Clouds of glittering, golden dust filled the keep.

Light from the giant eyes of the keep laced the dust with fire, shining on the wreckage of twisted silver too. Never opened his birch hand – two crushed seeds. He walked on. The rasp of his breath filled the hush but whenever he paused to spit the blood that continued to pool in his mouth, the hissing of the disintegrating trunk came to the fore.

Never pushed himself onward; he had to see.

He swore when a tangle of branches forced him to detour. His boots crunched the remnants of golden seeds as he walked but he could not care.

And finally he found Snow.

His brother was no more. The huge branch had

completely crushed Snow, leaving only a still-growing pool of dark blood at its edge – that and a single wing, pure white feathers tainted with blood.

Never fell to one knee, then slowly twisted himself around to sit against the branch, favouring his good wing. He squeezed his eyes shut until the pain eased. When he could move again he gathered the bloody white feathers into his hands and simply sat, staring down at them as tears fell, splashing against the blood and the soft white.

Chapter 33.

Never gradually became aware of a chill.

He opened his eyes. Darkness ruled the keep, yet pale blue moonlight cast more than enough light to see. How long had he slept? When had he fallen asleep? His aches had receded enough that he was able to think about standing and making his way back to the stair – swift healing continued to be a blessing.

Blood on the feathers had turned black in the night. The Evache woman had told him he would hold blood-covered feathers – he'd been wrong about his own wing. Never lifted a feather free, tucking it into his robe and placing the others beside his brother.

An end to it all.

He hadn't known what to expect, had not dared to think so far ahead and could make little sense of the aftermath. There was relief and even grief, yes, but more, it seemed emptiness ruled. That wasn't right, surely?

But he could not sit in silence forever.

Never stood with a soft groan and started on his path

back to Isacina. Elina was still being held by Cog, how would she fare? And were Luis and Tsolde safe from Andramir? He quickened his pace a little, still having to thread his way through the broken canopy. Flying would have been swifter, but fast healing or no, he wasn't sure his wings were ready.

When he finally reached the edge of the keep, Never paused. A single unbroken seed rested in the ridge between flagstones, glinting in the moonlight. He lifted it and slipped it too, into his robe before turning back at the top of the steps.

He could not see Snow, nor his resting place.

"Fare well, brother."

And then he stepped outside and felt around for the triangular piece of quartz, pulling it free. A rumbling followed and Never started down the steps, the stone grinding closed behind him. It did not matter what remained inside, for there was no-one left who could even reach the keep; he had no surviving family now.

At the bottom of the steps, Never continued directly to the stair. Standing beneath it and looking up, he did not have to wait. The white light appeared, burning his eyes. He looked away and felt himself descending.

Part of Never knew he had narrowly averted a disaster like no other – or, like none since the Amouni seemingly inflicted it upon themselves in the ancient past. Snow would have slaughtered uncountable numbers of people to create his new world, and any survivors would have been robbed of their humanity, of hope, surprise and chance, of self-determination.

Another part of him only felt the growing emptiness; a deeper loneliness. Even when Snow was distant, even when he was pursuing his madness, Never had a brother. A brother that might not have seen the truth about his dark plans, but a living relative at the least. A brother that had seemed to care for Never, despite everything else between them.

And now he was gone.

The world was better off for Snow's absence but Never didn't know yet if he would be. Nor did he know how that could be true. How could he miss a madman so? Never sighed as he ran a hand through his hair, fingers snagging on blood-caked locks. But he wasn't truly alone, such thinking wasn't fair – Luis, Tsolde and Elina. Even Vantinio and dozens of others he'd met over the years; he still had a different kind of family.

So long as Cog or Andramir had not taken revenge for the death of their master – Never had no doubt they would somehow be aware of what happened. He fought the urge to pace; there was no room anyway. But a renewed sense of urgency had crept over him. How much longer?

When at last the stair deposited him at Snow's doorway, he leapt through, stumbling into the tower – blinking at the rising sun which lanced through the windows, tinting everything orange. He couldn't leave the doorway open. Taking one of the pots, Never poured the paints over his hands and slathered the colours across Snow's complex designs – stone reappearing before he'd finished – then he stumbled down the stairwell.

When he finally reached the bottom, bursting through the door, he crashed into a Steelhawk. "My Lord, forgive me," the man said. His eyes widened when he saw Never clearly, no doubt reacting to all the dried blood.

Never glanced at the fellow, who gave no indication

that anything was amiss with his master. "Guard this door," Never said. "No-one but I or the Prince enters this room, understood?"

"Sir."

Never ran along the corridors, heading for the grand hall. His body still ached but he pushed himself on and it seemed movement helped with the stiffness. And obviously his cheek had healed enough that his speech was not impaired, seeing as the Steelhawk had understood him.

As he neared the Grand Hall, raised voices rang out from within. He thundered along the carpet, rounding the corridor to stagger into the hall, chest heaving, his arrival bringing all voices to a halt.

Two men, one holding up his hands in a calming gesture and the other a Steelhawk, stood before the dais and throne – where Sacha held a knife to Elina's throat. Never froze. Sacha's face was streaked with tears and her eyes narrowed when they fell upon Never.

"You killed him," she shouted.

"No," Never said, keeping his voice even. "The tree of Memory Seeds fell upon us. And though it cost him his life, Snow saved me."

"That's what I've been telling you," Andramir told her. "I saw it myself; you know he linked us. You have seen it before."

Fresh tears welled and it seemed for a moment that Sacha would release Elina, but then her nostrils flared. "Then what do you care if she dies? Someone has to pay for his death."

"But not Elina, for she means something to Never," the other man said, and Never finally recognised Cog, dressed in his usual nondescript clothing.

"What?" Sacha was frowning.

"We have our orders: Never is the new Master," Andramir replied.

"Yes," Cog agreed.

The new master? That was not something Never wanted but he could hardly deal with it now and more, it would doubtless aid him. Never approached the dais, moving slowly. Sacha pressed the knife against Elina's throat, drawing blood and Elina flinched. Her hands were tied and she was unarmed. The distance between them was still too great, even if he were to fly. "Snow chose his own path, Sacha," he said. "I tried to turn him from it but he would not listen."

Sacha's jaw was clenched. "You know what I have lost, Never."

"And I lost my brother and now I have no surviving family," he replied, moving forward again. "Please do not take my friend too."

Silence.

Never continued his approach and Sacha watched him, her pale eyes red-rimmed from her tears. It seemed no-one breathed in the hall.

Sacha hurled Elina forward.

Never caught her, then stepped before Elina as Sacha started down. Yet the First Hawk did not draw a weapon, nor did she stop, striding past with her back straight and shoulders set. Elina breathed a sigh of relief and Never turned to her. "Are you hurt?"

"Nothing that won't heal," she said. Elina raised her bound hands. "Cut this already, will you?"

Never produced his Quisoan blade and sliced through the rope. Elina thanked him as she rubbed her wrists. "Where are her weapons?" Never asked, directing his question to the others.

"I have them," Cog said, and offered a short bow before striding off.

Which left Andramir. "And what do you need from me, Master?" he asked.

"Watch Sacha; I don't want her leaving yet."

"Of course." He hesitated. "And our men?"

"Will be pulling out."

"I see. On whose orders will I say this has been given?"

"Prince Tendov. If the commanders resist... make it convincing," Never said, certain Andramir would understand what he meant by 'convincing'.

He too, bowed. "Very well. I assume I will be able to find you in the Spire?"

"You will."

Andramir left and Never turned to Elina. "It is done."

"I know. Andramir explained it to Sacha. He spoke of it as if he saw Snow's last moments himself," she said. An expression of concern came over her face. "How do you feel?"

"Somehow... empty even of relief," Never said. He shrugged; there would be time to discover what he truly felt later. He led Elina toward an exit at a stride. "I want to check the Spire, I have to know that the others are safe."

"We're not flying?"

"I don't have the strength yet."

"Slow down," she said. "What do you expect to find?"

Never shrugged. "You know me, My Lady. I'm just used to expecting the worst. It saves time and prevents nasty surprises."

Chapter 34.

The great banded doors of the Spire were gone. The very stone surrounding the space where they should have stood had been melted to a blackened maw. Despite the low hum of a city gradually stirring, preparing for a new day, a hush lay across Pacela's temple.

It was clear what had happened. He swore. Had Sirgeto defeated Jardila's seal, or had she been given no warning?

Never pointed. "I think we can guess what would melt stone."

Elina fitted an arrow to her bow and Cog shuddered, his eyes flashing grey. "Is it Sirgeto alone or has he found others once more?" the man asked.

"We have to find out," Elina said.

"Right." Never drew his own Amouni blade and led them into the Spire. The antechamber was empty, along with the cold altar room. He started up the stairs, checking the occasional room, but all were empty. Signs of a hasty departure were evident in the disarrayed furniture and the lack of common, small Pacela statuettes.

"Higher," Never said.

In the dining hall there was naught but kindling – benches and tables smashed sometimes to splinters. Scuff marks from boots too, at a glance Never estimated a dozen men or more. But still no sign of priest, acolyte or Sirgeto.

"They will have barricaded themselves within the inner chambers," Never decided.

"Will we be able to reach them?" Elina asked.

"I'm hoping not," he said. "Since that means Sirgeto won't either."

Elina nodded. "Why is he here?"

"I don't know." Never rubbed at his neck. "Can a sword crave revenge?"

"Perhaps an Amouni one can," Cog said.

Never sought the main stair and pushed his weary legs into the climb, passing gashes in the masonry, from the steps themselves to the walls. At the first landing he paused to rest. While his healing continued, his weariness was not really easing off.

But he had no choice. His friends were counting on him.

When at last he stopped to catch his breath once more, this time beyond Jardila's chambers, it was to the sound of something striking a hard surface and muttered cursing. Never glanced at Elina and Cog, struck by the strangeness of it all; how suddenly everything had changed now that one of his enemies fought alongside him. "If the odds are too great, I will use crimson-fire," he said.

"We will protect you," Cog said.

"Good. Ready?"

Nods.

Never kicked the doors open and leapt into the council

room. Bodies littered the floor, yellow priests and a mixture of Marlosi men and Vadiya soldiers alike, all motionless beneath the blue glow.

Surrounded by half a dozen men all tinted blue, the bright figure of Sirgeto hacked away at an invisible barrier that prevented him from reaching a few Priests, Luis and Tsolde. Also within the bounds of safety stood Vantinio, who held Jardila upright, her breast rising and falling in rapid breaths. Her hand was outstretched, as though she held Sirgeto back with the gesture. And perhaps she did; her face poured with sweat.

But hope sparked in her eyes when she caught sight of Never.

"Sirgeto, I am here," Never shouted.

The man spun and a frown passed over his haggard features. But he only opened his mouth, pointing his sword. Or perhaps the sword lifted his arm. No sound issued from Sirgeto's lips, but the men with him charged, allowing the man to resume striking the barrier. Elina drew and fired, her arrow flying just wide of the lead man. Her next shot struck an arm, causing the fellow to stumble and she cursed.

Never gave her a look as he readied his sword.

"I haven't been shooting much lately," she snapped.

Yet her next arrows felled two Marlosi in quick succession, one arrow striking a fellow in the chest and the other piercing the next man's eye. Then the remainder were upon them. Never swung his sword, cutting one and then a second Vadiya down, his weapon shearing through steel and flesh alike.

Never surveyed the room. Bodies collapsed around him as Cog unleashed his smoke, finishing the last of their attackers. Elina had already moved on to firing upon Sirgeto. The arrows thudded into his back but did not prevent the man hacking away at the invisible barrier. He simply kept raining blows down, arrows jutting from his body.

And with each blow it seemed Jardila's barrier shrank; as Sirgeto drew closer. If unchecked, he would either hem them into a corner or break through.

Never approached from the opposite angle, allowing Elina to fire another shot. Her arrow struck the man in the back of the neck. He paused, turning once more. His eyes were black orbs within a glowing face and Never flinched back. The creature that was no longer Sirgeto opened his mouth again, this time lifting his free hand.

Cog muttered a curse and Elina cried out.

Bodies were stirring where they lay, both Marlosi and Vadiyem but not the priests. Elina stomped on a head and kicked at a grasping hand. Cog issued more smoke and Never sliced through every limb that stood in his path, grunting as he worked. If he stopped Sirgeto, he'd put an end to the corpses. Hopefully.

When Never reached the creature, Sirgeto leapt to attack, swinging an overhand blow. Never caught the weapon with his own, and was driven down to one knee by the force. He winced as he unleashed a counter-slash. Sirgeto sidestepped, allowing Never the chance to regain his feet.

Never blocked another blow and stepped closer, lashing out with his birch hand.

Sirgeto's head flew from his shoulders.

It bounced from the barrier and rolled away, but Never didn't see where it came to rest, since the body continued to attack him. He deflected a slash and pivoted, hacking through Sirgeto's sword arm. It fell to the floor with a thud. Like the neck, it did not bleed but the sword thrashed about on the floor. Never kicked the arrow-riddled body over and stomped on the wild Amouni blade, stilling it.

His boot began to hiss.

Glancing up, he saw that the bodies had not come to a halt yet.

Sheathing his own Amouni blade, Never took a dagger and sliced open his palm again, avoiding the lines of pale scars. Then he drew forth crimson-fire, letting a globe envelope his hand before gripping Sirgeto's hilt.

Steam rose, purple light bathing the room – but the sword was melting. Once the hilt and cross piece were no more than a liquid heap, he ran a hand across the length of the blade until all that was left of the steel was a puddle of steaming liquid. Finally the corpses grew still and the purple glow faded.

He offered a weary smile to everyone behind the barrier. "Now, don't be angry because we're late."

Chapter 35.

Once Never had sent Cog back to the palace to secure Snow's rooms, and then arranged for everyone to restore the dining hall to some semblance of order, and once he had managed to organise bread, cheese and wine for everyone – even the still-weak Jardila – he had Tsolde continue her story from where she leaned against Luis' shoulder.

"When Sirgeto and his men broke in, waving their blue weapons, Jardila roused the alarm and we helped everyone flee the Spire," she said.

Jardila nodded. "I could not protect all. There is an ancient passage that leads beyond the city; you will be pleased to hear that Acolyte Lina was among those who escaped. I must send for those who are still hiding."

"After you eat," Never said, pleased to hear that Lina had survived.

The High Priestess took a sip from her wine, raising an eyebrow at him.

He grinned back.

Tsolde shook her empty cup at him. "Take your own

advice and listen so I can finish, Never."

Never popped a piece of bread into his mouth and started chewing, a burst of salty olive a fair reward.

"Some of the priests agreed to stay and help defend Jardila," Tsolde said, her voice taking on a sombre tone. "But even were Pacela's faithful warlike, I don't know how they would have fared against Sirgeto's weapons. He and his men were possessed, Never – you saw what he'd become."

"Why did he attack the Spire?" Elina asked.

"We don't know," Luis said. "Perhaps he sought the silver man?"

Never swallowed his mouthful. He'd wondered the same thing himself, yet what need would Sirgeto and the sword which controlled him, have of the artefact? "And so you diverted him and prepared a last stand."

"Yes," Jardila said. "He brought a small force with him and we were able to reduce their numbers but I could see, even with help," she paused to offer Luis, Tsolde and Vantinio a smile of gratitude, "we were not going to prevail. I invoked the Blessing and held it – I do not know for how long."

"Most of the night, Lady," Vantinio said, respect clear in his voice.

Just as Never had suspected – there were still mysteries to the Goddess' power. "And Andramir? Did he return?"

"No," Tsolde said. "He must have been busy elsewhere."

"He's busy now too," Never said. "I have him organising the withdrawal of Vadiya forces."

"You do?" Luis asked. "How did you manage that?"

"He seems to think I'm his 'master' now," Never said. "Like Cog, he obeys me as Amouni, now that my brother is gone." He caught Elina's look; she was no doubt still thinking of their conversation at the palace wall. And she'd been right, of course. The feeling of emptiness in his heart was a reminder of that; but he offered her a small smile. Being surrounded by friends did ease the darkness.

Tsolde reached across the table to take his hand. "No-one will think less of you if you miss him," she said.

"Thank you." Snow might have been right about humans being prone to war and violence, borne of the most base motives but that was hardly the sum of humanity. "But you know I just might."

"Don't try and figure it all out this moment, Never," Elina said.

"He was more broken by our past than I," he said with a sigh. "I didn't realise it at first. He always seemed the stronger one..." Never then launched into his own tale, pausing only for small bites and sips of wine – his voice still hoarse by its end. While he had left out the true details of his father's crimes, he did not conceal the man's attempts to sire more Amouni children. "I have no doubt I stopped my brother from bringing death and destruction on a scale that I can barely fathom... and I do take comfort in that, even if it doesn't seem so right now."

The table was silent a moment, expressions reflective, sombre.

Finally Jardila spoke. "I must thank you, Never – perhaps you are truly a Messenger," she said, then added, "even as you are also simply a good man."

"Thank you, My Lady."

"What's next?" Tsolde said.

"Ever-practical, aren't you?" he said with a smile.

"You try running an inn without a practical nature."

"I wouldn't dream of it." He refilled his cup and tapped his finger on the rim. "Next I'm going to ensure Andramir is doing as instructed." Which included checking on Sacha. Who knew what her grief and pride would drive her to. "I want to seal off my brother's rooms for now and then I'm going to send word to the Empress so she can come back and clean up here."

"And then what?" Luis asked.

He shrugged. "I don't know... I have to think about that." It was a daunting position to find himself in.

*

Never stretched his wings as he flew across the palace courtyard, pleased with how they were healing. His injured wing gave him a little trouble but he was still able to ride wind currents and eventually swoop down before a large group of Vadiya soldiers, all marked with the red talon. Sacha addressed them from where she stood, one hand on her hip.

Murmurs rose as he landed and approached Sacha, who'd raised a hand to halt the men who'd been reaching for crossbows.

"Why are you here?" she demanded.

"I wanted to see you."

She folded her arms. "You wanted to be sure we are leaving, yes?"

"That too."

Sacha strode closer and her voice dropped to a deathly whisper. "I may be leaving here now, Never, but if I ever see you after this day, you will not draw another breath. I swear it before God."

Never stared back at her, unable to muster any anger or

outrage, despite the venom in her voice. He could not even find hurt, as there ought to have been after what they'd once shared.

There was only regret.

He rested a hand on the hilt of his Amouni blade, not a threat but more a promise that any such meeting would not be a one-sided affair.

Sacha sneered as she turned back to her men, waving them toward the palace gates, the rattle of their armour as they walked in step echoing across the lawns. Never strode after, following all the way to the main gate.

He knew Sacha would not turn and doubtless she knew he would be following to ensure that she left. As he watched, a short figure scurried from the gatehouse, joining her party. He blinked. The lad wore a motley of colours and it seemed he carried a blue-skinned puppet... could it be the young jester who'd helped him escape Harstas? Why would Temilo do such a thing?

Never started after them but Sacha's warning rang in his ears – it was not the best time to start a fight, in the middle of a frustrated army that had just been ordered to leave a city, to leave the spoils of a war they had won so soundly.

"I hope you know what you're doing, Temilo," Never said as he watched Sacha's party start along the road. Maybe Temilo did, maybe he'd found someone who valued his skills – after all, the truth was a valuable thing indeed.

Nearby, Vadiya soldiers continued to break their camp and file onto the plains. Other groups of Vadiya were leaving too, sometimes in a less orderly fashion, with muttering and dark looks as they looted the buildings near the gate. Yet after Never melted a few groups with a blast of crimson-fire, word – and terror – seemed to spread.

One group of Vadiya he kept, those who bore no markings of family – Andramir's personal unit, those sworn to Snow. Those men, whose loyalty appeared to have simply been transferred as effortlessly as Andramir's, Never had tasks for.

*

In the palace Never searched all of Snow's various rooms and chambers.

He had the materials he found within transported to the inner chamber of the Spire, unable to think of any place that was both equally safe and accessible for him, since he wouldn't have the run of the palace forever. To such items Never added much taken from the hidden Amouni chambers Snow had also used. Some of the items were made of silver, bearing the look of smaller war machines or items such as he saw in the rooms of Elina's grandfather. Others were more innocent in appearance yet he did not know what they were.

Beyond the door with the rune marked for Thought, waited floor to ceiling shelves crammed full of Amouni texts in the form of books, scrolls and loosely bundled parchments, heavy quartz pieces not dissimilar to those found at the Amber Isle. Of all the items that he had found and sent to be hidden within the Spire, these were the ones that he could have locked himself away with.

But there would be time for that later.

He also moved his father's skeleton, though he did not know what to do with it. He should have cast it into the ocean... but could not make himself do so.

When he'd finally done all he could bear to deal with

for the day, he called Andramir and Cog to the Grand Hall where he rested on the throne, lying his head back against the seat a moment. It was, without a doubt, the least comfortable piece of furniture he had ever sat upon.

Both men came to stand before him. Never shifted on the throne, leaning forward, meeting their eyes one at a time. Both waited with similarly patient expressions. "You must know why I have called you here," he said.

"I believe we do, davishca," Cog replied, glancing at Andramir, who offered only a nod.

"Tell me, what are you both? What did my brother do to you?"

Andramir shrugged. "He improved me."

"He saved me," Cog said.

Never smiled. "Perhaps that is true. I mean, how did he change you? Was it with some lost Amouni lore?"

Andramir spread his hands. "The details are unclear to me, but yes. That is the simple truth." His expression changed to one of pride. "I was the first to survive the experiment. Before me, dozens had not."

"That doesn't fill me with a feeling of warmth, you know."

"Your brother expected as much," Andramir said. "Part of his orders were that I should tell you which texts to study if you were one day willing to continue his work. They are known as the Hor Pyrilh. Their bindings are green."

Hor Pyrilh – or, The Human Maps. Would they be as detailed as the Memory Seeds? If so, perhaps he ought to destroy them. "One day?"

"Yes, I suspect he held scant hope you would be curious."

Never sighed. "A fair assessment. And how do you feel, Andramir?"

"Me, My Lord?"

"Yes – I imagine you miss my brother."

He nodded.

"You must know that I will not follow in his footsteps, yet you are willing to serve me?"

"Yes." Andramir's answer revealed no emotion.

"Then once the city is cleared of Vadiya, I release you," Never said. He had not taken as much time as he'd have liked to think upon what to do about Andramir, but it was unlikely that the man would find a home in Marlosa. Nor with Never. "That is my final order, upon which you will be free to return home and seek your own path."

Andramir frowned, confusion clear. "My own path?"

"Yes," Never said. "Though I understand that some find it a burden."

"It is certainly a disconcerting thought," Andramir said softly.

Never raised a finger. "There is a condition."

"Yes?"

"I would hate to hear of any... warmongering, upon your return home and I believe that while Snow understood Amouni lore better than I, I would have little trouble dismantling you. I hope I am not being too subtle?"

"Hardly," Andramir said with a bow.

"Good. Now I would have you continue the fine work you and your men have began in the evacuation. Were you able to reach those at Monasema?"

"I believe so, they will soon be in the act of withdrawing and returning home."

"Wonderful."

"Then I will take my leave," Andramir said, striding from

the hall.
    Never turned to Cog.

Chapter 36.

"What do you have in mind for me, Master?" Cog asked.

"I am no-one's master, Cog – understood?" Never sighed; he hadn't meant to be quite so terse. "You said Snow saved you? Is this before or after he changed you with the Hor Pyrilh?"

"The changes were not wholly from the Pyrilh," Cog said. "I am from deep within the Hanik forests in a hidden valley. My people made up a small village only, births had been in decline for generations." He pulled down his collar, revealing the scarring. "I'm sure you've noticed this before?"

"I have."

"Well, it is a gift from Jenisan's men – I had been left to die, twisting on a hangman's rope when your brother cut me down. I owed him my life."

"For what crime?"

"The crime of birth," Cog said.

"Birth?"

"You are aware of Jenisan's hatred of the Amouni?"

"I am, but why would..." Never trailed off.

"My village sheltered the dying line of two heritages – ancient Hanik and Amouni. As far as Snow could tell, the last bloodline aside from your own. A strain far, far weaker than yours of course, but traces remained within us."

Never leant forward. "How?"

Cog spread his hands. "It is a long story. If you wish me to share it now..."

"Summarise, please."

Cog nodded. "Of course. My people were among those few Hanik smiled upon by the Amouni, favoured servants in truth. In the dying days of their rule, we were allowed to intermarry as a desperate measure on behalf of the Amouni to save their bloodlines. Then we were sealed within the valley. It was meant to be a temporary measure, I suspect, long enough for the hatred to recede. But something went wrong and we were only uncovered when, many, many centuries later, King Noak, who loved Amouni lore, found us. He fell in love with a woman there, betraying Jenisan's mother."

"And so the son's hatred," Never said.

"Yes. His hunt was relentless; I am the last of my village."

Never sat back, no closer to deciding Cog's fate. "This is an incredible story."

"But true," Cog said. He drew a small belt knife and held it over his forearm. "You need but to read my blood to be certain –"

"No, no, I mean incredible in terms of wonder, not credulity," Never said.

"Ah." Cog waited.

Never stood and began to pace. "Did Jenisan survive?"

"No, davishca."

Never sighed, not that he'd truly miss the man but it would hurt Elina to have her fears confirmed. And it would create instability in a land probably on the brink of collapse after Snow's meddling. "I do have a request for you, Cog."

"Yes, Master?"

"Fine – I have two. The first is no more 'master' and no more 'great one' either."

He smiled. "And the second?"

"I want you to accompany Elina and Tsolde to Hanik, I want you to help them both with whatever they need."

A nod. "You seem to be well-informed of their wishes – where will you be? I imagine Luis will be travelling with Tsolde, are you planning to go rampaging with the mercenary then?"

Never chuckled. "I don't think I will at that – and I may still travel with you all. At least at first. I still have questions without answers." One of which was a pressing question about his father's time in Kiymako, and the possibility that he might have a sister. Something he had forgotten in the chaos and rush of tasks that followed; something that offered a shred of hope. Perhaps he had not lost all of his family.

"Ah." Cog said. "Your true name."

"Yes," Never said. "That is one of them." Another was the glowing tattoo on his chest; its purpose eluded him still. Had Snow borne the same marking? And even the little man in the sphere – another Amouni artefact or something else?

"I wish I could help."

"So do I," Never said. He stood. "And so what do you say, Cog? You haven't accepted my request."

"I will go to Hanik as you wish," he said. "And I believe I will welcome it."

*

Never met his friends beyond the city walls, in the very same grove they'd used to disguise themselves mere days before. It seemed many moons longer. He carried with him new knives to add to the Quisoan blade, the Amouni sword and scant supplies, mostly water and some travel bread. Not too much, for he hardly wanted to make flying any more difficult than it would already be, having the sword strapped to his back as it was.

Hidden within his inner pockets was a map he'd copied from Snow's collection, along with a bloody white feather and the golden seed. Whether he would need all or any of the items, he could not be sure. But he was certain the touch of hope from before was growing stronger, despite the doubt that nestled beside it. There was no guarantee his last search would bear any more fruit than the others.

Yet he had to take it.

And if nothing else, the sky was clear of rain, despite the chill to the air.

"Are you sure you won't stay?" Elina asked. Her own expression was far from cheerful since learning the fate of her King. "Word is that the Empress will arrive in two weeks, it's not such a long delay."

He shook his head. "I unearthed some Marlosi nobles and a few Imperial officers, they'll have to do."

"You might be back before then," Luis offered.

"True – my old village is not so distant. And I'm a lot faster than I used to be," Never said with a grin.

"We will wait for you anyway," Tsolde said. "I don't think

my inn is going anywhere, though I don't know who's in charge."

"I may take longer," he warned.

She shrugged. "How much fun is crossing a mountain in winter anyway? Maybe we'll just wait for spring."

Now he laughed. "Looks like I cannot avoid it. Very well, I will be back by spring. Or perhaps earlier, I cannot say." He looked to Vantinio. "And where will the winds blow you?"

The mercenary scratched at his unshaven cheek. "There's plenty of work around, despite your efforts to single-handedly stop the war. Might find myself playing caravan guard for a while; they'll be good imperial gold reopening trade lines."

"If the Vadiya didn't spend it all," Luis said with a grin.

Never laughed and even Vantinio chuckled. Never looked to each of them. "Watch over each other until I'm back."

"We will," Luis replied. He placed a hand on Never's shoulder. "I hope you find it, Never."

Never gripped his friend's hand with a nod and once Luis stepped back, he slipped between the trees and took a running leap, climbing with his wings until he found a rising wind to take him the rest of the way.

*

Never walked the dirt street, kicking at hunks of ash and charred wood.

The village of Pirchys, his village, was gone.

Had the people escaped in time? Whatever Vadiya raiding party had come in months past had spared no effort in razing the place. Not even the foundations of the buildings remained, just the clear spaces that would have been the dirt floors, now home to naught but passing insects.

Despite the bleakness of the place, Never could find little to mourn of the people who'd died or fled. Pirchys housed few fond memories. Even the single bare stone that represented his own home was of little meaning.

It was more the single gravestone beyond the village that gave him pause.

Someone had kicked it free of the earth, doubtless when they took the time to burn the tree that once shaded Mother's grave. It was hard, in that moment, not to be reminded of Snow's scathing damnation of humanity.

Never lifted the headstone back into place, the hard edges biting into his hands. Then he sat beside it, trying to recall, and then hold the image of her where she sat at the table, before his Father appeared. For just that moment, she'd been happy.

And not once after, it seemed.

Snow had not forgiven their father, and neither could Never – that was not something he ever questioned; it would not happen. But could he forgive Snow? Never found no simple answer there. Snow had stolen or ruined so many lives in his desperate search. But he seemed to truly care for Sacha. And he had saved Cog. And he had saved Never... or so Never wanted to believe.

Yet Snow's eyes lingered in his memory.

The moment when Snow turned from the canopy, knowing he would not survive, and hurled Never to safety. There was a fierce desperation in his brother. Had Snow been trying to save the seeds Never held? Or save Never? The thought was impossible to banish, impossible to answer. And Never didn't know if he could forgive Snow without an answer. "And maybe not even with an answer," he murmured.

Never lifted a vial from an inner pocket. Within, he carried the fruits of hasty research; he had replicated the concoction Snow had made, which would allow him to experience the memories stored within his mother's bones; perhaps a chance to learn his true name.

If he was willing to desecrate her grave.

Never twisted the vial between forefinger and thumb, watching the silver liquid swirl.

He was not willing.

Had he ever meant to do so? Doubtful. Making the draught was no more than evidence of his confusion. He uncorked the vial, letting the contents slide free to soak into yellowed grass. He had a name: Never. It was the name he remembered, the name his friends knew him by, the name of the man that changed the world – though few would ever know what he did for them, which was just fine.

No, 'Never' was good enough.

Just as he'd given Snow a name, after his brother's secret wish to one day see snow drifting across the slopes of Kiymako, so too had Snow's choice for Never seemed fitting. "You always say 'never', did you know that?" Snow had asked that day. "Whenever I ask if you'll stop searching. What if we can't find the truth, will you give up?"

And Never answered 'Never', just like he always did when Snow asked the question and Snow had shook his head, even as he smiled.

Never stood.

His doubt had worn away; worthy tasks lay before him yet. Luis and Tsolde, Elina. All needed to be seen safely to Hanik. Even Cog.

And then his sister.

He did not know how old she was, had no clues to her appearance and little to go on when he started searching but he knew, as he knew his own past, that her cursed heritage would have been responsible for many trials. She would have experienced crushing doubt, bitter loneliness and self-loathing. Was she outcast? Scorned and hated?

He would find her. For there was no doubt that she existed; why else would Father have returned to the Kiymako temple and painted a rune of protection upon its door.

A Note from Ashley

Hello! Hope you enjoyed Imperial Towers and thanks for reading.

I'd like to ask if you could help me out by leaving an honest review of the story at your place of purchase? Long or short, bad or good, it all helps!

And if you'd like to sign up to my newsletter you'll be able to stay up to date on the possibility of future Never adventures and you'll also be automatically added into the draw for my other print and ebook giveaways.

Ashley

City of Masks (Bone Mask Trilogy #1) - Sample, Chapter 1

The chill of prison bars against his temple did little to ease Notch's headache. Decades of dank didn't help either, nor snoring from another cell, where someone was impersonating a bear. Or dying. In the poor light it was hard to tell.

Notch squinted. Noon sun barely crept through the small, grated windows on his side of the building. Even cells across the way were shadowed. Sunlight, in addition to a piece of bread and some water, were high points, while the straw 'bed' and stale body odour of criminals were typically unpleasant. Worse places than Anaskar City prison existed. At least he hadn't been beaten yet – a twinge in his shoulder reminded him how much some guards enjoyed their work.

His cellmate raised his voice and Notch turned. The man had probably been speaking for some time; his drawn face was expectant. Years of imprisonment had washed out his Anaskari tan.

Notch leaned against the bars. "What is it, Bren?"

"Did you kill her, truly?"

"No."

Bren nodded. "Innocent then." He knelt in the corner, his fine coat of blue long since gone to grime, his face pressed against the stone wall. "Listen to this one." He scratched at an armpit with some vigour. "It's hard to see but I think it says 'death to the Shields of Anaskar' and it's got a signature, but I can't make it out."

Notch grunted. Nothing special for a convicted man to write; since waking on a pile of old blankets that morning and meeting his cellmate, he'd heard a dozen similar sentiments. Through Bren's meandering introduction, Notch had winced, probing his body. Both arms and chest were heavily bruised and his head so fragile he wouldn't be surprised to learn a wagon rolled over it last night. Possibly twice. He wasn't drunk, though the smell of ale was on his breath. One damn drink, that was all.

And there was blood.

His leathers and tunic were splattered a dark red. Not his own blood, the City Vigil told him as much when they hauled him off the street, as if he couldn't figure that much out. But whose? His own memory was unreliable, which made no sense. He hadn't been drunk, truly drunk, since right after the war. When he bore another name. A name he left on some tavern floor, after making a convincing go of drinking the memories away. A good bath did for the sand on his body, but the blood-soaked sand in his mind? No amount of ale had washed that away.

And now the Vigil were telling him he'd been so intoxicated he had to be dragged to the prison?

Unlikely.

"The Shields probably caught him doing something bad, that's why he wrote this," Bren continued, tapping on the wall. His too-bright eyes looked up at Notch.

"I'd say so."

"Like us, Notch. We've done bad things, we have."

"So you keep saying."

Bren laughed, its shrillness cutting through Notch's skull. If it hadn't been unsettling, Notch would have thumped him, but there was something wrong with Bren. Any fool could see that.

"The guards say you've got a few days. That they can't hang you sooner, because there's too many in the queue. Waiting to hang."

"Thanks, Bren."

A moment of quiet fell between them. Distant voices drifted from beyond the prison walls. Notch clenched his jaw. He should have been out there. On his way to another job. The Blue Lady, a fat merchant ship, would have sailed with most of his possessions on board.

His father's sword.

No chance of seeing it again. He wrapped his hands around cold bars and squeezed.

"The guards say it too, the guards say you killed her," Bren said, unperturbed.

"I know."

He crept forward. "So?"

"So I don't remember." He frowned. "But I wouldn't harm a child."

Bren grinned, as if he thought it all a joke, and went back to the wall. A scraping sound followed. "This one says 'down with the Shields' and has no name. I wonder how many people have been here before us, eh Notch?"

"Maybe just you, Bren," he muttered, rubbing at his temples.

Bren prattled on. "I could deal with the Mascare too, you know. They aren't so powerful. It's just their precious bone masks. And their robes. All that crimson. They scare people, the faces. And the eyes too. Did you ever meet any, Notch, before you murdered that girl?"

He ignored the last bit. "I've seen the Mascare plenty of times."

"And were they protecting 'the city, the people and its history' as they love to claim?"

"Each time?"

Bren laughed. "Ever ask them why they won't show their faces?"

"They aren't very talkative, Bren."

Bren stopped scratching and moved to a spot beneath the window, running a set of cracked fingernails over the stone. "This is my favourite. I think it's the oldest one."

The clank of a key in a lock did not deter Bren from his examination, but Notch took hold of the bars again, letting the man's voice recede into the background. At the far end of their row, the guard, a scruffy man who'd made some effort to straighten his blue and silver uniform, led three figures toward the cell.

"Quiet now, Bren," he said as the group approached, their footfalls echoing. A slender woman – a Lady no doubt – stopped before Notch's cell. She was accompanied by a girl and a stony-faced man with broad shoulders, the orange tunic and gleaming breastplate of a Palace Shield in stark contrast with the prison keeper's appearance. The woman's hair was pulled back from her face, fanning down around her shoulders and covering the collar of an impeccably clean white dress. Bone earrings swung when she turned her head. A sneer that must have been permanent marred her otherwise smooth face.

Notch adjusted his grip on the bars. To come to Anaskar Prison in such clothing – she was either mighty vain or mighty important. Most likely both. Which meant trouble.

The girl stood in similar attire and shared the sneer but had trouble meeting his gaze.

"Here's the mercenary, my lady." The prison guard pointed with his key, making a low bow before scurrying off.

The woman took a single step forward, glaring at him. Her footfall clapped. "Your name?"

He blinked. Her distaste was like a battering ram. "Notch."

The palace guard bristled and she waved a clean hand at him. "Bring the torch, Holindo."

"Yes, my lady." His voice was a rasp.

Behind him, Bren shrunk back into the corner. He did not resume his scraping.

The woman levelled a finger at Notch. "You will address me as 'Lady Cera,' or not at all. Now, do not move."

"Can I ask why, Lady Cera?"

"Because if you do not I will have the Captain here gut you."

Notch did as he was told. The impulse to wipe her face clean of its expression was strong enough that he had to school his features. Palace folk. Even before he'd taken to the life of a hired sword, they'd looked down their noses at him. 'Mountain Family', they'd say to each other and snigger.

When Captain Holindo returned, the soldier thrust the

torch forward, catching Notch's shoulder with his free hand. He narrowed his eyes but said nothing, only adding a crease to his brow. Did Holindo recognise him? Notch couldn't place the man.

"Be still now," the solider said.

The flames singed a little of Notch's hair and he started to sweat. No-one moved or spoke, though the girl he took for Lady Cera's daughter stared wide-eyed at the blood on his clothing.

"Well?" The Lady snapped. "Look. Is it him? Is that the man?"

"I… I think so, mother," said the girl.

Lady Cera and her captain shared a glance before she addressed her daughter again, her tones becoming honeyed. "Dear, are you sure? This is the man they caught by her body, in the street on our way from the harbour –"

"It's hard to tell. I didn't see him that well." She met his gaze. "I suppose it could be this man."

Captain Holindo withdrew the torch. "We have other witnesses, my lady. You've done far more than enough by coming here; it will satisfy the Justice. Furthermore, your own daughter identified the prisoner, that's enough for any man of law." Such a long string of words strained the man's voice, and for the first time Notch noticed a long, faded scar crossing his throat.

She gave a short nod. "Truly. I've had more than enough of this stench in any event. Take my daughter back to the palace."

"Of course, Lady Cera."

He ushered the girl toward the exit. Lady Cera did not follow. "I don't know the whole truth of what happened. But you are a criminal, of that I have no doubt."

"Mercenary, Lady Cera."

"Do you think there's a difference?"

"There can be."

"Well, Notch the Mercenary, I will ensure you hang for this. The girl might have only been a pale-skinned, half-blood brat, but I can ill-afford to replace her."

Notch sneered. "That all she was to you? Something to be replaced?"

She raised her arm but he stepped back.

"Fool." Lady Cera spun and stormed off.

Notch spat. He was already going to hang, what did it matter if some bone-headed noblewoman wanted him dead? Bren shuffled forward and placed a hand on his shoulder. Notch had forgotten him. "She knows what you are. What we are."

"You might be right," Notch said, sitting on the floor and scratching at a new, disturbingly persistent itch in his hair. "But I didn't kill that girl."

Acknowledgements

If you've read any of the Never books you know that I like to thank those who help me most and the same people deserve my gratitude this time too - my wife Brooke, my editor Amanda and also David for the formatting, along with all of the Alchemists :)

As before, I also owe thanks to Lin Hsiang for the amazing cover to Imperial Towers and also Vivid Covers for that title work!

And to those of you who have followed Never on his quest across all the books and who still have questions, I hope to return to him one day soon!

Thanks for reading

Ashley

About Ashley

Ashley is a poet, novelist and teacher living in Australia. Aside from reading and writing, he loves volleyball, Studio Ghibli and Magnum PI, easily one of the greatest television shows ever made.

You can find him online at Twitter or on his fiction blog, City of Masks and at ashleycapes for poetry. As if that's not enough, you can also sign up to his newsletter for free books, competitions, giveaways and sneak peeks of forthcoming titles!

Also by Ashley Capes

Fiction
The Fairy Wren
A Whisper of Leaves
Crossings
Somnus and the March Hare

The Bone Mask Trilogy
1. City of Masks
2. The Lost Mask
3. Greatmask

Book of Never
1. The Amber Isle
2. A Forest of Eyes
3. River God
4. The Peaks of Autumn
5. Imperial Towers

www.ingramcontent.com/pod-product-compliance
Lightning Source LLC
Chambersburg PA
CBHW020517110726
47899CB00004B/1142